Emily

AND

Daisy

Emily

AND

Daisy

PAUL YATES

Matador
9 Priory Business Park,
Wistow Road, Kibworth Beauchamp,
Leicestershire. LE8 0RX
Tel: 0116 279 2299
Email: books@troubador.co.uk
Web: www.troubador.co.uk/matador
Twitter: @matadorbooks

ISBN 978 1800465 466

British Library Cataloguing in Publication Data.
A catalogue record for this book is available from the British Library.

Printed and bound by CPI Group (UK) Ltd, Croydon, CR0 4YY
Typeset in 11pt Adobe Garamond Pro by Troubador Publishing Ltd, Leicester, UK

Matador is an imprint of Troubador Publishing Ltd

For Susan

Chapter 1

MISS HEWITT PICKED UP THE BRASS HAND BELL FROM THE table in front of the Honours Board and positioned herself in the middle of the Grammar School building, a symmetrical Palladian mansion showing signs of wear. She flipped up the small fob watch on the lapel of her tweed jacket and, as the hand reached the minute, began to swing. The clapper hit the bell at four o'clock precisely and would continue to do so for two minutes.

Daisy rushed out of the library, down the wide staircase and hurried along the corridor. Running was against the rules. The cloakroom smelt of damp and sweat. It doubled as the girls' changing room for the daily Physical Exercise. Most girls loathed it. Jumping about in the playground in your knickers was mortifying. To avoid it, Theresa Moore had forged a letter saying she suffered from asthma and had got away with it. Daisy quickly shrugged on her navy blue mackintosh, pulling the belt as tight as it would go around her waist. Jamming her hat on her head, she swung the stuffed satchel onto her shoulder, and dashed out of the cheerless building. She must not miss the old coach that dropped the girls, like so many parcels, at the villages and hamlets around Marleigh.

Daisy got off at the Market Cross in Porthwiel. She walked down the High Street to near the edge of the village. The shop was one of several in a row. Passing the bootmaker, the haberdashery and the bakery she came to one painted dark green with the legend – Eric Lanyard and Son, General Stores – written in white paint across the top of the window. Pushing open the door carefully, she tried to grab the little bell before it sounded. Usually she failed, but this time she just managed to get her hand to it before the vibration of the door made it ring. Daisy closed her eyes and made a wish. Her mother came out of the back room, drying her hands on her flowered pinafore.

'Hello, love.'

'I'm that tired,' Daisy said, 'any chance of a cup of tea?'

'I expect you are. After all, the brain must be like a muscle, if you have to use it a lot it gets worn out. I expect your dad will be wanting one. I'll put the kettle on.'

She went through to the back parlour and down a step to the small kitchen. Daisy followed.

'Take your school shoes off, dear.'

'Oh, mum, do I have to? There's holes in my slippers and the floor is freezing.'

'Don't talk nonsense, that lino takes the chill off the flags lovely. You can put some cardboard in your slippers,' her mother said. She took the filled kettle to the enamel gas stove and clicked a lighter, until with a little thumping noise, she got a flame.

'There was a sack of sugar come in today, so your dad will want you to bag it up, only in four ounces mind.'

'Mum, please. It's my higher exam year, you know that. I've got French, Geometry and English homework tonight. I've got to do it. If I don't get the work done it's just wasting your money sending me to the Grammar School.'

'That's as maybe, but if you don't bag the sugar this evening then you just get up early and do it before you go tomorrow.'

'Then I'd be fagged out before I get to school.'

'No matter, it has to be done and you have to do it. There's a war on and your dad will be out with the ARP wardens again tonight, though don't ask me why it takes so many grown men to supervise the blackout in a little village. And stop answering me back all the time, he'll be home in a jiffy.'

Daisy said nothing. Taking off her shoes, she hung her coat on a hook behind the door. Passing the mirror above the fireplace she piled her long brown hair on her head and stuck out her tongue. She put on her dilapidated slippers and went through to the windowless storeroom, redolent with the dismal smell of stale Woodbines.

The sack of sugar didn't look as big as Daisy had feared. She spread some newspaper on a low table, to catch any spills, and took down a pair of grimy brass scales. The sack was lugged over to the table and a stool set before it. Taking a pile of stiff blue cartridge paper bags, she opened out the first twenty and put them on the table. Carefully undoing the stitching at the top, she rolled down the sack to expose the white granules. Daisy put two fingers in her mouth and wet them down to her knuckles. They were stuck in the sugar and then put back in her mouth. She did it a second time. Using a small cylindrical shovel, she weighed out four ounces and tipped the sugar into a bag. She deftly folded the top of the paper to make a sound seal and put it to one side.

She was soon into a rhythm where her mind could disengage. Her mother came in with a cup of tea. Daisy drank half and then poured some sugar in, drinking down the syrupy concoction in one draught. Wiping her mouth with the back of her hand, she again set to. Working fast helped her to keep warm in the unheated storeroom and got the boredom over more quickly.

The previous Wednesday had been Speech Day. All the girls sitting cross-legged on the floor of the hall while stacks of unspeakably boring books were dished out to goody goodies and brown-nosing teachers' pets. No one ever got nylons or nail polish, or even a packet of chewing gum. A former Head Girl had given out the prizes. The inevitable speech had been full of dull exhortations, urging the girls to put country first and do what they could for the war effort. She had at least kept up the tradition of visitors in asking that the school be awarded a half-day holiday. Everyone had cheered and clapped her for that, until, fearing a breakdown of social order, they were quelled by the Headmistress, standing up in her black gown and moving her forearms up and down with splayed hands. The holiday would be tomorrow, for an unknown reason they were always on a Thursday afternoon.

Her friend Alice was going to the pictures, but Daisy had made no plans. No doubt her father would find things for her to do, stifling complaint as always by telling her how hard he had to work to pay her school fees, a chance he had never had, and that giving him a hand was the least she could do. She never said that in her opinion, even given the chance, he would have been too stupid to benefit from it. Of course, French was due in last period on Thursdays and so she could postpone the homework until the following evening. This meant she would have time to write her journal before she went to sleep.

For supper, Daisy's dad had supplied a rabbit, acquired from an old farm labourer in the pub at lunchtime. Fresh bread was on the table, even if it was the stodgy National Loaf. The law forbad the baker to sell bread until it was one day old, but her dad seemed able to persuade him. He was always doing little deals, or big ones for all Daisy knew. She had weighed up not mentioning the half-day holiday, but there was nowhere to hide, and they'd probably find out anyway.

'If you've got the afternoon off you can help me with the deliveries. So, make sure you're home sharp. There's a lot of groceries to go to the camp tomorrow.'

'Let her be, Eric,' her mother said, 'the girl's got schoolwork to do.'

'She can help me and still have time for that. Can't you, love?' he looked across at Daisy but did not smile.

Daisy avoided his gaze and said nothing. After the meal she helped her mother with the washing up. Surreptitiously she took her coat off the peg and went to the storeroom. Her mum did not like her wearing it indoors, she said it made her look like orphan Annie. Daisy finished bagging the sugar and put it in the shop, stacked neatly under the counter. At last, keeping her coat on, she went to her attic room. It was better to do homework in the cold than stay in the smoky parlour with the chattering radio.

Daisy put up the blackout before turning the feeble light on. Sometimes, after a while, it made her eyes swim. She felt under the iron bedstead for the red exercise book she used for writing her journal, a word she preferred over diary. It was elegant. She found her lovely Waterman pen that auntie Hilda had given her when she passed her scholarship. It had a gold tipped nib that moulded itself to your particular way of writing.

Loosening the buckle on her coat she got into bed, balancing the books on her lap. Homework first, then writing. Out came compass, set square and protractor. Geometry would be the most difficult, so get it over with. English was a précis. It would be easy and enjoyable. Daisy opened, The Essentials of School Geometry [without answers], at page thirty-six, exercise six, theorem ten, headed, Congruent Triangles.

∽

They lunched on tinned pilchards and boiled potatoes. As her mother cleared away, Daisy went and changed into her old gymslip. Down in the shop she sorted out the order for the NAAFI, ticking items off as she went along, margarine, cooking fat, powdered egg, and the sacks of washing soda that looked like diamonds and stripped the skin from your hands. After checking the order was complete, she looked into the parlour for her father. He was on the telephone, so she went and sat in the van. The seat had long ago collapsed and was filled by a lumpy cushion. Pulling her skirt over her knees she hid the ladders in her thick black stockings, at least from herself. The polished toes of her dark brown school shoes she buffed against her calves.

It was Daisy's task to go to the quartermaster's office and collect the order for the coming week. The way back to the NAAFI took her through the maze of Nissen huts in the centre of the camp. In the narrow alleys between the black slatted buildings little light penetrated. Daisy didn't see him. There was the sound of crunching gravel and, before she could turn, a hand from behind was clamped over her mouth and an arm came round her body, pulling her roughly backwards into the shadow of the eaves. She felt her dress being lifted and rough fingers probing the skin around her waist. The hand grasped the top of her knickers pulling them down. Her body twisted and she tried to bite the fingers that pushed into her face. The hand tightened round her mouth pulling her head back so she could barely breathe. Kicking with her heels against the man's legs, she pulled at the attacking arms. Hot fingers were groping at her sex. The man was grunting and swearing, the smell of his breath was sickening. Daisy kicked back again and tried harder to struggle free, pushing with her elbows, her body writhing to try and evade the awful prying hand. An incredulous panic invaded her.

A whistle sounded. Daisy was released and shoved violently onto the ground her face grazing the gravel. She lay still. There was a sound of running and then a soldier was bending over her.

'Holy heaven, what on earth's been going on? You alright miss? Can you get up?'

Daisy felt another, gentler, arm around her. There were now several soldiers. Slowly, she regained her feet.

'That's right, you lean on me,' the soldier said, and turning to one of the men in uniform, 'you best go get Captain Blount, and an MP if you can find one.'

'You've been set upon haven't you love?'

Daisy nodded. She began to tremble violently.

'Get a chair, quick,' said the soldier who continued to support her. One was brought and she carefully lowered herself onto it.

A young officer, not much older than Daisy, came running up.

'What's going on here, corporal?'

'Well sir, I heard what I thought was a fight and so blew the whistle and come running. I saw a man, in uniform, shove this young girl on the ground and run off towards the range, sir. As the girl wasn't moving, I thought I'd better see to her rather than chase the squaddie, and then I called for you, sir.'

'Thank you corporal, you've done well.' He pushed back his hair from his forehead and did up the top buttons of his tunic as he came over to where Daisy now sat huddled, staring at the ground.

'I'm told you've been assaulted, miss,' he said, 'and that the man was in uniform. Is that the case?'

Daisy nodded. 'But I never saw his face, it was too dark, and he got me from behind.' As she tried to pull up her knickers and straighten her dishevelled dress she began to cry.

The captain handed her a clean white handkerchief. Daisy held it tightly but did not dry her eyes. He seemed open and kindly and it comforted her.

'Come along,' he said putting his face level with hers and placing a hand on her shoulder. 'We need to get you warmed up with some hot tea. I'm so sorry this has happened, and on my watch.'

Daisy sat, an army greatcoat around her, in a wooden swivel chair in an untidy office. The captain stood behind the desk talking on the telephone, his eyes on Daisy. He replaced the receiver. Taking a chair, he came and sat opposite her. Slightly built, with a clear complexion, he seemed barely old enough to be an officer. There was a faint blond moustache on his upper lip. He had large brown eyes, with long lashes, like a doe. He looked directly at Daisy.

'My dad, he'll wonder what's happened to me, he mustn't find out, he'll blame me. I should have been more careful, I didn't think where I was walking.'

'Your chin is grazed,' said the captain, 'we'll get that seen to. Don't worry about your father, I'll talk to him. I'm afraid we can't allow this to pass, it is too serious. Can't let the men imagine they can get away with it. I can explain to your father that you are not in any way to blame for this incident.'

'Please, don't. I'm alright now and I'll never hear the end of it.' Tears began to flow, she wiped her face with the handkerchief she continued to tightly hold. 'He didn't get a chance to do anything really terrible to me.'

The captain's orderly came in with tin mugs of tea and handed one to Daisy. She took it with both hands.

'There you are miss, hot, sweet and strong. That'll put you to rights.'

He gave a second mug to the captain and belatedly saluted.

'I think we've got a good idea who's done this haven't we sir?' he said.

'Go and find the girl's father and bring him over here. Don't say anything about what's happened, and get some iodine, cotton wool and a dressing.'

The orderly saluted again and left. Daisy went to get up but found her legs still unsteady.

'Stay where you are and keep that greatcoat on, you're shocked, and you'll need to keep warm. I'll try and square things with your dad, but that's all I can do. By the way, I'm Captain Blount,' the officer said, holding out his hand, 'and what is your name?'

∽

On the drive back to the shop Daisy sat hunched into the greatcoat, staring straight ahead. Her hands were squeezed tightly between her knees.

'I don't know about giving you a turn. It fair gave me one when that soldier come for me. I didn't know what to think. You sure you didn't lead this bloke on? You're as soft as a brush.'

The van bumped slowly along the dark lanes to Porthwiel. The blacked-out headlamps threw thin slits of light a few feet ahead of them.

'I don't know where you get it from, Daisy. You know what right and wrong is, I didn't ought to let you out.'

'You hardly ever do. I get so much work given me. None of the other girls have to slave for their dads.'

Daisy's ear began to smart as her father's hand hit the side of her head.

'That's enough bleeding lip from you my girl. What the hell do we tell your mother? She'll be beside herself, she will.'

They parked in the street and went into the shop where her mother was serving a customer. Her dad, smiling, greeted the woman cheerily as he went through to the parlour. Daisy heard him filling the kettle. She loitered in the shop. As soon as the customer left her mother turned to Daisy.

'What you got that army coat on for, dear?' She asked.

Without waiting for a reply, she hurried into the parlour.

'Eric, that Stan Reynolds phoned while you was gone. He sounded in a terrible state, swearing and whatnot, horrible man. Any road, you're to call him urgent, as soon as you get in, he said.'

'Christ, what now? What's he been up to?'

'How should I know, he never said what it was about.'

He went to the phone, lifted the receiver and dialled four numbers. After each there was a slow whirring noise as the dial returned to its normal position.

'What's up, Stan?' As he listened his face became immobile.

'Jesus fucking wept. You must be joking. I thought we had an understanding. What if Jimmy…'

He fumbled in his pocket for a cigarette, lit it and listened for another couple of minutes.

'Fine, right, I'll do it now.' Banging the phone down he turned to Daisy and her mum who had stood transfixed throughout the call.

'You two better help me load up. There's some stuff must be shifted now. It's in the shed at the back. I'll get the van round there right away.' He took a key from a ring and handed it to Daisy's mother. 'This'll do the padlock. Look sharp.'

'Good lord, Eric, whatever are we doing this for? What's going on?'

Daisy's father went quickly out of the shop, the door slamming behind him. Her mother shot the bolt and they both hurried out to the long back garden, past the washhouse and the lavatory, the litter of old crates and pallets, and cases full of empty bottles. A wide lane ran along the backs of the houses in the High Street. The large, black, windowless shed stood at the end of the garden near to the lane gate. By the time the padlock and chains were off the double doors, the van had been backed up to the gate. Daisy's father came towards them out of the dark.

'I can't see inside the shed, dad, can we have a torch?'

'Course you bloody can't, there's a blackout, you'll have the ARP on us.'

Daisy went into the store with her mother and waited for her eyes to get accustomed to the gloom.

'Get a bloody move on you two.'

'Alright Eric, alright,' said Daisy's mother. She grabbed at a sack and began to drag it towards the door. Her husband swung it onto his back and disappeared into the lane.

'I don't know what you've been up to Eric, I'm sure I don't. I just hope you're not going to get us all into trouble.'

'Don't you worry, it'll all be fine, just keep moving. You too girl, buckle to.'

Daisy picked up a case. There was a clink of bottles as she carried it out to her father.

'Mind how you go with that,' he said, taking it from her and sliding it into the back of the van.

Soon the store shed was empty. Daisy's father shut the back doors of the van and locked them. Looking up and down the lane he opened the door to the driver's cab and turned to Daisy and her mother.

'I'll be gone for a bit. Lock the shed up and go back indoors.'

He jumped into the van, the engine fired, and the grey shape lumbered forward, disappearing into the darkness of the lane.

∽

'It's an officer from the camp, love. He wants to talk to you.' Daisy's mother had come up the stairs and into her room, rather than shouting from the bottom. She spoke quietly.

'It's not about dad, is it?'

'No dear, thank God. It's that nastiness that you got involved in. He wants you to make a statement.'

Daisy hesitated, then put her book to one side and swung her legs off the bed. She stood up and pulled the greatcoat across her chest.

'Do I really have to? It was horrible mum, disgusting. I've been trying to forget it.'

'I know love, but I think you've got to, and take that coat off, you know I don't like you wearing them indoors, you'd better give it back to him, it must belong to someone.'

Daisy put her hand in the pocket and felt the handkerchief before shrugging it off onto the bed. She smoothed the box pleats on the front of her school dress and retied the sash.

'You come down and I'll make a pot of tea. I've put him in the parlour.'

As Daisy came through the door, her eyes cast down, the captain got up from the dingy settee.

'I must apologise for this, Miss Lanyard, but I'm afraid I'm going to have to ask you about the recent incident at the camp in which you were involved. I do hope it won't be too distressing. I realise it's probably the last thing you want to talk about.'

Daisy looked at him and nodded. His uniform looked fresh with sharp creases in his trousers. The khaki tie was in a neat Windsor knot.

'How are you? I hope you've been alright – it must have been a horrible shock. I'm sorry I should have asked you that first, shouldn't I?' He smiled and offered his hand. Daisy took it. He had nice pink nails, with little white moons.

'Captain Blount – James,' he said.

Daisy went and sat on a chair at the dining table. The captain sat opposite her. He took a buff file from an attaché case and a black fountain pen from his breast pocket.

'It's in the hands of the Redcaps now, the military police, but they sent me to talk to you, or rather, to be frank, I insisted I came. MP's aren't known for their social graces and I thought you'd suffered enough recently.' He paused and looked at Daisy. 'I know it's not my business, but I heard of your father's arrest and I don't suppose that has made life any easier for you and your mother.'

Daisy raised her eyes and looked straight at the young captain. She straightened her back and folded her hands in her lap but did not speak.

'The soldier involved has been interrogated, has admitted to the crime and will, in due course, be punished. But we do need a statement from you as part of the formal investigation.'

Daisy cleared her throat. 'Of course, what do you want me to say?'

'I just need you to tell me exactly what happened. I'll write it down as we go along. Then you read it to make sure I've got it right, and if you're happy with it, then you sign it.'

'It happened very quickly. It was completely dreadful but all I really remember is the shock of it and the horrible smell of his breath and his hands…sir.'

13

'It doesn't need to be in great detail Miss Lanyard. Perhaps it might help if I ask you some straightforward questions and write down your answers. And you don't have to call me sir, you are not in the army. Captain Blount or better, James, will do. The army is rather like school, after a while you begin to forget you ever had a Christian name.'

'I don't mind being called Lanyard,' Daisy said, 'the girls think Daisy is so old fashioned. It was my granny's name, but please call me Daisy. I think it will make it easier.'

Daisy's mother came in with a tea tray and set it down on the table. The cups were china and there were two slices of seedcake on small scalloped plates.

'You be mother dear,' she said, turning the handle of the teapot towards Daisy. 'I hope you'll excuse me Captain Blount, I'll need to attend to the shop. Not that it's so busy since…' her voice trailed away. 'But there, you pour now Daisy, don't let it get cold.'

Daisy poured out the tea, remembering to put the milk in afterwards rather than first, as she would normally have done.

'Would you like a piece of seedcake, James?'

'Thank you, Daisy, that would be splendid.'

They began the slow and awkward process of recording her deposition to the military court. Daisy read it through and excused herself. She came down the stairs a moment later with her pen and duly signed the form. James blotted it and slid it into the folder.

'Thank you so much, Daisy, I hope we won't have to trouble you anymore. I'm particularly sorry to have to put you through this now. Your poor mother must be finding life difficult?'

'She doesn't seem so bad. My dad's friend Harry is helping out. He comes to tea. If they find dad guilty of this black market thing, Harry says he could go to gaol. That really would take the wind out of mum's sails, mine too. She's already saying I'll have to leave school, because of the fees.'

'That sounds very hard on you. Isn't there a bursary or some arrangement that could be made?

'I don't know,' Daisy said. 'I'm sorry, I shouldn't be talking to you like this. It's not your fault.'

'I would like to help if I can. The army owes you something. Let me look around for you. Even in war time there are foundations that might be able to help.'

'Oh dear,' Daisy said, 'I'm not sure my mum would let me take charity.'

'Let's wait and see,' James said, 'you don't have to say anything at the moment.'

Daisy reached for the brown earthenware teapot, cupping its curves in her hands.

'I've let it go cold. Shall I make some more?'

'Not for me,' James said, rising from his chair, 'I think I should be getting back to camp. The motor bike is much friendlier when there's a bit of light left.' He picked up his coat from the back of the settee. 'Thanks for your cooperation Daisy. I'll look into the matter of bursaries. It's the least I can do. I'll come back to you if I find anything useful.'

James wrapped a long khaki choker round his neck and under his arms before putting on his greatcoat.

'I've got to apologise again,' Daisy said, her face colouring. 'You were kind enough to lend me your coat and I'm afraid I've been wearing it. It's so lovely and warm. Wait a moment, I'll go upstairs and get it.' She started for the door.

'Please, don't worry now,' James said, 'as you can see, I've got another and there would be nowhere to put it on the bike. But I'd be grateful if you didn't wear it out and about. It might cause comment.' He smiled and pulled a pair of goggles over his fair hair leaving them loose round his neck. 'Best go and thank your mother for her hospitality.'

James returned and picked up the attaché case. Daisy opened the back door. It was near dusk, but the sky remained intensely blue. At first hesitating she walked down the garden with him to the back gate. The grey Bantam bike was in the lane, propped against the wall.

'I'm afraid we don't run to a jeep,' he said. He stood with his hand on the gate and turned to Daisy.

'In real life – outside of the war – I'm an artist. Would you mind if I came and did some drawings of you? I'm getting very tired of drawing camp life. I would have to ask your mother's permission of course.'

Daisy, her arms folded round her, shivered in the evening chill.

'I don't know. What sort of drawings?'

'Portraits,' James said, 'you would naturally be fully dressed – you could even keep your scarf and gloves on if you wanted to.'

Daisy paused. 'That sounds nice, I'd like that. I don't think mum would mind. I'll speak to her about it and perhaps you can call in the next couple of days and talk to her.'

'It's very kind of you to agree and I'd be very grateful for the favour.'

James went through the gate and sat astride the bike. He secured his attaché case to the petrol tank and settled the goggles over his eyes.

'Thank you, Daisy, I very much hope we'll meet again.'

'Yes,' Daisy said.

Reaching down he opened the choke on the petrol line and kicked the starter. The engine settled as he pulled away down the lane. Daisy watched him fade in the haze of the setting sun. She shut the gate and turned towards the house.

'Goodbye, James,' she said.

She went through to the shop where her mother looked up from packing a cardboard box with groceries.

'Give me a hand, dear,' she said, 'Harry will be along with the van shortly. There's only a couple more to do. They're in the book. Has the captain gone then love?'

Daisy opened the book and began collecting packets of tea and tins of polish and stacking them on the corner of the counter.

'Yes, just now. It took much longer than I thought, but it was alright. He asked me about what happened and then wrote down what I said. It was helpful in a way – to talk about it made it less frightening – and the man who did it is going to be punished. By the way, he told me he's an artist in civvy street.'

'That's nice dear. I think we'll have corn' beef for tea. I'll make a hash. Harry likes that and you do as well, don't you?'

'Anyway mum, he wanted to know if you would give your permission for him to come over and draw me.'

'Whatever for? He wants you to be his artist's model? I couldn't think of such a thing. Haven't you been in enough trouble?'

'Mum, listen, you don't understand. He just wants to do my portrait. I'll have all my clothes on, and you'll be here.'

'Well, I don't know. I'll have to think about it. I'll ask Harry.'

'That's ridiculous. It's got nothing to do with him. He's not my dad.'

'No – more's the pity. He's got ten times as much sense.'

'Listen mum, James is a kind man. Nothing will happen.'

'Oh, James is it now? That was quick work my girl.' Her mother paused shaking her head. She took a little handkerchief out of her pinafore pocket and blew her nose. 'As I say, I'll have to think about it.'

Daisy closed her eyes and leaned against the counter.

'Now, put the orders by the door where Harry can pick them up, and then find something useful to do.'

Daisy did as she was told. Returning to the parlour she took her pen from the table and slipped it into her pocket. The tea things were collected onto the tray and taken into the kitchen to be washed up in the stone sink. She filled the kettle and put it back on the stove. Daisy carefully washed the cup that James had drunk from. She stacked the crockery on the draining board. The cold made it difficult to get the cups and plates to dry properly. Traces of lint stuck to the china.

Back in her room she put up the blackout before turning on the light. She picked up the greatcoat and read the printed label stitched across the top of the inside pocket – Capt. James B. Blount. What did the B stand for she wondered, pressing the coat against her face. It smelled spicy – Bay Rum – that's why his hair shone. Putting it on, she held it tight against her body. She did up all the nubbley brass buttons that she could and turned up the collar. For some time, she lay quietly, her hands deep in the pockets, clutching the handkerchief. Leaning over she fetched her journal out from under the bed and found her pen. Drawing up her legs, and tucking the skirts of the coat round her, she balanced the exercise book on her thighs and began to write.

∽

Rinsing her long dark hair in tepid bath water with an enamel jug was not a pleasure. Her mother had made it clear that she saw the bath as an unnecessary extravagance not warranted by having one's picture drawn. Daisy disagreed.

She flicked her hair forward and dried it as best she could on the thin towel. After brushing, she tied it loosely with a brown silk ribbon at the back of her neck. While her mother was busy in the shop, she surreptitiously ironed the pleats and the blue sash of her best school dress. Daisy pulled an orange woollen jumper over her still wet hair and stepped into her dark blue dress. She tied the sash carefully and pushed it low over her hips. In her mother's bedroom she looked at herself in the foxed mirror. Rather pale, too tall and skinny, pretty eyes, big ears, a well shaped mouth, she pinched her dress out from her nipples – flat chested. A proper dress would be nice. The couple she owned had not kept pace with her growth. They were too tight under her arms and across her bum, and too little girly. Her mother had been cautiously sympathetic to the idea that a new one was needed.

'We've all got to make do and mend, love. We'll think about it later. We could see if auntie Hilda's got any material. She was always the sister who was handy with a needle. I never had the patience.'

∽

James arrived with a large flat, black case. Daisy had been waiting, listening for the sound of his bike and resisting going into the garden to look for him. Her mother had thought that propriety demanded that Daisy and James use the parlour, a place where nothing untoward could possibly be imagined, let alone enacted. She greeted James rather formally, even warily.

'It must be very nice to be an artist,' she said.

Daisy stood quietly in the background hands clasped in front of her.

'Would it be alright, Mrs Lanyard,' said James, peering over the half lace curtains into the garden, 'if I move the table. I'd like to put Daisy in the light.'

'I suppose so. You clear the things off Daisy and then help the captain move it. Now, if you'll excuse me, you know where I am if I'm needed.'

They moved the table to the far wall and James angled a dining chair near to the window. He rubbed his hands together and pushed his corn-coloured forelock out of his eyes.

'You sit here, Daisy.' She did. 'That's perfect. There's good contrast between the orange and the dark blue and the pale sash breaks it up nicely.'

He moved his chair to different positions in front of Daisy – sitting and looking at her intently at each station.

Daisy pulled up her black stockings, smoothing out the wrinkles as best she could without revealing her garters.

'Do you want me to sit in any special way?' She asked.

'No, just sit naturally and comfortably. Perhaps you could turn a fraction to the window to increase the light on your face.'

Daisy moved slightly and raised her chin so that her eyes focused above James' head.

'That's good,' James said, 'but just hold your head naturally and look towards my left shoulder – that's it.'

'It doesn't feel very natural,' Daisy said.

'Don't worry, it soon will.'

James took off his tunic and loosened his tie, he undid the top button of his khaki shirt and ran his thumbs behind his braces. Putting his case on the table he took out a drawing block, several pencils and a putty rubber.

'I like the way the shine on your shoes picks up the light. Could you slide your right foot forward a little and move your left back, so the heel is against the chair leg – that's it – perfect.'

'Do I have to stay as still as a statue?'

'No – but try not to move too much.'

'Am I allowed to speak?'

'Yes, as long as you don't move your head a lot.'

Daisy began to laugh.

'And most important of all,' James said, 'you must never giggle.'

Daisy recomposed her features.

'I'll try,' she said.

James flicked his hair out of his eyes and began to draw in quick deft movements, looking from his block to Daisy every few seconds. The only sound for some time was the faint scratch of graphite on paper.

The proximity of James was disturbing. It was curious to be in the familiar parlour sitting so still and trying to keep a bead fixed on his shoulder.

'I'm aiming to do a couple of watercolour full length portraits of you.' James said, 'pretty much as you are today. I like the composition we've got now. The first thing is to get to know you with some pencil sketches. Your skin tones are lovely, but they'll have to wait.'

Daisy felt her face colour.

'Don't blush Daisy, it's only a technical observation.'

Daisy tried to hold her pose. She lost the sense of time passing. James changed the position of his chair. He came over to Daisy and carefully tucked her hair behind one ear.

'I need to see your jaw line.'

Intermittent faint sounds of her mother talking to customers came from the shop. Daisy's legs were going to sleep, and her neck ached.

'Can we stop for while?' She asked.

'Of course, the light's not so good now in any case.' He put his drawing block down on the table and wriggled his fingers.

21

Daisy stretched out her legs, pushed her shoulders back and down and moved her head from side to side.

'I haven't done anything, but I feel quite tired.'

'It's the concentration,' James said, 'it'll be much easier next time.'

'Shall we have some tea?' Daisy suggested.

'I'd love some, thank you.'

'Can I look?' she asked, getting up from her chair.

'I'd like you to, you can tell me what you think – whether I've captured the real Daisy.'

James stood beside her at the table and lay out the sheets of drawings. He smelled of soap, Imperial Leather and spice. Daisy wanted to touch him, to stroke his arm, even to lay her head on his shoulder.

She looked down at the images of herself. There were two full sketches and some studies of her face, her loosely clasped hands, the angles of her feet and ankles.

'That's me,' she said, 'but not me.'

'It's the best I can see you today,' James said, 'I'm pleased with them – I think it's going to be good.'

'I think it's magical,' Daisy said. 'There are some snaps of me, but I always look like a long thin ghost – you've made me look like a person.' She turned her face to his. 'It must be wonderful to be able to do that.'

'Well it is, and it isn't, after you've been painting for a few years it's like a job – but it still feels special to me. I could have been a bank clerk.'

'You don't look like one, for a start, your hair is too long. I'm sorry that was rude. I'll go and make the tea.'

'I'll take it as a compliment,' James said. 'Let me come and help or perhaps I should go and see if your mum would like one?'

'That's a good idea.'

James smiled at Daisy and went through to the shop, she to the kitchen.

Daisy heard the voices of her mother and James, first in the shop and then in the parlour. As she came in with the tea tray her mother was looking at the drawings.

'Aren't they good Daisy? I think the captain has really caught you. It's a wonderful likeness, you must be very pleased?'

'I am, mum.'

Daisy's mum poured herself a cup of tea and made for the door.

'You two sit and have your tea, I'll take mine through, if that's alright.'

༄

Softened by an amber light from a falling sun, they sat, facing one another, in the chairs as they had been set for drawing.

'I think my mum's coming round,'

'I hope so,' James said, 'after all, I don't look much like a Parisian ravisher of demoiselles, do I?'

'No, not much like a bank clerk either. I expect you look like who you are.'

A thick silence fell between them. Daisy looked down the garden to where a light mist was blurring the lane.

'We'd better move the table back,' James said, barely audibly.

'Yes, we had,' Daisy said, gathering the tea things onto the tray.

'I've spoken to the vicar,' James said, doing up his shirt and putting his tunic back on.

'Oh.'

'He's the chairman of the trustees who administer an ancient parish fund, for the education of the deserving poor and such like, not that you necessarily qualify on either count, Daisy. There's not much call on it nowadays and he thinks your school fees would be very likely to fit the bill.'

'Thank you, that is so kind of you,' Daisy said. 'I didn't like to ask but it has been worrying me. It looks like mum's set on going to London. Harry says that there's plenty of factory jobs going. That's where he's off to.'

'Sounds a bit hard on you,' James said.

'It will be fine. My auntie Hilda's only the other side of the village and I could move in with her at least until I finish school.'

James collected his drawings and took the block over to the window. Daisy joined him.

'They look even lovelier in this light,' Daisy said.

They shifted the table and reset the chairs.

'It would still be very disruptive, surely,' James said, 'isn't this your exam year?'

'I think I'd like it at auntie's, there's more room in her cottage, she's on her own and I think she's fond of me. She gave me my pen and a beautiful geometry set, she even knitted this jumper,' Daisy said, lifting her arms to show it off.

'Then I'm grateful to her,' James said. 'That doesn't sound half bad.'

Daisy waited while James took his leave of her mother. They walked together down the garden and she opened the wicket gate to the lane. Out of sight of the parlour window, Daisy took his arm.

'If we walk down to the bend,' she said, pointing, 'there's a place where we can watch the sunset.'

They stood before a crumbly red brick wall and looked across a paddock. Two horses with blankets snuffled the scant pasturage. Beyond them the filigree outlines of trees were blackened by the light of the sun, rippling as it dipped towards the horizon.

'I think you've saved me,' James said, 'I was beginning to forget what it meant to be an artist.' He turned to Daisy and took her hand.

'You may be awfully young, but you are a perfect subject – you've got real presence – and that is what I want to show.'

'I don't quite understand what that means,' Daisy said, 'but the person I saw in your drawing makes me happy to be who I am – thank you. Also, I'm nearly eighteen, so not that young.'

Shoulder to shoulder they watched the final shimmering crescent drop behind the distant trees. For a while they stood enjoying the gathering dusk.

'I asked your mum if I could come back on Thursday,' James said, 'she was fine as long as it didn't interfere with your schoolwork. After I chatted to her about the rigours of the artistic life, she seemed almost keen.' He smiled broadly, which dimpled his cheeks.

'I'd like that,' Daisy said. 'I can work at break and lunchtime. It'll take my mind off mum's bloater paste sandwiches.' They turned and began to saunter back up the lane. 'After today I shall want to tell the girls I'm an artist's model, but it sounds like swanking.'

'You could say you're sitting for your portrait, that's even grander. And now I must get a move on or I'll be on a charge.'

They reached the motorbike and James put on his choker, turned up his collar and got astride the bike. Daisy stood close. James tried to kick start the bike, but nothing happened.

'I'm being too slow, and I've flooded the carburettor. Daisy, be an angel and give me a push – I'll have to jump start it.'

Daisy held on to the pannier behind the saddle. James pulled his goggles on and turned round, giving the thumbs up.

'Thanks awfully, I'll see you Thursday about four.'

'If I'm spared,' Daisy said, laughing as she started pushing the bike, running along behind it. The engine fired with a jolt and James accelerated away. He turned and waved a gauntleted hand at Daisy who stood in the middle of the road, waving back until he was out of sight. She walked slowly down the lane, mist in her eyes.

'So, this is what it feels like,' she said to the tortoiseshell cat from next door that sat on the wall, purring as Daisy stopped to stroke her.

'So, this is it.'

Chapter 2

'Where are we?'

'Sussex, it's a populous home county with manicured countryside and properly metalled lanes. It's the late twentieth century's answer to Metroland. We can't be lost.'

'Just keep driving, something will show up, there must be a sign.'

'Sounds ominous.'

'How about a signpost?'

'That's better – I think there's a crossroads ahead. This magical navigation aid refuses to believe we're in England – won't relinquish France.'

'I don't blame it.'

'Emily, and you an English girl, how can you say such a thing?'

'I don't feel like an English girl papa. Look, there's a pub. Can we stop and have something awful to eat, please?'

'Sure thing. They might know the way to Campiston House. I am sorry. It's not as though we haven't been here before.'

Toby braked and swung the car into a gravelled space beside a low pink building. Inside, light shafted through small leaded panes and played on bleached kitchen tables and comfortable looking chairs. The low ceiling had the amber patina of ancient smoke. Behind a polished copper bar, they glimpsed a cool taproom with barrels racked against the wall. A yeasty scent drifted towards them.

'This is what pubs smelt like when I was young,' Toby said.

'It smells a bit like champagne.'

'But only a bit.'

An elderly man in shocking pink cords and a check jacket sat on a sofa by the unlit fire reading a broadsheet. On the hearthrug a fat tabby was stretched out, audibly snoring.

'I'd give that bell a ring, if I were you,' the man said, lowering his paper, 'Belinda will be about the place somewhere.' Emily struck the domed bell producing a sharp clear note. A young woman in skinny jeans and a leopard skin sweater appeared.

'Hi, what can I get you?' She picked up a cloth and began polishing the bar.

'Can we have some coffee, please,' Toby asked, 'and perhaps something to eat?'

'Of course,' Belinda handed them two plastic covered menus. 'I'll get the coffee while you decide.'

'Looks more like an aid to euthanasia than a menu. Pies, pasties, chips and sausages – it reminds me…'

'No Toby, not again – Gus Fraser said that Shane Warne's idea of a balanced meal was a meat pie in each hand.'

'Sorry darling. But you will remember to tell it at my funeral. I think a list of my favourite jokes instead of a eulogy is a good idea, so much better than being remembered for being inoffensively nice.'

'Of course, but I wouldn't worry too much, Toby, seeing as currently you're a long way even from retirement. But then you do behave rather oddly and talk like a Henry James novel, plus, there's no real chance of you being thought of as nice. Is there anything here we can eat?'

'Ploughman's looks the safest bet. Shall we risk it?'

'Yeah.'

Belinda brought a tray with a cafetiere, cups and saucers and two little biscuits. Emily immediately unwrapped and ate both the Lotus caramels. They ordered the ploughman's which arrived with equal dispatch. The coffee was fresh and mellow, the fat wedges of yellow brie, ripe, the bread soft and crusty. Some apple jelly cut the cream of the cheese nicely.

'I've noticed before how a simple, but unexpected, culinary pleasure can lift the spirits.'

'Ace nosh,' Emily said, 'let's try the apple pie.'

'Fine, I'll ask about James' place.'

'I wonder if you can help us,' Toby said, as Belinda put two slices of Dutch apple tart dark with spices and sultanas onto the table.'

'I'll try.'

'We're looking for Campiston House. We know it's somewhere round here, because we've been there before, but today it's being elusive.'

'I know the name,' Belinda said. 'Was that your friend's place, Dr Quimper?'

The doctor lowered his newspaper. 'Campiston House, why yes, of course. James' old place, end of Monk's lane, about two miles south of Barcombe. Been shut up since he died. Is it on the market?'

'We are relatives of his,' Toby said, 'we've come to look it over. We rather hope it's habitable.'

'Couldn't call James house proud,' said the doctor, 'but there was an old girl who kept it clean for him.'

'Thanks a lot,' Emily said, and tucked her straight blond hair behind her ears. 'Do you think you could direct us from here?' She scrabbled around in her bag for a notebook. Dr Quimper joined them at their table and drew a sketch map of the route.

'He was my great uncle,' Emily said.

'Yes, you were at the funeral, of course.' Dr Quimper said. 'Quiet, lovely man – spent most of his time painting, right to the end.' There was a pause. 'We'd play chess and have lunch here every so often, do a bit of fishing when the weather was good. He used to go to the West Country in the spring, not sure why – but then men don't talk much, do they?' The doctor wrote a number on Emily's notebook. 'If you need anything, please call, I live close by.'

'Thank you so much,' Emily said.

∼

Outside Barcombe they stopped at a farm shop and bought some basic supplies. Toby drove slowly up Monk's Lane avoiding the worst of the potholes and the occasional speedbump. The carriageway petered out and disappeared into a wood.

'It's round here somewhere, but I do remember needing one's wits,' Toby said.

They drove, even more slowly, back the way they had come, and this time found a trackway leading from what Toby had earlier identified as merely a passing place. A small faded wooden sign nailed to a post, with Campiston House and an arrow pointing up a tree lined path, was reassuring.

The track led to a large clearing with a circular gravelled drive designed for horse drawn carriages. The square house sat on rising ground with a south facing front. The façade was Georgian, with long windows and an oriel above the door. The low double roof, a mixture of stone and slate, suggested earlier origins. Crumbling masonry steps led up to a faded main door. Gravel paths, green with weeds, led off west and east, disappearing round the sides of the house.

Toby and Emily got out of the car and stood looking up at the shuttered windows.

'Let's make some tea and then look round.'

'Sounds good,' Emily said. 'How odd it feels to be back here.'

The heavy door swung open and they stared into the dark interior. Toby stood to one side while Emily hesitated at the threshold. Inside she peered around looking for a switch. Once found, it failed to deliver the expected flood of light.

'Bugger,' Toby said, 'I'll go and get a torch, we can open the shutters and find the fuse box.'

Emily stood alone, the hallway gradually revealing itself. In front of her was a wide central staircase of bare wood. On either side dark doors cut into the walls. The shape of a chandelier was discernible hanging from the ceiling above the oriel. After the warmth of the sun the air struck chill and musty. Emily tried a door to the right of the staircase. It was unlocked, two sets of windows on the far wall were outlined by pencils of light seeping round the edges of the shutters. She crossed the room, dominated by a large kitchen table. Her steps sounded on the stone floor. The room gradually came into focus as Emily folded green painted slats back into recesses beside the window frames. The black mass of a coal range with an antique electric cooker beside it revealed themselves. Between the windows were two deep porcelain sinks with dull brass taps, flanked by wooden draining boards. In one corner stood an ancient fridge, its cream paint spotted with rust. She opened the door, inside were patches of pink and black mould. A dresser stood next to the door leading back into the hall from where footsteps could be heard.

'Toby, I'm in here,'

'For a moment I thought you'd been spirited away,' Toby

said, coming into the kitchen and giving Emily a hug. 'What's all this?'

'It's the kitchen. I dimly remember having breakfast in here, now it seems about five hundred years out of date.'

Toby went over to the sink and turned on a tap. It gurgled and vibrated before emitting a stream of clear water.

'That's good,' he said. 'Now, I'm going to look for something attached to a wall that might possibly contain the fuse box and perhaps you can look for a kettle.'

∾

They sat at the kitchen table drinking tea from large white mugs, Emily ran her fingers along the ruts of past knives. She tugged open a reluctant drawer under the table and uncovered a cigar box. Inside were car keys and a large ring hung with a variety of others. There was no indication of what locks they might open.

'It's easy,' Toby said, pulling them one by one around the ring, 'size, shape and type of key are the clues. These long ones with simple square ends are going to be internal doors, the stubby fussy ones are for padlocks.'

'That's pretty obvious Toby, but which doors and padlocks?'

'Trial and error, is always a good plan.'

'Didn't need any in here,' said Emily, looking around the kitchen, 'none of the cupboards were locked. They're all full of stuff. If I were Escoffier I'd be really pleased. I recognised the jelly moulds, but a lot of the old gadgets look like instruments of torture.'

'They probably were to the poor scullions who had to use them. We'll get what we need tomorrow, an electric kettle would be an addition. There was quite a bundle of post on the hall table, I wonder who picked it up? There's likely to be stuff from the solicitors or the bank, we'd better have a look at some point. Let's do the tour, bring those keys,' Toby said. He got up and took the mugs to the sink. 'Downstairs first?'

The spacious sitting room faced south. Two sets of French windows opened out onto a paved terrace. The cracked plaster ceiling was apparently supported by fluted pilasters.

'Ridiculous affectation,' Toby said, grimacing at them.

The generous fireplace was topped with a heavy mantel. High backed armchairs, designed for draughty rooms, were to each side. Closer to the garden there were occasional tables and sofas. Iranian carpets covered most of the floor.

'I used to wind that,' Emily said, going over to a casement clock, 'the key was kept underneath it.' She fished it out and wound the clock. Tipping it gently to one side for a moment she got the pendulum to swing evenly. 'If it's still going tomorrow, we can put it right. It can take ages because of the chimes.'

Emily sat on the sofa and looked around the room. The walls were everywhere covered in paintings.

'Are these all uncle James'?'

'Pretty much all. As I remember the whole house is full of his paintings. He didn't bother to sell a lot when he got older, or perhaps he simply went out of fashion.'

The dining room was dull, and the morning room had only a writing table and a few upholstered chairs, all slightly bigger than necessary for the average human. Everywhere the house seemed well ordered, the furniture polished, if dusty, the mirrors offering clear reflections. The study was alone in having an immediate sense of occupation. Papers and books still littered the desk and spilled over onto tables and floor. Old, clubbable, leather chairs had large cushions nestling in their sagging seats. A basket of wood sat beside a log burning stove. Old fashioned glass-fronted cabinets were filled with books. A humidor, half full of cigars, perched on top of a pile of notebooks.

Emily and Toby sat down in the club chairs facing one another.

'Well?' Toby said.

'It's like revisiting a dream, familiar but not quite real,' Emily said, pushing the flat of her hands down the outside of her thighs. 'We'd better try and sort out a couple of bedrooms,' she said, getting up. 'Let's have our supper in here, we can light a fire and be cosy, better than chilling in the kitchen.'

'I'll do it now,' Toby said, 'give the room a chance to warm up.'

The oak staircase creaked beneath their feet, their steps making a faint echo. At the top a gallery ran along three sides of the house. On the walls, out of the direct light, were lots of watercolour sketches, mainly landscapes. Doors were let into the walls at irregular intervals. In one corner was a thin door raised about ten centimetres from the ground.

The first door they tried was locked. Employing Toby's logic, Emily selected a likely looking key from the ring. She tried several keys before she was rewarded with a click and a slight giving of the door. The room felt chilled and curtains moved in the wind. The two windows were shattered. Glass shards crunched beneath their feet. Toby looked through the jagged hole into the garden, now returning to a natural disorder. He stooped and picked up several stones the size of walnuts.

'Naughty boys?'

'Bloody nuisances,' Emily said, pulling her jacket close round her. She began dragging the glass into a pile with the side of her shoe. 'It's a lovely bedroom.' In the middle of the wall facing the windows was a red mahogany four poster.

Emily launched herself onto the thick mattress and bounced around.

'Smells a bit musty,' she said, 'we'd better check the other rooms. If all the windows are smashed, we'll have to go to a hotel – if we can find one. Come on Toby,' Emily jumped off the bed and grabbed his hand.

One other bedroom had similarly suffered, and another had been converted to a bathroom some time ago. That left three, good sized, bedrooms in reasonable shape.

'It's all a bit damp,' Emily said.

'If we can find some bricks and heat them in the oven – if it works – we can wrap them in pieces of blanket and use them to air the beds. It's what my granny used to do. I wonder why it's called airing?'

'*Aeration* – that's what they do down South, hanging their duvets out of the window – not filling their beds with hot builders' materials,' Emily said.

'No matter. I suggest we stay and reclaim the house, what's a bit of damp? I'll get the suitcases, at least our sheets will be nice and dry.'

∾

The sun was gone and the air much colder. Toby found the plugs and switches for the squat enamel stove and turned on all the plates, leaving the oven door open to heat the kitchen. As he began to assemble their supper, the smell of hot dust stung his nostrils. He opened the back door and stood peering into the darkening garden trying to recall what was out there. He put their food and a bottle of wine on a butler's tray and went to find Emily who was toasting herself by the stove in the study.

'It's only a cold collation,' Toby said, 'the bread and ham

should be alright, but the tomatoes will be red bags of seeds in water, welcome to England.'

'Don't grouch, at least my phone works. I've just spoken to Jean-Marie, he says he'll come over if we decide to stay for a while, and he misses me, which is sweet.'

'That would be good, I'm sure we'll have uses for a strong young man.'

'Stay cool Toby, we are talking Jean-Marie here. Given the choice he'd always do some light dusting over chopping wood.'

'Silly me. Of course, the countryside's a setting, not a habitat to the average Parisian,' Toby said, getting up from his chair and feeding a couple of logs into the open door of the stove. 'So, now you are the chatelaine of your own country estate.'

'It's probably no more than a few hectares, Toby. It feels weird. Being here – the house – knowing that it's mine. If uncle James had left it to you that would be understandable. I'm the wrong generation and he only knew me for a few years, those lovely summer holidays in my teens. We did get on well, I was really fond of him, I suppose in a way I loved him. But, it's still, I don't know, what am I meant to do with it?

'That's something for you to decide, and it's why we're here.'

∽

'I have had better nights' sleep,' Toby said, 'it's certainly a sight colder first thing than we've been used to. I'm wearing nearly everything I brought with me.'

He kissed Emily's cheek as she sat at the kitchen table wrapped in her outdoor coat, with a woolly hat pulled down over her ears, her straight blond hair sticking out at right angles.

'I think a couple of pairs of socks would be a good idea?' she said, getting up. 'Would you like some tea? The kettle takes about three days to boil, so I could get one to you by Wednesday at the latest, and we must get some mould cleaner for the inside of the fridge.'

'Yes, thanks, I'd love some, in your own time. How did you find the shower?'

'What shower? There's just a wobbly hair washer stuck on the wall, can't be directed, no water pressure and about as hot as the Arctic Ocean.'

'Poor cherub, I hate to think of you suffering.'

'And there is absolutely nothing to make coffee in.'

'Better stick with tea for now, we'll get a cafetiere.'

'And there's no fresh bread. And the croissant you bought taste as though they were made with pig fat – and don't say 'welcome to England,' I thought it was supposed to be civilized now.'

'Emily, darling, you're a chatelaine, not a diva, get a grip. We'll make a list of everything we need for an emergency civilization kit and go into Lewes. You'll be beguiled by its metropolitan pleasures.'

Emily put her arms round her father's neck and kissed him.

'Sorry Toby, didn't mean to be a princess.'

Toby squeezed Emily's hand. 'No matter, we'll put some effort into making ourselves comfortable while we're here, no expense spared, promise. Let's explore the garden and then set off for adventure.'

Outside, reflected through the cold dew of an autumn morning, the light was dazzling. In front of them was a wide swathe of what once was a lawn and, a large area of overgrown beds, now run to seed. A path led to a dilapidated summerhouse. Emily peered through a grimy window and pushed open the door. Inside was a jumble of garden furniture and faded cushions.

'Look, a barbecue. Steak for supper,' Emily said, 'I suppose it still works?' She knocked some flakes of rust off the fire holder. 'It looks as though it might have been left by the Romans.'

'Then it probably will work,' Toby said.

Running along the end of the garden was a ragged woodland.

'I remember this,' Emily said, 'I used to make dens in the woods and spend hours in them, reading and dreaming.'

They walked back in silence. Emily clutched the ring of keys and began to investigate the collection of outhouses that lay on both sides of the garden. Most imposing was a pantiled barn with oxeye windows. Emily found the key to the padlock and released a rusty chain. Inside the dark interior, under a tarpaulin, they discovered a dilapidated Peugeot estate.

'Did uncle James leave me the *mobilieres?*' Emily asked.

'Yes, they're called chattels in English. You've got some car keys, let's see if it really is *mobile*.'

Toby had to get his car and use jump leads. After some coaxing the engine stuttered and fired and Emily drove out onto the gravel.

'That's great, Toby, almost as exciting as the house, and it means if you go back to Paris before me, I won't be stranded, although I've never had to drive on the wrong side of the road.'

'It's easy. We'll put, 'car insurance for Emily,' on our to do list, along with the glazier,' Toby said, 'and do you think we should get a washing machine, there doesn't seem to be one in the house?'

'Yeah, sounds good, but let's finish looking round and get that civilisation kit before we do anything else, living out here a freezer would be useful.'

The back of the barn was piled high with logs. Not as

neatly stacked as they would be in France, nor as big, as Emily observed, but a hundred euro's worth at least, Toby calculated. Beyond the barn was an enormous glasshouse with peeling paint and a lot of broken panes.

'Tomatoes,' Emily said.

Next to this was a gardener's shed with a long trestle table, packed with tools and clay pots.

On the other side of the garden was a low building with large windows and a skylight. At one end was a chimney. A path was discernible between the door and the back entrance to the house.

'It's James' studio, of course,' Toby said. He took the keys from Emily and tried several without success. She looked under a doormat. Toby ran his fingers along the top of the lintel and found a key. Before he could use it, Emily had turned the brass doorknob and pushed. The door opened.

'What a gorgeous space,' Emily said, pirouetting on the wooden floor, 'the light is wonderful.'

'Positively Gothic. St Denis would have loved it,' Toby said.

'Too arcane Toby – St Denis – uncle James?'

'As you know, St Denis built the first recognisably Gothic cathedral in the eponymous, but now sadly unfashionable, Paris suburb. Light was a big feature.' Toby lay on a chaise by the fireplace, Emily looked around her.

It was about the same size as the drawing room and smelt of linseed oil. In the centre of the room, to the side of the skylight, was a heavy easel caked in paint. An unfinished oil of a man at a desk was clamped on it. To the side was a tea trolley covered with tubes of paint, mostly without caps, pots of brushes, mahl sticks and bits of old rag. On the top was James' pallet, still loaded with paint and with brushes stuck through the thumbhole.

'When I used to stay, I wasn't allowed in here, the

housekeeper made it very clear that I mustn't disturb the master at work. I did like her, she spoilt me, but she was a bit fierce, one false move and...' Emily drew her hand across her throat.

Emily was rifling through loose sketches and notes that lay strewn over a long table under the windows facing the garden. Against the wall was a deep, unbelievably filthy, sink and a metal stand with a gas ring attached to a red canister. Next to it was an old saucepan encrusted with what looked like hardened treacle. There was also an electric kettle with an original rubber lead that was almost deliquescent with age, some open packets of coffee and a percolator that Emily thought might constitute a danger to public health.

'There are so many canvasses and piles of sketchbooks around the place,' Emily said, 'it makes uncle James look almost obsessive. He must have worked so hard.'

'And for a long time,' Toby said. 'He was a bit like Turner, who'd manage at least four sunrises over Petworth park before elevenses, speaking of which, do you think we should be moving on?'

'I guess so. There's only one painting that's hung in here, it's that picture behind the chaise,' Emily said, pointing to a small watercolour portrait of a girl in a black tunic sitting on a chair. 'It's beautiful – she looks so alive.'

Toby stood up and came to look at the painting. 'That's Daisy, James' only love, as far as I know – she was at school when he met her and, after the war, she may have come and lived with him here for a while. I don't know what happened to her, it wasn't something James would talk about.'

'It's such a tender picture, and she looks, I don't know – enigmatic, I guess. There's so much behind her dark eyes – I love it.'

As they went to leave Emily noticed an old Barbour hanging behind the door.

'Do you think uncle James would mind if I borrowed his jacket – it's got a quilt and it would be so nice to be warm?'

'He'd be delighted. Now, off to the city of lights and laughter,' Toby said, opening the door.

Emily swung the coat over her shoulders and pulled the heavy zip up to her throat. As a child she remembered trying on Toby's jacket, enjoying its warmth and protection. The portrait of Daisy drew her eyes once more as she left the studio, locked the door, returned the key to the lintel and followed Toby back to the house.

∾

The smell of searing steak and garlic drifted into the kitchen where Emily stood at the stove. Outside the back door a barbecue glowed in the dusk. It lit the front of Toby as he stood with a fork in one hand and a watch in the other.

'Two min's either side or ninety seconds?' he asked.

'Depends. The Lyonnaise is ready when you are,' Emily said, using both hands to toss the potatoes and onion in a cast-iron frying pan. 'I'd better open another bottle of that ridiculously pricey Bordeaux – how do people afford to live in this country?'

'Beats me, but then apparently nobody drinks more Champagne than the English.'

Toby had set up a small table in the study so they could be warm. Supper was a partial success, the meat juicy and tender but lacking depth of flavour, the Epoisse, thought to be a lucky find, was unripe and chalky.

'We could have ripened it in the microwave if we had one,' Emily said.

'For that matter, we could have coated it in breadcrumbs and deep fried it,' Toby said, 'but thankfully we didn't. I've sorted the post, there are only a couple of things that need attending to and there's a packet from the solicitors addressed to you. It's on the desk behind you. More wine?'

'Thanks,' Emily said, getting up and going to the desk. She took the package and sat in one of the armchairs by the stove, tucking her legs underneath her. Toby filled her glass and brought it over before clearing the table.

'Looks exciting,' he said, 'I'll make coffee.'

She shook the contents of the package out onto her lap. There was a letter detailing what she had yet to do, and a range of papers including the deeds to the property, the car registration and a bundle of financial documents. There was also a sealed handwritten envelope from uncle James. Emily sat and stared at it in the firelight.

Toby put the coffee down on a low table and sat in the chair on the other side of the fire.

'Is that from James?' he asked, recognising the writing on the envelope. 'You may as well open it.'

'I'm a bit scared. I don't know why.'

'Would you like me to read it?'

'Thank you, I would,' Emily said, and handed the envelope to Toby.

Emily sat looking into the fire as Toby unfolded a sheet of writing paper.

Dear Emily,

If you're reading this, I will be dead, although right now I feel very much alive. But I am old and rather tired and doubt if I have many years left. I have decided to make you my sole heir, not that it will enrich you hugely, but it is my wish.

It has undoubtedly come as something of a surprise to you, and to others as well. Perhaps I should have discussed it with you, but I reason, perhaps cowardly, that it might be easier to hear from me in absentia.

I settled my will some time ago. My intention was to make Toby my heir, although I have been a neglectful uncle, I have always been deeply fond of him, and I hope that I have not unduly upset his expectations. He will get my cottage in Devon.

The decision for you was made in a second and has ever felt completely right. The logic of that decision can only be described as poetic.

For a few years, when you were young, your father thought you might prefer the English countryside to the pleasures of Paris during your summer vacation, especially as he was tied to work and often away. In those years I came to value your company enormously and realise that this was because in your youth, your sense of yourself in the world, simply the way you were – all these powerfully recalled for me the joy I experienced in the brief time I shared my life with Daisy. You reminded me what it was like to truly value being alive, to live for someone else. It helped me at last to grieve and come to a new understanding of love as a moment of grace.

Giving you the house is not a thank you for the innocent gift you gave me. I merely wanted you to feel that this place could be yours as it was mine, that even if you decide to sell it tomorrow it would contain something of you as it did of Daisy. There is much in the house that speaks of her and through you I was able to make that voice once more a positive force in my life, something to cherish, free of regret. Enjoy the house if you can, it is given in love.

With fondest regards,
James

Emily sat quietly for some time. She got up and knelt by Toby who hugged her, gently stroking her hair.

'What a beautiful man,' she said.

Chapter 3

Two suitcases, three cardboard boxes and two Huntley and Palmer biscuit tins, cleaned out and lined with brown paper, were assembled at the bottom of the stairs. To take them all up to Daisy's attic would have left no room to do any packing, and one suitcase had already been filled with towels and bedding by her mother. Daisy took the other up the steep stairs and laid it open on her bed. Folding her clothes neatly she put them in the case, including the dresses she could no longer get into. There was so little in the small chest of drawers she had soon emptied it. Daisy took off her slippers and stuffed them behind the chest.

Taking James' greatcoat from the peg behind the door she put it on. Books were packed into the boxes. There were several Blackie's Girls' Annuals. Auntie Hilda gave her one every Christmas. Daisy tried to ration herself to a story a day over the holiday, but never could. A pile of classic novels in cheap editions, a complete Shakespeare and, a clutch of romantic poets with a very pretty calf bound Keats that she treasured, completed her library. Boring jigsaw puzzles of pastoral England, a board game she had never played and, a couple of dolls, neatly dressed but rather dusty, went into another box. The tins were for smaller things, some miniature china ornaments, a pincushion, an inlaid box and a Book of

Common Prayer, covered in soft red leather, tooled in gold, that had belonged to her maternal grandmother.

Most of her schoolbooks she crammed into her satchel. Daisy got her journals out from under the bed and stuffed them in with her other exercise books, before changing her mind and putting them under some seashells in one of the biscuit tins. She moved the case onto the floor and, lay on her bed for the last time, hands clasped behind her head. She looked round the little room that had been her haven since she was old enough to climb the stairs.

'Goodbye,' she said, 'I'll probably miss you.'

Daisy reluctantly took off the great coat and packed it into a suitcase. She closed the lid and sat on it, fastening the catches behind her legs. She descended the stairs backwards bumping the case down the steps as she went. Her mother was waiting at the bottom.

'Do be careful dear, they're not real leather you know.'

'Don't worry mum, I know you need them back for your things.'

They stood in the parlour that had already lost the sense of home.

'You'll be alright love, won't you?' her mother said. 'It's good of Hilda to take you in for your exams. I've told her, as soon as I'm earning, I'll send her something regular. Don't forget to give her your ration books as soon as you get there. I'm going to miss you, Daisy. You will write me?'

'I will mum, just as soon as you send me your address. Can you give me a hand with the other stuff?'

They both went up the stairs to Daisy's room. Her mother stood by the window with her arms folded, looking out over the littered garden.

'If I'm honest, I'll be glad to get away,' she said. 'Everyone knows there's a lot of black market going on, but people are such hypocrites, and I do feel ashamed, though I've no reason. We didn't know anything, did we?' Framed by grey light, she turned to face Daisy. 'We were deceived, weren't we love?'

'Yes mum we were.'

'And you will be careful, Daisy? I can tell the captain is a good man, but he's a man for all that.'

'Of course I will mum, I'll miss you too you know.'

Daisy put her arms round her mother's thin frame and hugged her.

'Miss my nagging more like,' she said, squeezing Daisy tightly. She let her go and fished in her pinafore for her handkerchief.

'Come on, mum,' Daisy said, 'we'll be alright.' She handed her mother the two tins. 'You take these, I'll take the boxes.'

They set Daisy's things down on the parlour floor.

'I'll just go and make sure I've got everything,' Daisy said, 'can we have a cup of tea, mum?'

They sat opposite each other across the dining table.

'It's all happened so quickly, mum, I can barely believe it.'

'It's hard for me to say this, especially to you Daisy, but I don't want to see him again, ever.' Tears welled in her eyes and she reached again for her handkerchief. 'He wasn't doing it for us, was he? He must have made money, but I've no idea what he did with it, and look what he's brought us to.'

Daisy went and put her arms round her, nestling her head on her mother's shoulder.

'Try not to worry mum, we'll come through. You'll get a good job and I'll pass all my exams.'

Her mother turned her crumpled face to Daisy.

'I know you're right love, thank you.'

Daisy went back to her chair and finished her tea. They sat quietly.

'The shop will be locked up when I go,' her mother said. 'Hilda's got keys. I want you to check on it from time to time, it'll keep my mind easy.'

'Course I will, mum'.

An unusually loud rapping sounded on the door of the empty shop.

'I expect that's James,' Daisy said, getting up from her chair and smoothing her dress.

Shutters had been fixed to the outside of the shop windows and the blinds were down inside. As she opened the door a corridor of light spread across the room. James stood in the frame his hair bedewed by the light drizzle that blew in the wind. Daisy reached out and held his hand, pulling him into the shop.

'My bits of luggage are in the parlour,' she said, leading him through.

'It's very good of you to move Daisy, Captain James, now we haven't got the van,' Daisy's mother said.

'Not at all, Mrs Lanyard, I'm only too happy to be able to help.'

'There's not a lot to take,' Daisy said. 'If mum and I take the boxes, James, could you take the suitcases, please?'

'Of course,' James said, picking up a box and handing it to Daisy. 'The car's right outside. I'll put the cases in the boot, better put the boxes on the back seat.'

They loaded the khaki staff car that dully glistened in the grey light. James and Daisy went back into the shop.

'Thank you for all your kindnesses, Mrs Lanyard,' James said, 'I have much appreciated your hospitality. I promise I'll keep an eye on Daisy for you, while I'm at the camp.'

'Thank you, Captain James, it is good of you to take an interest. Perhaps when all this is over…'

'We'd better go now, mum,' Daisy said, hugging her

mother. 'I'll come back and say goodbye properly before you leave for London.'

'Take care, love, do as auntie Hilda tells you and, don't leave your bedroom in a mess – now, off you go.'

Outside, James opened the door of the car for Daisy. The small figure of her mother stood in the doorway, twisting her handkerchief round her fingers. Daisy hesitated, then went back and hugged her.

''Bye, mum,' she said, and quickly got into the car.

∽

Daisy sat, hands folded in her lap, looking ahead. Her mind was numb, and she could not tell what she felt except for butterflies in her stomach. James drove up the High Street, past the church and the market square, through the outlying lanes of jumbled houses, towards the fields and pastures that surrounded the village.

The cottage was one of several, randomly placed, either side of a wooded bye-way. It was a whitewashed oblong of indeterminate age. From a central stack a plume of grey smoke rose slowly and dissolved into the mist. A black oak door was flanked by windows, with smaller lights tucked under the eaves beneath a mossy slate roof. Outbuildings clustered close to the cottage. Chrysanthemums and Michaelmas daisies bloomed in beds at the front of the house, and the clucking of unseen chickens could be heard.

Daisy and James drew up and auntie Hilda appeared at the front door. A taller and more substantial presence than her sister, her hair was coiled in a bun and she wore a khaki jumper and woollen trousers. She came through the gate, leaving it open and smiling broadly at the pair getting out of the car.

'Daisy, darling, welcome,' she said, holding out both hands and kissing Daisy on the cheek. 'And you must be Captain James,' she added, pumping his hand. 'Come on, let's get your things in out of this weather.'

James opened the boot and took out the suitcases. Hilda grabbed one and started up the red brick path to the cottage door, James followed, with Daisy behind carrying two of the boxes.

The centre of the cottage was taken up by the chimneystack, with an ingle on the living side and a range on the other, kitchen, side. A fire burned in the hearth and a large faded Persian carpet kept out the draughts. Furniture was plentiful. A walnut writing table stood under the front window, with a vase of cheerful daisies on it. In front of the fire, on a chintz settee, a tabby cat sprawled, oblivious. A pair of carvers stood to the sides of the ingle and small Victorian upholstered chairs were dotted about the room. A dining table, with barley twist legs, sat under the gable end window. On the walls, where one might have expected picturesque watercolours and framed samplers, there hung Chinese landscapes and seascapes and a set of Japanese prints of geishas in swirling dresses, negotiating snow flurries or making tea in simply sketched interiors.

Hilda waved a hand towards a narrow door in the corner of the room.

'Put everything down by the stairs,' she said, 'we'll take them up later. Your room's ready for you Daisy. I hope you're going to like it.'

'Thank you, auntie, I'm sure I will.'

'I'm glad to have you. You'll be company for me. It gets very quiet on your own. I just hope you won't feel too isolated. Can you ride a bike?'

'I used to have one, but it got too small, or I got too big.'

'We'll find one for you. I've got a little cart that I can tow behind mine. It makes me look like an eccentric old maid – but then I suppose I am one,' Hilda smiled at them both.

'I don't think you're quite old enough, auntie.'

'The kettle's on,' Hilda said, rubbing her hands together, 'you two get warmed up while I make the tea.'

James hovered, looking uncertainly at the cat on the settee. 'Just shove Winny on the floor,' Hilda said, 'I shan't be a moment.'

She disappeared through a door to the kitchen side of the cottage. James took a look at Winny and stood with his back to the fire looking around the room. Daisy pushed the cat to one side of the settee and sat down, he meowed briefly before resettling. They heard the noise of a kettle whistling and crockery being assembled. Hilda came in with a pile of crumpets and a long brass fork.

'You get on toasting these, my love,' she said to Daisy, 'and perhaps the captain would come and get the plates and the butter.'

'Of course, Miss er…,' James said, getting out of the chair.

'Hilda, will do nicely, and you're James, is that right?'

'Yes, it is,' James said, coming through to the kitchen. There was a space the size of the sitting room, partitioned at the cooler, outside wall end, with a larder and storeroom. A door with a porch let out onto the back garden. The kettle was singing on a small black coal range. Hilda deftly tipped it to fill the teapot that she put on a tray and covered in a brown knitted cosy.

'It's a struggle to get the coal sometimes,' she said, 'and it burns that much wood if I have to use it, but so far I've managed.' She handed James plates and a butter dish. 'Take them in and I'll bring the tea and some jam,' she said.

James did as he was bid, putting them down on a stool. Daisy knelt on the rag hearthrug. She impaled another crumpet and held it to the glowing base of the fire, checking every now and then to see it did not burn.

Hilda put two buttered crumpets on a plate with a generous spoon of strawberry jam.

'From the garden,' she said, passing it to James, 'special treat as it's Daisy's first day.'

'Thank you,' James said, 'it's kind of you to include me.' He spread the dark red jam over the buttery crumpet, pushing pieces of strawberry into the surface, and took a large bite.

'That's delicious,' he said, fishing for his handkerchief to wipe his buttery chin, 'I think NAAFI jam is made of parsnips and cochineal. It's a lovely cottage you've got here,' he added, looking round.

'Yes, it is,' Daisy said. 'I've always meant to ask you why it's called Yew Tree Cottage when there aren't any yews?'

'There were when I bought it,' Hilda said, 'enormous trees that hadn't been looked after, either side of the front door, and taking all the light, I had them chopped down, they burned better than oak.'

James got up to take a closer look at a pair of Japanese geisha prints.

'I do find your choice of art interesting,' he said.

'Thank you,' Hilda said. 'Some people think they're unpatriotic, which annoys me. I worked out east before the war, nothing grand, just in a bank, but I loved it. I got out of Shanghai, just before the Japs arrived. I was lucky, a lot of people didn't.'

Daisy put the last of the crumpets onto the plate by the fire and shifted her position. Her cheeks glowed from the heat. She stayed on the rug, pulling her dress over her knees.

'I'm so glad you did come back, auntie. I love your cottage, it's warm and feels like a real home. I've never lived anywhere except the shop.'

'It'll be yours for as long as you want it, Daisy.' She took James' cup and re-filled it. 'I was very taken with the art out east, James,' she said, 'so beautiful, delicate and tender, and yet people died on the street with no-one caring a fig. I could never understand it.'

'I know what you mean,' James said, 'my art is all rooted in the everyday. I want to paint what's real, but those geishas are sublime, I could never get there.'

'It sounds more like poetry than pictures,' Daisy said.

Hilda laughed, 'This is the first intelligent conversation I've had in this cottage. We sound like the Brains Trust.'

'Did you always want to be an artist, James?' Daisy asked.

James stretched out his legs and stroked Winny, who had insinuated himself onto his lap.

'It wasn't like that,' he said, 'there was no burning zeal, but, yes, I suppose I can't remember ever wanting to do anything else, certainly not become a soldier, but I am one now.' He looked at his watch and picked Winny up putting him on the hearthrug. 'I'm afraid I'd better be getting back, I had to borrow the major's car for this jaunt.'

Daisy stood up, brushing crumbs from her lap and fetched his coat.

'I'm glad to have met you,' Hilda said, proffering her hand, 'you're welcome to come here and draw Daisy whenever the pair of you want, or even just to visit.'

'That's very generous of you,' James said.

Daisy smiled at her aunt.

'Thank you,' she said.

'And thank you, Hilda, for the delicious crumpets and jam. I'll think of them tonight in the mess, as they serve the watery stuffed marrow, with even more watery cabbage and spuds.'

'You must come here for a proper meal,' Hilda said, 'when you can get away.'

'Thanks, I would very much like that. Can I take the suitcases upstairs for you before I go?'

'No, we can manage. You see James out Daisy and then we'll get you settled in your room.'

Daisy and James stood by the car. The rain had stopped, and the feeble sun cast a milky light. She stood close to James looking into his face.

'Hilda's nice, isn't she?' Daisy said.

'Yes, she's warm and clearly fond of you, I'm sure you'll be well cared for.'

'I've only come from the other side of the village and it's as if I'm in another world. It's odd, I feel sad, as though something has ended.'

She moved closer to James and briefly held him. He wrapped his arms around her. Pulling her head gently onto his shoulder, he kissed her hair. 'Daisy,' he said quietly, stroking her cheek.

'I'm going to miss you,' she said, 'am I allowed to say that?'

'It's time one of us spoke.' He paused, still holding her. 'I've been unsure, scared, perhaps because lately, whenever I catch myself thinking, it's of you, Daisy.'

'That makes me happy,' she said, 'I can't think of a nicer place to be than in your thoughts. You're always in mine, you've made me feel new.'

James kissed her forehead and held both her hands. They stood without speaking, looking into each other's faces.

'If I can, I'll come after school on Wednesday, that's only three days,' he said.

'I do hope you can get away.' Daisy lifted her head and kissed James softly on the mouth.

'That's the first time I've kissed a man.'

'I'll treasure it always,' James said, kissing his finger and placing it on Daisy's lips. He opened the car door. 'I think you may be right, this is another world. Take very good care, Daisy.'

'And you, James.'

He drove off and Daisy turned back to the cottage.

∽

Daisy and Hilda struggled up the narrow staircase with the suitcases and dumped them on the floor inside the room. Daisy looked around her new quarters. The long room stretched from the gable end of the cottage to the central chimney. There were windows on two sides. Curtains were heavy, against the inevitable draughts. Primrose wallpaper decorated with sprays of pink flowers covered the walls. Small Japanese prints hung beside the windows.

The iron framed bedstead faced the morning sun. A plain deal chest squatted at its end. The linen shone with starch and a quilted blue counterpane hung almost to the floor. A writing table and a tallboy stood either side of a small grate. In front of the fire sat a little button backed armchair.

'Auntie, I can't believe it, this was your old box room and now it's so beautiful. Did you really do this for me?'

'I've just cheered it up a bit and made it comfy. You'll need somewhere to work, if you're going to do well in your school certificates, won't you? Let's bring the boxes up and then I'll leave you to unpack. The weather's cleared up so I'll be in the garden if you want me.'

They clattered down the stairs and up again with the boxes.

'I've managed to get some chops for later, so we can have a nice meal together.'

'Thank you so much, I know I keep saying it, but I do

mean it, auntie.' Daisy hugged Hilda, kissing her downy cheek. 'I'll help you as much as I can, I promise, and I'll be as good as gold.'

'I'll keep you to that. Perhaps when we're sat down and cosy over supper you can tell me all about Captain James. He seems a very fetching young man.'

'Yes,' Daisy said, 'he is.'

When Hilda had gone, Daisy set about unpacking. Singing to herself, she first got James' greatcoat and put it on. Winny came into the room purring, and presented himself to be stroked, before curling up in front of the unlit fire. Daisy hung her dresses in the wardrobe. She put blouses and knickers and stockings in the tallboy, each drawer had a little muslin bag of lavender in it. A wide exposed tie beam ran between the walls at the gable end. Daisy put her books on it and arranged her ornaments. The dolls, which had been ignored for years at the shop, had their little outfits flounced before being put on the velvet chair. The current journal was put in the drawer of the writing table, along with her pen. Everything was put in its place slowly, with deliberation. When she had finished, she sat on the bed and looked around her. Laying back she closed her eyes and was very soon asleep.

Chapter 4

WAKING WAS MOSTLY A PLEASURE. THE MORNING WAS bright, the air still and cool. The gathering polyphony of the dawn chorus filtered into her consciousness. The moment of languor was interrupted by the sound of whistling and the rattle of the chain that held the barn doors. It was Dan, and time to get up. Emily had never known anyone who whistled. She had tried it herself, pursing her lips and moving her tongue into different positions, but to little effect. She was too shy to ask advice. Today she had agreed to help Dan in the woods. At his suggestion they were going to create a coppice. Emily had agreed without knowing what it meant.

'It's transformative. It'll give life to the wood and be great fun to do,' he had said.

When Emily looked it up it seemed complicated, labour intensive, at least at the start and, a long-term commitment to woodland management. It would take years to become fully functional and, it was not clear that the product, which seemed to be long thin poles, would be of any use to anyone.

Hands in pockets, she tripped down the stairs and stopped to check her face in the hall mirror. Toby sat at the kitchen table in a warm pool of sunlight reading yesterday's newspaper.

'Smells good,' said Emily, and leant over his shoulder to peer at the photograph of a smiling man.

'Is that the PM?' she said.

'Spot on. It's their wunderkind, Tony Blair. Looks a step up from Drybones Jospin and shabby Chirac, and he's very pro-Europe.'

'Good for him,' Emily said, her nose poised over Toby's coffee cup. 'Seen Jean-Marie?'

'Briefly – he never seems to leave the morning room – is he staying long?'

'Don't be mean, he's got to finish his *Diplome* or he won't be able to do his doctorate next year.'

'I do understand, but then what's the use of him coming over here if all he does is closet himself and work? I recall you saying he'd be no good at logging but so far, he hasn't shown much aptitude for light domestic work either. I'm surprised he hasn't asked me to valet for him.'

'Was that Dan I heard in the garden?' Emily asked.

'Yes, I think he's already started work,' Toby said, 'he came in to say hello and grab some coffee about half an hour ago – the good Dr Guy sends his regards. I suspect he's just a little warm for your form.'

'The doctor?'

'Hadn't thought of that, but it's not beyond all possible imagining.' He smiled briefly and held Emily's hand as she passed him.

'You're vile. I'm going to have some coffee with Jean-Marie in the morning room and then help Dan. We are going coppicing.'

The room faced south and was filled with morning light. Books and papers littered the floor and the chairs. Jean-Marie had moved a table in front of one of the windows where he sat looking intently into the screen of his Powerbook. He stood up as Emily came in and ran a hand through his auburn hair.

'*Salut cherie,*' Jean-Marie said.

'*En Anglais, s'il vous plait*,' Emily said, '*c'est bon pour toi.*'

Emily put her arms round him and kissed him, then dropped her hands and jiggled his buttocks. 'Are you losing weight?' she asked, 'you look a bit pasty.'

'Probably,' said Jean-Marie, 'it's all the anxiety of this thesis, everything depends on it. Am I good enough?'

Emily stood by the window looking out over the garden. 'I shouldn't worry too much,' she said, 'you've already been promised an *allocation*, so the School must think you're going to make it. You're nearly as clever as me you know.' She looked into his dark eyes and kissed him again. '*Delicieuse*,' she said, 'come and sit over here and have some coffee. The Madeleines are actually from home.'

They sat side-by-side, sipping coffee and eating the little bright yellow cakes. Emily talked about the house and what Dan was doing in the garden and Jean-Marie nodded abstractedly, his gaze drifting to his computer screen. Emily leaned over and stroked his thigh.

'I'm going to help Dan in the wood this morning and then I thought I might go into Lewes. Would you like to come?'

'It sounds nice, but I'd better see how the writing goes, if that's alright with you.'

'I'll drop by later,' said Emily, she jumped to her feet and collected the coffee cups, 'I expect a break will do you good.'

'Yes,' Jean-Marie said.

∽

Emily judged Dan a definite addition to the limited local amenities. He was Dr Guy's grandson and at a loose end. Dark, not very tall and overweight, he not only whistled but drank English beer, which only increased his exotic lustre. Emily had been amazed at his performance in the pub. How could anyone down litres of warm brownish, slightly cloudy liquid for pleasure?

The morning air was soft and still damp. The garden was beginning to make itself known, less melancholy, it was becoming friendly. Approaching the barn, she could hear a rhythmic rasping sound. As she got closer, she saw Dan, in jeans and T-shirt standing in a shaft of light. He was sliding a tube of grey stone along the curved edge of a scythe. He saw her and called 'Hi' but did not stop sharpening the blade. Emily kissed his cheek.

'Hi, yourself,' she said, 'are we going to start today?'

'I thought we might. I've done a reconnaissance and a feasibility study, and we can't do the whole lot, a life's work I'm afraid. We could do, say, a twenty to thirty metre section in the middle, facing the house. It will look good and will let some light into the wood, which it badly needs.'

'That sounds reasonable to me,' Emily said.

Dan looked serious. 'I'm afraid I've been baking again, and I've brought you a proper English loaf, help you get over a lifetime's lack of real bread.' He lobbed what looked like a brown boulder over to Emily. She caught it with two hands and immediately fell forward, the loaf touching the ground.

'Thank you so much,' she said, slowly lifting the loaf off the ground and groaning.

Dan feinted a cuff round her ear and Emily moved her head back out of range.

'No, honestly, thanks.'

Emily picked up the small chain saw that Dan had brought along, weighing it against the loaf.

'Vicious,' she said.

Broad shafts of sunlight slanted through the tall wooden doors creating warm smells of wood and earth. Empty crates, ancient hay bales and stacked tools took on depth and texture.

Dust milled slowly upwards. Dan handed Emily two small scythes and a rake and swung the chain saw onto his shoulder.

'Can you manage?' he asked.

Emily nodded.

'Are you sure we're doing the right thing?' She said. 'From what I can understand we're about to embark on a lifetime of small wood management, it's a big commitment.'

'Woods aren't just for Christmas,' Dan said, as they walked down the garden. 'I've cut the honeysuckle right back over there and I left the clumps of self seeded foxgloves, they'll be out soon, hope there's some white ones,' he indicated a curved bed with a sweep of his free hand. 'It's your chance to invest in posterity,' he said as they came to the edge of the wood. Emily set down the tools and put her hands on her hips.

'Am I up to it?' she said. 'I've no notion of how long I'll have Campiston.'

'Let's look on the bright side. You could still be around when you're a granny.'

'Is that appealing? I'm enjoying being here at the moment but I'm not sure I could live here. What would I do in the winter? And in any case now I've finished my degree I have to go back and think how to earn a living while I'm being a bright eyed intern. I can't live off my dad for ever.'

Dan pushed a peg in the ground and looked up towards the house.

'That's about the middle,' he said, 'take a peg and pace fifteen metres that way and I'll go this, then come back to the middle and we'll get cracking.'

Some hours later they had cleared a section about ten metres deep. Emily fetched rolls and coffee and they sat on the ground leaning against one of the neat piles of wood and brush that Dan had constructed, in a line, at regular intervals about halfway into the strip.

Emily had abandoned the gardening gloves in order to better grip the scythe. Her hands were now scratched, and her nails chipped and dirty. She looked round at the wood.

'In the brief time Toby and I have been here it has really changed character,' she said. 'The trees have filled out with bright green leaves. All the bluebells have gone and now there are ferns and grass and loads of little flowers, none of which I could name.'

'I'll loan you a book, British Flora,' Dan said, 'there will be lots more flowers now the sun can get to the floor, you've seen how there's no ground cover in the middle of the wood. If we thin it out a bit, things will change.'

'Seems a shame to cut down all this life,' Emily said.

'All in a good cause,' Dan said, flicking his coffee grouts onto the ground.

∽

None of the keys fitted. Emily guessed that behind the door was the attic stair possibly leading to the servants' rooms. She tripped down to the kitchen, took the key drawer completely out and tipped its contents onto the table. Sifting through the scissors, string, knives without handles, bent spoons and other oddments yielded no more keys. The contents of the drawer were being swept back into place when Toby came in to make some coffee.

'Fancy a cup?' he said, holding one up and waggling it seductively.

'Yes,' said Emily, 'thanks. Would you like a *gallette*?'

'Mmm, please.'

'I want to get into the attic. I've been saving it up and it's time I gave my imagination a rest.'

'Gothic fantasies I suppose, they're certainly in vogue. Are you hoping for a handsome young vampire in a frockcoat who's been up there since seventeen thirty, just waiting for you.'

'No Toby, that's asking too much. But I hope there's something more interesting than old newspapers and broken furniture.'

'If at supper you're wearing a deathly pallor and demanding steak tartar, then, I shall know the worst. However, I must get on, research reports don't write themselves.'

'Can I please look in the study to see if I can find any keys? I'll only be a minute. I thought perhaps those little drawers and compartments at the back of the desk, with the cute fretted brass rail running along the top of them, might be a good place.'

'Of course, petal. I'll go and annoy J-M for a while, the boy needs taking out of himself. The pair of you should go to London for a few days.'

'He'd pine for his *diplome* and I'd miss you and the house,' said Emily, stroking her father's arm.

'I do worry about you,' Toby said.

Emily sat at the desk and looked out at the acid greens and muted yellows of the garden. She pulled out the first little square walnut drawer. It was full of used sticks of red sealing wax. In the next drawer, with some faded airmail stickers and postage stamps, were some short keys. One was very small with a gilded filigree haft, pretty enough to be on a chain. Emily looked around the room. It fitted the humidor, presumably to stop the butler smoking the master's cigars. As to the thin door, there were three that might fit the bill.

Upstairs all the keys fitted the keyhole, but none would turn. Emily stood for a moment staring at them and then tried again. This time she wiggled and probed more carefully, waiting to hear some give in the mechanism. She bent her ear closer to the lock, though with no clear notion what she was listening for. The most worn key, after some random manipulation, finally made the lock yield.

The door opened inwards onto a tiny space before a dark varnished flight of stairs. The narrow treads rose steeply and curved. There was no rail and the plaster walls were badly scuffed. At the top was a corridor with four doors, laid with a threadbare runner. In the sloping ceiling, green glass tiles let in a grimy light. Emily turned a brown wood handle and felt for a switch. The light that came from an unshaded central pendant was both feeble and harsh. The switch began to fizz and Emily quickly turned it off. Her eyes became accustomed to the light that filtered through two dirty windows set in a dormer. The floor was covered in brown linoleum with a rag mat by an iron bedstead. A cupboard had been used as a wardrobe, and still contained a few wooden hangers on a rail. She sat on the edge of the bed frame, elbows on her knees, chin in her hands.

The next two rooms were full of furniture in various stages of decomposition and boxes of household junk. Emily lifted the dusty lid of a trunk, full of old board games, chess, backgammon, a large black lacquered box of Mahjong tiles in little trays, yellowed with age, black dominoes and packs of cards for Pit and Happy Families. In a wooden box there were racks of coloured chips, an ebony wheel and, a baize marked out for roulette. Somehow Emily couldn't quite see uncle James playing the gambler. The door at the end of the corridor had a small brass knocker depicting a fox's snout and brush. It was locked but the key to the stairwell opened it.

The room was almost twice the size of the others. The floorboards had been painted white. An Iranian carpet ran across the middle of the room. One wall was covered with sketches in pencil and watercolour. Black and white photographs of people and landscapes, of trees and interiors were pinned to a large square of cork. Most were faded and curled. A small Victorian sofa, with a grey silk tasselled shawl hung over the back, was angled towards the fireplace. An oak table stood by the window. It was covered with books and paper, pens and pencils in a blue ceramic pot, and black boxes of watercolours.

An old kitchen chair sat half out from under the table, as though someone had just got up. In a tarnished silver photo frame she stared at the image of uncle James, in shirt sleeves, standing in front of the studio, his arm resting on the shoulder of a slight young woman as tall as he. He was looking at her, she at the camera. Neither were smiling but Emily was pleased by the easy intimacy of their pose. This was what Daisy actually looked like and this room had clearly been hers. She put the photograph back on the desk and sat on the sofa, looking round.

The windows were hung with chintz curtains on brass rings. Beside the blacked hearth was a scuttle, still with some coal. Under the table an old black deed box was marked along the front edge where shoes had rested on it. A small chest sat under the window, painted sepia with trompe l'oeil swags. On a narrow shelf beneath an oval mirror was a Mason Pearson hairbrush. Emily pushed the spines down with her thumb, it still had some spring in it. In front of the mirror she pulled the brush across her head and down to her nape with a faint rasping noise. The light caught the hair among the bristles, a few blond and some darker. Emily stood for a while looking out of the window. Next to the sofa a cardigan lay on the floor, where it had fallen, goodness knew when. She picked it up and put it on the sofa. With one last look she quietly left the room, locking the door behind her.

Downstairs, she lay on her bed looking at the portrait of Daisy she had moved from the studio. The face was young, dark eyed with a strong mouth. She was half profile, looking to the side of the viewer, umber hair pushed behind a pale ear. Emily liked the way the light caught the knees of her black stockings.

~

As they drove the few kilometres to Lewes, Jean-Marie listened to music on his Walkman. Emily was entirely occupied by the business of driving the old Peugeot. It was an adventure, like driving a tractor. The long gear stick required some strength to shift and seemed to move much further than one might have supposed. She liked its deep untidiness and the ancient muddy scuff marks on the inside of the door. It had a radio that didn't work, and the absence of entertainment emphasised its utility. The lack of power-assisted steering was a novel sensation, combining elements of being both in, and out, of control. At slow speeds the capacity to steer was intimately connected with having the strength to turn the wheel. Since being at the house, Emily had noted, with some pleasure, the beginnings of muscle definition in her upper arms. This was elemental car.

They rattled over a cobbled bridge on the way to a less frequented car park on the edge of town. Across the road a hill rose at a vertiginous angle towards the downs. A converted barn selling antiques nestled against the chalk.

They sauntered up the High Street, stopping occasionally to examine a shop front.

'There seem to be so many antique shops around,' Jean-Marie said, 'it seems to be the major local industry. It's not much like a country town.'

'Yes, it's odd. Toby says that when he was a kid it was all corn factors and agricultural machinery. There's a pretty little cafe in a courtyard around the corner, we could have tea and English tea cakes before we go back, if you like.'

'Sure.'

Emily stopped at a church with a leaning bell tower. She dragged Jean-Marie inside and pointed out a leper squint set into a wall with a view of the High Altar.

'I used to think this was so spooky. I imagined groups of hideously misshapen peasants in rags, jostling for a view of the priest – and it really did happen,' she said, widening her eyes.

'Sounds gruesome,' said Jean-Marie. His phone sounded in his pocket and he stopped to answer it, moving out of earshot.

Emily entertained herself with the church notice board, mindlessly absorbing the times of masses and parish meetings.

'Alexis,' Jean-Marie said. 'Where to now?'

'Is there anything you want to get?' Emily asked.

'I'd like to buy Toby some good wine, a sort of thank you, is that possible here?'

'It is, but what are you thanking him for? You're both guests of mine.'

'Yes, of course. But it would still be mannerly. I don't think he likes me, do you?'

'Darling Jean-Marie don't be so silly. He's always teasing and sardonic, it shows he accepts you.'

'I still find it very difficult. I don't know how to speak to him.'

'What do want me to do, tell him off?' Emily said.

'You might be a little more sympathetic. It's alright for you…'

'And how is Alexis?' Emily said.

'He seems very well. Sounds as though he is having a great time and doesn't miss me at all.'

'Are you missing him?'

'Don't be jealous Emily.'

'And why not? Because it's petit bourgeois and morally absurd and doesn't suit you?'

They had stopped outside Harvey's Brewery Shop.

'This is probably the best wine shop in town,' Emily said. She made no move to go in.

Jean-Marie looked at her, waited a moment and then went down a couple of steps into the fragrant, gloomy interior. Emily walked on past the brewery gates and stood staring at a jeweller's window. Her eyes smarted. Jean-Marie appeared with two bottles wrapped in blue tissue paper.

'Do you mind if I wait for you in the car?' he said.

'No, I just have to go and buy supper.' Emily took the keys out of her jeans pocket and lobbed them over to Jean-Marie. She started across the bridge towards the supermarket without looking back. A shared boy – what would Daisy and James have thought?

⁓

Emily enjoyed cooking. Over the years she had learned from Toby and shared his confidence that all things being equal, it would be fine. She made some tarragon butter and pushed it under the skin of the breasts of a large chicken. Half a lemon was squeezed and put into the cavity, along with a couple of squashed garlic cloves. Rice and a lemon sauce would be good. She took a bottle of Creme de Loire out of the fridge and swapped it for the one in the freezer.

Going into the hall she called out to Toby and Jean-Marie – 'drinks in the garden, right now.'

A loaded tray was carried to where a small wooden table had been set to catch the western light. Wine fizzed in the glass as she poured. Toby appeared, and they watched the sun gently lowering behind the crumbling glasshouse. Dan had said they could have it up and running for the cost of three days' labour and some glass and putty. Emily liked the idea. They could grow big lumpy Marmande tomatoes and sell them at local markets. Some pathetic little squidgy ones had made an appearance in Safeway and they had gone in moments. But if she sold the house what would it matter? She had already said yes to the coppicing, and that would take ages to bear its dubious fruit. The fantasy gently faded.

'Heavenly smell of, what is it, tarragon?' Toby said. He poured himself a generous measure, collected a handful of nuts and sank into a rickety chair.

'Tarragon chicken, lemon sauce and rice.'

'Let joy be unconfined. Shall we eat out here? There aren't that many chances in an English summer.'

'Let's, you can carve, and we'll put it all on a big meat dish and help ourselves, like Morocco. Then it's just bread, cheese and fruit.'

'Perfect. Hi J-M – good day?' Toby said, as Jean-Marie came into the garden.

'Yes, just fine, thank you.' He filled Emily and Toby's glasses before emptying the bottle into a third.

The church clock across the fields struck the half hour.

'Hope there's another of those,' Toby said, nodding towards the empty bottle, 'slips down like mother's milk. By the by J-M, many thanks for the handsome accompaniments to tonight's victuals, they'll be delish. Hope the chatelaine here chipped in, must have cost an arm and a leg at English prices.'

Jean-Marie, who was often baffled when Toby slipped into his own version of the vernacular, smiled and nodded.

'I just thought you might appreciate a glass of good wine. It should go perfectly with Emily's meal.'

'Yes.' Toby said. 'Are you enjoying being in England?'

Emily came out of the house with another bottle and handed it to Toby. It opened with a soft hiss and he handed it back.

'Unlike the English, I don't think the French travel very well,' Jean-Marie said, 'unless of course they are bankers, in which case they travel to Kensington and stay there.' He smiled. 'It is lovely to be here. The old house is beautiful, and I can hardly believe Emily's luck.'

'Surely you have rich old aunts queuing up to leave you substantial villas on the outskirts of Beaulieu-sur-Mer,' Toby said.

'Not that I know of,' said Jean-Marie. 'I've found this a great place to work, peaceful and no distractions. But I guess I'll have to go back soon to prepare the thesis for presentation.'

'Of course. Shame you haven't had time to see a little more of the English countryside. Emily's had a riveting introduction to the mysteries of English rural culture from young Dan.'

'You'd love dwyle flunking,' Emily said. 'People in fancy rustic dress and occasional Viking helmets dance in a circle to some fiddle music, all holding hands. The man in the middle has a bucket of stale beer dregs with a mop head in it and he fishes it out with a stick and tries to smack someone in the face with it.'

'Fun, perhaps,' Toby said, 'but neither good nor clean.'

Jean-Marie's shoulders tightened, and he closed his eyes. 'Surely – not even the English?'

Emily laughed.

'I doubt it's a national sport,' Toby said, 'sounds more of a Sussex lads' thing to me, wouldn't you say Emily?'

'I don't know,' Emily said, 'but I'd love Jean-Marie to try it, just once. I must get the supper. Would you two lay the table out here please and see to the wine. Toby come and carve, and Jean-Marie get the hurricane lamps and candles from the sitting room.'

'Just try and stop us,' Toby said, leaping to his feet and heading for the house. 'Come on J-M. Last man to the cutlery drawer is a sissy.'

Jean-Marie raised his eyebrows and followed Toby. Emily stood and looked down the garden to the wood and then at the darkening house and what she now recognised as Daisy's window. Picking up the debris she returned to the kitchen.

∽

The fragrance of the meal mingled with that of the evening. Jean-Marie's choice and generosity were duly appreciated. As the light slowly faded, they talked of Paris and politics. Emily waited for the moment in a meal when formality gives way to something else, a certain ease of being and communicating. It didn't happen.

Dark gathered on the horizon and Toby went off to smoke in the study. Emily lit the hurricane lamps. The evening was warm and soon a variety of insects began flirting with death around the flickering candles. For a while she and Jean-Marie were silent, looking down the garden to the dark shapes of the newly coppiced wood.

'I'm sorry,' Emily said.

"Me too. I know I have not been much use to you. You have been patient and looked after me as you always do. I understand that Alexis calling could upset you.'

'It's not your speaking to him that hurts. It's that he always seems to get what he wants. I think he called to get you back to Paris. That's why, during supper, without mentioning it to me first, you said you would have to go back.'

Jean-Marie said nothing. He got up and put his arms round Emily, kissing her ear.

'You know how I feel about you Emily. Our relationship is important to me, I rely on you. We are a couple, aren't we?'

'A while ago, I would have said yes without hesitating,' Emily said, 'but right now I don't know.'

Jean-Marie poured the last of the wine into their glasses and sat down beside her.

'We have both had a lot to think about lately,' he said, 'we must not let those things affect what we have, who we are together.'

'Perhaps they already have,' Emily said.

'I won't go back if you don't want me to.'

Emily looked at Jean-Marie. 'You would stay to placate me when you would rather be back in Paris with Alexis.'

They stayed silent neither looking at the other.

'I'm tired,' Emily said. 'I'll clear up and then go to bed.'

She got up and began collecting the dessert plates. Jean-Marie started to help.

'That's alright there's not much to do, I can manage,' Emily said.

'Things might be clearer in the morning,' Jean-Marie said.

'Yes, they might.'

∽

Emily sat at the kitchen table her hands folded under her chin. She did not want to wash up. She checked everything had been brought in from the garden and blew out the lamps. At the bottom of the stairs she hesitated, about to call good night. The light was on in the study where Toby sat in one of the big leather chairs, reading and smoking. Seeing Emily, he lifted a bottle of Calvados and raised one eyebrow.

'Just a tiny one please.'

She took the drink, and sat in the matching club chair, tucking her legs under her. Toby took a slow draw on his cigar and let out a thin stream of blue grey smoke.

'I could get used to these,' he said. He turned the lit end of the cigar towards him and gave it an admiring look.

They sat quietly together in the lamplight watching the thin eddies of smoke rising to the ceiling. Emily took a tentative sip and raised her head.

'Fuck it, papa.'

'I thought fuck it might be the case. It was hard not to notice a certain froideur at supper. Such things always make me act hearty. Very annoying and I do apologise.'

'You were good Toby, you always are. I'm afraid I'm not.'

Toby returned his attention to the cigar.

'My grandfather used to put a thread of cotton through the middle of his cigars with a long thin needle. He said it stopped the ash falling off and making a mess of one's waistcoat and, incidentally, helped to keep the smoke cool. Always seemed a bit anal to me. After all, if you're cigar ash, falling off is the whole point of being.' He paused and looked into Emily's face.

'I'm instinctively loath to get involved in things that are properly private to you and not my province. I'm also aware that you don't have a mother. I can't be an omni-parent but, if you're happy to engage me in your current concerns then you know I'm for you.'

Emily nodded and paused. She rubbed her eyes. 'I thought I knew what I was doing,' she said, 'but now I don't.'

'There may be a problem of the general and the particular here. I've been surprised by how the house has impressed itself on you. This may be the responsibility of owning it. But that is not all. You have changed in the time we have been here. Something is going on in you that is new, you seem to be carrying, not exactly a burden but something unresolved. Then J-M arrived, almost from the past. He has stayed for a while but perhaps has not been at his shining best.'

Emily groaned and sipped her Calvados.

'I imagined him coming over and being interested in the house – and me. But he's not. I know he doesn't love me, but I thought we shared real sympathy. He hasn't helped in any way. I sort of understand, he's a bit lost here, and it is a stressy time for him, but what about me? He just plays the important Frenchman.'

'I've noticed that,' Toby said. 'He's adopted an air of preoccupation that at his age merely looks dangerously close to sulky. He may even be stooping a little in anticipation of his chair at a Grande Ecole. He should smile more. But that's not the problem, is it?' Toby stopped and carefully put out his cigar in a small brass ashtray.

'Menage a trois, so I'm told, are never easy to be a part of. Jealousies and discontentment are almost bound to occur. That is what we are talking about isn't it?'

Emily said nothing.

'I can see it from J-M's point of view,' Toby said. 'Paris, unlike London, is not a hugely gay friendly town and he wants an academic career. He could join the gay Mafia. This would give him a measure of protection but also limit his options. And they are not a happy fraternity. Some doors would open but more would probably shut. Alternatively, he could appear, at least in public, to be firmly attached to a filly from a proven stable – if you'll pardon both the metaphor and the boast. Setting aside the question of love, you are so clearly good for him. What is more difficult to determine is an answer to the question, is he any good for you?'

Emily drained her glass and poured herself another. She looked quizzical and Toby nodded.

'I'm not sure I can just set love to one side. Jean-Marie never gave any promises or pretended to be anything other than he is. I naively assumed he couldn't fail to fall in love with me, but he seems to be managing quite well, I thought I knew him better than I do, but then today Alexis calls and he's straight back to Paris.'

'It does seem sudden, even callous but that is where his life is, and for that matter ours as well, I will have to go back very soon and so will you. Internships at major institutions don't grow on trees and I can't ask them to hold it open for much longer.'

'I'm sorry,' Emily said, 'I do seem to have unravelled a bit since I got here. Uncle James has involved me in a past that I feel a part of now. I'm intrigued by Daisy. It's like I'm getting to know her, and I want to know more. It sounds stupid but I am really fond of her.'

'Then we will find out more.' Toby finished his drink and put his glass down with firm finality. 'But not tonight, cherub. Enough?'

Emily unfolded her legs from under her and ran her hands down her calves. She yawned and nodded.

Toby stood up and stretched. He briefly caressed Emily's cheek.

'Jean-Marie is a good friend to you, and they are not that easy to find, but don't stay with it if you will be made unhappy. We will talk soon, about you and Daisy and James and the house. And now, for me at least, bed.'

He took Emily's face in his hands and kissed her forehead. She put her arms round him and lay her head on his shoulder.

'Toby, why aren't all men like you?'

'Don't be absurdly sentimental, that's Calvados talking if ever I heard its siren voice. To bed.'

⌒

Upstairs Emily turned her top pillow on end and propped herself against it. She gazed at the portrait of Daisy. In the faint light from the bedside lamp the luminosity of her face was intensified, and her dark clothes receded into the background, losing form.

The late hour and the Calvados had not made Emily soporific but rather the reverse. She was full of inchoate anxiety but could not focus on any train of thought. Might she rouse Jean-Marie? In bed he was always attentive, not so obviously concerned with his own orgasm like most boys. He was like a good waiter, anticipating, creating and fulfilling needs, so that his pleasure seemed identical to hers. Sometimes after she had come, he lost interest in his own orgasm. Sex with Jean-Marie was friendly, personal but never passionate. She wondered if it was like that with Alexis. Jean-Marie had asked for his own bedroom when agreeing to come and stay. That was fine, she had expected it though it was difficult to say why. But they rarely spent a whole night together even in Paris.

Toby was right, Jean-Marie was a good friend. He could be affectionate, and they enjoyed being together, he had opened a new Paris to her. He was her guide and she his consort. Why now did it seem not to be enough? Perhaps he sees me as what Toby might call, a contextualised asset. I mean something, am worth something, in Paris. But the contract seems not to extend to me in the world more generally, that I suppose would be love. It has never occurred to me that I might want it, even need it. Emily lay still, looking at Daisy. The pillow she had been resting against was shoved onto the floor as she pulled back the covers and slipped into bed.

∽

Emily braked hard as the lights on the level-crossing ahead began to flash and the flimsy barriers to descend.

'Whoops. Sorry,' she said, as Jean-Marie was jolted forward. His green case fell off the back seat with a thud.

'That was a Paris moment,' said Jean-Marie, smiling, 'Being driven round the *peripherique* by you is never less than interesting.' He leaned over and kissed her cheek. 'I'm going to miss you.'

'I'll be home soon,' Emily said, 'there's not much more I can do here for now.'

'You still have not decided what to do with the house?'

'No, Toby says we can hang on until Christmas and then decide in the new year.'

'It will probably be best to sell. Everyone I know with a country house moans about it the whole time. It's fine for the rich, they dump their old nannies there and make them keep house.'

'There's always Nicole,' Emily said, 'I loved her, and she pretty much brought me up, but she wasn't keen on the flouncy teen years and went back South to be near her family.' Emily laughed. 'She would hate the English countryside.' The car nosed down the narrow roadway to the station car park, Emily found a spot away from the rookery which ran all along one side. 'We've got loads of time. Let's get some coffee from the buffet, it's on the platform for the London train.'

Emily hauled Jean-Marie's luggage out of the car and pulled it along. It had wheels with superior bearings and was almost noiseless. She linked her arm with his. Emily kissed him as they came to a stop outside the buffet. She bought coffee and they sat on a bench.

'Thank you for coming over,' she said, holding Jean-Marie's arm and tilting her head momentarily to his shoulder. 'It's been lovely to have you with me, outside our natural habitat.'

'The global triumph of humans is largely down to our adaptability, whatever the conditions. I suspect that is not quite what you mean, is it?

Emily was quiet.

'Things will be different, good, back in Paris, it's where we belong, make sense,' Jean-Marie said. 'Perhaps England, the house, will seem like a fantasy when you are back home.'

Emily looked at Jean-Marie's face. The sun gilded the lashes above his brown flecked eyes. He did look lovely. White linen shirt, black 501's and a tight Russian tunic, all topped by his Botticelli curls. She lay her forefinger against his olive lips.

'You are so pretty,' she said, and kissed his forehead. 'I am going to miss you. I may even have started.'

The train sidled into the station. Jean-Marie hugged Emily and the doors closed behind him. She stood and blew kisses as the carriages disappeared into the tunnel that went under the castle and on to London.

∽

'It's like Eton,' Dan said, 'get your name down at birth or forget it. The waiting list is years and years long – and now the old are refusing to go quietly, it's only going to make things worse.'

He and Emily were carrying a wicker hamper across an immaculate lawn that ended in a ha-ha beyond which sheep safely grazed.

'This way,' Dan said, 'let's head for the lake and try and get a spot under a tree. That's at least a hundred points to us if we manage it.'

'I didn't realise the opera was a competition, isn't it meant to be sedate?'

'Nonsense, it's cut-throat stuff. People send their servants down here at dawn to set up tables and mount guard. I was a picnic porter here one summer. It was great, but my gang got sacked for finishing off too much of the punters' champagne, irresistible I'm afraid. That's a lovely dress. Grey silk and gold hair, it really suits you.'

'Thank you,' Emily said. 'I found it in a chest that must have belonged to Daisy, I'm sure she wouldn't mind. It's got such a pretty neckline.'

'Look,' Dan said, 'straight ahead and left. An apple tree – dappled shade and free hanging facilities for coats and stuff. Come on Emily take your shoes off, we don't want a bunch of hoorays to nab it before we get there.'

Emily did as she was bidden, and the pitch was secured.

'Just in time,' Dan said, as a group of elegantly dressed young men with willowy young women, all heavily accoutred for feasting in comfort, came down the hill from the car park and passed on insouciantly to find other grazing.

Dan spread a large chequered blanket on the ground. He positioned it carefully at an angle that firmly excluded any other party taking advantage of the shade. He removed his black tie and stuffed it into the pocket of his dinner jacket that he took off and hung on a spur. Undoing the top button of his dress shirt he turned to Emily who laid full length on the blanket with her hands cupped behind her head.

'I'll go and help the oldies with the chairs and the eski, you do a bit of nest making.'

'Fuck off,' Emily said with a smile, 'I'm going to bask and

wait for the Bolli.' She sat up and pulled the long dress over her knees and linked her hands in front of her calves. Shortly, Toby and Dan appeared with the picnic gear, Guy followed with some cushions.

'I'm so glad the sun's shining,' Guy said, 'if it rains, we have to eat in the marquee, and that's awful, like a well dressed refugee camp.'

Dan took the lid off the eski, pulled out a bottle and handed it to Toby. Guy put up a tiny rickety table and found four glasses. Emily put a round blue tin on the table.

'A few delicious grammes of almost Beluga,' Toby said, 'my contribution to the feast. It'll be bread and water until Christmas after this.' He handed round small French toasts piled with shiny black roe, 'Eat up. Purists say it has to be gone within minutes of opening or it begins to resemble mouse droppings.'

'That is so lovely, just made for champagne,' Emily said, draining her glass and holding it out to Dan.

'It's very good of you,' Dan said to Toby, 'I could eat loads of this, it seems to be full of natural MSG.'

'Despite that dubious observation do please have some more,' said Toby, proffering the plate.

Dan did.

'If I were a member, I'd be here every week,' Emily said, standing up and going over to Guy.

'And I'd be penniless in no time,' he replied, 'I would still have to buy the tickets, and find friends like Toby to provide the caviar. I've been coming here for so long,' he paused and raised his glass, 'absent friends,' he said.

'Absent friends,' they echoed, though no one except Guy could think of any in particular.

'I wonder if uncle James and Daisy came here?' Emily said.

'Yes, I'm fairly sure they did, when things began again after the war,' Guy said, 'the opera would have interested Daisy, with her theatrical background.'

'I've found a lot of her water sketches and pen drawings in her room. Was she always an artist? Is that why they came together?'

'I'm not sure. She was a lovely girl, not unlike yourself,' Guy said. 'In fact, there is something about you today…'

'I'm wearing her dress,' Emily said, holding it out and pirouetting.

'Good Lord, how wonderful,' Guy said, 'rather poetic in a way. Dan tells me you've become interested in Daisy.'

'I have. I feel her around me at the house somehow. I want to know her better.'

They fell silent. Sounds of voices and laughter drifted across the gardens. Emily sat with her back against the apple tree. She closed her eyes, the dappling light registering behind her lids. Leaves rustled in the barely palpable breeze. Indefatigable small birds sped around the trees. Emily opened her eyes, stretched and got up.

'Is there time for a walk?' she asked, pulling Dan to his feet.

'Plenty.'

Emily put her arm in his and they strolled around the lake path.

Small groups of elaborately dressed people occupied every niche and clearing, all doing precisely what Emily and Dan had been doing, eating and drinking, talking and laughing.

'Is this what it means to be English?' Emily asked. 'It's like a wonderfully surreal pantomime.'

'And we are in it,' Dan said, 'parading around the gardens, dressed for dinner in nineteen thirty, as though it were a perfectly normal way to spend a summer's afternoon.'

'I would never even think of the opera in Paris, too formal. But being in costume and picnicking is so extraordinary. I suppose it softens us up for those mad fairy tale plots that operas seem to have.'

'I think it creates the perfect mood for being charmed by the place. When Guy first brought me here, I thought it was ghastly, but if you just let it flow, it can be quite a treat. The nosh has to be good though. What's for the interval?'

'Luckily I managed to mortgage the house and buy a Chateaubriand from the butcher by the church,' Emily said, 'we can have it with tomatoes, stuffed with garlic and anchovy, and a cous salad.'

'Great, something to look forward to if the opera's crap, or for that matter even if it's brilliant.' He smiled and squeezed Emily's hand. 'It's been great meeting you, Emily,' he said, 'I've loved working on the house and garden, and I'd like to carry on renovating what I can, while I can, if that's alright with you?'

'I think that would be great and I'm sure we can come to an arrangement. I'm so glad you turned up, you've been utterly brill,' Emily said, pointing, 'look, there's a little champagne tent on the lawn over there, loan me some money and I'll buy you a glass.'

Chapter 5

'CAN YOU DROP ME AT DENCHER'S LANE PLEASE, IT'S JUST before we get into Porthwiel.'

Every day this week there had been a different driver for the school coach, thus Daisy had to repeat her request to each of them.

'Right you are my lovely,' replied the stout lady in a shiny blue serge suit, who sat wedged behind the enormous steering wheel of the old coach, 'you just give me a shout when we're there.'

Overweight people puzzled Daisy. Now that almost everything edible was rationed, even a little tin of peas, where did they get their food? They must all be farmers.

Usually, Daisy enjoyed the coach rides home. The school day was over and she could sit watching the fields and farms go by, listening to the banter of the other girls, joining in from time to time. It would be nice to talk to Alice sometimes, but she went on the Marleigh coach. Today was Wednesday, and Daisy sat quietly, in hope. Hilda had no telephone. This meant the end of messages from James. There was often only one post a day and that arrived after she had left for school.

Daisy thanked the driver for putting her down at the end of the byway and hurried to where a bend in the lane gave her a view of the cottage. The motorcycle was not there. She slowed her pace. There was no reason why he should be there already. If she could find an acorn before she got to the gate, then he would come. Looking round she could see no oaks, only beech and hornbeams, so she scolded herself for being superstitious and for not thinking of beech nuts, of which there were thousands.

Daisy's purse was on a black ribbon stitched into her coat pocket. She took out the latch key and let herself into the still cottage. She stood inside the door. An amber light warmed everything it touched. Winny appeared and rubbed his muzzle against her ankles, purring. She had not realised how different an ordinary home would feel after the shop, nor how much she now resented the time spent having to endlessly make up orders and weigh the meagre rations of sugar and raisins into the little blue bags. The freedom and comfort of being with Hilda was a wonder. Best of all, Hilda understood how she felt about James. Rather than seeing him as potential danger, she was welcoming and approving. For Daisy, it had come as a revelation.

On the kitchen table there was a note from Hilda and a letter. She was to make up the range, light a fire in the sitting room, have some tea and, cut herself a slice of cake from the tin. The address on the envelope was written in black with an italic nib. It was from James.

Daisy stoked the range and put on the kettle. In the sitting room she cleaned out the hearth and kindled the fire, sitting on the rug to watch it catch and quicken. Back in the kitchen she made the tea and, holding the envelope in her mouth, she took the cup and cake into the living room and sat on the settee with Winny. She had prepared herself for the disappointment that it must contain. Some senior officers had been called to HQ and James had his watch extended until midnight. Tomorrow, almost without a doubt, he would be able to see her.

...I could not be more disappointed, Daisy. I am thinking of you all the time and look forward so much to being with you again. I find it difficult to quite adjust to how I feel, indeed, to know what it is I am feeling. I am sure that when I see you, the mist will dispel and perhaps we will both understand more. At least I know the signing off word of a letter will for once mean what it says.

Yours,
James
X

Daisy liked his writing, the way it flowed and the small Gothic flourishes. She had noticed it on his first visit to the shop when she had signed the deposition. She read it several times, imagining his voice saying the words. Her fingers ran over the cross at the bottom of the page, and she pressed it to her lips. The letter was carefully folded and tucked into her knickers and the envelope put into a drawer.

Fetching her satchel from the hallway Daisy began her homework, writing up a chemistry experiment from the notes in her rough book. Every now and then she stopped and looked into the flames, wondering what James might be doing at that moment and, what it meant to be thinking of her, Daisy. Nobody, as far as she knew, had ever done such a thing before. The idea was miraculous.

It became too dark to write. Daisy pulled the real curtains and the heavy blackout curtains. and put on the light. In the kitchen she found a pile of carrots and potatoes on the draining board beside the sink. Daisy washed them and peeled the potatoes, putting the peelings in a bucket for compost. The water from the tap seemed colder at the cottage than it had been in the shop. Selecting a small, misshapen carrot,

Daisy ate it. It was sweet and crunchy. Finally, she refilled the kettle and put it on the side of the hob.

Singing to herself she went upstairs to get the greatcoat before going out into the garden. Walking between the beds to the henhouse, she could smell the coming autumn, moist with decay, the leaves on the trees barely moving. The first windy day would bring them tumbling off the branches, especially if it rained. The chickens were given a bit of feed and then put into the coop for the night. She locked the precautionary padlock and slipped the key into her pocket. Hilda had said that it was not only foxes that were interested in her hens and their eggs.

Twilight deepened and the air grew markedly cooler. Daisy stayed in the garden, enjoying the feel of the keen air on her cheeks. She wandered around, examining all the beds, poking about in the gloomy outhouses, and admiring the small orchard at the back of the garden, heavy with Egremont Russets, Cox's Pippins, and fat, waxy Bramley's. The Victoria plums had already been picked and bottled or made into jam when there was the sugar.

Hilda's bike sounded in the lane and Daisy went to meet her as her aunt pushed open the gate and wheeled her black Raleigh up the path.

'You startled me in that coat, I must say it suits you, very Marlene Dietrich. That James must be soft on you to let you keep it.'

'I love it,' Daisy said, 'it's so warm and snugly, and so elegantly cut. I wish I could wear it to school.'

'I bet you do, my love,' Hilda said, taking off her gloves and chortling, 'that would set the girls' tongues wagging alright.'

They walked round the house to the shed where Hilda kept her bike. She wheeled it in and shut and bolted the door.

'How was the WI?' Daisy asked.

'If I never see another pair of knitted socks it won't be too soon. Some of the specimens were dreadful. If you can't turn a heel, don't knit socks would be my advice.'

'Must be terrible trying to fight a war in socks with dropped stitches, what if you're taken prisoner, what would the Germans think?'

'Get on with you, girl. I've got plenty of spare wool and needles. We'll get you started on a balaclava after supper.'

'It's no good auntie, they tried to get us knitting at school. I managed a dishcloth made out of some brown stringy stuff, they wouldn't let me near any real wool. But I have been in the Horticultural Society since the first year. I'm brilliant at vegetables, so I'll help you in the Victory Garden, my contribution to the Home Front.'

'Thanks for shutting up the hens. Did you lock the coop?'

Daisy nodded, slipping her arm into her aunt's as they walked round to the front door.

'I've got some sausages for supper, though goodness knows what's in them, it won't be much meat that's for sure. I've rarely seen a sausage so pale.'

Hilda sat on a stool in the kitchen with her legs out in front of her.

'I know it's hard on your mum, losing you, but I'm glad to have you, Daisy. It makes a lot of difference to find someone in the cottage, and the fire lit, when you get back of an evening. You are better company than Winny, and better looking as well, though I doubt you're as good a mouser.'

'Let me.' Daisy grabbed hold of Hilda's Wellingtons by the heel and toe and tugged.

'I'd better make sure that fire's still in, I banked it before I did the hens.'

Daisy disappeared into the sitting room, put a couple of logs on, watched them catch for a moment, and returned to the kitchen.

'James couldn't come over today, he had to do an extra watch.'

'So that was his letter this morning.' Hilda said, putting on a rumpled white apron and tying it behind her back.

'Yes, it's the first time he's written to me. He'll come tomorrow, if he can. Is that alright?'

'Of course, Daisy, whenever you want. Now, let's get the supper going. You've made a start on the veg – good girl – just chop those carrots up, slice an onion, lay the table and that will be your lot.'

Daisy set to, dropping her lids to tiny slits in an attempt to avoid her eyes stinging from the onion. Laying the table took seconds. Before she left the kitchen, she deftly undid the bow at the back of Hilda's apron.

Homework put to one side, Daisy sat on the settee, gazing into the fire, stroking Winny and imagining James at the camp. Comfortable sounds of sizzling and boiling came from the kitchen.

Sausages had only recently been put on ration and, it was difficult to think of them as in the treat category. They had a flavour, but neither Daisy nor Hilda could definitely identify them as either pork or beef, or any other meat for that matter.

'Probably horsemeat, if I know that butcher,' Hilda said.

'I wonder which bits they use? I do hope mum writes with her address soon. I've already written her a letter so I can post it as soon as we know where she is.'

'I shouldn't worry love, she'll be staying in a hostel. It won't take her long to find something permanent.'

'It must be quite frightening with all the bombing. I can't see mum coping very well.'

'I think London's been quieter recently. I know she'll manage alright, she always has done. We'll hear soon.'

'Yes, I'm sure you're right.'

After supper they washed up before sitting by the fire. Hilda, incongruous in jodhpurs and carpet slippers, sat in the carver, reading a Margery Allingham whodunnit. Daisy let a meowing Winny out of the back door, returning to finish her homework. When done, she tucked her stockinged feet under her and lay her head on the arm of the settee.

Later, they drank hot milk listening to Alvar Liddell read the news on the wireless. Continuing allied successes in North Africa was the main item.

Since the advent of James, the war had taken on a new meaning for Daisy. Previously, it had seemed like an escalating series of personal privations of food, clothes, opportunities and the general material support of a developing young life. Thinking about the war had got no further than wondering, when on earth it was going to end, if ever. Whenever the idea of a possible invasion came up, it made Daisy think that perhaps she should have done German as well as French.

'Your feet are going to get cold with no slippers,' Hilda said. 'I've got a nice pair of soft court shoes I never wear that you can have, we're about the same size, I'll look them out for you directly.'

'Thank you, auntie, I'd like that very much, it is kind of you. What colour are they?'

'Chestnut brown, same as your school shoes.'

'They sound lovely. I couldn't bring my slippers with me – the soles were almost all cardboard, and they were too small.'

Daisy uncurled herself, yawned and stretched.

'I think I'll go to bed.'

She stood on tiptoe and stretched up her fingers touching

one of the massive crossbeams that spanned the cottage walls. Daisy leaned over and kissed Hilda's cheek.

'That's chilly tonight,' Hilda said, 'hark at that wind. We could do with a hot brick in our beds. I'm going to stay down for a while, I've just come to an interesting bit in the story. I'll get those shoes out for the morning. Sleep well my love.'

Upstairs Daisy quickly got undressed and pulled a flannel nightdress that Hilda had given her over her head. James' letter went into a pocket in the greatcoat. She was tired, too tired to write her journal and, unsure what to write about. Life was both full and suspended. The room wasn't cold, the heat from the central stack kept it from chilling. Daisy spread the coat over the counterpane. It wasn't as good as wearing it, but it was a comfort and, the extra layer would help her to sleep.

~

Running out of school to get the coach, coat undone and hair flying, outside the gates Daisy stopped. Across the road James stood next to a motorcycle. She was halfway across the road before he saw her and waved. She kissed him quickly on the cheek. Girls milled round them on their way home, many turning to stare from a safe distance. Those already on the coaches were all craning at the windows, their faces animated with curiosity.

'James, how lovely of you to meet me, I wasn't at all expecting this.'

'I'm sorry, I should have asked you first, but this bike with a pillion was free and I couldn't resist. I've brought you a helmet.'

'Gosh.' Daisy stuffed her school hat into her satchel. 'I've never been on a motor bike, do I have to wear a helmet, you're not?'

'You did actually push my bike once though, and yes, you must wear it, I don't want Hilda to think I'm risking your life and limb.'

Daisy grimaced and pulled the helmet down over her hair. It was heavy.

'Let me fasten it,' James said, buckling the strap under Daisy's chin.

'I must look a fright in this.'

'You look charming,' James said, getting astride the bike. 'Get up behind me, there are little pedals for you to put your feet on. Move your satchel to your back, put your arms round my waist and hold on.'

'James, this is so exciting.'

James started the bike and they pulled away. Leaving the school, the girls and the coaches behind them, they were soon in the country. To be moving so fast in the open air took Daisy's breath away. To be doing it with her arms round James was barely credible.

As they rode through Marleigh Wood the bike slowed and James turned off down a track between the trees. He braked gently to a halt on a bed of wet leaves, putting his feet on the ground to steady the bike.

'Jump off Daisy,' he said, pulling off his goggles, 'I thought we might have five minutes to ourselves before we go back to the cottage. It's such a lovely afternoon and the wood is so peaceful.'

James pushed the bike over to the side of the track and leant it against a tree. Daisy took his hand.

'James, that was thrilling. I'd love to have a motorbike, perhaps a little one like the telegraph boys. Can you teach me how to ride?'

'I will, I promise, it's dead easy, but not right now.'

They stood together, in the afternoon light, their arms

91

round one another, listening to the sounds of the forest. They walked along the springy track towards the setting sun. A slight breeze moved those leaves still on the boughs, flashing silver and gold as they turned. The autumn sun cast long enchanting shadows, blurring the outlines of trees and bushes and sharpening the contrast between the yellow light and the dark forest forms. James was the first to speak.

'I thought we might need to talk. Something has happened to us. But right now, I have no idea what to say.'

Daisy stopped and smiled, running her hand down his sleeve. Holding the lapels of his coat she pulled his face close to hers. She put one hand on his neck, feeling the cleft of his nape, and tilting her head, she kissed his lips. They were still cold from the ride. She kissed his cheeks and forehead before pressing her lips against his with a gentle pressure. She pulled away and they continued to walk.

'James, I can't believe this.'

James held her to himself, stroking her hair.

'Darling Daisy, how has it happened?'

She cupped his face in her hands and looked into his eyes.

'I don't know, but when we do need to talk, I'm sure the words will come. Right now, I am just happy to have this moment. It's more than I ever hoped for.'

They stood quietly, neither wanting to move away.

'We'd better start back,' Daisy said, 'auntie will be expecting me.'

Before they re-mounted the bike, they kissed, it was impossible not to.

⌒

Daisy unlocked the front door to the shop and pushed it open. She hesitated, peering into the gloomy interior, before crossing the threshold followed by James. With the light on, the place looked unreal, it was difficult to connect it with the whole of her young life.

'It's only been a few weeks and already it seems a world away. I know every scratch on the counter but it's as if I was never here,' she reached out for James' hand, 'it's like I never existed.'

James put his arms around her.

'I can swear to you that you did and I've got the drawings to prove it. But I do understand. When my parents died in Malaya the house in Sussex seemed meaningless without them. It was as if I'd been cut adrift.'

Daisy wedged the door open.

'It smells musty. Will you come with me to check everything?'

'Of course.'

They went through to the parlour, where the main pieces of furniture had been covered with spectral white dustsheets.

'I didn't know mum had such things,' Daisy said, lifting the sheet on the table and running her hand across the wood. 'It seems a bit posh for us.'

The empty kitchen smelt of mice and looked dirtier than Daisy remembered. The sharp tang of tobacco still lingered in the storeroom. Upstairs there were no shutters and the natural light made the rooms feel more normal, only dustier than they once were. They climbed the steep narrow flight to Daisy's attic.

'So, this is where Daisy laid her sweet head,' James said.

Daisy sat on the bed.

'It feels odd. I don't know whether this was my refuge or my prison.'

'Perhaps it was a bit of both,' James said. 'At school I never had a room of my own, and I stayed at a dingy hostel off the Euston Road when I was at the Slade.'

'You poor thing,' Daisy said. She pulled him towards her and kissed his lips, keeping hold of him as she looked around her.

'I would have died without my little space to hide,' Daisy said. 'When did you get a room for yourself?

James rubbed his chin.

'Not until I went back to Sussex after college and tried to become an artist. And then the war arrived.'

'You were called up.'

James nodded.

'Life as a soldier is like school, cleverly organised to avoid the possibility of a private life.'

Daisy got up from the bed and smoothed her skirt. They stood looking out of the attic window at the overgrown garden. She put her arm through James.'

'Do they know about me?' she asked.

'You bet they do, Daisy, although, needless to say, I've never told anyone, except Watson, my batman, who, I'm sure, is entirely loyal.'

'It must be osmosis.'

'Little signs,' James said, 'I'm off camp more, constantly trying to scrounge vehicles that two might use. It adds up. Camp life is very tedious for the men, nothing to think about except an uncertain future. Officers are fair game, especially if one is young.'

'Do you mind?'

'No, it makes me more human, more effective.'

'That's good,' Daisy said. She took hold of James' wrist and looked at his watch.

'There's only the garden and the shed left to check, and then we'd better get a move on.'

'Do you know what's for lunch?' James asked. 'It is kind of Hilda to invite me.'

'She likes you. It's rabbit and bacon pie, though God knows where she got the bacon, it's probably from Tom Dacre, he's sweet on her.'

James looked slowly round the room and followed Daisy onto the tiny landing at the head of the stairs. With her hands on the thin banister rails Daisy's feet barely touched the treads on the way down.

'It's funny how your body remembers,' she said.

Daisy put on her helmet and mounted the pillion. As James pulled away, she looked back at the shop before putting her arms round him and resting her cheek on his back. The autumn sun still had some warmth and the air smelled sweet. Daisy closed her eyes.

∽

'I've got my provisional licence and my motorcycle learner's permit, couldn't you let me ride it just a little way. I know how to operate the clutch and I could stay in a low gear.'

Daisy put her hands on the handlebars and sat astride the bike. She looked directly at James.

'I daren't, Daisy, if there was an accident, even a minor one, I could be up before a court martial. The bikes don't belong to me, they belong to the King. I'll talk to Hilda and we'll see what we can do, but I can't promise anything.'

'I'm saving what mum sends me to buy some jodhpurs. I could join the ATS.'

Daisy got off the bike and pushed her hair back before putting on her helmet.

'Come on, let's get to this secret cove,' James said, 'you'll have to direct me and let's hope the war office haven't sealed it off.'

'They hadn't last time I was there. It's so difficult to get in and out of. We'd be able to shoot the Germans easily, if they tried to land.'

'Then let's hope we don't meet any,' James said.

Leaving the bike at the top of the cliff, they wound their way down towards the sea along tracks barely wide enough to place two feet together. The way was precipitous and increasingly slippery as the rocky soil underfoot gave way to flat, damp, shale. They walked in single file, Daisy leading. A few faded sea pinks and clumps of coarse grass clung to the narrow verges. The higher reaches of the cliff were streaked brown from the ferrous ore, constantly washed out by water silently coursing from fissures in the rock. Closer to the bottom of the cliff these were joined by vivid streaks of green algae. Samphire sprouted from patches of sparse mineral soil. As they entered a cleft in the rock the way became steeper, with sudden sharp drops. There was little light and the sound of the sea was barely audible. Abruptly, they came out on a ledge towards the back of the cove. A hard light bounced off the white sand and a fine salt spray drifted from the rolling breakers along the strand.

Daisy led as they scrambled over boulders and skirted rock pools on their way to the water's edge. Behind them, the black triangles of cave entrances appeared to disgorge massive coloured boulders. In front of them the rhythmic crash of waves mingled with the cries of birds.

'Isn't this wonderful, James,' Daisy shouted, running towards the waves, 'Let's paddle. Hilda says it's a tonic for the feet. You should get your men to do it. They'd march better.'

'It's a kind invitation, but do I have to?' James said, running to keep up with her.

'Course you do, silly.' Daisy kicked off her shoes and rolled down her stockings, stuffing them into the toes and leaving them on a rock ledge. She fell to her knees on the soft wet sand and undid the laces on James' boots.

'Now get your socks and gaiters off or you'll get drenched, and be ready to run backwards if a big wave comes.'

Daisy tucked her dress into her knickers and walked to the edge of the water, still fizzing from a spent wave.

James put his boots next to her shoes and joined her, his trousers rolled up to his knees. He took Daisy's hand. Her face was in profile, lit by bright sun. A blush coloured her cheeks and her hair moved with the wind. James kissed her forehead.

'You are beautiful,' he said.

Daisy squeezed his hand and moved forward towards the advancing line of white rimmed water. They stood looking out towards the dark blue of the horizon.

'My feet are freezing,' James said.

'That's not the way to think of it,' Daisy said, kicking up some foam. 'It's cooling your blood and making you feel more alive, it's elemental, it's nature.'

'You've been reading the Romantics again. It's just perishing cold.'

'I wanted to bring you here,' Daisy said, 'because it's a place I've loved all my life. It changes with the light and the weather, and sometimes, after a big storm, it's barely recognisably itself. But whenever I come here, whatever's going on, I feel alright, like it's holding me. It's good for being happy and for being sad and I want to share it with you. Let's go and look at the caves.'

She took his hands and pulled him up the sloping beach to where they had left their shoes. Daisy put her leg against James' so that their feet were together.

'Look how different they are,' she said. 'Yours are so big and knobbly, and mine are tiny little thin things.'

James shivered.

'Sit down on the rock,' Daisy said, 'and you can put your feet under my arms to warm up.'

'Thanks, but we'd better not.'

'Why not? There's no one here and I bet it's not against army regulations.'

'Damn, I left my copy in barracks,' James said. He lay back on the rock with his feet in the air and Daisy tucked them into her armpits.

'Gosh, they are cold,' she said, holding her arms tightly by her side, 'and a bit wet too.'

'It was a very kind thought and thank you for sharing this place.' James said, gazing up at the cloudless sky. He eased his feet from under Daisy's arms and sat up. He pulled her towards him, nestling her head in his chest. Daisy stroked his shining hair.

'It has nothing to do with kindness,' she said.

'I know, Daisy,' he said, 'I know.'

Daisy took his head in both her hands and looked directly into his eyes, saying nothing.

'I haven't said it Daisy, because I'm not sure if it's fair or reasonable, and I'm a little afraid of the consequences, but I do love you. I feel like somebody different in an unfamiliar world.'

'It's like that for me too. Everything looks the same, but nothing is, especially me. In chapel, at school, we have to love God with all our heart, soul, strength and mind, that's how I feel about you.'

They stood alone on the sand, entwined in each other's arms.

'What will become of us, Daisy?' James said. 'I lecture the men against falling for local girls. We never know how long we will be here, and when we go, if we will come back. I had decided to leave women alone until after the war was over. We could not have met in a more dreadful way, but that was it. I seemed to have no choice, and you are so young.'

'So are you, there's no more than three years between us, cradle snatcher. Come on, it's all uphill on the way back, and at your age and in your condition...'

Chapter 6

'GIVE ME YOUR LEFT INDEX FINGER,' SAID THE HOTEL receptionist. Emily obeyed. He pressed it against a glowing blue pad. A tick appeared in a box on the computer screen.

'And now you, sir.'

Jean-Marie complied.

'You simply press your finger against the red pad on the street door and again on the hotel door, here on the first floor. No keys, antique hotel and modern technology,' he looked up at them and smiled, 'except, of course, the key to your room.' He handed Jean-Marie a latchkey attached to a reproduction miniature at the end of a silver chain. 'Just hang it here when you go out,' he said, with one hand languidly indicating a walnut art nouveau cabinet. He picked up their bags and recommended the lovely sea air, and the long beautiful beaches, as he led them through narrow, dimly lit corridors, crammed with paintings, cabinets and small pieces of furniture, that failed to coalesce into any known style of décor.

The room was long and thin. At one end, floor to ceiling windows opened onto a wide terrace shared with other rooms along the corridor. The view was obscured by a dense tangle of ferns and potted palms that screened the street. Along the terrace, large baroque tables were adorned with elaborate candelabra and bowls of outsize china fruit. At intervals tiny songbirds, flitted, or sat staring, in ornate cages. The combination of the greenery and the awning over the terrace reduced the fading natural light of a November afternoon.

'What is this place?' Emily said, looking around their room crowded with a melange of random furniture, mostly tawdry reproductions of classical and baroque. A faint sweet smell of something like talcum hung in the air.

'I'm cold,' Emily said, sinking her head into her shoulders and wrapping her coat tightly about her. She looked up at the air conditioning grille some metres above them set into a plaster frieze. Jean-Marie found the thermostat and turned it up.

A massive Murano glass chandelier hung from a gilded lozenge in the ceiling. The switch was a dome of white fluted porcelain, with a toggle that rotated to turn on the current.

'Isn't that heaven.'

'No,' Emily said.

'Just let your Romantic imagination flow.' He folded Emily in his arms, and then stood back holding her hands. 'Don't you like this place?'

'I can see the point, I think, total camp abandonment. But it's laid on so thick, it's all a bit like treacle. And the art is vomit making.'

'You're absolutely right. The art is a bit nymphs and shepherds, alright, unspeakably awful. The whole thing is de trop but then that is its thing. It's vulgar, random, that's the point. It's about as far from Best Western as it's possible to get.'

∽

Breakfast, cold, had to be ordered the night before and they chose to risk taking it on the terrace, at nine thirty. Emily, wrapped in her towelling robe, answered the door at nine fifteen the next morning. A young waiter in a bright white jacket, stood there with a trolley, smiling a good morning.

'Excuse me Madame, may I come through your room to lay up breakfast on the terrace. Unfortunately, this is the only service access,' he said, intensifying his smile.

'Of course,' Emily said, after a few moments' reflection.

As she went to the shower Jean-Marie was helping the waiter lift the trolley over the sill, onto the terrace. Thin streams of water cascaded from the large sunflower showerhead and trickled over her hair and body. What am I doing here? What am I doing?

Smelly patio heaters, their cylinders dressed in frills, hissed amongst the greenery and shed an uneven and airless heat. Emily had put on a tight cashmere vest that flattened her breasts, a woollen jumper and a jacket.

The table was needlessly fussy. Crockery was ornate and ill matched, as was the cutlery. Hot water was in a small Samovar with a tea light underneath it. The only hot element of the meal was some limp, and rapidly cooling, toasted *pain de mie*.

'I'm sorry I haven't been more reliable since you got back, working on my dreaded thesis and moving apartments has mopped up all my time. I thought it would be good to have a couple of days together.'

'You like your new flat?'

'Yes, Denis is older and it's much quieter.'

Emily put some jam on the end of a cold croissant, nibbled it and dropped it on her plate.

'Why didn't you move in with Alexis? I thought you might.'

'He didn't ask me,' Jean-Marie paused, 'and I'm not sure it would be a good idea.'

Emily touched the side of the samovar. It was warm. Maybe tea was possible. She selected a bag from the velvet casket on the table and put it in her cup. The spigot released a trickle of tepid water.

'Why not?'

She rhythmically squashed the bag against the side of the cup with a teaspoon and watched the water slowly darken. Emily picked up the cup in both hands and raised it to her lips, sipped and looked directly at Jean-Marie. She opened her eyes wide and raised her brows.

'Emily, please, let's just enjoy our breakfast.'

'I'm cold.'

Emily got up and, taking her tea with her went back to their room. She sat on the small gilt chair by the dressing table, cluttered with toilet bottles and round glass containers with outsize powder puffs. Her reflection looked back at her from the foxed mirror. It can't be hormonal, so why so spiteful? Jean-Marie was just his normal self-interested self, nothing special. The reason why he wouldn't move in with Alexis is that it would mark him as unambiguously gay. I do not want to be here in this awful hotel, she thought, it is simply absurd. This is not 'sharing a passion' it's being subjected to some mad queen's appalling whimsy. She closed her eyes and sat still.

Jean-Marie came quietly into the room and put his arms round her.

'I'm sorry,' she said.

'No matter.' Jean-Marie bent and kissed her cheek. Emily smelled the fragrance of his hair and turned to kiss his lips.

'What are we doing today?' she asked.

'What everyone does in Moulegate. We walk along the beach and then go to an English tea shop.'

'Come on, let's get out of this gimcrack museum,' Emily said, 'the relentless camp wears me down.'

'Like the Ladyboys of Bangkok?'

'No, they made me laugh.'

'I'm sorry you don't like it here. I thought you'd find it amusing.'

'I'll get over it,' Emily said, and stood up. 'Hats and scarves, I think. It's bound to be blowing a gale.'

∽

Eddies of fine grains of sand coursed along the wide promenade. Emily could feel the salty grit on her lips. Family groups and middle-aged couples, well wrapped and leaning into the buffeting wind, made up the majority population. Emily and Jean-Marie went down the steps to the long flat beach. A light mist hovered over the grey sea and the slap of a slight swell was muted in the wet air.

They walked along the water's edge, stopping occasionally to examine stones and shells or pieces of flotsam that caught the eye. At their approach, small crabs darted sideways over the mud into the safety of shallow pools. Emily collected some tiny shells and put them into her pocket.

Shafts of suddenly brilliant sunlight illuminated moving patches of land and sea, as the breaking clouds blew westwards. The warming day gradually dispelled the mist. Emily stuffed her hat into a pocket, took off her coat and tied it round her waist by the arms. She thought she might take her shoes off and paddle in the chilly rivulets that ran down from the head of the beach, but looking at Jean-Marie she detected early signs of boredom as he stood, hands in pockets, looking back up the beach to the town.

'Coffee?' he said,

'OK.'

They walked slowly up the gentle slope to the promenade.

'The architecture is wonderful,' Jean-Marie said, 'lots of modernism and art nouveau, some of the mansions are like fairy tale castles, and such bold colours. It must have been so elegant once, glorious to live in.'

'Horrible,' Emily said, 'all swirly bits and pregnant looking balconies, everything overstated. It's like they're really trying to get noticed. Wouldn't you feel like it's living in someone else's dream?'

'Emily, so philistine, no I would not. This town is a casket of jewels, each one unique. I'd be inspired.'

'To do what?' Emily asked. 'It would only make you more camp and you wouldn't like that.' She laughed. 'Alright, they are a lot of fun and the salt stained paintwork does have some allure. Come on let's find a hot drink, it's getting chilly.'

The salon of the eponymous English Tea Shop was snug, with a pleasant buzz of amiable conversation, mostly in English.

'Do you have Darjeeling?' Emily asked the elderly waiter.

'Of course,' he replied, 'milk or lemon? And would mademoiselle like a cucumber sandwich, or perhaps an English muffin?'

He took their order and moved smartly on to the next table.

'Very snooty.' Emily said.

'He's just trying to be authentically English,' Jean-Marie said.

Emily grimaced. She put her elbows on the table and cupped her face in her hands. She looked at Jean-Marie.

'Beautiful, hazel calves' eyes,' she said.

'Thank you,' Jean-Marie said. He sipped his tea, looking over the rim of the cup at Emily.

'Do you think it would be wise for us to get married?'

'I very much doubt it, but I'll get back to you. It must be the sea air. Of more immediate importance, what am I going to do, Jean-Marie? I'm hopeless at making decisions. Toby does it effortlessly and, I've rather let him make most of mine, but this time he's insisting it's up to me.'

'It didn't take much reflection for you to dismiss my proposal, I could be feeling hurt, and I guess this is the English house again. How long can it go on?'

'Yes, I'm sorry, it was very kind of you to ask me, but I'm not ready, I'm too young and I have to sort out my future. As to the house, I honestly don't know how long.'

'Just sell it. English houses are worth ridiculous amounts of money. It's what their mad economy is based on, more and more unrealisable assets tied up in crumbling real estate. But you, my pet, already have somewhere very nice to live in Paris, and so you can just take the money.'

'I know I'm ridiculous,' Emily said, 'I'm supposed to understand economics. If I don't cash it in it will turn into a liability. We're already spending unnecessary money through all the work Dan's doing, and he's beginning to develop ideas of his own. I should get planning permission for a house in the woods and put the package on the market. But I can't make up my mind to do it.'

Emily took a bite of her cucumber sandwich.

'I know they're meant to be peeled,' she said, 'but without it there is no flavour at all.'

'Have a bit of muffin,' Jean-Marie said, cutting her a quarter and lifting it on his knife.

Emily put it in her mouth and licked her buttery fingers.

'Delicious,' she said, 'so what stops me?'

'I cannot say.' Jean-Marie turned his head to look out of the window. 'Maybe your English genes make you crave property.'

'It is feeble minded of me, but I keep coming back to Daisy, she's why uncle James left me the house, though I don't quite follow the reasoning. I just want to know what happened between them. James never spoke of her to me and yet I found her room in the attic, left untouched. Did he expect her to come back or was it like some mausoleum?'

'I'm not convinced you truly want to know. It cannot be hard to find out. People leave traces, and by what you say, lots of them. You could borrow some money on the house and get a detective to search for Daisy.'

Emily absently opened her sandwich, removed the limp green discs of cucumber and ate the bread.

'I couldn't. It wouldn't feel right. I don't want to know in that cold way, I want to be involved in her story.'

'Then just do it. It's not as though James was a significant figure for you. You had hardly mentioned him before he died.'

'That's true, but then I didn't realise that I had meant something to him. It has changed my past. I know it's not reasonable, Daisy is just a small watercolour and uncle James no longer exists. They are remote, but I care.'

Jean-Marie drained his cup.

'This Darjeeling is good,' he said, 'amber velvet, with a fugitive hint of woodland smoke.'

'Shut up, you poof,' Emily said. 'Let's power walk the prom and then wrestle with an enormous *assiette de crustaces* and a bottle of Sancerre.'

'I knew you liked the seaside,' Jean-Marie said. He swung his coat over his shoulders and followed Emily out of the *salon de thé*.

∽

Emily got off the Metro at Abbesses. There were queues for the lifts and so she toiled up the long decorative staircase and turned right, towards Rue le Pic, into a freezing raw wind. She needed to buy supper. The streets were full of tourists, shops glowed with the promise of warmth and delicious things. *Paupiettes de Veau* would be good, but must make sure they are not turkey, a common substitute nowadays. If she sautéed them well, they could be quickly roasted instead of braised. A golden square of Dauphinoise would be perfect and, could heat alongside them. For cheese, a mature Comte, dark as beeswax, just as Toby liked it. Nearer the apartment she stopped at an *epicerie* for some dates and clementines, and at the *boulangerie* for some bread.

Away from the main streets the world was becalmed, anonymous. Apartment blocks, mainly twentieth century, rose up darkly on either side of the road. Emily mounted the few steps to the high double doors and punched in the code. Inside it was cold and gloomy. They no longer had a live-in concierge. Manon came in every day to clean and to see to the post. Emily liked her, she was friendly and good hearted, but she left mid-afternoon for a northern suburb, to look after her children.

Emily tramped slowly up the stairs to the fourth floor. She could hear Toby coughing from outside the apartment.

'Hi, Toby,' she called, on the way to the kitchen to drop the groceries. Toby sat in the living room that overlooked the street, reading a newspaper. He always read both *Liberation* and *Le Monde Diplomatique* in order to synthesise a balanced appreciation of events. Emily went over and kissed him. She sniffed the air.

'You've been smoking again,' she said, unbuttoning her coat.

'That's nothing to what Chirac's been up to. He's such an egotistical tripe hound, it can only be the aphrodisiac of power. Hardly counted as smoking. It was the smallest cigar you will ever see. Indeed, I doubt it ever aspired to be more than a cheroot.'

Toby laid his paper down on the sofa, got up and headed for the kitchen to look in the bags.

'What's for supper, *petite ange*?'

'*Paupiettes.*'

'*De veau?*'

'*De veau.*'

'Delicious, you spoil me. Can I get you a glass of wine?'

'Yes please. I'll get the supper in a minute. It won't take long.'

Emily went into the sitting room and closed the curtains. The high ceilinged room was sparsely, but comfortably furnished. There was warm wood, large mirrors and deep comfortable sofas. Emily kicked off her boots and propped herself up lengthwise on a sofa opposite Toby. She raised her glass.

'*Tchao,*' she said.

'*A votre santé,*' Toby said.

Emily stared at her toes as she wriggled them in pale grey tights.

'I quite like being at L'Institut,' she said, 'and I'm meeting lots of people who will be useful if I decide to follow you into development. I think I should. It's well paid and one of the more interesting areas of economics. My current problem is that they don't seem to have a clue what to do with me. Have they had many interns before?'

'Yes, but they're mainly Americans, who don't need supervision because they're programmed to intern themselves. I'm afraid it's not such a big thing here. I do sympathise, not to have a clear role in a complex organisation whose major activity is the personal pursuit of power is not easy, but it could be fun and useful. Which is why I thought it might suit you for a while, as well as aiding the major decision of what to do next.'

'That's very helpful, Toby. Being powerless explains my sense of invisibility and, why I have a desk and a computer, but no-one seems to have any responsibility for me, I'm liminal.' Emily scratched her scalp with both hands and vigorously shook her hair from side to side. 'That's why I get random, low level, editing type jobs from just about anybody in the building. Alain actually asked me to get him a coffee and, I had to explain that I was not his gofer – he took it quite badly. French men can be surreal.'

'I fear you're right, angel, but don't worry. The fact that you are free and capable will soon sink in.'

Toby, smiling, held out his glass and Emily refilled it before going into the kitchen. Cooking, even assembling a simple supper was soothing, a tangible and worthwhile achievement. Toby always cooked at weekends and when he was entertaining, occasions to which Emily was invariably invited and sometimes accepted.

After supper Toby stacked the dishwasher and retired to his study. Emily lay on the sofa, checked various locations on her phone and read for a while before running a bath. Jean-Marie texted. *Des Cineastes*, which was close to the apartment, was screening, *Ma Vie en Rose*, he was going, would Emily like to join him? She thanked him but declined.

Laying in the bath she could hear Toby's muffled coughing. She hoped he wasn't smoking. Absently, she pushed her breasts together and created little waves on their release. Perhaps she should try again to get Toby to quit with nicotine patches? Emily got out of the bath and towelled herself vigorously before putting on a long flannel nightshirt that she had bought in Lewes. She imagined Jean-Marie sitting alone in the dark cinema.

The morning air struck chill as Emily walked briskly back with the bag of croissant. When she got to the apartment Toby was still in bed. She called out to him and made some coffee. Toby, swathed in a dilapidated Chinese silk dressing gown that reached the floor, came into the kitchen, walking slowly. His face was grey and his hair awry. He sat down heavily, holding the gown tightly to his neck.

'My back aches, I'm going to work from home today.'

'Good morning, Toby,' Emily said, going over and placing her palm on his forehead. It was hot and clammy. She went to the bathroom and came back with a fever strip, placing it above his eyes.

'You've got a temperature and the pain in your back might just be your lungs, and whatever you say, I'm calling the doctor.'

Toby slowly raised his head and looked at her.

'I don't need to see one, even if we could afford to lure one here. A couple of aspirin and a day in bed and I'll be fine. I do know how I feel.'

'I'm going to call Dr Lendais – now.'

'Don't be so hysterical, Emily, it's not like you to be melodramatic.'

'Don't call women hysterical, Toby, Freud's dead. And bloody stop it, you're scaring me, and I've had enough. You've not been well since we got back, you won't do anything about it, and you completely ignore Dr Lendais' advice. Dear God, if you are like this now what sort of old man are you going to make?'

Emily left him to find her phone. Toby sat, looking down, his hands holding on to the edge of the table. He stood up, walked unsteadily to his bedroom and lay on the bed. His breathing had become fast and shallow. He could hear Emily in the sitting room talking on the phone.

'Dr Lendais will come at eleven o'clock. His first question

was, had you stopped smoking. I said, no. You must take some paracetamol to bring down your fever. Stay where you are. I'll get them and bring you some coffee and croissant. You'd better call L'Institut and let them know you're sick.'

Emily found things to do around the apartment to fill the time. When Dr Lendais arrived, after a brief examination, the diagnosis was immediate.

'Toby, you are a fool. It is probably a bacterial pneumonia, which in a healthy man is no problem, but with your lungs.' He spread his hands in front of him. 'We will have to get some tests done and, some Xrays and probably pump you with antibiotics until it goes. I'll get you a room in the *Assis Publique*. Depending on how you respond you should be home in a matter of days, convalescence may take a lot longer. I'll drop in and see you tomorrow. You are a very lucky man to have Emily, Toby, I hope you know that.' As Emily showed him to the door he turned and put his hand on her arm.

'Toby is still young, but he's overweight, he doesn't exercise and switching from Havanas to Sumatran cigars is fooling himself. They may look less lethal but that is as far as it goes. He's not going to be able to work very effectively for a while and he will not take kindly to it. See if you can get him to leave Paris and get some rest away from the winter smog.' As Emily held the door he looked back and smiled. 'Take care of yourself.'

'Thank you, I'm grateful.'

Her eyes began to smart as she closed the door.

∿

Toby spent a week in hospital on an antibiotic drip and was then allowed home. The paramedics from the ambulance helped him slowly up the stairs to the apartment. A bag of medicaments was given to Emily and the dosages and frequencies explained. She was warned that Toby might suffer from extreme fatigue for a while.

Toby sat on the sofa, panting after his exertion.

'Holy heaven, thank God that's over,' he said, 'and why were those young women instructing you in the mysteries of my medicaments? I'm the fucking patient and I'm not senile.' He leaned forward with his head in hands. 'I'm sorry darling, I must keep my temper, I'm just so cross with the whole business. I'm parched, how about a *pousse café* if I promise not to smoke.'

Emily picked up his bag and took it to his room. Toby followed and flopped on the bed. Emily sat on the edge and took his hand.

'Maybe those women thought you were older than you actually are. Right now, you look like an exceedingly ancient and, rather badly stuffed, teddy bear.'

'Now you're patronising me, where is this going to end?'

'I'm not, papa, I'm just scared. You've suddenly become mortal and you are all I've got in the world. I'm going to make sure that you last just as long as you possibly can.'

Toby pulled her to him and hugged her.

'My darling Emily, I'm not going anywhere, I'm simply ill, it's a temporary condition.' He stroked her hair and kissed her forehead. 'I do understand, and you're right, we need a conservation project. I've always been neglectful of the infrastructure, my rackety ways didn't much matter at twenty-five.'

Emily stood up and wiped the tears from her eyes. 'I'm so relieved to have you back home. I'll get you an espresso and a small Calvados, but I'm afraid all your cigars have gone down the garbage chute.' She leant over and kissed him.

'Oh, God,' Toby said.

The queue at the *Musée Luxembourg* snaked along the road and around the corner into the park. The afternoon was bright, but people were hunched into their coats, rubbing their hands together against the cold.

'Who cares about Gauguin? He's just a chocolate box painter of underaged girls, which is all he ever wanted to be. By the time he got to Haiti all those adolescents with lovely tits had been shown the error of their ways by the missionaries. One hopes he painted them from imagination but fears the worst.'

'That's unfair, Emily,' Jean-Marie said, 'and I care. He had a unique way of handling colour and form and his work is so evocative.'

'Given the crowds, the only thing this exhibition is likely to evoke is the Metro. Great art needs to be savoured and we'll be queuing for hours for fast food bolted down in a crush, definitely indigestible.'

'I promised Alexis I'd go because he can't make it, and he wants a catalogue.'

'We needn't disappoint Alexis. You can get a catalogue from the shop and pretend you went to see the exhibition. We'll save money as well.'

Emily sucked in her cheeks and began to stagger.

'If I don't eat soon, I might collapse, and you know how you hate me making a fuss in public.' She put her arm through his and dropped her head onto his shoulder. 'We could have a brisk walk round the gardens and go and find supper.'

Jean-Marie frowned, but was walking with less determination. Emily stopped and held on to him.

'The simplest cost-benefit analysis says, eat,' she said. 'I'll even pay for the catalogue, and it won't be cheap, will it?'

'I can't pretend to have been to an exhibition I haven't seen. I would feel a fraud – it would be absurd.'

'Then tell the truth, or better, blame it on me. He might

like that. He'll have the catalogue, that's probably all he wants.'

Jean-Marie's shoulders dropped his face relaxed. He cupped Emily's chin in his hands and kissed her nose.

'You may be morally dubious, but I admire the acuity of your thinking and, the way you uncover the true dynamics of a situation. You're a better philosopher than I am.'

'Dear Jean-Marie, it's kind of you to think so highly of low cunning. I'm hungry and Gauguin's a bore. Let's get the book and then go and count the lovers round the lake.'

A little later, with the catalogue safely in Jean-Marie's bag, she took his arm and they walked past the end of the queue and out into the gardens. The bright, cold sunshine had attracted elderly Parisians, who chatted or dozed on the green slatted chairs lined up against the wall. Despite the cold an old lady rolled her stockings down to her ankles to air her legs. The gardens were always popular and the respite from the long greys of a Parisian winter gave an early impression of Spring. Couples strolled under the bare trees with arms entwined, all enjoying that hermetic intimacy that green space encourages in the city. The windows of the *Palais* burned white with reflected light. Without intention they walked towards the sheltered depression that held the lake. Jean-Marie put his arm round Emily and kissed her ear.

'I do love you, Emily,' he said.

Emily stopped and looked at him, her face close to his, taking his hand they walked on.

∽

Emily sat at her desk, she stretched her neck upwards and arched her back. The précis of an OECD multi–nation report on adult skills was not presenting much of a challenge. If it were, she might have resented having to do it as an intern, but the fact that it was easy made the work boring. Emily liked economics, she enjoyed, to an extent, constructing tightly written reports based on a critical analysis of the evidence. Tonight, it was proving difficult to bother.

She looked up at the portrait of Daisy that hung above her desk. It was all she had brought back from Sussex. The familiar pale, intent face, small hands white against the folds of her tunic, dark eyes looking past the viewer. I want to know Daisy I want us to be friends. The idea had come unbidden. Emily turned over in her mind the impossible sentiment.

'Emily.'

Toby was sitting upright in bed wearing a baggy green sweatshirt.

'Darling, I am sorry to call you, but I've left my phone somewhere, probably the study, but right now I lack the energy to go hunting. Would you be an angel?'

Emily found the phone and handed it to Toby. He let it rest in his hand against the covers.

'I wish you'd take things a bit more slowly, Toby. You're never going to recover at this rate, you're constantly exhausting yourself.'

'I know, but I promise you I'm only doing things that have to be done and stuff is just piling up.' He lay his head back against the tapestry cushion that allowed him to work, more or less comfortably, from bed.

'I'm getting fed-up with all this,' Toby said, 'it's been going on for far too long and I still feel as though I've been recently run over.'

Emily sat on the bed and looked at him. He was pale and had lost weight. Unshaven, the probable impact of age was discernible in the contours of his face, if indeed, he managed to get old.

'We could go away for a while,' Emily said. 'Dr Lendais reckons getting out of Paris will speed up your convalescence. L'Institut wouldn't miss their intern for a while. We could go South it would at least be a bit warmer.'

'Thanks, but I'd prefer not to be pushed around Nice in a bath chair. The South is ruined, it's full of the worst sort of English.'

Emily stood up and looked out of the window.

'What about your friend Raoul's house in Burgundy? I'm sure he would let us stay as long as we wanted.'

'I'm sure you're right, but Burgundy is so empty. There's no-one left and it's all a bit depressing, especially in winter. I'm sorry, I'm not being very helpful, am I?'

'No, you're not, Toby. I must go and finish this summary.'

She leaned over and kissed his forehead.

∽

Emily checked her email. There was a long message from Dan. They had left him to work on the garden and grounds when he could find the time, and he had kept in sporadic touch. It was good to hear about the house. Dan wrote much as he spoke. For subject he had put '*Campiston Restoration Society Bulletin.*' She imagined his voice as she read.

The barn is now fully cleared of old straw bales, bits of rope, decayed bushel boxes, broken implements and other useless impedimenta. The priceless collection of old quart beer bottles I've taken to Guy's place and they are now filled with my peerless home-brew. The exciting news is that [roll on drums] behind a partition in the nether recesses of the barn, under some ancient tarpaulins, I have found the mouldering remains of an old motorbike.

The leather saddle has turned to dust, the tyres have perished and melted away, but the rust on the metalwork doesn't seem too bad. It was a lightweight classic of its time, and I asked a mate to come and take a look, to find out if it is worth trying to restore –YES – all I need is the owner's consent. Also, me and another mate, have at last finished re-glazing the hothouse and we've removed all the old soil, not an easy task I might tell you. After fumigation, fresh soil will be installed, ready for some Coeur de Boeuf, we can get the seeds here [couldn't get Marmande], 75 days to harvest, so start sowing in the spring. My very best to Toby and hope that he is still the model patient. Guy sent his regards to you both. You won't recognise the old place when you see it.

Your respectful retainer
Dan

Emily was warmed by the enthusiasm in Dan's tone. She imagined the garden in winter as she went into Toby's bedroom. He lay propped up, spectacles on the end of his nose, leafing through a sheaf of papers.

'Listen, Toby,' she said, 'let's go to Sussex and stay there for Christmas.'

Toby dropped his head and looked blankly at her over the rims of his spectacles. His face wrinkled with the effort of thought.

'Sounds good to me, I used to like an English Christmas, Midnight Mass and a great stuffed goose. I'm definitely languishing here – and if I don't get back to work soon, I'll find myself written out of the script. It's a deal. When do we go?'

Emily clapped her hands and hugged Toby.

'I'm so glad you like the idea. It'll be a treat. We should be able to go in a few days. I'll mail Dan and get him to warm the house up. There are a few things I must see to and, then we can be off as soon as you're ready.'

'Likewise,' said Toby, 'we enjoyed the summer and got the house quite cosy. We could go and drink stirrup cups with the hunt, I don't think it's been abolished.'

'Imagine trying to ban hunting here,' Emily said.

∽

Emily eased herself into the strapless lace bra. She leaned forward to admire the shadow created by her cleavage. The split front of her black shift made delicate reference to the ogee of her curving breasts. She ran a finger over the gentle incline formed by the artful constraint. Men, and some women, had stared at her tits since she was fourteen. It was unpleasant to be slavered over in public, but in more civil circumstances, where desire was checked by the weight of formality, nice tits could be an advantage. A choker of seed pearls would serve to draw the eye. She slipped her feet into plain black court shoes with satin bows and, glided elegantly into the sitting room, where Toby sat with a newspaper enjoying a glass of wine. Emily took the glass from his hand and sipped before returning it.

'I'm not sure I want to do this,' she said, 'I feel a bit pimped. I told Jean-Marie to take Alexis to this dinner, if he needed to take anyone, but he won't. If he wants to stay in the closet, that's up to him, but I don't think he should use me as cover.' She sat on a sofa, her hands folded in her lap, and faced Toby.

'Should he?' she asked.

'That's a difficult question,' Toby said. He stretched out his legs and crossed his ankles. 'It's one that you and Jean-Marie must work out, or distrust will work like a canker in the fragrant rose.'

'Do I trust him? I'm not sure what it means. It's not a normal relationship, is it?'

Toby spread his hands.

'There are going to be lots more dinners in the future to consider,' he said, 'and you are partly complicit. You agreed to go with him, even delayed our crossing to England to accommodate him. That should tell you something.'

'I'm sorry, I feel attached, dependent even. I want him to do well, to get what he wants. But I am fuzzy about the future. I think we're a bit like incestuous sibs, connected, but not in the usual way.' Emily got up, smoothed her dress and looked in the mirror, turning her head a little to the right.

'That sounds ridiculous even to me. The truth is I don't know what we are, or where we are going.'

Toby crossed the room and put a hand on Emily's shoulder.

'You're still very young and nothing is yet pressing. I don't mind if we leave Paris a few days later. I'm beginning to feel better at just the prospect.'

'I am sorry, it's selfish of me, but Jean-Marie made it sound like his career depended on my being there.'

'Then go and try and enjoy it. The food should be good, the wines impeccable and, if you can find someone eminent to flirt with…'

'French formality gives me indigestion, and most eminent men have paunches and damp hands. Will I need a reticule?'

Chapter 7

'TIME FOR YOU TO GET OUT MISS AND LET YOUR AUNT have a go, before the water freezes over.'

Hilda stood in the door to the scullery. The walls shone with condensation. Daisy lay partly submerged in a short and narrow zinc bath, her knees necessarily sticking out of the water.

'Throw a few herbs in and you'd pass for Ophelia,' Hilda said.

Daisy frowned and hunched her shoulders.

'I might die of exposure if you make me get out.'

'And you'll get waterlogged if you stay in, what's more, your skin will begin to look like ten-day old suet pudding.'

Hilda advanced on the bath holding open a large white towel.

'Step into this, quick, it's been warming by the fire.'

Daisy rose slowly, shivering, her arms wrapped round her slender torso. Her teeth began to chatter.

Hilda briskly rubbed her with the towel. 'Get on with you. Go and dry yourself by the fire. Then get the big kettle off the range, that'll warm it up a bit for me. I know we're only meant to have five inches of water but there are two of us.'

Daisy came back wrapped in the towel and poured the kettle slowly into the foot of the bath.

'I shan't be very long,' Hilda said, 'and then we can have some tea.'

They sat in their customary places, Hilda in the corner to the right of the ingle, Daisy knelt on the rug, toasting slices of bread that Hilda took off the end of the fork and spread thickly with beef dripping, scraping at the bottom of the basin to get at the dark brown jelly.

'I was saving some of this for James,' Hilda said, 'but we haven't seen him for a while, have we love.'

'He'll have to make do with Marmite,' Daisy said. 'There's a lot going on at the camp right now. He says they may be getting ready to leave, but I can't even think about it. It makes me feel sick.'

Hilda put down her cup and stroked Daisy's hair. 'You really are fond of him, aren't you?'

Daisy looked at her aunt and nodded but could not immediately speak.

'He wrote today that he's got an overnight pass coming up. Could we let him stay here? He's got no family to say goodbye to, please auntie.'

Daisy sat up on her knees and put her hands in Hilda's lap. She looked directly into her eyes. Hilda moved her gaze.

'I'm not at all sure about that, Daisy. It's partly because we're out of the way here that I've let you see so much of him. But having him under the roof all night? I don't know. We haven't even got a bed for him.'

Hilda shifted in her chair, and Daisy removed her hands sitting back on her heels.

'Couldn't we make up a bed on the settee? It might be my only chance to see him before he goes.'

Hilda clasped her hands together and looked at Daisy.

'You must appreciate it's not easy for me. I don't want to be hard on you, but right now I'm responsible, and I have to do what I think is best. I've tried to be accommodating, you know that, and I haven't said no very often, have I?'

Daisy got up and put her arms round Hilda.

'No-one could have been kinder, auntie. I've never felt so looked after, so safe, ever. You can trust me, I promise you. I know what I owe you.'

'Let me sleep on it, Daisy, and you don't owe me anything. You've brought some life to the old place, and to the old girl who lives in it.' She pulled Daisy to her and kissed her cheek. 'Now listen. I might be speaking out of turn, but James and I have a surprise for you, so cheer up, and we'll see about the other thing.'

Daisy had only managed brief meetings with James over the last few weeks. He met her from school, an occasion so often repeated that it had lost all novelty for the other girls. It was well known that Daisy had an officer for a boyfriend. On the way back to Hilda's they would stop for a walk in the woods if there were time. Despite James' reservations, she had finally persuaded him to let her practise riding the motorbike down the lane to the cottage, with him on the pillion giving instructions.

One day he brought his art materials over to the cottage, folders of paper and an attaché case full of paint boxes, charcoal and putty rubber, rolls of sticky paper and drawing pins. Hilda had agreed to look after them. They were put in the ottoman with the oriental prints. Daisy extracted one of the original sketches James had drawn in the shop parlour and pinned it on the wall in her room. Art now engaged her, and she wanted to try it for herself. She was working her way through the art books in the school library and, sketching from life and copying the paintings and prints round the cottage.

When she had some time, Daisy worked in the Victory Garden. Apples needed to be checked for bruises, wrapped in newspaper and packed in trays. With luck, some would keep until well after Christmas. The last of the beans were salted, marrows laid out on straw on the cold floor of the shed and onions hung in skeins from a rafter. Beds were weeded and dug over for the winter. Everything that could be was composted. Hilda refused to use horse manure, on the ground that one might as well sow weeds broadcast, as so many seemed to survive intact and fertile. Daisy collected all the canes, rods and nets to stand in the corner of the large shed, along with the wood. Lengths of garden twine that still had a bit of strength in them were rolled up and kept for next year. Geraniums were dug up and potted. They would go under cover at the first sign of a frost.

❦

Hilda relented. It was only for one night and it did look as though the army was preparing to leave. Everyone could read the signs. There were fewer soldiers in the pub of an evening. Commerce between the camp and the local tradesmen was dwindling. Visitors to camp noticed it was busier, with a new sense of purpose, and that security was tighter. The village began to brace itself for leaner times. James was to arrive on Saturday and be picked up by Watson after lunch on Sunday. It would give them a bit of time together and who could say what their futures might be.

On Saturday Daisy was out of bed, washed and downstairs early. She wore the greatcoat as a dressing gown. She rekindled the range and set the kettle on to boil. Winny came in with his tail up and rubbed against her legs, purring. She chopped some lights and melts and set the bowl in front of the crackling fire. Outside, the crisp air brought tears to the corners of her eyes. Singing quietly to herself, she let the chickens out of their coop and fed them before checking the egg boxes. In the fuel shed she broke up some coal with a sledgehammer and filled the scuttle, returning for an armful of logs. Daisy made some tea, and toast and jam, and took them upstairs to Hilda with an invitation to have a lie in while the kitchen floor was swept and mopped, the sitting room spruced and the furniture polished.

By ten o'clock the cottage was warm and it sparkled in the sharp autumn light. Hilda, dressed in her familiar land girl style, went off on her bike to do errands in the village. Daisy, who had been giving a last prune to some fruit canes, came inside, leaving her boots by the kitchen door, and went upstairs. Keeping the greatcoat on she lay on the bed, hands behind her head, and stared at the ceiling. She got up and stood in front of the mirror. She brushed her hair, shaping it with her hands. Daisy opened her eyes wide, pushed out her chest and pouted. The effect was not convincing. A finger, dampened with spittle, smoothed her pale eyebrows. Biting her lips to make them red seemed to have no effect. Pinching her cheeks made them look chapped rather than rouged. Daisy grimaced, went downstairs and put her boots back on. She turned her collar up, secured the neck flap and went out to walk slowly round the cottage to the front gate where she stood looking down the lane. The russet oak leaves, always the last to fall, rattled in the breeze. Daisy breathed in the comforting mellow smells of autumn. Soon the sound of the wind would be shrill and the air, now invigorating, would turn perishing.

The throb of a motorcycle engine presaged the sight of James appearing round the curve of the lane. Daisy's heart pounded and her mouth dried. She blinked back an involuntary tear. As soon as he came to a stop, Daisy put her arms tightly about him. She pulled down the muffler covering his mouth and kissed him.

'James, it's so lovely to see you.'

'And you, my darling Daisy, and, what's more, we've got some time together, more than we've ever had.'

Daisy held the gate open and James wheeled the bike round to the side of the cottage. It was smaller than those he normally rode and it had no pillion seat, only a rack over the rear wheel where James had strapped his kitbag. He pulled the bike onto its stand and stood back, looking at it as he took off his gauntlets.

'What do you think of her?'

'Not a lot if it means we won't be able to go out together.'

James handed her the stiff gauntlets.

'You had better have these. They're a bit big, but you'll be glad of them when it gets colder.'

Daisy held the gloves and looked at James' beaming face.

'James, what is this, it can't be.'

'Daisy, it is, it's all yours.'

Daisy screamed and rushed at him, smothering him in kisses. She turned to stare at the bike.

'I can't believe it. You do really mean it?'

'Yes, I do. Go on, get on it.'

Daisy, her jaw slack with amazement, swung her leg over the bike, tucked the greatcoat under her, and settled on the saddle. She leant forward, her hands on the grips.

'You're absolutely sure it's for me? It's too generous. What will auntie say?'

'That's all settled, she thought it would be useful for you and we paid half each.'

'James it's so wonderful you're both so kind to me.'

Daisy pushed the bike forward off its stand. She leaned it to the right and the left, using her legs to take the weight.

'It's nowhere near as heavy as yours.'

She flicked the starter pedal out with the toe of her left foot, shifted her weight onto it and pushed it down. The engine immediately fired. Gently, she opened the throttle. Resisting the temptation to put it into gear and ride round the garden, she switched the engine off and closed the choke. Shaking her head, she got off the bike and pulled it back onto its stand.

She stroked the petrol tank inscribed, Francis Barnett, in elegant script.

'I can't wait to take her out.'

'You certainly shall, we'll get you used to the machine over the next couple of days. I want to know you can ride safely before we have to decamp.'

Daisy's face fell.

'We'll talk about all that later,' he said. He put his arms round her and kissed her.

'My love,' he said.

They undid their coats so as to hold each other closer and that is how Hilda found them as she came out of the back door.

'Steady the Buffs,' she said, 'you're not in the back row of the Essoldo.'

Daisy sprang away and hugged her aunt.

'Thank you so much, I shan't expect presents for Christmas or birthdays for years and years.'

'I'm glad you're pleased, Daisy, though I didn't doubt it. James and I thought it would be a sensible thing to do. It's practical and will give you a bit of independence.'

'Do you think I can go to school on it sometimes? No one else in the VIth form has got one.'

'I'm not sure love. We'd have to get permission, we'll see. First thing is to learn to ride it safely. And now let's make some tea, I'm sure you two could do with one and, after a couple of hours with the WI committee I'm near fainting myself.'

'It's a safe little bike, Hilda,' James said. Daisy held his arm as they went into the cottage. 'Small engine, cruises at twenty-five to thirty, and looked after, it'll do close to a hundred miles to the gallon. Being young and female pushed up the insurance, but it still wasn't much.'

'Sounds like you should be selling them,' Daisy said.

The afternoon was spent with James running behind Daisy, now decked out with helmet, goggles and gauntlets, shouting instructions and encouragement. By mid-afternoon she could read the pitch of the engine to change gear, and let in the clutch gently, so as to avoid stalling. By teatime, Daisy was able to stop and start smoothly and, turn both left and right without mishap.

As the light began to fail, she reluctantly relinquished the sensual pleasures of powered movement. The machine was padlocked in the shed with Hilda's pushbike.

'I absolutely love my bike, it's so beautiful,' Daisy said, as they went into the cottage, 'let's see if Hilda wants a hand with the tea.'

'Hang on,' James said, as he fished in his kitbag. He took out a booklet and some papers, rummaged again and produced a rolled up green oiled cloth.

'Here,' he said and handed Daisy some papers. 'That's the insurance and most importantly, the logbook. You must fill it in as you're the new owner. This is the manual, it's a bit dog-eared and oil stained but it's all there. It tells you exactly how the bike fits together and what you need to do to keep it running well, cleaning the plugs and that sort of thing, so read, mark and learn. You absolutely must keep an eye on the level of engine oil, or it'll seize up.' He spread out the green cloth that had compartments containing tools. 'You'll need these, they'll help you take the bike apart and, of course, put it back together. You will have to get your hands black and oily I'm afraid.'

'I don't care,' Daisy said, 'learning how she works sounds almost as exciting as riding her.'

'Do you know the nickname for Frances Barnett bikes is Fanny B.'

'Then I shall call her Fanny, it's a nice old-fashioned name, like mine, and I'll enjoy looking after her. I'll get my jodhpurs next week they'll be just the job.' She hugged James and kissed him. 'I just can't tell you how good this feels.'

The sitting room was dappled with pools of fading light as Daisy put up the blackout and James mended the fire. Hilda could be heard talking to Winny in the kitchen as she prepared supper. When she came through to the sitting room, wiping her hands on her apron, Daisy was sitting on the hearthrug, her face lit by the fire. James, in the carver, a tablet of paper propped on his knees, was sketching her.

'What a lovely picture you two make, charming and peaceful.'

Daisy sprang up to James' annoyance.

'Sorry, James, I forgot. Do you need a hand with supper, auntie?'

'No thanks, dear, it's mince pie and veg' tonight. Tomorrow there's a real treat for lunch – pheasant and apples. Young Billy Oakley, over the way, said he found them dead by the side of the road and he'd let me have them cheap as I give his mother eggs when there's any to spare.'

'Isn't that receiving stolen goods, auntie?'

'If they'd been in someone's copse then, yes, that would have been poaching, but on the King's highway…'

Daisy lay her head on her shoulder and let her tongue loll out of her mouth.

'They used to hang people for it,' she said.

'You two lay the table, and James, if you'd like some, there's beer in the back porch. After we've eaten, if you wash up sharply, we can all listen to ITMA before the news.'

After the news Hilda got the cards and they played a

game of Pit. Daisy won, vociferously cornering the market in barley, corn and sugar.

'You know that officially just about everything is meant to be a secret,' James said, 'but it must be pretty clear to everyone around here that something is going on at the camp. Most likely we are pulling out imminently, which is why I have to be back tomorrow evening.'

He looked at Daisy who sat without expression, her eyes cast down.

'I still do not know for sure where we are to be posted.'

Hilda and Daisy did not speak.

'Granting me this furlough was a surprise.'

'I'll be so glad when this war's over,' Hilda said, getting up from her chair. 'Go and put the kettle on Daisy, I'll get some bed clothes for James.'

Daisy went into the kitchen and Hilda shut the door.

'I'm sorry we can't offer you a bed, James, let alone a bedroom.'

James sat his head bent and hands on his thighs.

'It's very good of you to take me in. I'm deeply appreciative of you welcoming me into your home, and for the way that you have allowed me to be with Daisy. I couldn't be more fond of her, you know that.'

'Me neither, James, between us I think she's well looked after now, which wasn't always the case. Her dad was not exactly cruel, but he never showed her much kindness, and made her work all hours in that shop. I'm not surprised he's where he is, I just hope he doesn't come round here when he gets out.'

'I trust he won't. I never knew the fellow myself, and Daisy barely mentions him, though she does worry about her mother, alone in the smoke.'

Hilda got up and stirred the fire.

'She's coping alright, according to her letters. I know she's my sister, but there wasn't much resourcefulness there, no sense of independence, and as you can tell from the man she married, not much of a judge of character.' Hilda paused. 'I love seeing you two together. I've never quite had it in my life, but I wish you two joy with all my heart.'

James looked up and smiled. 'Thank you, Hilda, I'm grateful.'

Daisy came in from the kitchen, carrying the tea tray.

'I've just been to say goodnight to Fanny, she's so beautiful and shiny, I'm going to polish her every day, and clean her carburettor, or whatever it is, every week. Would you like some tea, auntie?'

'See what we've done James, we've turned the girl's head, tea in just a mo', love, I must stir myself and fetch the bedding.'

Hilda came down the stairs with a pillow, sheets and blankets. Daisy took them from her.

'That looks like luxury to me,' James said, 'I'll be very snug.'

Hilda and Daisy made up a bed on the settee and James banked the fire.

Hilda paused at the bottom of the steps. 'I'll say goodnight and I expect you to follow me shortly, young lady. I'll see you in the morning James and trust you'll get a good night's rest.'

James stood up and pulled Daisy towards him. Daisy put a hand on his chest gently pushing him down onto the settee. She sat on his lap and stroked his hair. Taking his head in her hands she pressed her lips against his with gently increasing pressure.

∽

When Hilda came downstairs the following morning the bedclothes were neatly folded on a chair. She found James in the kitchen, washed and dressed, pouring water from the kettle into the teapot. Winny was stretched out in front of the range.

'Good morning, James, looks like my timing is perfect. I'll get some milk from the scullery. You must have been up betimes. Did you sleep well?'

'Like a log, thank you. I hope you don't mind my making some tea?'

'Course not. Shows a nice domestic side.'

'I've had to develop one, living on my own and now a soldier.'

'I think it's good for a man to be independent in that way,' Hilda said, 'less likely to take a woman for granted. I'll go and let the hens out, see if Ariodante's going to give us any breakfast today.'

'That's a grand name for a hen.'

'It's one of Daisy's hens, apparently it's an opera by Handel. She heard it at school. There are two others called Rodelinda and Orlando, both good layers. She's got hidden depths, that girl.'

They looked at one another and laughed.

Daisy pushed her hair behind her ears and bent her head over the basin of cold water. She splashed her face and rubbed her eyes. Voices and laughter sounded in the kitchen. It made her smile. That Hilda and James got on together was important, for her sake. She cautiously dabbed her mouth and chin. When she raised her head and looked in the mirror her skin glowed pink, as though it had been sandpapered. Her lips felt bruised. She hoped Hilda would not notice. After all, it might just be chapped by the wind.

There were two eggs and Daisy insisted that James and Hilda have them, as all she wanted was some toast. Breakfast was cleared away. Daisy cleaned the hearth and laid a fire, before helping James get the fuel, bring in some potatoes and cut a cabbage.

'You two can go off now and I'll get the lunch ready,' Hilda said, tying on her apron. 'We'll eat about two o'clock.'

Daisy took hold of James' hand.

'Come on, let's go and see how Fanny is. We'll be back in good time auntie.'

'I didn't know you liked opera,' James said, as they walked out to the shed.

'I'm in Music Society at school. It mostly means listening to Miss Chalmer's records, which are nearly all opera, and any others that she can borrow. I really love Handel.'

'There's an opera house near me in Sussex,' James said, 'closed for the duration of course. It's in a lovely old house with a big country garden. I hope it opens again after the war.' He squeezed Daisy's hand. 'One day perhaps we'll go there,' he said. 'Now, shall we spend a bit of time with Fanny? You know how everything is done, but you need to put in some practice hours, like a pilot. You're already confident, which is the most difficult bit. Then perhaps we'll have time for a walk before lunch. My batman is picking me up around four.'

Daisy was quiet and it was a while before she could look at James.

The pleasure of Fanny was every bit as tangible as the day before, enhanced by the established fact of ownership. At the corner of the lane Daisy skidded on some wet leaves and righted the bike instinctively. This gave her a great fillip. After stowing Fanny away, they set off to climb the tor that rose gently at the end of the byway. The sky was filled with restless, fair weather, cloud. A fresh wind stirred the boughs as they walked down the lane hand in hand and followed the narrow sheep tracks that led, erratically, to the rock-strewn crown. From their seat on a boulder they looked out at the undulating countryside, rolling green and brown towards the sea. Daisy pushed her hair back from her face, put her arm through James' and lay her head on his shoulder.

'I hope I wasn't too disappointing last night. I didn't want to lose my virginity on auntie's settee, wondering if at any moment she might walk in on us. It's not that I don't want to, James, I do, wanting you hurts, I didn't know it could.'

James put his arm round her and kissed her hair.

'Darling Daisy, I do understand, but it's hard to feel responsible when the future is so obscure, if we are not lovers now, we may never be.'

'If we were, I don't think I could bear to see you go. I'm not sure I can cope with it in any case. My mind refuses to imagine me continuing without you. The future looks so empty and dangerous, it frightens me.'

'Me too, Daisy, I just hope with all my heart that providence includes a place for us. I want to come back to you more than I want to live for myself. I don't want to fight Germans, Daisy, I want to be with you.'

James put his arms round Daisy and tenderly kissed her lips.

'So quickly we've become one thing, James. I can't imagine being myself without you.'

Daisy stroked his hair and felt his face, her fingers tracing the contours, feeling the roughness of his beard. She kissed him, wetting his cheek with her tears.

'I thought I would ask you to marry me, Daisy, that you might be comforted by being engaged. But it could be more of a burden than a blessing, and at your tender age, I have to face the fact that, whatever you are feeling now, you might find someone else. It would be quite natural if you did. But at this moment, I am completed by you.'

Daisy went to speak but James put his finger gently on her lips. He took the heavy gold signet ring from the little finger of his left hand and, put it into her palm, closing her fingers over it. Daisy opened her hand and looked at it. She stood up and put the ring on the middle finger of her left hand, the only one large enough for it to be secure. She put the ring to James' lips, and he kissed it. He took her hand and put the ring to Daisy's lips.

'Know I love you Daisy and, with grace, we will be together.'

They stood holding on to one another for a long time. Daisy took James' wrist and looked at his watch. Hand in hand, they began the descent to the lane. As they neared the cottage Daisy looked at James and broke a long silence.

'Do you truly not know when?'

'I'm not sure, it could well be tonight. Everything is ready and, the men will start to ferment if they have to hang around much longer. As to where, I used to think North Africa, but Italy seems more likely now. It doesn't matter to me. I just want to do it as best I may and come back to you.'

Daisy stopped and stood in front of James. She slid her hands under the lapels of his coat.

'Hold me,' she said. 'I don't know what to say. Words seem useless. Nothing can stop you going away, or how much that is going to hurt.'

James put his arms around her and stroked her hair.

'My darling girl, we will be separated, and it will hurt, but it will be a hurt that we share. You'll be with me, in my heart, every second, and all my love will be with you, Daisy. We can write often, you'll have my BFPO address and the army makes a real effort to get letters to the men, and to get theirs back home.'

'James, James, James,' Daisy said, dashing tears from her eyes. 'You are so lovely to me. Each night, before I go to sleep, I shall tell you that I love you. If you're able, will you, sometimes, do that for me?'

'That's a beautiful idea, I will, and please write whenever you can.'

'Of course.'

She looked again at his watch.

'We'd better shift, Auntie's been planning this feast. We must make a fuss of her. She's been a fairy godmother to us.' Daisy sniffed and nuzzled James' cheek. Her arm went around his waist and, she matched her stride to his, as they kicked through drifts of decaying leaves that carpeted the lane.

∿

Daisy chopped the gizzards and tiny hearts, that had been roasted with the birds, and put them on a saucer for Winny, who growled his appreciation. The pheasants, served with roasted apples, were succulent and, for pudding there was a baked jam roll and custard.

'This is better than Christmas, auntie.'

'It might well be, Daisy,'

'Thank you so much, Hilda, I couldn't have imagined a nicer furlough than the one you've given me.'

'It's my small gift to the pair of you, and when you get some leave, James, you'll always be welcome to take pot-luck here. Now, we can go and sit by the fire while Daisy clears and makes us a cup of tea.'

'Of course,' Daisy said, jumping up. She kissed her aunt. 'Thank you, I'll go and put the kettle on.'

'Give the fire a poke and put a couple of logs on, James,' Hilda said. She sat in her carver with James on the other side of the hearth. 'I hope you don't mind my asking, but I do feel responsible and it would put my mind at ease. I don't have to worry about Daisy, do I?'

James coloured, he shifted in his seat and cleared his throat.

'You can rest assured, you have my word, that there is no possible cause for anxiety.' He paused and looked down. 'I do love her, and it's my intention, my hope, that I will come back to her.'

'Thank you, James, I'm sorry to embarrass you. I noticed the ring. That was a lovely thing to do, I'm sure it will help her – along with your greatcoat, which is pretty much a second skin.'

'She'll need it on the bike in the winter, and with us gone she'll get away with wearing it,' James said, smiling. 'It will make my mind easy, knowing that she's here with you, Hilda. She's a different girl to the sad waif I felt such pity for not so many months ago.'

'I'm not sure it's me put the roses in her cheeks,' Hilda said. She reached into her pocket and handed James a manila envelope. 'Here's my half of Fanny, sixteen quid was a good price. I'll make sure she never goes out without a helmet. Daisy couldn't be more chuffed. Thank you for that.'

James handed it back and sat rubbing his hands along his thighs. 'Keep it, Hilda. She'll need petrol, when she can get any, and oil and new plugs. Daisy must be costing you a fair bit already and that will help you keep the bike on the road.'

'You're a good man, James, she's a lucky girl to have you.'

Daisy brought in the tea and they sat, grouped around the hearth, as the day faded, each immersed in their distinct and connected worlds. None of them could say what was in their hearts. Daisy sat on the rug in front of the fire, her head resting on James' knee, as he gently stroked her hair.

They heard the sound of the staff car in the lane, shortly followed by a single toot on the horn. They all stood up. James grabbed his kitbag and went over to Hilda and they hugged.

'Goodbye, I have so much to thank you for. So many moments of real contentment and especially for your sympathy and kindness in letting Daisy and me get to know one another, to find each other.'

Hilda squeezed his hand. 'Make sure you write and come back just as soon as you can.'

In the hallway Daisy held him tight and kissed him, looking intently at him before reluctantly loosening her arms.

'I wanted to give you something wonderful,' Daisy said, 'a gold locket with a tress of my hair or a beautiful miniature portrait, but I don't have anything to match your ring.' She put a fine gold chain with a small cross on it in his hand. 'I'm giving you all my jewellery to remember me by. It was a confirmation present, and now it's yours to keep.'

'Daisy, it could not be more precious to me. Thank you.'

He lifted both her hands and kissed them. They looked into each other's faces and James softly ran his hand down Daisy's cheek.

She opened the door and followed him down the path to where Watson waited in the staff car with the engine running. James threw his kitbag in the back. He turned and they briefly hugged. James opened the passenger door of the car. Daisy heard Watson say, 'Good evening, sir,' and he was gone. It was some while before she turned back to the dark shape of the blacked-out cottage.

Chapter 8

EMILY TOOK UNCLE JAMES' BARBOUR OFF THE PEG BY THE back door. Mottled, grey and stiff with age, it felt heavy on her shoulders. She pulled the sturdy zip up to her throat, picked up the brass coalscuttle, shaped like a warrior's helmet and headed for the barn. Chill mists floated round the garden obscuring the fringe of the wood. Sounds were muted as the chain fell from the doors. Emily pulled them wide to allow as much light as possible into the interior.

Inside were neatly stacked bags of coal that Dan had brought in from Lewes. She slit open the top of one with his Swiss Army knife, which she had borrowed and failed to return. The shiny black nuggets rattled into the scuttle. The barn, now brought to new purpose, was a good place to be. Logs from the wood were stacked high, in layers, to season. A space for the old Peugeot had been marked out in whitewash. The debris of past purposes was now cleared away. A tiny red tractor and trailer dozed in a corner. Near the door, where the light was better, the skeleton and metal innards of a small motorbike lay on pieces of hessian, brown against the pitted rose brick floor. The metal frame, painted a dark green, shone where it lay.

Emily picked up the scuttle, collected a bundle of kindling and returned to the house. It was a trek to the attic and she imagined Daisy, or perhaps a housemaid, hauling the coal up the narrow stairs to the tiny rooms.

The grate was very small. Emily scrunched up some old newspaper, tucked the balls into the grate and put a criss-cross of sticks on the top, with some coal and a small log. The kindling caught easily, but the smoke, instead of being drawn up the chimney, billowed out into the room. Emily sprang to her feet, coughing, her eyes smarting. Her impulse was to leave, but thinking it might be dangerous, she opened both the windows. The kindling had caught light but not the coal, so she removed the pieces with tongs. With her head, and one arm, out of the window, she phoned Dan.

'Fire doesn't work,' she said, when he answered, 'and, yes it's your favourite feeble female here. I would have called Toby, but the place is full of smoke.'

She heard Dan laughing.

'Where are you?' he asked.

'I'm in the attic, Daisy's room.'

'Very short flue, could be a bird's nest, probably hasn't been swept since Armistice day. Get a sweep, or if you can wait until the weekend, I'll bring my brushes round, mate's rates for you.'

'Dan, is there nothing you cannot do? Have you really got one of those round brushes and lots of poles?'

'Yes, it's easy and, it's a way of making money.'

'If you honestly don't mind doing it, I'll wait. It'll be surreal. Do I have to cover everything in dust sheets?'

'Not nowadays, we collect all the soot in a vacuum cleaner madam. I'm a bit busy right now, see you Saturday, bye.'

He rang off. Emily knelt in front of the grate and raked it out with a poker, making sure there was no possibility of it reigniting. Closing the windows, she left the room.

∽

There was a gap in the hedge that led directly onto the downs. Narrow flinty pathways, worn by the grazing sheep, tracked back and forth. As she passed, their heads lifted to stare at her, seemingly dislocated jaws continued to rhythmically grind grass. At the top she came to a long ridge. Below, the plain was bifurcated by the shining meander of the Ouse that melted into the mist on its way to the sea.

The sheer number of people one passed on the downs always surprised Emily, compared to walking in the country at home, they positively thronged. Young people bounced by on wide tyred bikes. Small groups of middle aged, rain-proofed hikers, with oversized boots and thick socks rolled at their ankles, smiled greetings as they passed. There were lots of dog walkers, mainly women. Others like herself were simply out for a walk. As she sauntered along the wide droveway the undulating landscape opened before her. Everywhere was green, mainly pasture, with long crescent copses on steep slopes, from which the cuk, cuk, cuk, of pheasants could be heard. Occasionally, rounding a bend, Emily would disturb a group of foraging birds that, after a short, and surprisingly rapid, run across the ground, would scramble into the air, keeping strategically low. Emily left the path and sat on a tumulus overlooking a valley. Below her a train, green and yellow, like a segmented caterpillar, silently slid through the fields.

Emily relaxed her body and let her mind drift. She had lately become aware of Toby's mortality, something never considered before. At some point, however distant, he would die. It was an uncomfortable thought and it added a frightening dimension to her own being. Her need for a career, what to do with Campiston, her feelings for Jean-Marie, and in a vague way, the barely understood pursuit of Daisy, everything else now seemed to be coloured by this shift in perception. Emily stuffed her hands deeply into the breast pockets of the Barbour, snuggled her chin down into her scarf and looked out across the soft lines of the weald. Perhaps she had become too dependent on Toby? But he was her father, and there wasn't much that could be done about that.

∽

Emily sat on the low bench in the back porch, pulled off her boots and padded through the kitchen in her thick marl socks. They were new and a treat. She had two pairs, one of which she wore in bed.

'Toby,' she called.

'In the study, cherub.'

Logs crackled in the stove and the room was very warm. Toby sat in the dark leather chair, reading. A stack of papers stood on a small table beside him.

'I know it looks like work,' he said, waving a sheaf, 'but it isn't really, just catching up on organisational chaff. It's a way of addressing anxiety but I can't say my heart's in it. Dan came over while you were out, he cleaned the attic chimney and offered a competitive price for doing the whole house. I think he's still about the place somewhere.'

Toby put the papers down on the table and rubbed his eyes.

'Guy has offered to come and give me a game of chess. Seems a bit of an old man thing, he must be twice my age, but churlish to turn him down.'

Toby got up and looked out at the garden, fast disappearing as the night gathered. He turned to Emily.

'You're looking ruddy and busting with vim. The English winter plainly suits you. Why don't we ask them to supper, if you're up for it? Perhaps, Dan could bring his inamorata, the blessed infanta Isabel?'

Emily looked in the mirror and stroked her cheeks, they definitely were reddened by the wind. She scowled.

'Her name is Annabel, and from my brief meeting with her in the pub, betrays no pretensions to the Spanish throne.'

'Angel, you're getting waspish, not an attractive quality in the young. It comes with having spent too much time with me. We need Dan to pack the infanta off for a while and pay some attention to you.'

Emily stood warming her bum by the fire, rubbing her hands down the backs of her thighs.

'I don't need attending to, Toby, I just dropped by to see if there was anything you might want…'

'A bottle of Yquem and a Romeo y Julieta, half corona will do.'

'…within the bounds of possibility and sanity.'

'Tea and crumpets would be nice, it's what the English do about four o'clock.'

'Sounds good. We seem to drink an awful lot of tea here, but Dan says the real English are giving it up in droves. I'll think about the dinner idea. I'm not sure you or I could get through an evening with the infanta.'

'See,' Toby said, 'I knew it was a good name for her without ever having seen her.'

'Yah, can be inflected but, if having said it you've more or less shot your conversational locker, it gets tedious.'

'Even more waspish,' Toby said, 'do I detect a hint of the green-eyed monster?'

Emily, whose bum was now scorching, moved to the door.

'No Toby, Dan and I belong to different tribes. I like his style, but we don't really share much in the way of cultural space. I'll get some tea and then I'll have to work for a bit.'

'I think it's beyond the call of duty, making an intern work when she's nursing a convalescent father.'

'I guess it's worth it. I'm going to need some help with my CV and a couple of job applications over Christmas. I'm wondering if I should look in London as well. Should I say I'm applying for a research degree, even though I'm not sure I want to do one?'

'No, you're not thinking clearly. If you're looking for jobs where a research degree is expected, you won't even make the long list. If you're applying for something more lowly they may think you'll be off as soon as soon as you get a place, and that, in any case, your heart is elsewhere. I've told you, if you want a career in economics, rather than a job that pays the rent, you'll need to put in the slog and get a doctorate. If you do it in Paris, say, EDE, I'll be able to get you a supervisor and, it's all over in four years. If you go to London, you can do something you're interested in but, it usually takes longer.'

Emily linked her hands on the top of her head and grimaced.

'Sorry, I'm not focusing properly, am I? I want to be an economist, I love it, but the years of academic slog, can I face it? Can I afford it?'

'If you sell the house you can, easily, if not, I'm sure we could manage it somehow. Now, please get me some tea. I can't be expected to tackle this weighty stuff wracked, as I am, by hunger pangs.'

Emily disappeared and slid across the parquet hall floor in her socks. In the kitchen she practised whistling as she slotted crumpets into the toaster and filled the kettle. Best to have a quick look for Dan, she wouldn't want him to feel neglected. What would she want him to feel? Being with him was always good, though his joshing could be irritating. All the rural stuff, Morris dancing and dwyle flonking, was diverting, but only once. His addiction to English beer was pretty much unfathomable, if not unforgivable, and it was making him podgy. Outside, through the misty winter twilight, Emily saw the barn door etched in orange from the lamps Dan had installed. She tried to whistle and then called his name. Moments later he emerged, his unkempt hair falling forward over one eye. He pulled a grubby handkerchief from his pocket and wiped his hands.

'*Bonjour*, Emily, *ça va?*'

'Don't even pretend to speak French, Dan, please.'

He came over and kissed her on both cheeks. Emily took his arm and walked him back to the bright kitchen.

'Damn chilly in that barn, cold hands, especially for fiddling with that little two stroke. It's amazing, it's so old but most of it is in perfect nick. You are going to love it. Parts are easier to find than I thought, we're getting there.'

He grabbed a crumpet as it popped out of the toaster, smothered it in butter, and took a large bite. He wiped the grease from his chin with the back of his hand.

'Got any jam?'

They sat in the study, all three of them momentarily absorbed in the perilous matter of ingesting buttery crumpets.

'These must be so bad for us,' Emily said, 'especially with jam. That's animal fat, bleached white flour and, concentrated sugar you're eating, Dan.'

He scowled briefly and continued munching.

'I hope you don't mind, Toby, about me and the bike. Once I knew there was a chance of being able to restore it, I couldn't resist. That little Villiers engine is a thing of beauty, and it's almost mint. It must have been loved by someone.'

'It's very good of you, especially as you intend it for Emily. You must let us know if it's costing you money, and I do hope you're not devoting great swathes of time that you can ill afford. How's the search for employment, any joy?'

Dan's shoulders dropped and he put down his half-eaten crumpet.

'Nothing solid yet, just jobs for farmers and, 'hanging about the hiring fair,' as Guy puts it. He has let me have the tiny flat above the garage, which is great, and I do whatever he wants about the place. I kind of manage.'

'Life's tough for the young, but you and Emily will still have to find a way of keeping the wolf from the door.'

Dan howled and Emily grinned.

'He doesn't have to overdo it, Toby. A lot of people make casual livings nowadays.'

'No, Toby's right. Annabel's been at me pretty relentlessly lately, and I do have a plan. On reflection I'm happiest when I'm in a wood, so it's agri' college studying sylviculture, I start after Christmas.'

'Is that the study of wood nymphs?' Emily said.

'...then perhaps the Forestry Commission, National Trust or, if I'm lucky, persuade someone to give me some woodland to manage. The bottom of your garden would do nicely. We've already made a start with our little coppice, haven't we Emily?'

'That's serious Dan,' Emily said, 'if you get a real job, what will we do? You've transformed Campiston for us, pretty much on your own.'

'I've had help from various mates, it's been good. Bringing this place back to life has radically improved my skills base. I like this place, and it's great to have you both back.'

Emily kissed his cheek.

'You're gold,' she said.

'I worry that we've exploited your good nature,' Toby said, 'I know we don't pay you much.'

'It's better than the farmers and I don't have to haggle or get up before dawn.'

Toby coughed, his shoulders hunched and his chest heaving.

'I was going to say that being here I feel much better but trying to get it out between coughs rather belies the message.'

Toby gripped the arms of his chair and hauled himself to his feet. Emily stood up.

'It's alright darling, I'll go and rest for a while.'

In silence they heard him slowly mount the stairs.

'Is he really OK?' Dan asked.

'I don't know. It seems to be taking him a long time, and I get anxious. He's lost weight, which he could afford to do, no reference to present company...' she added, prodding Dan's gut. He pulled in his tummy and slowly let it swell out.

'...but not in a good way. His clothes are beginning to hang on him, which makes him look a little bit decrepit.'

'He's still young,' Dan said. 'I'm sure he'll be fine. Guy says pneumonia's not much more than a bad cold these days.'

'I know. Campiston helps, he's relaxed a lot, being out of Paris. I love being here myself, I feel comfortable. We agreed that I would give myself until Christmas to make a decision, it's only a week away and I'm no closer to it than I was in the summer. I thought it might be easier, being here, but it's not.'

Emily looked up at Dan who was munching the last, cold, crumpet.

'What would you do, if you were me?'

'Keep it and make it earn its keep.' He pulled his grimy handkerchief from his pocket and rubbed it over his chin. His brow furrowed.

Emily was silent for a while. She leaned forward, elbows on her knees and cupped her face in her hands.

'But how? Toby has already put money into it and I've no way of paying him back. I don't want to exploit his kindness. He says he might sell the Devon cottage James left him.

Before we go back, he wants to drive down and see it. If it's sound he might let it out.'

'You could always do the same.'

'For me the point of keeping the house would be that I could use it. Stay here when I wanted, grow tomatoes, extend the coppice, keep bees and find out more about Daisy. I've been thinking that, if I did sell, it would create another problem. It's not a good time for holding money and so I'd end up buying a flat in Paris and, we've already got one.'

'It's a problem I think I could cope with,' Dan said.

Emily leaned forward and stroked Dan's arm.

'I'm sorry, it is a bit of a spoilt princess problem.'

'You can't help being rich, Emily. I don't hold it against you. I mean it's not as though you did it on purpose, it just happened. You should talk to Annabel. Pallant's, where she works, sell loads of big county piles. You could have it valued. It might help you decide. I'd love it. I'd buy it in a flash if I could. And, on Daisy, I think you're a bit half hearted, perhaps you're spinning it out to delay the house decision. You haven't talked to Guy yet and you haven't really been through the studio. There must be more clues to be found in the house. You discovered her sitting room, and now you can even keep warm, have you really taken it apart, searched every cupboard and box. You wore her dress in the summer, a bit tight admittedly, but you looked stunning.'

'You cheeky bastard,' Emily said, and poked him again in the ribs, which made him curl up and laugh. 'But you may have a case. Let's go up to Daisy's room now, light a fire and see if we can open that box under the table.'

Dan went to get some tools and Emily laid the fire, waiting for him to come before putting a match to it. As it began to catch and the smoke rose, Emily clapped her hands and hugged Dan.

'This is brilliant, thank you so much,' she said.

They sat on the sofa with the box on the floor between them. Emily had tried every likely key she could find and, Dan had fiddled around with pieces of bent metal for some time, before she allowed him to use force. He inserted the end of a large screwdriver under the lip of the lid of the small chest and levered it gently. It sprang open. Inside was a tray of black lacquered compartments which Emily lifted out to reveal the body of the box.

She knelt down and began to turn over the contents. There were the bundles of rolled papers that had been held by rubber bands, now perished, some exercise books, two dilapidated dolls, several annuals and a chocolate box, that she lifted out. The paper covering the cardboard was the colour of burnt cream, now faded. Pictures of chocolates floated on its surface around the legend, Dairy Box. Emily carefully prised off the lid. Inside were some letters and theatre programmes. Folded in the bottom was a large white handkerchief. Some conkers and acorns desiccated with age almost disintegrated on touch. Emily picked up an envelope, heavily marked with blue crayon. It was addressed to Daisy. Postmarked, Field Post Office, with a date in 1944, across the top was written 'on active service,' to the side of the address was a red stamp which read, 'passed by unit censor'. Emily took out a single sheet of thin white paper. The creases, where it had been folded were frayed. It was uncle James' writing.

My Dearest Daisy,

Enough to say that things are hectic and I'm dog tired but, so far, still in one piece. Congratulations on your exams, that's very good news and I bet Hilda's proud of you. However, I'm afraid that even your exam results are not enough to swing a furlough in the foreseeable future. But the sooner we get the job done the better for us. The Italian countryside is very beautiful, in another world I'd love to have my paints with me. The men keep cheerful and that's about as much as I can say without attracting the censor's blue pencil.

I could not miss you more. I think of you as my guardian angel. I feel your love every moment and it is a great protection. I had no idea how powerful love could be. Your letters are so precious to me, so please keep writing, even if there is no news on the home front. Know how much you are loved and missed. I live to see you again.

 Ever yours
 James X
 P.S. Give Hilda a hug from me.

Emily handed the letter to Dan.

Dan held the paper by the edges and read it slowly.

'It's beyond imagining,' Daisy said, 'how could anyone cope with the person they loved being God knows where and, in constant danger of being wounded, taken prisoner or even killed.'

'It's so real,' Dan said. 'It's also very brief. I know people would sometimes write every day, it was a way of keeping going and hoping, I guess. James sounds very young,' Dan added, after a pause.

'He was only our age. Toby said that was quite normal for junior officers, they could go pretty much straight from school with a detour to train at Sandhurst. Daisy was a bit younger. I wonder what exams she took. Perhaps in war time people have to grow up fast. Like the middle ages, things are done younger if you think you might never have the chance to grow old.'

'I've never fallen in love like that,' Dan said, 'I can't imagine it.'

Emily reached out and held his hands.

'There's still time,' she said.

⌒

'You're too good for me, Guy, I'll have to get more practice. I could try one of those little chess computers.'

Guy collected the chessmen and put them in a box. They sat across from one another in the study. A wooden chessboard lay on a small three-legged table between them.

'Those little blighters are fiendish,' Guy said, 'I've tried them. I don't like the way they instantly know their next move. I know they're only computing, not thinking, but all the same I feel patronised.'

'Can I get you anything?' Toby got himself to his feet.

'If it's after four thirty I normally have a sherry,' Guy said, 'it's too late for tea.'

'Sherry's not much of a thing in France. I think I've seen a couple of bottles of fino or oloroso around here.'

'Can't drink fino in the winter,' Guy said.

Toby went to a painted cupboard in a corner of the study and brought out a couple of glasses and a grubby bottle. He uncorked it and made a purring sound. He poured out a large glass of the heavy wine and put it down by Guy. He took a much smaller glass to his own chair. They sipped silently. The back door slammed and shortly Emily appeared, pulling off her hat and gloves and discarding her Barbour.

'Hi, Guy, it's good to see you here. Been thrashing Toby?'

Guy stood up and Emily went over and kissed his cheek.

'Hello, Emily, and no, he's a worthy opponent.'

'We played three games and I lost them all,' Toby said.

'It's nice to be back in the old house,' Guy said, 'it feels like a home again.'

'You're very welcome,' Emily said.

'I've had plenty of intelligence. Dan reports minutely on developments here. He finds any excuse to come over and potter. Especially now he's got the bike to play with.'

Emily removed a pile of papers from a chair and sat down.

'Lewes was weird,' she said, 'Safeway was packed with demented shoppers, stripping the shelves. You'd think war had broken out rather than Christmas is coming.'

'Very English,' Toby said, 'proximity of feast brings on fear of famine.'

Toby refilled Guy's glass and raised one eyebrow at Emily, who shook her head.

'Not too much old man, I'm driving,' Guy said, but failed to say, 'when.'

'Dan tells me you're still interested in Daisy, and as I said in the summer, I'm happy to help. I saw something of James in those days, but I was the very junior partner, and they were treated by Fraser. Later, when she had gone, he didn't talk about her.'

'I'd be thankful for anything you might remember that would help me get to know her.'

'Someone who used to talk of her very fondly, was old Mrs Gauge. She lived out at Fletchton and was housekeeper here for a time after the war.'

'I don't suppose she's still with us,' Toby said.

'Long gone,' Guy said, 'but she had a spinster daughter who stayed in the cottage. I haven't seen her for a couple of years.'

Emily jumped up and went and stood in front of the fire.

'I'd love to meet her. Her mother must have told her about Daisy, she may have been to the cottage. She might have known Daisy herself.'

'I'll find out if she's still around and if so, we'll arrange a visit. Best take Dan, she'll be more forthcoming with a local lad.'

'I'd be so grateful if you could, Guy. Would you like to stay for a bite. It's only pea and ham soup and some cheese omelettes, but you're very welcome.'

'That would be a treat,' Guy said. 'I'd better phone Dan and see if he can pick me up later, so that in the event of my being offered a glass of wine, I can accept.'

'I guarantee you will be,' Emily said.

'You know that cottage James left you, Toby. There might be a connection there. For years James used to go to the west country every spring, and I know that Daisy came from round there somewhere. Also, James spent some of the war in Devon.'

'Excellent,' Toby said, 'Emily and I are going down for an inspection before we go back.'

'I mustn't get excited,' Emily said, 'it's all such a long time ago, I can't expect much.'

⁓

Annabel stood in the hallway and looked around with evident pleasure. She tossed her head and flicked her long brown hair behind her shoulder. Her solitary earring, a slender gold bar, caught the light as she moved.

'What a gorgeous house you have, Emily. I've lived round here most of my life and I never knew it existed. It was good of you to invite me. I hope you did. I never quite know with Dan, he didn't just assume, did he?'

'No, it's great you're here,' Emily said.

'He thinks everyone is as laid back as he is. It's particularly kind of you after our night in the pub. I don't think I was very forthcoming. I'd had an absolute bitch of a day at work and was hungry and tired, and the prospect of a few hours spent watching Dan and the lads sink the amber fluid wasn't really speaking to me.' She smiled. 'I must be firmer.'

Dan, after kissing Emily on both cheeks, had preceded them, with Guy, into the sitting room, from where the voices of the three men could be heard amongst the clinking of glasses.

'I'm totally with you, even if I've had a good day. I just don't get pubs. An ice cold Leff, sitting in a leafy square, on a hot summer's day is a pleasure, but doggedly swilling litres of the stuff in the middle of winter, it's so Prussian. How about a civilising glass of wine?'

'Yes please, yummy.'

Emily ushered Annabel through the wide sitting room door.

'Emily, if your hostessing on your own tonight, please let me help, I'd be glad to.'

'Thank you,' Emily said, and poured Annabel a large glass of Chablis. 'I would like that. Now, come and meet Toby.'

It was a comfortable sight. Toby and Guy stood by the fire. Dan, resplendent in ancient dinner jacket and jeans, unruly black hair falling into his eyes, sat in a spindly armchair to one side. Emily did the introduction and she and Annabel sat on a sofa and made bright conversation. As things began to flow, Emily went and fetched some small filo pies of lamb with chestnuts and anchovy.

'Fabulous,' Annabel said.

They ate in the dining room, now hung with some of James' paintings that Emily particularly liked. These included an oil portrait of a young woman in a khaki greatcoat, standing in a garden, three quarter profile, looking out beyond the viewer. It reminded her of the watercolour portrait.

'That's Daisy, isn't it?' she asked Guy.

'Yes, she wore that coat a lot, especially on the motorbike. Thought nothing of women on motorbikes after the war, much more rare nowadays. They shared a big bike, beautiful looking thing, gleaming chrome. Sometimes James would ride pillion and sometimes Daisy. One could certainly hear them coming.'

Toby ladled out partridges with cabbage and bacon onto deep white plates and Annabel handed them round while Emily saw to the wine.

'They look amazing,' Dan said, 'can I have two, please?'

'No,' Annabel said.

There was the polite clatter of silver on porcelain as the meal got under way. Emily had seated herself next to Guy.

'Were they happy here do you know?' she asked.

'They certainly were initially. James adored Daisy and she thought the world of him, but the county didn't take to her.'

'Parvenu?' Toby said.

'No, it wasn't that, Daisy had no airs. They were both, in their way, unworldly, despite James' military experience. They came from equally narrow, if different, upbringings. There were a lot of artists living round here at that time and James, more or less, fitted in. But he was quite conventional, not at all bohemian, unlike that lot in the Lewes farmhouse, never knowing who had sired whom and by what dam.'

'It's called Bloomsbury, Guy,' Dan said, 'and the house is at Charleston.'

'No matter. The county couldn't make head nor tail of Daisy, she knew nothing about farming, wouldn't shoot and didn't appear to have any "people." And the bohemians were all toffs and she didn't fit in there either. James knew just as little about the land, but at least they knew where he came from.'

Emily had bought some good cheeses from the French stallholder in Lewes, who gamely came over from Dieppe. Toby thought good cheese wasted on the English and refused to serve crackers of any description, even those with a Royal imprimatur. He had compromised by making some walnut bread. Dessert was crème, caramelized by Dan with a small blowtorch. He had insisted on wearing goggles.

Emily appeared with a bottle of port she had found. It definitely looked old and may or may not be good, she didn't care. She uncorked it carefully and put it in front of Toby. He poured out a little of the plum, viscous fluid and sniffed the glass.

'Raw beef, raisins, and spice' he said, 'parfait.'

'Just to prove to the county we know how to behave, Annabel and I are going to retire. Actually, I'm going to show her the house. Be good boys and remember you're driving, Dan.'

Emily went over and kissed the top of Toby's head.

'Please don't smoke, Toby,' she whispered.

He squeezed her hand.

Dan looked at Emily and Annabel, widened his eyes and let his jaw drop. Emily returned his gaze and smiled, before taking Annabel's arm and heading for the door. Toby filled Guy's glass to his right and pushed the bottle to his left. Dan poured a large measure. There was no offer of cigars. Emily and Annabel returned to the long sitting room.

'It was lovely in the Summer,' Emily said, 'French windows opening onto the garden, the scented evening air. Toby doesn't like this room, he thinks, "the Doric columns make a false partition of an otherwise well-proportioned space." I like them.'

'I can see his point, but I'm with you, they are certainly not original, but they give a touch of elegance to what is, at base, a small country mansion of uncertain age with its last makeover a century or more ago.'

Annabel walked round the room as Emily sat down by the fire.

'Emily, I hope I'm not here on false pretences. I don't know what Dan told you, but I couldn't possibly give you a reliable valuation. You need a surveyor and agent for that, but I could give you the general range for a house like this. I'm not an expert on country houses, although I love them, and I can already see that this is a gem.'

'Dan was trying to help,' Emily said. 'I cannot make up my mind what to do with it and he thought some idea of its worth might clear my thoughts.'

'What I can tell you, from what I've seen already, is that I could sell this to a developer at nine o'clock tomorrow morning and, in no time at all, there would be three or four luxury apartments in an historic country house with private drive and extensive gardens and woodland. It's happening all over the county. This is close enough to London to attract foreign buyers, not the Gulf, but French, they don't care about the absence of lifts.'

Emily laughed.

'That's so true, I have to climb three flights to our apartment, Toby finds them definitely uphill at the moment. Do you want to see upstairs?'

Emily went to the kitchen and returned with a bottle of wine.

'Lovely wide central staircase,' Annabel said, as they mounted it side by side. 'That's a great dress. Pale grey silk goes beautifully with your blond colouring.'

'I found it here,' Emily said, 'it was Daisy's. Guy even remembered it or said he did. Dan thought I looked fat in it.'

'Bit of a nerve coming from him.' Annabel stopped at the

top of the stairs and looked around. 'This gallery is fabulous, masses of light from the oriel window, gives a huge sense of space. I love vernacular buildings, you never know what you're going to find.'

Emily showed Annabel the bedrooms and the ancient bathroom, still with yellowed enamel bath and pretty tiled fireplace.

'Would you like to see Daisy's room?'

'I'd love to. I've heard all about her from Dan.'

Emily opened the door in the corner of the landing and led the way up the narrow stairs to the dim servants' corridor. Inside Daisy's room she turned on a heater and lit several candles to augment the meagre electric light. Annabel stood in the middle of the room and slowly looked around.

'Wow, this is definitely somebody's room,' she said, 'those walls covered in photos and sketches are wonderful.'

'That was my reaction when I first saw it, that chair by the table was at an angle, as though someone had just pushed it back and got up. There was a jumper on the sofa where it had been dropped, goodness knows when.'

They sat side by side and Emily poured some wine.

'It's got a lovely feel to it,' Annabel said, 'like an imprint. You can feel it gave someone pleasure to be here.'

'Yes, I'm sure Daisy must have loved it.'

'It's such a gentle name, how could you not love Daisy?' Annabel said.

'I feel bound to her in a way. I owe her my good fortune, she seems almost present when I'm here and also unknowable, which of course, she is.'

'Dan said you found her portrait that your uncle had painted, and that's how it started. Being here I can understand that. I don't want to pry, but do tell, right from the beginning. Perhaps Daisy is the key to you and this house?'

Emily got up and brought the wine bottle over to the sofa and filled their glasses. She slipped off her shoes, tucked her legs under her and turned to Annabel.

Chapter 9

DAISY PULLED HER ORANGE JUMPER OVER HER HEAD AND put on a pair of trousers that she had tried to make under Hilda's direction, but had needed so much help that it could barely be described as a joint venture. Plain grey, they fell straight from the hip, the simplest possible pattern. She didn't like them much, but they were good for the bike. When Hilda let her borrow her boots, she would tuck them into the tops and look quite Russian, which was nice. Daisy looked out of her bedroom window. The sky was clear, and the trees barely moved. It was bright, early spring and Saturday. There was enough petrol to get her to Marleigh to meet Alice. The greatcoat was grabbed from the bed and shrugged on. Hilda insisted she wear the crash helmet and so Daisy had her hair cut in a pageboy. Being on the willowy side, she thought it made her look like Joan of Arc and importantly, when the helmet came off, could be restored to shape by a couple of vigorous shakes of the head and some finger raking.

Guided by her hands lightly sliding along the banisters, her feet padddled down the treads of the stairs. She rounded the massive chimneystack and ran into the kitchen. Hilda sat by the range warming her feet on the fender and knitting steadily. Daisy kissed her cheek.

'Hallo love, you do look the part wrapped up in that great thing.'

Daisy lifted her chin and secured the throat flap of the greatcoat.

'Well, at least I'll be a warm part on my bike. Me and Alice are going to the pictures if we can afford it. I'll try and be home before it gets dark and, of course, I'll ride carefully. Is there anything you want me to get while I'm in Marleigh?'

'No, but before you go would you be an angel and go to Pierce the butcher for me. I've got another puncture in my back wheel. That inner tube is more black patches than it is original rubber, but I can't find a new one for love nor money.'

'Oh auntie, must I? What if there's a queue? Some of those old women natter on for ages.'

'Then you'd better move smartly, or there'll be nothing for your supper.'

Daisy frowned and held out her hand. Hilda took a shilling out of her purse and Daisy slipped it into her pocket.

'And I want the change.'

In the shed, with a soft cloth, Daisy polished the petrol tank with its Frances Barnett signature and wiped the condensation off the saddle. Cleaning round the engine she noticed a small patch of oil on the brick floor. She took out the dipstick, wiped it, and checked the level of engine oil, fine for a few miles yet. Fanny was eased off her stand and wheeled out to the road. Daisy swung her leg over the saddle and flicked out the starter. In a single swift movement, she lifted herself and put all her weight on the pedal. The engine fired. Daisy took an almost unconscious pleasure in the rhythmic pulse of the little two-stroke. Fanny delivered Daisy to the butcher's in a few minutes and Hilda's order was ready when she walked into the shop. The morning was so lovely she couldn't resist opening the throttle wide on the way back, it increased petrol consumption but the extra speed was a treat.

Daisy put the meat in the pantry and then went to say goodbye to Hilda who was in the garden, turning over a bed. She gave her the change.

'I've left it in the pantry,' she said, 'I didn't open it so that it will be a surprise and, for all I know, it's rump steak.'

'Not for eight pence ha'penny, I'm afraid,' Hilda said. She put her hands on the top of her buttocks and arched her back. 'I hope victory comes soon. This garden will wear the pair of us out.'

'I'll do some tomorrow,' Daisy said, 'I quite like digging and it'll leave you free to start on the planting.' Hilda put the change into her purse and took out two sixpences and gave them to Daisy. 'There you are. That'll help pay for the pictures. Don't be late back and ride carefully.'

'Thanks auntie, that's very kind,' Daisy said, pocketing the coins, 'and it saves me borrowing from Alice, she's never short. Her dad must be made of money.' She pecked her aunt on the cheek. 'Won't be late, promise.' She ran down to the lane and was urging Fanny along the road to Marleigh in moments.

The small market town was busy with shoppers. There were queues wherever anything useful, or better still edible, could be found.

'Do you think it's true that some people join queues when they don't know what they are actually queuing for?' Daisy said.

'Dunno, seems a bit desperate to me. I could see Miss Simmons doing it. She may be good at physics, but she never knows what day of the week it is.'

They stood gazing at the paltry offerings in the ladies' section of Dosset's department store, a favourite haunt as it was warm and filled with occasional objects of desire.

'Look at those awful lace collars,' Alice said, 'three shillings and sixpence and they look like doilies. I wouldn't be seen dead in one. I'm fed up with rationing. I bet hardly anyone had a proper Christmas pudding this year. I think ours was made of carrots it was awful. Still, you're jolly lucky to have that great big garden, plenty of fresh vegetables, good for the skin.' She narrowed her eyes and peered into Daisy's face but made no comment.

'We don't starve, but too often all we can do is boil stuff. It's hard to get excited over a cabbage however hungry you're feeling.'

Alice tugged at Daisy's sleeve.

'See that shop walker over there by the ladies macs, he's looking at us. No, don't turn round yet,' she added, as Daisy moved her head. 'Let's pretend to pinch something and then make for the exit.'

'No. If we annoy him, he might frame us, put a pair of gloves in our pocket or something.'

'Your imagination must be warped,' Alice said, 'who'd want to frame two schoolgirls?'

'He might get a bonus for every thief he catches,' Daisy said.

'Alright, you win, I just thought it would be fun. Let's go and find some boys to tease.'

Daisy readily agreed to this plan, knowing that with Alice, it rarely got beyond the window-shopping stage. When it did, it was not necessarily an enjoyable experience.

'Remember that boy who paid for both of us to sit in the back row, so that he could snog you,' Daisy said, 'I've never been so embarrassed in all my life.'

'Embarrassed, you got off lightly. He didn't spend the whole time trying to undress you, did he?' She shuddered. 'What a creep. Thank God it was a Western. If it had been a film I wanted to see I'd have been doubly cross.'

'It's the only time I've left the cinema before the National Anthem,' Daisy said. 'We ran so fast and were giggling so much I nearly wet myself.'

'Come on, let's get to the Essoldo. It's Saturday so we'll have to queue. Front stalls?'

'I suppose so,' Daisy said, 'it'll ruin our eyesight, there might be noisy boys and it'll give us a headache and possibly a crick in the neck, but on the bright side I'll have enough money over for a cup of tea afterwards.'

'We might be spared the noisy boys,' Alice said, 'with a film called, The Gentle Sex.'

'Depends how you read it,' Daisy said, and they both laughed as they walked, hand in hand, down the broad market High Street to the cinema.

∽

'It's curious how the world always feels slightly odd when you come out of the flicks,' Alice said, as they stood outside, squinting after a couple of hours in the smoky darkness of the Marleigh Essoldo.

'We expect it to have stood still while we were away, but time has passed and it's darker.' Daisy yawned. 'There were loads of men in there. They must have been so disappointed that it was all about women and the war effort and nothing romantic at all.'

Alice tugged Daisy's sleeve. 'Let's go to Lyons and look mysterious.'

The vast tea house was packed and chaotic. They had to go upstairs and wait to be seated. Waitresses in black, with short white frilled pinafores, negotiated the tables carrying large round trays laden with teapots, milk jugs and crockery.

'Perfect,' Alice said, as they were directed to a table at

the far end of the room. 'I love upstairs window seats. You can watch passers-by and they don't know because they never look up.'

'I think that's called voyeurism,' Daisy said.

'I thought that was watching people at it, peeping Toms.'

'Give over Alice, don't you think about anything else.'

'It's alright for you, you're spoken for. I could be left on the shelf.'

'Don't be daft, you're still at school.'

'I won't be by the time we manage to get a waitress to take notice,' Alice said, 'it's a shame you're not tall, dark and handsome.'

'Well, I'm one of them,' Daisy said, straightening her spine and trying to engage the eye of a passing waitress who hurried on without a look.

'If we ever get served,' Alice said, 'I'll treat you to a cake.'

'Thanks, a Chelsea bun would be lovely, or an Eccles cake.'

'Sorry,' the waitress said, when finally taking the order, 'the only cake is Madeira, it would have been Seed Cake, but there's no caraway.'

Daisy poured. She stirred her tea although they had run out of sugar. Alice cut a small piece off the slab of yellow cake and chewed it.

'It tastes of absolutely nothing, unless sand is a flavour.'

'I'm just grateful for cake.' Daisy said. She sipped the hot weak tea. 'How do they make the cake bright yellow it certainly can't be eggs?'

'They boil up old onion skins to make yellow dye,' Alice said, 'least, that's what Susan Ellis told me.'

Daisy sniffed her cake and scowled.

'In the film, all the women were from different places, like posh girls and poor girls, but they all wanted to help us win the war.'

'Some more than others,' Alice said.

'All those scenes in the munitions factory upset me,' Daisy said, 'they made me think of my poor mum.'

'I hope they don't make us go to London and make shells and things when we leave school.'

'I'd be terrified,' Daisy said, 'but I don't think they can force us, it's not like the call up. They'll just make us guilty with all the propaganda.'

'I suppose we could both join the Women's Land Army. My granny was in it in the First World War. She loved it and I really like the land girl's uniform.'

'That's a good idea. Next time you're out at the cottage I'll teach you which end of the spade to dig with.'

'Very amusing,' Alice said, and stuck out her tongue. 'You're only in the Horticultural Society so you can get into the green house at lunchtime in the winter. Anybody can do gardening. I'd train as a tractor driver and leave the muddy stuff to types like you.'

'We'll have to do something when we leave school,' Daisy said, 'and if I could make this war a day shorter so that James could come home, then I would do it.'

They fell silent. Daisy bit her lower lip and sniffed. Alice squeezed Daisy's hand.

'I'm sorry,' Daisy said, 'it's just always there. It's like an illness and there's only one cure and they won't let you have it.'

'I don't properly understand, I've never loved anyone passionately. It must be unbearable. I think I'd go doolally.'

'Sometimes I'm so scared he'll die I can barely breathe. He must come back. If he doesn't, I shall die.'

'Poor Daisy, all the girls envy you like mad, having a serving officer in the front line as a boyfriend is dreamy. They don't think what it might actually mean, we just remember him meeting you from school on his motorbike, it was so romantic, the two of you speeding off into the sunset. And, I hope you don't mind me saying this, but it surprised everyone, because you were so quiet and a bit nervous at school in those days, and certainly weren't known as one of the boy mad things, like me.'

'It's hopeless sometimes, I try not to think of him, it makes me so anxious. What if he's in a battle while I'm imagining him? But that is all I can do. He's not here and no-one knows when, or if, he might be.'

Daisy licked the tip of her finger and picked up the last crumbs of cake from her plate. The din had lessened, the crowd thinned. The waitresses were now serving the evening menu to early diners.

'I think we'd better go,' Daisy said. 'I told Hilda I'd be back before dark. She doesn't like me riding in the blackout. What time is your mum expecting you?'

'About half an hour ago. It'll do her good to worry a bit, make her appreciate me more.'

'Might just make her cross and stop your pocket money.'

'My dad would never allow it, I hope.'

They found their waitress and paid the bill.

Outside, the air was markedly crisper. Shops were closing and fewer people were in the streets. Young men were already sporting their white shirttails as token protection in the blackout. In the half-light they set out for the bus station where Fanny was parked, and Alice could get a bus home.

'I've enjoyed today,' Daisy said. 'I like it when we are together. We're just girls looking for adventure and even if we rarely find any, I always feel there's a possibility. Although, I suppose when you get a proper boyfriend, you'll drop me like a hot brick.'

'Never, I'll let you share him 'til yours comes back.'

Alice grabbed Daisy's hands and danced her round in a circle in Marleigh High Street.

∽

Alice jumped out of bed and put on thick woollen socks and yellow garters.

'Staying with you,' she said, 'is worse than guide camp. You should train your aunt to come in and light a fire in the mornings.'

She picked up her new jodhpurs, a gift from her mother, from the floor where she had left them, and pulled them on. Only then did she take off her nightdress. After gazing briefly into the mirror, she tugged a cotton vest over her head followed by a khaki shirt, still buttoned from its last wearing, and a ribbed green pullover with leather patches. She put her hands on her hips and tilted her head at a rakish angle.

'What do think, Daisy? Every inch the land girl, ready to dig for victory.'

Daisy poked her head out from under the covers.

'Looks more likely you're off to a fancy-dress party to me. Your hair's looking a bit Gorgonish.'

Alice turned back to the mirror and pushed back her mop of umber waves. She reached for her hairbrush and, tipping her head forward, she raked with gusto from the nape of her neck towards the crown. Daisy got out of bed and put on her greatcoat. She took the brush from Alice, sat her down and, began to brush her hair in long steady strokes.

Your barnet's beautiful,' Daisy said. 'It's so shiny and full, you're so lucky.'

'What's a barnet? If mine's beautiful then I'm glad to have one.'

'It's Cockney, slang that rhymes, Barnet fair, hair. Billy

uses it all the time. He thinks it makes him sound like a geezer.'

'Isn't that a thermal spring?'

'Not in this case,' Daisy said. 'I think it's a sort of wide boy or gangster. Poor Billy, he's a poacher with nothing to look forward to except the call up if the war lasts that long. Too many Jimmy Cagney films.'

'I thought he was a bit weird when I met him,' Alice said, 'I couldn't stop thinking of him offering you half a crown to feel your breasts. I know I laughed when you told me, but seeing him in the flesh, and imagining, was creepy. Were you scared?'

'Shocked, I think. I can handle Billy. But it brought back me being attacked at the camp, and that scared me half to death, I was terrified I might get murdered.'

'But you met James, so it had a happy ending.'

'Yes, it did,' Daisy said.

'What are we going to do today to win the war and bring James home to his love?'

Alice hugged her friend before she could reply.

'You'll live and die in that coat, won't you? When I saw you get it as we came up stairs last night, I thought you were going to sleep in it, not just lay it on the top. Please, can I borrow it for a minute, I've got to have a wee and I can't possibly use a po', it's like something out of Dickens, so I have to go to the lav' in the garden. I honestly don't know how you do it. But then I suppose it's your sort of gel that props up the Empire.'

To refuse was not possible and so Daisy reluctantly slipped out of the coat and draped it round her friend's shoulders. Alice put it on and struck a few poses in the mirror.

'Move over, I thought you were dying for a wee,' Daisy said. She stood at the washstand and let her nightdress fall to her waist. Alice stopped at the door.

'Gosh, I think I might faint,' she said, as Daisy poured cold water from the ewer into the basin.

Daisy heard her exchange cheery greetings with Hilda, followed by the slamming of the back door. Soap being bad for the complexion, she scrubbed her face with a wet flannel and then washed her hands and arms, before getting dressed. She was ready to go down to breakfast by the time Alice returned.

They sat at the kitchen table, warmed by the range. Hilda had got some honey that she stirred into the porridge and Daisy and Alice shared a boiled egg.

'It's good of you to give up your time to help us in the garden,' Hilda said, 'and you certainly look the part, though it might be an idea to change those lovely brown boots for a pair of wellingtons.'

'Of course, Mrs Thursby, thank you,' Alice said. 'I've not much experience of the country, and I don't have any practical skills, so I'm looking forward to working and learning. I'm sure I'll love it.'

'I hope that you do, Alice. We need all the help we can get this time of year. Spring and autumn, it's all hands to the pump. That Billy says he'll help, but all he does is moon round Daisy and mess about with the bike, shiftless youth. You don't have to call me Mrs Thursby, I'm not Mrs, but I am Hilda.'

'Can I call you auntie, like Daisy does. I haven't got any aunts, you see.'

Daisy went to speak, and Alice kicked her under the table.

'Well, you can if that would please you,' Hilda said.

'Thank you, auntie,' Alice said, 'what are we going to do today?'

'Plenty, I hope. There's the onion sets to get in. Broad beans and carrots to sow, and then tomorrow we'll make a start on the potatoes and leeks. And there's some potting on to be done in the shed, Daisy can show you how to do that, and there's always beds to be dug over and weeded.'

'That all sounds a bit daunting, auntie,' Alice said, 'but now Daisy has shown me which way up a spade goes, I'm sure I'll be fine. This honey porridge is heavenly.'

'I'm sure you know which way up a spade goes, and the honey came from the old boy who keeps the bees, I was lucky he'd still got some this time of year, and as with anything that sweetens nowadays, he's able to charge well for it.'

Hilda got up and stretched. Those black boots by the back door will probably fit you, Alice. I'll make a start on the onions. When you're ready, rinse your plates and join me.'

The back door closed, and the two young women were quiet for a moment.

'Why did you say that?' Daisy said.

'What?'

'About not having any aunties, when it's not true.'

'I don't know. I just thought it would be nice if we could share one. It doesn't matter, does it?'

'I suppose not. It just seemed an odd thing to do.'

Daisy picked up the bowls and ran them under the tap in the stone sink.

'Let's get going. A bit of work will warm us up. We can do the digging this morning while we're fresh and strong, and then potting shed this afternoon while it's still light.'

Daisy picked up a large pot-bellied saucepan that Hilda had filled with pearl barley, vegetables, water and a piece of pork rind and put it on the range.

'Can you get me the flat iron from the scullery shelf, please, Alice,' Daisy said, as she stirred the mixture. She jammed the lid on tight and put the heavy iron on top. Alice stared at her.

'I've not gone daft. It helps keep the moisture in and increases the pressure inside the pan and that makes it cook faster. Ask Miss Simmons, it's basic physics.'

∽

'I like working in the potting shed,' Daisy said, 'It smells lovely and earthy and taking tiny plants and giving them space to grow in their own little pot is satisfying. Get that tray of seedlings from the bench and I'll show you how to pot on.'

Daisy shook the little green shoots onto the table.

'Fill a pot to three quarters, make a hole with this thick bit of stick, it's called a dibber, pick up a seedling by the green leaf shoots, don't touch the root, fill up gently leaving space to water, and very carefully firm the soil round the root so it will be able to drink.'

'Do a couple to show me.'

Daisy did as she was asked and they were soon working quietly and efficiently, side by side. When they had finished Daisy cleared the table for the next task. Alice gripped the backs of her thighs and groaned.

'My legs will never be the same again. They hurt.'

Daisy squatted down and vigorously rubbed Alice's thighs and calves.

'Cripes, that's agony.' Alice said.

'Just get some blood circulating, they'll be fine. It's only because you're not used to using your muscles, we'll rub them with White Horse Oils before you go to sleep.'

'But I'm not a horse.'

'It's only camphor and herbs and stuff, it's just good for strained muscles, whatever sort of animal you are.'

'Seems like it's a hard life in the country. I didn't know I had any muscles 'til I met you.'

Daisy pushed the arms of her shirt up above her elbows and twisted her wrists.

'Muscles are not very ladylike,' she said, 'but I think they're elegant, I like the way they change shape under my skin as I move.'

'You do have lovely arms,' Alice said, 'let's arm wrestle on the table.'

'If you must,' Daisy said. 'If Hilda comes in, she'll think we've gone potty, not meant as a joke, promise.'

With their sleeves rolled up they stood at the end of the narrow table, one on each side. They put their elbows together and joined hands. Daisy's arm stayed upright as Alice went red with the strain of pushing. Daisy relaxed a little of the tension and her arm was pushed flat on the table.

'You let me win, didn't you? We'll have to do it again.'

'No, I didn't.'

They stood up and Daisy put some small pots on the table and sacks of soil mixed with compost and rubbed to a fine tilth. Alice put her arms round Daisy and squeezed her, laying her head on Daisy's shoulder.

'I'm so happy to be here with you.'

Daisy turned around and, with her hands on Alice's hips, leaned slightly forward and softly kissed her lips.

'Come on,' she said, 'I want to get these runners done while we can still see what we're doing. Three or four to a pot, about half an inch deep with the eye pointing upwards, then put them in trays where they'll get the light and water them.'

⁓

Daisy and Alice made the supper. They listened to Alvar Lidell reading the evening news. The seemingly interminable Italian campaign was making early gains in the spring offensive and the allies were in sight of Rome. The news cheered Daisy greatly. Alice rose stiffly and helped her move the small table near the fire. The three of them sat and played Pontoon for matchsticks.

'I think I shall have to go to bed,' Alice said, after a while, 'I seem to be aching everywhere, and I want to be fit for tomorrow.'

'I'm sure you will be love.' Hilda said. 'I hope Daisy hasn't been working you too hard on your first day in the garden?'

'Not at all, I've learned how to do so many things already. Generally, I'm not very active and so I expect it's going to take a bit of getting used to.'

As they said their goodnights Alice did not call Hilda, 'auntie'.

⁓

After the warmth of the sitting room the bedroom struck cold and they changed quickly into their nightdresses. Daisy had brought up a bottle of white fluid. Alice held her nightdress up and Daisy poured a little into her palm and rubbed the oil into Alice's calves and thighs.

'That is so cold,' Alice said, as the oil made contact with her skin, 'and it smells like mothballs.'

'It will smell nice when it warms up,' Daisy said, 'a bit like sage and onion stuffing.'

'Can't wait,' Alice said, 'you do say the loveliest things.'

Daisy spread the greatcoat on top of the counterpane and they quickly slipped between the sheets. Daisy lay on her back and Alice turned to face her.

'I'm so tired but I'm loving it here,' Alice said, 'it's invigorating and different, I feel like someone else.'

'Who might that be?' Daisy said. 'You certainly will tomorrow. We've got to go to church.'

'Blimey, chapel at school is ghastly enough, those awful hymns. You never told me you were religious.'

'I don't think I am, although, I suppose there must be a God, somewhere. I just think I owe it to the vicar because some fund of his pays my school fees. We can go at eight o'clock, which is a short service, or half past ten, which has got hymns and a sermon and feels like it goes on for days, but you do get a bit more time in bed.'

Alice closed her eyes and groaned.

'I suppose we have to. If we wake up in time, let's go to the early one and get it over.'

'Are you confirmed?' Daisy asked, 'because the eight o'clock is a mass.'

'I don't know, I could always pretend I am if anybody asks me.'

'I'm sure you could,' Daisy said.

Alice shivered.

'Your bed is so cold, and I've been thinking about heat transference. You're not the only one who can apply physics to the problems of everyday life. If we lay side by side in this narrow little bed, the one on the outside, that's me, is in danger of falling out, plus, any heat generated by our bodies simply goes up to the ceiling. We should lay on our sides and take turns in cuddling one another, that way heat is both generated and shared.'

Daisy raised herself on her elbows and looked at Alice.

'Gosh, that's probably worth a Nobel prize. However, clearly the cuddle-ee is in a better position than the cuddle-er, who is losing heat through her back. Also, some bed socks would be good, and hot bricks, I'll ask Hilda tomorrow. We'll be as snug as bugs in a rug. As it's your idea you should get first go.'

They arranged themselves spoon fashion. Daisy put her arm round Alice and nestled into her hair. Soon Alice's breathing slowed, and her exhalations sounded like little sighs. A faint odour of camphor drifted up from her nightdress. Daisy lay awake, thinking of James, and wondering.

∽

Daisy and Alice walked quickly along the frosty lane. They were not late, but they were cold. Trees showed black in the early light and the hedges were rimed white. Alice turned up the collar of her blue woollen coat and pulled the belt tighter. Daisy's hands were stuffed deep in the greatcoat. Their visible breaths mingled with the damp morning air. The church gradually revealed its bulk as they neared the top of the incline on which it stood. A single bell tolled. The unheated interior did not welcome as they slid into a pew in front of the chancel arch. They both kept their gloved hands in their pockets. The priest, his back to the people, said the familiar words of the Book of Common Prayer, communicated his small flock of mainly elderly women and returned to the vestry. He reappeared briefly at the porch to offer a cold, bloodless hand, nobody lingered.

'You acted the part beautifully,' Daisy said, as they waited for a lorry loaded with rattling milk churns to pass them on the road. 'You crossed yourself like you'd learnt it in the cradle, and demure is the only word good enough for you at the communion rail.'

'I liked it, very English, but I didn't realise it was catholic and that seemed strange. My legs didn't want to get me up after kneeling for that bread and wine. It tasted nice and warming, I wouldn't have minded a glassfull.'

'It's Anglican catholic, my mum's family, Hilda's one as well. Goes back hundreds of years. It's a bit odd, but I'm used to it, and you are clearly meant for it. You'd make a lovely nun.'

'I couldn't wear one of those coalscuttles on my head, and there would be no boys, ever. Do you want to marry James in a church?'

'Of course, although we are not even engaged yet. He said he didn't want to tie me to him because I was so young, and he might not come back. Had he have asked me I would have said yes.'

Alice took Daisy's arm as they walked along the Marleigh Road.

'But you are young. Don't you want to see what other men are like before you get hitched for life?'

'That's what Hilda says, I should go out with boys my own age. I can't dance, you've seen me at school, I've got all the grace of a lame donkey. Nobody ever wants to partner me, not even you. Hilda might be right, she says you're only young once and that I may live to regret it, but you can't force yourself, can you?'

They stood watching while a woman in oilskins coaxed her herd of cattle across the road from the milking sheds to a warm barn.

'I understand you love James, and it is hard to meet boys, unless you belong to social clubs or something. But everyone seems to manage to get married at some time or other, so it must be possible.'

'Hilda didn't,' Daisy said.

'You said she lived abroad,' Alice said. 'They have dances at Marleigh. My mum would never let me go on my own, but she might let us go together. I'm sure you don't have to dance at dances, you can just stand about looking frightfully bored like Marlene Dietrich and boys will fall at your feet. What do you think?'

'I don't know. I'm probably too scared. You would go off with some bloke to snog, like you did at the pictures, and leave me sitting there terrified that someone would ask me to dance. And then, when nobody did, I'd just feel awful. Why not ask somebody confident, like Jennifer Theakston?'

'Too pretty, she'd get all the boys and I'd be a wallflower.'

'So, you want me to go and be your monkey and make you look beautiful. Thanks a lot, Alice.'

'I didn't mean it like that.'

'Well, that's how you said it.'

'I'd much rather go with you, we could dance together, girls do.'

'Doesn't that miss the whole point? If it's a dance you want we could waltz round the beds in the Victory Garden.'

For a while they walked in silence, listening to the birdsong and the sound of their boots on tarmac.

'There's always Billy,' Alice said.

'Don't, just the thought. I'd rather eat mud.'

They burst into laughter as they turned the corner to Dencher's Lane.

'Come on let's run back to the cottage,' Daisy said, 'It'll put roses in our damask cheeks.'

'Last one to touch the front door has to sleep with Billy,' Alice said, and sped off down the lane.

Chapter 10

EMILY AND DAN CLIMBED THE STAIRCASE TO THE FOURTH floor, their footsteps echoing in the concrete stairwell. A slight, elderly woman wearing a bright floral dress opened the door. Mrs Gauge's daughter, Enid, no longer lived in the cottage, but in a small, neat council flat on the edge of Petersham, a village about ten miles from Campiston.

'Come in, come in,' she said, and ushered them into the sitting room. 'It's a long time since I've seen you Daniel, you're looking quite the young man. And you must be Emily. Now sit down the pair of you.'

They sat in easy chairs in front of a convection heater, cheered by flickering faux coal.

'How's Mr Guy, Daniel? I expect he's been retired a few years now, getting old, like me. I'll get the tea.'

A cherry Madeira cake was served with strong tea out of a brown pot, in green cups with saucers.

'It's very good of you to see us,' Emily said, 'I'm trying to find out more about uncle James and Daisy. By the time I got to know him he wasn't with Daisy anymore, but the house is still full of remembrances of her and I'm intrigued. In a way it's family history.'

'That's very popular now, you see it on the telly, people looking up their family trees and whatnot. It can be very interesting.' Enid settled in her chair. 'Daisy was a lovely girl, tall with long dark hair. Naturally elegant I would say, even in jodhpurs and an old army coat, which is all I ever saw her in. She wasn't pretty but she had a strong face. You wouldn't forget her. It was all a long time ago now, and of course I was only a kid. My mum was Mr James' housekeeper and he kept her on after they got married. Mum took to Daisy, felt protective I think, thought she was a bit of an odd one, hadn't had much looking after as a kid apparently.'

'Can I have another slice of that delicious cake, please, Mrs Gauge?' Dan said.

'Course, my love, you help yourself. I must give you a slice to take with you.'

Dan cut the cake and picked out a glace cherry to pop into his mouth.

'Daisy did have an aunt who she talked about a lot, looked after her during the war, near where Mr James was stationed, West country I think it was. I know later Mr James used to visit the aunt, because he'd send us a drum of clotted cream through the post. Seems funny now doesn't it, cream coming through the post. Anyway, mum got took bad and had to chuck it in. Ida Russell used to do for Mr James, but not like mum, Ida couldn't cook, or wouldn't.

'I must have been about thirteen I suppose when Daisy just dropped out of the picture, all very mysterious like. Whenever I asked after her, mum would just fob me off with some tale or other. I think there were some letters from her, but I couldn't swear to it. Later, of course, mum died and I got evicted because the cottage was tied. I didn't mind too much. These new places are easier to manage when you're getting on, but I do miss the garden. I've got a suitcase of mum's stuff on top of the wardrobe. I'll look through it for you, Emily, when I've got a moment, and if there's anything about Daisy I'll let young Dan here know.'

Emily asked a few more questions but it was clear that for Enid, Daisy, was just the wife of someone her mum had worked for. Dan chatted about himself and Guy for a while and then, clutching a large slice of cake wrapped in greaseproof paper, they said their grateful goodbyes to Enid Gauge.

∽

The drive West seemed interminable. The battered Peugeot, that had a certain chic on the run into Lewes, was now simply sluggish and unresponsive.

'It's only four hundred klicks, it's beginning to seem like a thousand,' Toby said. 'We should have hired a car.' He sat next to Emily, his overcoat collar turned up and a tartan blanket wrapped around his knees.

'Sorry about the heating, Toby. The garage said it was beyond repair. We'll stop as soon as we can spot a source of hot food, even one of those burger shacks with the British flags would do.'

The terrain became increasingly rugged the further west they drove. Fields of plump sheep in rolling pastures had gradually changed to a more uneven landscape of boulder and scrub, with occasional tors, shrouded in mist. Single carriage roads wound round hills, dipped into hollows and rose on wooded slopes. There was little traffic and the countryside was strewn with hamlets and farms.

Annabel had warned that, gastronomically speaking, the West was still largely in the dark ages and had been able to advise on where to stay. Emily's idea was simply to go for the most expensive but as all economists know price and quality are not inevitably benevolently linked. She had put a few bottles of wine in the boot, just in case. They pulled up in front of the White Hart in Porthwiel. It had once been an inn but was now a B&B, with a posh restaurant where the proprietor was chef. The façade was painted in two complementary shades of light green and its double front faced directly onto the market square, in the centre of which was a Victorian version of an Eleanor cross.

The door opened into a wide hall with a wood burner at the end. Two hefty Labradors got to their feet and with tails wagging, came to greet them. A young woman in jeans and a cream shirt appeared from the back of the building.

'You must be Dr Blount, and you Emily,' she said and shook their hands. 'You're very welcome.' She picked up Emily's bag. Emily picked up Toby's. 'I'll show you your rooms and then perhaps you'd like to have some tea downstairs, I expect you're ready for some after your journey?'

'Thanks a lot, that will be great,' Toby said.

The staircase creaked amiably as they made their way to the first floor. Their rooms were spotless and thoughtfully comfortable. Toby checked the radiators under the slider windows.

'Gratifyingly hot,' he said, 'let's see what's for tea.'

'The nosh should be good,' Emily said, and it was.

At breakfast, Toby, whose appetite had recovered, ordered English. Emily, for whom English sausages, mushrooms, eggs and *boudin noir*, held the same allure as warm beer, had toast and coffee. Outside, in a grey cold light, the aged Peugeot spluttered into life. Within a few minutes they had found the byway that led to Yew Tree Cottage. Emily stopped the car and sat shivering for a moment before she got out.

They stood in the lane, side by side and looked over the boundary, marked by sections of collapsed fence, towards the grey weather stained façade. Thick clumps of emerald and orange moss glistened on the roof, where gravity defying pigeons ambled up and down the steep rake, pecking vigorously. The skeleton of a formal grid of garden beds was discernible through the tangle of bramble and wild grasses. Here and there, collapsed frames for soft fruit, draped with rotted netting, littered the overgrown beds.

'Ripe for development, or some such glossing phrase, comes to mind,' Toby said.

'I'm not sure what I was expecting,' Emily said, 'but nothing quite so sadly neglected.'

'It's got atmosphere,' Toby said and pushed at the wicket gate. It caught on the ground and had to be lifted. The brick path to the cottage was slippery and green, the oak door, bleached by sun and rain. Toby found the latchkey, the lock yielded.

'It's much bigger inside than it looks,' Emily said, as she went into the sitting room followed by Toby. The furniture was dulled by dust. The wide hearth flanked by its chairs, was uninviting. She went over to the window and pulled the faded lace curtains back as far they would go. A wintry light filtered through dirty panes. With his hand, Toby rubbed some dust off one of the paintings that covered the walls. It revealed a small watercolour landscape.

'Does that look like James?' he asked.

Emily came over and squinted at the picture. There was a track running through woods with a clearing visible in the distance, an umber palette lent the picture a melancholy air. A low light gave form and depth to the view. In the bottom right hand corner were the initials, DL.

'It's not uncle,' she said, 'it's by Daisy, her name was Lanyard, and of course this was where she lived.' Emily lifted the picture from its hook and took it to the window. On the grey paper backing was inscribed, Marleigh Wood 1944. 'I wonder if uncle tutored her,' she said, and laid the frame on the table. 'Let's quickly look round the rest of the cottage and then I'll get the flask of coffee they gave us. It will warm us up and we can talk about what happens next.'

'Looks like someone's been camping out,' Toby said as they rounded the massive chimneystack leading to the kitchen. Opposite the hearth the old black coal range was covered in newspaper. A small electric cooker sat on the hob. Emily opened its oven door to reveal a mahogany encrusted interior. The sink and draining board were clean and, the deal table was clear, with the kitchen chairs tucked underneath it. Toby pulled one out and sat down, looking around him.

'It's not as bad as I feared,' he said. 'Judging by the outside. I was half expecting some wreckage.'

'It's even got provisions,' Emily said, opening a cupboard door. Dried milk, tea bags, tins of steak and kidney pudding, sounds disgusting, some gloop called sago. I guess uncle James must have stayed here, but how did he come to own the cottage that Daisy lived in? Do you think he bought it?'

'It's hard to say. I can't think why he would.'

Emily went back to the range and looked at the yellowed newspaper.

'It's only five years old.' She returned to the cupboard and took out some tins. 'Some of this stuff is almost within its sell by date. He must have been here quite recently. Let's check the bedrooms.'

The room over the kitchen side of the house was still functional. The simple wooden bed frame was made up and covered with a patchwork counterpane. Hanging in a bow fronted wardrobe was a paint stained overall alongside a baggy tweed jacket, underneath were a pair of black plimsolls and some well scuffed brogues. A dirty white shirt was rolled up in a corner.

Emily picked up the brogues. 'These dead people seem so real, like uncle's studio, still inhabited.'

Toby sat on the bed, his palms flat on either side of him.

'You carry on looking around, Emily, I'll rest a bit.'

Emily crossed the landing to the room directly above the sitting room. The floorboards, caulked against draughts, formed the downstairs ceiling and Emily's steps had a faint echo. Windows in the gable end let in a bleak January light. Emily looked round at the comfortable low chair by the fireplace, the single bed covered in deep blue silk. Small, black and white photographs, watercolour sketches and drawings, were held by rusting pins to the broad wall plates. Heavy black rafters rose and disappeared through a plaster ceiling. Next to the fireplace was a washstand and three rusty biscuit tins, one on top of another.

A sketch of Daisy sitting on a chair was stuck onto a beam. It was probably preliminary to the portrait by James. The paper was yellowed and foxed but the graphite lines were as fresh as when it was drawn. Emily carefully removed the pins and took it over to the window. The tenderness she saw in the lines made her eyes prick. She perched on a beam under the window and looked around the room. On the top of a brown painted cupboard was a battered cardboard suitcase. She took it down and put it on the floor. The corners were worn away and the spring clasps were broken. She blew some of the dust from the lid and opened it. Inside were clothes, folded and loosely wrapped in brown paper.

Emily opened one of the parcels. Inside she found a threadbare cotton dress with a flower pattern. Beneath were two navy blue school tunics. She stood up and shook one out. The pleats still held their shape but, the wool felt damp and oily with the faintest tinge of green. In a paper carrier bag was an orange jumper. It was shapeless, unravelling at the neck and badly eaten by moth. Emily recognised it immediately and smiled.

'Toby,' she called, as she went across the tiny landing to where he lay on the bed, his eyes closed. 'Look at this.'

Toby started. 'Sorry, I must have dropped off.'

Emily dropped the jumper on the bed.

'You stay here, pull the blanket over you. It seems to be a bit warmer upstairs. I'll go and get the coffee.'

Toby propped himself against a pillow and took the coffee with both hands. Emily squatted cross-legged on the end of the bed, her back against the wall. She held up the orange jumper.

'It actually is the one Daisy is wearing in the portrait. It was in an old suitcase with her school clothes.'

'Amazing it has survived.' Toby stretched out and took the jumper. 'Bit of a moth fest over the years.'

'Perhaps the portrait was painted here?' Emily said, 'there's no background so it could have been anywhere.' She folded the jumper and put it down beside her. 'I wonder when she moved to Sussex. When did they get married? I suppose they did.'

'Of course,' Toby said, 'James wouldn't live in sin. Demobilisation took years after the war despite a buoyant labour market for reconstruction, but it must have been possible to get married while still enlisted. It probably took place here. They wouldn't have moved into Campiston before they were legally an item.'

'Church wedding, do you think?'

'Most probably at that time. It's easily checked,' Toby said. He swung his legs onto the floor.

'I expect you want to do more exploring, but I've seen as much as I need to and I'm getting chilled. I'll just look round outside and take a few pics, and then perhaps you would run me back. Then you can spend as much time as you want here while I think about what to do with the old pile.'

With Toby safely in the warm hotel, Emily drove to the cottage, asking herself, yet again, what on earth she was up to, what did she hope to find?

While it was still light, she explored the garden. It was largely impenetrable, but the ghost of order could still be seen. Dead brambles and dried convolvulus were everywhere and smothered the collapsed hencoop. The outhouses were mean in comparison to Campiston and in much worse repair. Doors were hanging off and hardly a pane remained intact. There was little of much interest. The wooden structures were full of broken boxes, sacks and rubble or just empty and dusty. Dan could have this looking great in a week, Emily thought. One small shed, near the cottage, was still in good repair and held a log pile, some garden implements and a pair of muddy, black gumboots.

Back in the cottage, the gloom of a January afternoon made for a dismal atmosphere. There was no central light, only a couple of standard lamps either side of the hearth that Emily hoped might still work. She pushed the red switch. The room was illuminated by a low wattage bulb that barely penetrated the dust accumulated on the fabric lampshade. The effect was to throw long shadows across the room and create pools of blackness in the corners. Emily tried the other lamp, but the bulb had blown. She went around the room opening drawers that were all empty. Under an embroidered linen runner, she found an ottoman and lifted its lid. Instead of blankets it was full of faded folders, books of prints and piles of small sketches and paintings secured with gardening string.

Emily took some of them over to the chair by the hearth and moved the lamp directly behind it. She looked at the grate. If she lit a fire, she'd be able to stay for a while without freezing. She was loath to go. Piling a few small logs on top of some kindling, she hoped it would not be a repeat of Daisy's room in Campiston. It drew easily and was soon flickering a yellow warmth around the room.

This work must be Daisy's. She sifted through the piles. Most of the paper was badly discoloured cartridge, but there were also some sheets of Not watercolour paper that had kept without foxing. The sketches were mostly outdoors, a churchyard, woodlands and meadows, some flower drawings, delicately painted, and a few inside the cottage, all very English. One, with flowers on a table by the window and a fat cat asleep on a cushion, full of summer warmth and light, had a strong sense of place that appealed to Emily and she put it to one side. Another was of the cottage, painted from just outside in the lane, with crowded flower borders either side of the path and under the open windows. She would take them and have them framed, along with the study for the portrait. They could hang in her room in Sussex.

At the bottom of the pile was a dilapidated folder of theatre designs. There were scale drawings of flats on a grid, medieval Italianate palaces, the bridge of sighs and a house with a balcony. There was also an exercise book with a school crest and motto on the cover, St Cedd's Grammar School for Girls. It was full of painted drawings of costumes. Emily recognised the work as Daisy's. Strong colours applied with a firm economical hand, all neatly annotated and initialled. A sheaf of drawings, tied with tape, were for a school play. Portia, Bassano, Jessica and Lorenzo embracing, she like a gypsy princess. The Merchant of Venice seemed an odd choice for a girl's school, but then, of course, Portia was the hero.

Emily sat in the gloom imagining Daisy around the cottage, wondering how her voice sounded, how she smiled, what did her hands look like. The light and the fire faded.

She went around the cottage fixing the images in her mind and collecting things to take away with her. Daisy must have been tall from the length of the tunics. How on earth did they keep clean without a bathroom? And an outside lavatory on a day like today? Emily went out the back to see if it was still functioning. It was but she hovered unwilling to let her bum hit the cold and grubby seat. Inside she took one last look around what must have been Daisy's bedroom. It was hard, having been awakened to another part of Daisy's life to simply leave the space, possibly for good. Her eye was caught by the three biscuit tins she had noticed earlier. She took the one off the top and opened it. It was empty. The other two held some school text books and exercise books. She decided to take these with her, and carried them down the steep, dark staircase and out to the car. She would come back early tomorrow for perhaps a last look round before heading back to Sussex. Emily started the car and shivered. She was cold and hungry and looking forward to dinner. However, she had determined that tonight she would tell Toby the news from Paris, and that would not be easy.

∽

The wine list was short and sensible. A Limoux Chardonnay for the scallops and smooth Buzet for the long-breasted mallards that formed the heart of supper. The plate of local cheeses was a delight.

'Character, flavour and in perfect nick – delish, but it's disturbing to have one's prejudices trampled on,' Toby said. He took his napkin from his lap and scrunched it up on the table before emptying the wine bottle into their glasses.

'You must be feeling so much better,' Emily said, 'that's the first bit of full on pompous snobbery I've heard from you in a long time.'

'Oh dear, I'm such a dreadful old caricature, I don't know how you bear it.'

'I've got used to it over the years, and it's good to hear you sounding like Toby again, regardless.'

Toby leant forward and stirred his coffee.

'Yew Tree Cottage, did you notice not a yew in sight, what to do with it? No smells or signs of damp which suggests the walls and roof are still sound, if in need of some attention. The garden is large and the outhouses a jumble but all that can easily be brought up to scratch. The general aspect is delightful and the location on the edge of the village could not be better. In short, it's an asset. We'll see what a surveyor says and if nothing ghastly comes to light, probably have it modernised and lease it out, as long as there is a local market for long lets. I can't see much advantage to selling it to a developer in its present state.'

Emily laughed.

'It has taken you a few hours to make a decision that I can't make after months and months.'

'Cherub, I have no personal investment in the property and its phantoms. How best to realise its potential is easy. I've also been thinking about Campiston. Were it mine I would sell it. However, it's clear to me and must be to you that for whatever reason you are not ready to relinquish it. Let's keep the house for now while you pursue young Daisy, but at some point, not that far away, either the house or you will have to make some money, or it must be sold. You could always buy something smaller and more practical in England if you wished.'

'Papa, thank you, that is so kind. I know I've been indecisive, but it will be a relief not to have to make up my mind right now, and I shall explain why.' She reached over the table and took Toby's hand. 'I've been meaning to tell you, but I keep putting it off. Jean-Marie didn't visit over Christmas because Alexis has not been well. He has been diagnosed HIV positive and so has Jean-Marie.'

Toby's eyes widened and he jolted back in his chair.

'And?'

'We've always been very careful, and I'm sure I will be fine. I'm going to a clinic in Brighton when we get back to make sure.'

'Dear God,' Toby said, 'that is appalling news. What the hell are we doing here? How have you kept yourself together with this hanging over you? Why didn't you tell me immediately? What on earth were you thinking of, Emily?'

Toby stood up and pushed his chair back. 'We can't talk here. Let's go upstairs.' He opened the door to his room and stood aside to let Emily through before shutting it. She put her arms round him, laid her head on his shoulder and cried. He gave her his handkerchief and she wiped her eyes, before sitting on the little sofa at the end of the bed. Toby poured some Calvados into two tooth mugs and handed her one. Emily looked up and smiled at him. He went and sat across the room in an armchair.

'I am so sorry,' Emily said. 'I was shocked, and I didn't want to stress you. You know I've never kept anything important from you, but you being ill has made me recognise that you are not immortal, and one day I shall be on my own.'

'I shall definitely die, Emily, but that is no reason why you should be alone.'

'I know, but there is something else I haven't told you I don't know why. I did not think it was very important at the time. That weekend we went to the seaside, Jean-Marie suggested that we might get married.'

'You mean he proposed?'

'In a way yes. We are not a very romantic couple, and I

didn't warm to the idea, I sort of ducked it. My first thought when he asked me was that it would shut his mother up and help his hetty credentials at the college.' She paused. 'Whenever I've done a cost/benefit analysis of marriage, I've struggled to find anything to put in the benefit column. He did say he loved me once, last spring, in the Luxembourg, but I didn't take much notice. I'm not sure he knows what it means, but then I'm not at all sure I do either.'

They fell quiet for a few moments.

'I hope there's nothing else, Emily?'

'No, that's it. But with you being ill and the rest of my life fraying at the edges, I'm feeling a bit at a loss.'

'Don't worry about love, cherub. Linguistically it's a floating signifier, nobody knows what it means, but everybody wants some. But love is as nothing beside the matters of HIV and marriage to J-M. Sweet of him to ask and of course it is up to you. However, please God you test negative, but still an HIV positive husband is something to think about carefully. Perhaps not insuperable, but it certainly is a complication.'

'I do realise all this, papa. Jean-Marie, needless to say is completely wiped out, devastated. He thinks it's the end of his career and his life and everything, and he's so angry with Alexis.'

'One can only feel enormous pity for them both', Toby said.

'I found myself thinking, if I say no to marriage will I be punishing him for being sick. But if I say yes will that be because of some obscure sense of duty to care for him, which I might end up doing. I've told him I'll see him as soon as we get back to Paris.'

'My dear Emily, you've been carrying all this, while I've been wittering on about my coughs and my comfort like some querulous octogenarian.'

'I know I should have told you earlier, but I didn't want to seem a drama queen.'

'You wouldn't know how,' Toby said.

For a while they sat in silence. Emily got up and clinked glasses with Toby before draining the last few drops of brandy.

'I've had it,' she said, 'I must go to bed, we're driving back to Sussex tomorrow.' She kissed Toby's forehead.

'Thank you for being my papa.'

Toby squeezed her hands.

'Goodnight,' he said, 'sleep like an angel.'

Emily smiled, then yawned and left, closing the door quietly behind her. In her room she fell onto the bed and lay there, her mind a void. The image of the rusty biscuit tins came into her consciousness. She got up and went into the bathroom and cleaned her teeth, trying not to think about HIV.

∽

'I still like this old car, Emily said, as she swung it across what felt like the ninetieth roundabout of the day, 'but on a long drive with minimal motorway it's hell. I guess all this ancient infrastructure means that wherever the UK economy is, it's not down here.'

'Absolutely right, such acuity,' Toby said. 'At least the sun is shining,' he added, wrapping the blanket more tightly round his legs and slapping his hands together. 'Driving in England has always been ghastly, terrible congested roads, no *aires*, only those gulags of service stations and endless suburban ribbons wherever you go.'

Emily stamped her foot on the brake as the traffic on the single carriageway suddenly came to a halt. Shortly, it began to crawl along in fits and starts.

'Papa, I'm so relieved I told you about Jean-Marie. He told me to go and get tested straight away, but I've been frozen. Having it in the open has made it easier to bear.'

'I understand that.'

For no discernible reason the traffic began to speed up. Emily grasped the chipped and faded plastic ball on top of the rusty gearstick and pushed her way through the elderly cogs.

'I've found a clinic in Brighton that gives fast results and I'm going first thing in the morning.'

'Would you like me to come with you?'

'That's a kind offer but I thought I'd risk asking Annabel and she's agreed to hold my hand. I like her, she has been so friendly, and she's almost as keen on Daisy as I am, which helps me not feel mad.'

'A much better notion, she'll have some distance that I couldn't possibly manage.'

'I feel sick, just thinking about it,' Emily said, 'and whatever happens I'm dreading seeing Jean-Marie. We must get back to Paris.'

'Of course, we must. Apart from anything else, I must get back to work. It doesn't seem so daunting anymore. I'm sure when you've had a chance to talk to J-M life will seem more manageable.'

'One step at a time,' Emily said.

∽

Emily and Annabel leant on the parapet, looking down at the grey sea slapping listlessly on the stone walls of the quay. As they waited until it was time to return to the clinic, conversation had been sporadic. Emily was shivering and her breathing shallow as they left the seafront.

The clinic was like reception in a good hotel. Polite solicitude and quiet efficiency reigned. They were immediately led to a consulting room by a smiling and spotless male nurse where a young female doctor, also smiling, asked them to sit down.

'You will be pleased to know that you have tested negative for HIV. Is there anything else we can do for you at this time?'

Emily sagged visibly, Annabel put her arm round her and handed her a tissue.

'I'm so glad,' she said.

Emily blew her nose and began to struggle to her feet as the doctor got up from her chair.

'No, don't get up,' the doctor said, offering her hand to Emily, 'just take your time. Shall I have some coffee sent in?'

'Thank you so much, but no. I'm ready to go now, I'd like some fresh air,' Emily said, and stood up.

Outside she found her phone and called Toby. Unable to face talking to Jean-Marie, she texted him and switched off her phone. Annabel took her arm.

'Do you fancy a glass of wine?' she said.

'I'm sorry, but I feel wiped out, emptied,' Emily said. 'I can't thank you enough for being with me. You hardly know me, and you've been so kind.'

Annabel squeezed her arm.

'I'm just happy I could help. Dan thought we might get on and he was right, we do.'

On the drive back to Campiston Emily had little to say. Annabel came into the house briefly and was thanked profusely by Toby, who invited her to come and stay with them in Paris whenever she wished and of course to bring Dan. Emily hugged Toby and they stood together in front of the fire savouring their deliverance.

'I'm afraid I'm exhausted and confused. I'll have to go and rest for a bit.'

'Is there anything you would like me to bring you?' Toby said.

'No – thank you. I just need to let things settle.'

Emily lay on her bed with her knees drawn up. Her eyes closed and she fell into a dreamless sleep.

∽

Toby brought some oysters, with a little jug of mignonette, from out of the kitchen. He noiselessly opened a bottle of sparkling wine.

'Dan called to see if I needed any shopping and, I thought I'd be optimistic.' He poured out the wine. '*Sante.* He recommended this, it's a local English winery, gold medals and all that.'

They clinked glasses and drank.

'Delightfully dry, but a bit like carbonated Sancerre, what do you think?'

'Toby, I think you are so better and it's lovely, but I must eat before I faint,' Emily said.

'It's some sort of game ragout. Dan's recommendation again, I couldn't concentrate to cook.'

'I don't care, bring it on,' Emily said, 'then I want to sleep again for a long time. We can just pick up a train when we get to London.'

Emily raised her glass.

'*Santé,*' she said.

'Absolutely,' Toby said.

Chapter 11

A THICK COLD MIST SWIRLED AMONG THE HEDGEROWS. Daisy lay on her back by the side of the road, half on the verge and half in the ditch. Fanny had slewed to a halt some yards away. The engine had cut out and the front wheel spun noiselessly. Daisy felt sick and closed her eyes. Her right leg felt numb and breathing hurt.

Something had come out of Tenby's Plat and hit her broadside as she rode past. It crushed her leg against Fanny's frame and, propelled her across the road and into the ditch. Brakes screeched and a land girl jumped down from a tractor and ran towards Daisy, followed by a man who had been sitting in the low loader hitched behind.

'Oh God, oh God, what have I done,' the young woman fell on her knees beside Daisy. 'I'm so sorry, are you hurt?'

Daisy, her face completely drained of blood was on the point of fainting. The man came up and stared down at her. He took her wrist, pressed two fingers against the inside, and held them there for some seconds.

'This is Daisy, the girl from Yew Tree Cottage,' he said, 'her pulse is fine. You stay with her and don't try to move her.'

The girl nodded, 'Of course, Tom.'

Daisy lay inert and did not speak. He picked up the bike and leaned it against a hedge.

'I'll go back to the house and call the cottage hospital,' Tom said.

He took off his coat and gave it to the girl, still kneeling beside Daisy.

'Take her helmet off carefully and put this over her. Make a pillow with your coat and put it under her head.'

Minutes later he returned.

'There's no ambulance. They want us to bring her in and splint anything that looks damaged before we move her.'

He took a flask out of his pocket.

'Have a sip of this, Daisy.'

Her eyes opened and she bent her head forward. Tom held her and trickled a little brandy into her mouth. Daisy spluttered.

'Your colour's come back,' he said, 'in a minute we'll see if you can move. There's no sign of any serious blood.'

Daisy looked down at her body and tried to sort out the signals she was receiving. Her right leg was now pulsing with pain and she felt nauseous.

'Water,' she said.

'There's some in a stone bottle on the loader, Jess,' Tom said.

The girl came back and held the bottle to Daisy's lips while she drank.

'I'm so, so sorry,' she said, 'the mist was too thick, I just didn't see you, and the noise of the tractor drowned you out.'

Daisy closed her eyes and lay back. Tom put his hand on her shoulder.

'We need to find out what damage there might be,' he said. 'you're moving your head fine. Try moving your arms, one at a time, now roll your wrists.'

He took off Daisy's shoes and gave them to Jess, before putting his hand flat against the sole of Daisy's left foot.

'Push,' he said, 'try again, if you can, that's good.'

Daisy tried again with her right leg, but no signals seemed to get through. Tom straightened it and she winced.

'You'll need to be brave,' Tom said. A splint was made for Daisy's leg with beanpoles and twine. He backed up the low loader and he and Jess lifted Daisy onto a pile of hessian sacks.

'We're taking you to the cottage hospital,' Tom said, 'it's only a couple of miles and I'll drive as carefully as I can. Will Hilda be at the cottage?

Daisy nodded. Tom turned to Jess.

'Tell Hilda not to worry. I'll bring her back if they don't want to keep her in, I can't be absolutely sure.'

∽

As Tom drew up outside the cottage hospital two elderly orderlies appeared and put Daisy onto a trolley. They kept up an amiable banter and wheeled her down a corridor into a green tiled, bare room that reeked of carbolic. They carefully transferred her to a scrubbed wooden table. One went to inform the charge nurse while the other put a pillow under Daisy's head and covered her with a grey army blanket. Tom appeared in the doorway.

'I'll wait and tell the doctor what happened,' he said.

A moment later a nursing sister came in and whisked off the blanket. She was stout with red hands that smelled of Lifebuoy soap.

'So, you're the young lady who got herself knocked off her motorcycle,' she said, 'dashing along in the fog and not looking where you were going, I suppose.'

'No, it wasn't like that,' Daisy said.

'And who are you?' The sister said, turning to Tom, who had followed her into the room.

'Tom Dacre,' he said, 'it was one of my land girls knocked her off I'm afraid, weren't that used to driving tractors, lot of mist about and not expecting to meet anything at the junction.'

'I don't think the doctor's going to be pleased whoever is at fault,' the sister said, 'it's an unnecessary accident and we've got quite enough to do, thank you. We all know the war is finished but that doesn't mean the wounded mend overnight.'

She took a pair of scissors out of her pinafore and released Daisy's leg from the beanpole splint. Daisy shut her eyes tightly against the pain.

'These trousers will have to come off if Doctor's going to find out the trouble. You go and wait outside,' she said to Tom.

The doctor, when he arrived was elderly and smelled strongly of tobacco that reminded Daisy of her father.

'Tell me exactly what happened,' he said as he began his examination, 'the main problem is this leg, is it?'

He gently manipulated the joints and felt along the thigh and calf, watching the pain register on Daisy's face.

'A good deal of swelling and contusion, that's to be expected, but basically a bad sprain much better than a break but just as painful. If your breathing hurts you've probably bruised some ribs. Bandages I think and let nature take its course, feel a lot better in a couple of weeks. Nurse will give you a bottle of aspirin for the pain. Get your own doctor round if there are any problems and his nurse to renew the dressing if need be. We can't let you have crutches they are all being used. An old broom with a towel wrapped round the head will help you get around. Try not to be too impatient and you'll be fine. We'll charge you to the parish so that will be alright and look where you're going in the future.'

As he left, Hilda, out of breath, appeared in the door.

'Oh, my Lord, whatever's happened to you. I knew that bike would be the death of you and it nearly has been. Have you broken any bones? Will you be able to come home? Tom Dacre's outside and he'll take us home if they'll let you go.'

Hilda put her arms round Daisy and kissed her. Daisy began to cry.

'I'm sorry love, taking on so, it's scared me, that's all.' She stroked Daisy's hair. 'There, you'll be fine, I'm sure.'

'It's alright, auntie, it's just a sprain and bruises, that's all. They'll strap it up and I can come home. We don't even have to pay.'

Two young nurses came in and shooed Hilda into the corridor. They set to binding Daisy's leg, tightly, in a wide crepe bandage.

'Leave it on for a fortnight and don't get it wet,' one of them said, and then they were gone.

∽

'Blimey, that hurts like the blazes,' Daisy said.

She gingerly put her foot on the ground, but it was too painful to bear any weight. Leaning on Tom she hopped out to the low loader and he lifted her onto the sacks. Hilda's bike was hoisted on next to Fanny, and Hilda climbed aboard and sat next to Daisy helping her to get as comfortable as possible

When they got to the cottage, Tom carried Daisy into the sitting room and put her on the settee. Hilda brought the pouffe and Daisy manoeuvred her damaged leg onto it. Hilda went to make tea and Tom to unload Fanny. Daisy heard the familiar noise of the starter and then the engine fired, the throttle was opened wide for a few moments and then closed, leaving the purr of the idling machine.

Tom came back and stood by the fire. He took a cup of tea from Hilda.

'Your bike is fine, just a few scratches. It had a nice soft landing on the verge, softer than yours I'm afraid.'

'Thank you so much, Tom, I'm truly grateful for what you have done. What would have happened to me?'

'The least I could do. It was my girl, Jess' fault after all. I shall have to report it as an accident to the police so they might come calling.'

'You don't have to do that,' Daisy said, 'Jess might get into trouble and she's probably feeling pretty bad about it as it is.'

'That's very good of you Daisy but I might get done if I don't.'

Daisy lifted her leg and slowly lowered it onto the rug. The pain increased and she lifted it back onto the pouffe.

'Don't forget,' Tom said, 'if there is anything I can do just send word, and any doctor's bills must come to me.'

'Thank you, Tom,' Hilda said, 'we'll see how things go.'

'I must get back to the farm,' Tom said, buttoning his leather jerkin, 'I'll drop by later and see how you are.'

Hilda pushed Daisy's hair away from her forehead and looked into her face.

'Now, my girl, something to eat if you can manage it, and then I'll help you upstairs and you can have some aspirin. You'll want to rest after all this going on. There's a letter from James today. I'll fetch it when we've got you settled.'

'Give it me now, auntie, please, I won't open it until I'm laying down'

The only way Daisy could get up the stairs was backwards on her behind. Every step jarred her leg. On the landing she used her hands and the good leg to awkwardly shift into her room where Hilda helped her get onto the bed. Daisy lay there clutching the letter.

'Oh, Hilda, this is awful. We must let the theatre know. I should be prompting tonight, and I have to finish the designs for The Good Companions, they're depending on me.'

'Then they'll just have to depend on someone else I'm afraid, but give me the phone number, I'll go across to the farm directly and call them.'

'That would be a kindness, it's Marleigh 157. Thank you that will be a relief. You'd better tell them I'll be off for a while, and I'll write to Rex tomorrow. I hope he'll hold my job for me, I'd die if I lost it.' Daisy stopped talking and bit her lip.

'I'm sure they will,' Hilda said, 'what with all the sets and stuff you do, you must be worth three times what they give you.'

Shortly, Daisy heard the banging of the front door. She lay back on the pillow, closed her eyes and let the pain and exhaustion fill her mind. Still clutching the envelope, she slept.

Daisy woke to the sounds of Hilda in the kitchen below. It was dark, a fire had been lit while Daisy slept, and shadows flickered round the walls. It took a moment to register where she was before the events of the day, unbidden and unwelcome, seeped back into her consciousness. Wincing with pain she leaned over the side of the bed to retrieve the letter that had fallen from her hand while she slept. She opened the envelope and slid out the familiar thin paper, by tilting the sheet towards the hearth there was just enough light to read by.

Dearest Daisy,

I don't know whether to laugh or cry. The CO called me in and I held my breath, thinking I was going to get my papers. But it wasn't to be. I've been such a good soldier they are thinking of posting me to the British zone in Berlin, which is plain awful. Charles reckons that as everyone hates it there so much the tours are all short and they probably won't keep me for longer than a few months, but he may have just been trying to sugar the pill. We can't argue with the army. It owns us body and soul until it doesn't need us anymore. Watson's got his papers but he's been put on reserve. He doesn't seem to mind, the thing that frightens him most, he says, is getting one of those de-mob suits, he's hanging on to his uniform. He's been with me through thick and thin and I shall miss him a lot. I'd like to do something for him when I get back.

It would be good to leave this makeshift camp. There's a sense of restlessness about the place waiting to be demobbed. I can't keep up with who is left in my battalion and who has gone back to Blighty. And, oddly, now the fighting is all over it's more difficult being an officer. Naturally the men want to get home and there's a limited amount we can find for them to do, so they get bored and frustrated and start chafing at the discipline. I don't blame them I feel the same, but I won't have them whitewashing stones at any price.

I hope all this avoids the censor's blue pencil. It probably will. Now the show's over it's hard for us all to keep going through the motions.

It must happen one day Daisy. It can't be that long now and you'll be in my arms as well as my heart. I miss you as ever and long to be with you.

Your ever loving
James X
PS Love to Hilda and a stroke for Winny

Daisy kissed James' signet ring and looked into the fire. Why if the war is over can't he come home? Why do they need him, out of all the Majors in the army, to go to Berlin? People are saying we might have to fight the Russians, but Hitler was fighting them a while ago, they're supposed to be our allies. They've been liberating Europe just like us and the Yanks. If James is sent off to fight, I shall die. I could not go through it all again. Please, God, send him home, but I don't want him to see me like this. If he took me in his arms it would hurt like hell. Perhaps they'll only want him in Berlin for a few weeks, it can't take that long to clear the place up. It would be best if I recovered before he got back. I'll write to him in the morning and pretend I'm much worse than I am, then, perhaps, he'll get compassionate leave. But officially I'm not even his fiancée, so that won't work.

Daisy lay back. A few minutes later, steps on the stairs interrupted her reverie. Hilda came in and switched on the light. Winny followed and jumped on the bed, rubbing himself against Daisy's leg and purring loudly. Daisy stroked him.

'I've called the theatre and they were very concerned but said not to worry, they'd get by and you're to let them know as soon as you're able to go back.'

'That's a relief, thank you, and for the fire, it's really cheered me up, which James' letter most certainly hasn't.'

Daisy told Hilda the news.

'It's hard to bear, Daisy. It's not as though he's a regular, and nobody could say he hasn't done his bit in Italy. It's not fair on either of you. We'll just have to hope his CO's got it right and he'll be home soon.'

Hilda closed the curtains, raked the fire and put a couple of shovelfuls of coal on. The dust hissed as it ignited and flew up the chimney.

'How's that leg feeling?'

'Unbelievably sore, but the fierce pain has died down.'

'Good, you'll need to get out to the lav,' so, I've put an old velvet shoe bag over a broom to help you get around.'

'That's brilliant, auntie, where would I be without you.'

Hilda picked up the scuttle.

'I'll get some coal in and bring you up a tray later on. I've ransacked the larder and made some rock buns. Do you want your writing things so you can reply to poor James? It's a wonder he doesn't go AWOL.'

'Yes, please, and I'll drop a line to Alice to see if she can get out to see me and to Rex. I think if you brought my pad and pens, I could do the designs, and someone could come out and collect the drawings. This is only the second time Rex has asked me to design, and I so want to do it. I've got some ideas for costume as well. Oh, why did this have to happen? And why is James not coming home?'

Daisy started to cry and Hilda comforted her. 'Forgive me,' Daisy said,' I mustn't feel so sorry for myself. It's just that the war's been over for ages and nothing seems to be getting any better. There's no James and anything you might want is still rationed. The only difference is, there's lots of men in horrible suits hanging about the High Street because they can't find a job. And now this has happened.' She squeezed her thigh.

'You mustn't mind too much, Daisy, it's only a setback, and you're young. Now, let's see how you can shift. I'll help you to the top of the stairs, and I've cut down a carpet slipper for you to put your foot in to get to the lav.' If needs be, we could always make a bed for you downstairs.'

'You're right, auntie. Let's test the leg and see just what I can do. I'd like to stay in my room if I can. At least Fanny's in one piece and that's something.'

Daisy swung her legs slowly onto the floor. As gravity filled the damaged tissue with blood it began to hurt a lot.

'I can just about put my foot on the floor but it won't take my weight.'

With Hilda's help she manoeuvred herself onto the landing and bumped down the stairs. With her foot in the slipper, she tucked the broom under her arm and hobbled out to the lavatory. Hilda waited by the door until she got back inside.

'It's a good job James can't see me now,' Daisy said, 'I must look comical.'

'With a cocked hat and a parrot, you could be taken for Long John Silver.'

'I think I'd like to do panto,' Daisy said and smiled.

Hilda gave her a hug.

'Now you're down here, would you be comfortable sitting for a bit?'

'I'll give it a try,' Daisy said, and lowered herself gingerly into a carver by the fire.

'I'll get some tea,' Hilda said, 'We'll be alright for supper. Tom gave me some bacon and a half pound of real butter.'

Daisy sat looking into the fire and sipped her tea. She took a large bite out of a thick slice of golden toast.

∽

'I feel like I'm back in the world this morning,' Daisy said.

'That's good to hear. If you write your letters, I'll get them in the early post, and they might be delivered today.'

'That would be wonderful. I'll do them as soon as I've washed, which might be a bit difficult.'

'A lick and a brush will be fine for a few days,' Hilda said.

'I can't see that dressing lasting a fortnight, you might be able to get a bath soon. I'll get Dr McKay to send his nurse round.'

'Thanks, auntie, last night I couldn't get comfortable and I lay awake for hours, still shocked I suppose. I should count my blessings. I'd never seen the inside of a hospital until yesterday. I had certainly never thought just how soft our bodies are and how easily they get damaged.'

'It's true, Daisy. I saw such things in the streets in Shanghai, people left to die on the pavement, starving beggars we used to ignore, just stepped over them. I soon learnt that life is not as solid as it looks at first glance. But don't let me get maudlin. Yours is all ahead of you, and once we get that James back, you can get on with it properly.'

Alice sat on the bed in jodhpurs and ribbed sweater, smelling faintly of dung. Daisy took her hand.

'I'm so glad to see you,' She moved her watercolours and block of paper to make room for Alice, who gave her a hug and kissed her.

'I managed to get the afternoon off. I exaggerated your helplessness a little bit. I said you lived alone in an isolated cottage. Brought a tear to my eye just thinking of your plight. Now I'm here you don't look half bad to me, apart from that rather alarming leg. Does it hurt?'

'Only when I try and use it as a leg,' Daisy said, 'it's odd not being able to walk about. I feel stranded like I'm on a desert island. What's been happening in the outside world?'

'Nothing much in the bits I've been in. Did some muck spreading this morning, which is about as attractive as it sounds, but it's better than being in college where it's all soil science and common diseases of the pig. Still, it's some use I suppose, which school science never seemed to be.'

'School, it hasn't been a year and it seems like another world, a long way away,' Daisy said.

Hilda shouted from the kitchen for Alice to come and get the tray. She clattered down the stairs and Daisy heard them laugh. Alice came in and put the tray on the washstand.

'This cake was made with a real egg and Hilda ground some sugar in a pestle to make icing. Such luxury. Your Hilda is brilliant.'

'I know,' Daisy said, 'I've been rather short with her lately, captivity is fraying my nerves.'

Winnie appeared and jumped on the bed. Alice tickled his ears and he purred.

'You're lucky to have a cat to cuddle. I've never had a pet, too messy for my mother, hairs on the settee. She's a strange woman, I think my mum might die if she had to spread muck.'

'Winnie keeps the rats down and even bags the occasional rabbit, so he earns his meatpaste sandwich.'

'Poor little soul, surely you can run to a cod's head.' Winnie settled into Alice's lap, sniffing her jodhpurs ecstatically.

'And how is Arthur?' Daisy said, and they both laughed.

'He is so boring a cod's head sounds like fun by comparison. Most of the time I have no idea what he's on about. He actually talks to me about cars and he hasn't even got one. He dresses like he can't wait to be forty and thinks being an articled clerk is some sort of achievement.'

'You must like him a bit, you keep on seeing him.'

'He's not exactly ardent, I don't have to see him that often. I don't really know why I do. I suppose partly it's a lack of choice, I'd prefer Bob Mitchum, with his come-to-bed eyes. Also, it's just easier to go on as things are. If I dumped him there'd be a scene and I'd have to explain it to mother.'

'Don't see why?' Daisy said, 'It's up to you, isn't it?'

'My mother thinks I should have a boyfriend, so she can tell her friends how popular I am. She keeps asking me, "when is he going to pop the question, dear?" to which I reply, *sotto voce*, "not this side of hell freezing over, I hope." Mother wants me to be normal, it would reassure her.'

'Has he asked you?'

'He's got close, but if I think I can see something brewing, I put a straw in my mouth and start talking about crop rotation and milk yields. He's pathetically easy to manage.'

'I suppose you kiss him, what's it like?'

'Just as you might imagine. A wet fish sums it up and I only do it when I have to.'

'Alice, it can't be as bad as all that?'

'It might be.'

'When we were at school you used to be boy mad, what's happened?'

'I still like the idea of them,' Alice said, 'the problem is that in the flesh they can be awfully disappointing.'

'I know what you mean. I remember being kissed by James, it was lovely, but I was just a girl. I don't know how I would feel now. Everybody says that the men who've come back from the front are changed and can't adjust to civvy street, and don't get on with their wives. So, when I think realistically about him coming back it might not be love's young dream, I just don't know. I want him to come back, but I'm scared that we will both be different people.'

'You certainly were in love, and the Berlin thing must have been awful. This war is mad. We had VE day and everybody was happy for about two days, and now it's back to just like it was.'

'In his latest letter he didn't seem so sure about the Berlin posting. He seemed a bit more hopeful, so, fingers crossed,' Daisy said.

'That sounds promising. I can't help feeling a bit jealous, when he does finally show, I'll probably never see you again.'

'Of course you will,' Daisy said, 'you're my best friend in the world.'

Alice swung her legs onto the bed and stretched.

'Just look at the holes in your socks,' Daisy said.

Alice looked down at her toes, poking through the brown wool, and wiggled them.

'It's really uncomfortable, but I hate darning.' Alice was quiet for a moment. 'What would make me happy is for us to share a flat in Marleigh, or even a little cottage, there's lots of them on the farms round here.'

'That would be dreamy,' Daisy said, 'but I guess we'd be pretty low priority in a housing shortage, and we might struggle to pay the rent. I'm paid in buttons and you're an agriculture student living on what your dad gives you. I suppose you could bring home mangelwurzels for us to eat.'

'I'd have to fight the cattle for them. I could probably get my dad to foot the rent. He's soft as a brush where I'm concerned.' Alice wiggled her toes again. 'Speaking of feet, I've got something for you.'

'Thanks, you're meant to bring something when you visit a sickbed. I hope it's not a ball of wool and a darning needle,' Daisy said.

'Don't be so ungrateful.' She rummaged in her rucksack and brought out a crumpled white paper bag.

Daisy took it, peeked inside and laughed. She put her arms round Alice and kissed her.

'Nylons, that is an amazing present and, now I've only got one good leg, they'll last twice as long.'

'You could save them 'til James comes back. He's not going to recognise that scrawny schoolgirl he fell for, is he?'

'I was not scrawny. I was slender with a waif like charm.'

Alice rolled her eyes.

'You've definitely matured. You're about as tall as him and your pageboy does make you look like Joan of Arc, before she went nutty, of course.'

'I just keep thinking about James coming back, it scares me. He's been away for such a long time and he's only been with other soldiers and fighting the Germans. I can't imagine trying to shoot people, can you? It doesn't happen in normal life.'

'But James is such a gentleman, Daisy. I can't see him getting moody or taking to drink, he'll just come marching down the lane, swishing his swagger stick.'

They both laughed. Alice raised herself on her elbow and turned to face Daisy.

'You'll be fine,' Alice said, and kissed her.

'Perhaps you're right. It's being stuck here. I'm getting anxious before I have any cause. But then I think, we were in love, but it was very sudden and then he was gone, and we hardly had time to get to know one another.'

'Do you mean no time to be – intimate?'

'No, I don't. I mean we barely talked about our lives or what we wanted to do. I feel that I have my own life now, and he'll want me to give it up. I'm determined not to end up like my poor old mum.'

'Don't worry, Daisy. James is nothing like your dad and nothing like mine either. I can't see James rattling his newspaper and moaning about the government going communist all the time, and how he, personally, is having to pay for it. If James loves you, he'll want what you want.'

'You're right. It's not very loyal of me to have misgivings, but I've got them all the same.'

Alice had loaded a sable with watercolour and was painting a flower on Daisy's bandage.

'Alice, no,' Daisy said, 'you'll get me into trouble with nurse Boothby. She's frightful, puffs up the stairs like an old battleship and it really hurts when she rips the bandage off.'

'She's probably got nine cats and spends her evenings putting them all in splints. Now, "look lively" as Hilda says. We'll get you downstairs and comfy by the fire and I'll toast you some crumpets and we can think about kitchen curtains for our cottage.'

'I'm so glad you're here.'

'Me too,' Alice said, and bounced off the bed.

Chapter 12

EMILY WALKED BACK FROM THE *BOULANGERIE* THROUGH the crisp early morning air. In the apartment she waited to hear the shower stop before making coffee. Annabel came into the kitchen in skinny jeans and a roll neck jumper, her long hair tied in a towel.

'Hi, that smells great,' Annabel said, 'fragrant coffee and warm butter. I'm impressed. Do you go out every morning for fresh stuff?'

'Most mornings,' Emily said, 'unless I'm on my own, or feeling lazy. Did you sleep alright?'

Annabel spread some strawberry jam on a croissant. It was a moment before she could answer.

'Yes, thanks, it's a fabulously comfy bed and so quiet for the middle of a city.'

'That's good, I often don't sleep well the first night I'm away. It's cold today but there's no rain so we can go out and see some Paris.'

'Great, I'll be guided by you, I've only been here once before, and that was with the school.'

'The power of Disney?'

'You got it.'

'We could go to the Louvre,' Emily said, 'but it's just hectares of stuff looted from the Empire. Like the British

Museum I guess, only more so, and always hideously packed. I suggest Cluny or the Carnavalet, which is all about Paris and it's not that far.'

'That sounds a treat, but I'm not much of a tourist. I just like walking about and hanging out, and I'm really looking forward to Daisy's journals.'

'I've only scanned them myself, but they look amazing. Let's give Carnavalet a go. It's a little bit old fashioned, but full of good stuff and rarely gets overcrowded. It's in Le Marais, which is the gay quarter and is a nice place for strolling around. We're meeting Jean-Marie for lunch, I'll let him know where we are going, and he can choose a bar for us.'

'Great,' Annabel began to vigorously towel her hair. 'I'll be ready in no time.'

～

They stood at the top of the steps outside Sacre Coeur looking out across the city. The Eifel tower and la Defense stood out in the distance amongst the intricate pattern of grey roofs.

'It's so not London,' Annabel said, 'It looks like a town where people live and send their children to school.'

'It is, the centre round here is a bit of a France theme park, but I've always loved it, great to grow up in.'

'I worked in the City of London for a couple of years,' Annabel said. 'Hated it, never taken seriously, groped on an hourly basis, and knowing that no-one would ever do anything about it. The bosses were the worst.'

'Yeugh, that sounds awful. Here you get patronised and flirted with. Most Frenchman have a ridiculously high opinion of their desirability, which can be a bore, but you're rarely invaded.'

'It was pretty grim. Many fewer bucks in Lewes, but you can, more or less, call your body your own.'

Emily and Annabel walked down to the Ile de la Cite. The myriad padlocks on the Pont de L'Archeveche sparkled in the sunlight.

'I suppose it's romantic. But lovers putting their names on a lock and leaving it on a bridge? It's a bit of a clunky way to do things. Can't see Dan doing it, he'd think it a waste of padlock. You can see them in London now, but nothing like this.'

Annabel stopped to read some of the dedications. 'Not many French names,' she said.

'No, it's mainly Asians, maybe they still think Paris is a romantic place.'

They passed over the Pont St Louis and the Pont Louis Phillipe and headed for the Rue de Sevigne.

'I'm looking forward to meeting Jean-Marie,' Annabel said, 'Is he keeping well?'

'Sort of. He hasn't got any symptoms, but he's finding it hard. He's always been pretty driven and very ambitious as well as a ridiculous closet. He says he can't come out because it will ruin his career but I think he's more scared of his family, especially his father who sounds rather grim. He has to try to reconnect with his life and especially with his doctorate, he is a bit obsessive about it. At the moment it doesn't seem very real to him and this makes him anxious. As far as he is concerned without it his life is over. He's not in a good place and it's hard to know what to do.'

They stopped at a Paul's and sat outside in the bleak sunshine.

'Best chocolate on the globe,' Emily said, as they sipped their bowls of hot, fragrant liquid.

'How is Dan getting on? It was a shame he couldn't come.'

'Early days, but he has taken to his course, it's all about

the stuff he loves. He's no academic but there's a lot of practical stuff and that gives him confidence. You are going to have to watch him. He's getting big plans for Campiston, coppicing isn't the half of it. He truly loves your house, you know that?'

'I do and it makes me feel good but also a bit guilty. I am grateful to him for bringing the house back from the dead. It's not just the hours and effort, he has had all the good ideas. I thought coppicing was whimsical, but it isn't, it's one way to make the wood productive. With any luck there's going to be loads of real tomatoes in the summer too, all knobbly and luscious, that we can sell.'

Emily stretched her legs out and tilted her face to the faint warmth. She pulled off her beany and pushed her hair back.

'If only he wasn't such a boy,' Annabel said, 'he'd be a complete treasure. He's been doing bits of work for farmers, but nothing has lasted, and no one has offered him a job. Campiston just does it for him, he's terrified you are suddenly going to sell.'

'I've just put any decision to one side. Toby's happy to support me for the time being. Selling would mean displacing Dan but I may well have to. Let's go.'

Emily pushed a note into the bill clip and took Annabel's arm.

'Is Dan a long-term fixture? He talks about you all the time.'

'I'm not sure, I sometimes think that if he had to choose between me and that bike he's restoring, the bike would walk it.'

∽

When Emily and Annabel reached the bar, Jean-Marie was already there, sitting on a high stool drinking coffee. He got up and embraced Emily and shook Annabel's hand. His shining auburn curls and tailored overcoat gave him the aura of a renaissance blade. He smiled and held Annabel's hand while he spoke.

'It's good to meet you,' he said, 'I hope you are enjoying Paris. Do you know the city?'

'No, not yet, but I'm hoping to. We've been to the Paris museum, which was great, what a history. By comparison nothing much has happened in London. I love the atmosphere,' she opened her arms and looked around her, 'it all feels so civilised.'

'A lot of people say that is its problem,' Emily said, 'it lacks the raw energy that makes London so successful.'

'You know that London is one of the largest French cities,' Jean-Marie said, 'that's why presidents go over there to canvas for elections. If I was a banker, I'd probably have to move to Kensington.'

'Then I'm jolly glad you're not,' Emily said, and stroked his arm.

They sat on stools round a tiny high table and ate steak frites with a carafe of red wine.

'Emily tells me you are doing a doctorate,' Annabel said, 'that must be very demanding. What is it you're researching?'

'Never ask a doctoral student that question,' Emily said, 'you could be here for days.'

'The short answer is, whatever my tyrannical supervisor tells me to.'

'We are going to spend the afternoon reading Daisy's journals,' Emily said.

'Daisy,' Jean-Marie spread his hands in front of him, 'my very real phantom rival. I know when I can't compete. It's been a great pleasure to meet you, Annabel, and I trust we will meet again. I shall stay and have another coffee.'

218

He stood up and again embraced Emily, this time he brushed Annabel's cheek.

'Wow,' Annabel said, as they walked to the Metro station, 'he is so gorgeous.'

Emily laughed.

'I know,' she said.

⌢

They sat curled up on opposite sofas with small piles of exercise books, filled with Daisy's round hand, the ink now faded, and read to one another anything they thought interesting.

'Listen to this,' Annabel said.

D. Lanyard 20th September 1944

Auntie was waiting for me when I got off the bus, so I knew something was wrong. I was so scared I nearly wet myself. I thought it would be James and that he must be dead. But it wasn't, it was mum. The hostel she was staying in had a direct hit and most of the women were killed. I just went numb, it didn't seem to be possible that somebody could suddenly die like that, without me seeing her or saying goodbye. Then I immediately felt relief that it wasn't James and that made me feel like a monster. My legs turned to jelly, and auntie couldn't hold on to me and so I sat on the ground and thought I was going to faint. My whole body tingled, and I felt sick. Auntie got me to sit on a tree stump and put my head between my legs and after a while she helped me stand up. We were both crying and holding on to each other. The whole world had suddenly changed into something horrible and I wanted to die myself. I don't remember

getting back to the cottage. Auntie sat me by the fire and
gave me hot tea with about a week's sugar ration in it. It's
good for shock and it did seem to steady me for a bit but
then I was sick. I couldn't eat so she put me to bed. I just
lay there thinking it can't be real, perhaps they've made a
mistake and she was out down the shops or something. I
kept seeing her, having a cigarette or eating a sandwich
and laughing and the next moment being blown to tiny
bits by a German bomb. I prayed for her soul, but she
was never very religious.

'How can you believe that?' Annabel said. 'Having your mother suddenly wiped out, not ill, not old but gone forever. The poor girl, and with the guy she loves somewhere being shot at. How did they manage?'

'I don't know, I have no idea. Annabel, I haven't said this to anyone before, but I have no idea about my own mother. I know she's American, her name is Lisa and she's an economist, and I know she and Toby were married and that she left him and went back to the States when I was a little baby, and I don't think they've been in touch much since, that's it.'

'That's barely credible, Emily, it's your mother, surely you have wanted to know about her, you must have asked Toby questions, he must have talked about her, surely?'

'She has never ever tried to get in touch with me, no birthday cards, no attempt to connect ever. Toby doesn't say anything, and I sort of feel there's nothing for me to say. It's a black hole.'

'But, Emily, there must be a story, you must be inquisitive?'

Annabel came and held Emily's hands.

'I might have been too frightened to ask. It's easier not to have a mother, I've never felt I needed one. Nicole looked after me 'til I was in my teens and then retired back down

South to be with her family. She helped me grow up.'

'But she wasn't your mother. I guess I understand your reticence, but maybe the longer it's left the more difficult it becomes.'

'You may be right, she's out there somewhere. I must find the courage to ask Toby. I hope you don't think I'm a freak. Can we get back to Daisy?'

They sat and read through the afternoon, rapt in the unfolding narrative of Daisy's adolescent self. Much of the writing was given over to the quotidian business of survival during the last years of the war, but always with the backdrop of uncertainty and longing.

D. Lanyard 24th September 1944

I haven't been able to face school. The world still hasn't come back. Some girls have lost relatives. Brenda Nash's dad is a POW somewhere and they can write to him, which seems odd somehow. Claire Brownly even lost her brother, but no one's mum has died. I hope I'll be alright. Sometimes girls can be unkind, not really meant but just not knowing what to do or say to help probably. A few of them had been to the shop and so they'll have known my mum. I suppose I'll have to go back soon but I'm not looking forward to it one bit. I must look after auntie. Mum was her sister, her only relative that I know of except some cousins in Canada. It's good that I'll be with her, but what will happen to us. I know mum was sending her money. What will I do if she can't afford to keep me? Auntie says dad must be out of gaol and he should help, but he hasn't been near, or sent a telegram or anything. I don't want to see him. I suppose he must have loved mum once to marry her. There are too many

frightening things to think about. Maybe going back to
school would be good for me. I still haven't written to tell
James I can't do it yet. If he died I would want to die too.

D. Lanyard 1ˢᵗ November1944

I let Billy Oakley come over and help me put my bike
back together after her service, which I just loved doing.
I could have done it all myself, but it would have taken
longer. If he comes over, he usually brings a rabbit or
something else he's poached and tries to sell it to auntie.
Most often he persuades her, but she always beats him
down a bit. He's good with engines and he's taught me
a lot about how they work and what to look out for
and now I feel quite confident and can understand the
manual that James left me. Bikes are like chickens, if
you don't keep them up to scratch, they don't work so
well. I had been getting on fine with Billy. We've walked
up the tors and he can be interesting, and he makes me
laugh. Then, while we were working, he offered me half
a crown if I'd let him touch my breasts. He got quite
worked up about it and I was a bit scared, he was really
close to me in the corner of the shed and it reminded me
of that man in the camp. I even thought of letting him
in case he got nasty. It's really upset me because it was
nice to have a boy to be friends with who liked bikes
and I don't think we can carry on as normal now. Mum
was always warning me about boys only wanting one
thing, and that I was to keep my hand on my halfpenny,
which took me a long time to puzzle out. Ever since I've
known Billy he's got more excited about engines than
girls. I'm certainly going to wait awhile before I decide

222

whether to see him again or not. I couldn't tell auntie, I'd die of embarrassment and she'd have a fit. I'll tell Alice at school, and she'll laugh and probably say my breasts aren't worth half a crown and she'd have done it for two bob. But then auntie says it's unnatural for me not to be interested in boys and that I shouldn't put all my eggs in one basket. She may be right, but I only want James. For me it stirred up all that bad stuff I felt after I was attacked. I felt scared all the time and carried a penknife with me for ages, God knows what I thought I could do with it. When I told Alice, she said I could always offer to sharpen my attacker's pencil with it. Billy has upset me. I couldn't sleep and so tried to think about James and him rescuing me and then painting me and us falling in love.

D. Lanyard 27th April 1945

Fanny is working beautifully. The engine is purring and I've just got a full tank of petrol and a big can of oil, so we should be all right for a while. There was a rumour that the GI's were coming to take over the camp, so all the VIth form is dreaming of nylons and lipstick and girls are chewing bits of their rubbers pretending it's gum and putting on American accents. They're nuts. Today was sunny and I rode to the cove where I haven't been for ages. I had to jump down to the beach because the sand had been washed away from the entrance. There was no one there. And I had a letter from James next to my heart that I was saving to open. Sometimes he doesn't say very much but it's such a relief to know that he is still alive and that we are loving each other from different

223

worlds. Some days I hardly think of James at all, and then when I do, I feel anxious because he might be dead. Love shouldn't have to be like that. Auntie says that now the Americans are in it we can't lose. I hope she's right but she's not a general. I was so glad I brought James to the cove. I remember his enormous white feet. They were not very lovely, but they were his. When I tucked them under my arms they felt like ice. I stayed for a long time and remembered every second of us being together. It was the first, and for that matter the only, time anyone had said that I was beautiful. I hope I'm not changed too much by the time he gets back, God willing.

I went to check the shop and definitely someone had been there. Things were out of place and one of the dust covers had been taken off a chair. I thought at first that there'd been a break in but none of the windows or doors had been forced though someone had been in the garden because the grass was flattened. It made me feel creepy as I checked the rooms because it must have been dad, as nobody else has keys. We know he's out of gaol, and now I know he's been to the shop, but I don't understand why he hasn't been to the cottage. I know he doesn't love me but surely he cares a little bit what happens to me.

D. Lanyard 5th May 1944

It seems so long since I kissed James goodbye in the rain and I've changed so much he might not even recognise me. I'm even taller than I was then. Auntie says it's all the nourishment from the Victory garden and she's probably right. We're almost vegetarians except we don't wear sandals. I can now boast a 32inch bust and my nipples are bigger and mysteriously have got darker. Even more mysteriously I've sprouted hair, not much but in all sorts of unlikely places. I'm used to more or less regular periods and certainly know why it's called "the curse." It's absolutely frightful with stomach ache and a terrible dragging feeling in my back, and it will go on and on until I'm old, taking up a quarter of my life. Also, my bottom is changing shape, from two apples to more like two pears, much more womanly auntie would say. I'm not positive but I think I smell different, I used to just smell of soap. Auntie says this is all to the good. She calls me "comely" which makes me sound like an 18th century tart. But I can't think about any of this. I must revise and then revise again. It gets me down.

D. Lanyard 13 May 1945

I've been staying over at Alice's house recently so we can help each other revise. It's modern and has gas fires everywhere and a swish kitchen with a cooker but it doesn't feel as comfy as the cottage, there's something missing. Alice's mum is so house proud, you can't put your cup down anywhere or get crumbs on the carpet so I'm a little bit on edge when she's about, worrying if I'm doing something I shouldn't be. It's got a warm bathroom with a lavatory in it so you don't have to go outdoors which must be lovely in the winter. Her mum can't cook either, not like auntie. She can't make pastry and has never boiled a pudding in her life. Alice and me get on really well it's like having a sister, especially as we share her bed. Sometimes we rub each other, and I imagine it's James. It's lovely but I shouldn't think sisters do it. It is so much easier to do revision when there's the two of us, and we've got the same exam timetable. So far, I've done the English's, Lit and Lang, Hist and the French written paper, we are all dreading the oral because none of us are any good, also done art and music, dead easy Winny could have passed. That leaves the four maths papers to dread, especially trig which is so pointless it's impossible to get the hang of, chem, physics, geog and RK. Poor old Holy Joe, who comes in to teach us, with holes in his jumper and his gown falling off, can't keep discipline to save his soul, so we don't learn anything, which is a nuisance because there's nothing hard about it, unlike chem and physics where's there's just yards and yards of difficult stuff to remember. Most of the girls say how much they hate the exams and how scared and exhausted they are. Actually, although I grumble, I'm enjoying them. Me and Alice went through all the proofs of every theorem in the geom book and I liked it, there is something lovely about the way they all fit together in their own world. I'm secretly hoping for a high grade in art, I might be getting good at it. I've been doing a lot of drawing and painting with James' stuff. In art club Miss Gaymer got the whole group to try out theatre and costume design for the school play and she said mine were EXEMPLARY. As she runs drama club as well, I'm hoping she'll let me help with the designs. Even though the exams are the sort of pinnacle of our time at school and terribly important I can't wait for them to be over because the school play is always the high point of the year for me. Alice is so sporty, she does everything, even shinty which is the most stupid game ever invented, it's like trying to play hockey with upside *down walking sticks. I get out of games whenever I can. Still, my muscles are bigger than Alice's because of the all the gardening and lugging things around I do at the cottage. I always beat her at arm wrestling and that annoys her.*

D. Lanyard 23rd May 1944

When I got back from school today auntie was very quiet. I knew a man had been there because I could smell tobacco. I had told her that I thought someone had been in the shop, so I asked her if it was dad. She said yes and started crying which made me cry. I can't bear it when auntie is upset I get frightened. She cheered up after a while and we went out to feed the chickens. Partenope has stopped laying but I'm still trying to save her from the pot. I come out early to check the eggs, so auntie doesn't notice. Then she told me that dad had come round in a car and said he wanted the keys to the shop because he had sold it, and so I didn't need to look out for it anymore. Then he asked her to keep me for the duration because I was happy at the school. He told her he was going up north to try and set up a new business and when he was settled, and the war was over he'd send for me. Auntie said he didn't stay above half an hour and just as he left, he gave her a bundle of bank notes, £150, to cover my keep, he said. And that was it. He didn't even mention mum. I was panting with joy that he hadn't come to take me away, but I felt so lonely and sad. It proves he doesn't want me and I'm as good as an orphan. I really do thank God for auntie.

D. Lanyard 30ᵗʰ June 1944

In a few weeks I shall leave school forever. I wrote to James about my results, which were better than expected and a great relief. They're good enough to matriculate. A few astronomically brainy [and of course rich] girls are going to University. If you get into Oxbridge you get your name in gold letters on the Honours Board, if it's only Durham or worse, a real redbrick, nobody cares. I don't think I want to go, even if we could afford it and we certainly can't. It's hard to imagine what it would be like. Auntie put £50 of the money dad gave her into the PO for me. James is really kind and sends her some money when he can, but it's not easy for him. I worry that auntie will run out of money and I'll have to leave, but she says the two of us will manage whatever happens, which is so kind it makes me cry. James says that on a captain's pay, once you've paid your batman and all the subs, [I don't know what they are, can't be submarines] there's not a lot left. I shouldn't think he gets much chance to spend it as the Italian war seems to go on forever.

D. Lanyard 7ᵗʰ August 1945

I now at last think I know what I want to do and it is [fanfare followed by drumroll] THEATRE DESIGN, darling. But, [and I like starting sentences with But] I haven't got a clue how to go about it. The problem with something like theatre design is that in the middle of a war [please God we've passed the middle, everybody is so sick to death of it] in the countryside in Devon, there are not going to be many openings for a girl with no training and no experience. I've loved doing the stuff for the Merchant, and if only the school had an orchestra we could have put on an opera. I'd like to do Partenope which is all about women and love, and even though everything I've heard of Handel's sounds the same, I'd love the music. Miss G thinks my best bet is to do a year at art college and then try and get a job as an ASM in a theatre. I'm not sure I want to do that and anyway there's no money. I want to do something with my life, like auntie did before the Japs ruined it. I want so much to be with James, but I can't be a housewife, like my poor mum, at my horrible dad's beck and call all hours. Her life was sad and it came to an awful end. Dad never got in touch after he came to see auntie and we have no idea where he might be. I've never been able to love him he was too cruel to me. I think I hate him, which is a terrible thing to say about a parent and I'd never repeat it in front of auntie. I love her so much and am so grateful. With a dead mum and a disappeared dad, I'd be in a home somewhere or in the workhouse, if they still have them. I wish I could do something marvellous and wonderful for her, like take her on holiday to Margate. Fat chance now but I hope to one day.

'They are all so real,' Annabel said, 'you can't help yourself feeling with her, even though it is so long ago and in a much tougher world than ours. The way she writes pulls you into her life. I can see why you're hooked.'

'I'm so glad you got into them, they are precious to me and I wanted to share them with you. Reading them together definitely lessens my sense of obsession. I do think a lot about Daisy, I feel involved with all the things that happen to her, as though they were part of my life. Her story seems so authentic and I feel tender towards her. Perhaps I want to live in her narrative because I'm not sure that I've got one of my own. She must have adored uncle James. He was the first man to show her any love.'

∽

Emily drove out to CDG to meet Toby off the plane. He had been away for more than a month, mainly in the Middle East, auditing projects in the bits where the west was still welcome. After a final few days in the L'Institut's regional office in Tel Aviv, they had flown back from Ben Gurion, where the security pantomime always annoyed Toby.

The evening traffic was slow, and it took time to park. Toby was waiting in the lounge his flight having landed early. He looked tanned and crumpled and needed a shave. He stood up and opened his arms when he saw her.

'It's good to see you, Toby,' she said, and hugged him tightly. He smelled rather dusty.

'It's great to be back. I find being away from my civil space increasingly irritating. It used to be exciting. The Middle East was such fun, especially Beirut, but it has evaporated. Since Iran, politics has been turning religious with a vengeance, and that goes for Israel as well, nobody wants to read the writing on the wall. God knows what's coming next.'

'Slow down, Toby, you're home.' Emily put her hands on his shoulders and looked into his face.

'Sorry, but you know how one has to constantly suppress what one is actually thinking on these jaunts. That too is becoming irksome. Enough, you are looking your fragrant self, I'm back home, what more could a man want?' Toby pursed his lips, 'Supper.'

'Gesier salad, slow baked shoulder of veal with Dauphinoise and Neufchatel.'

'Life saving provender, a nice flinty Graves would set us up for that.'

'You'll have to make do with Macon.'

'I'm sure I'll cope,' Toby said, 'let's get out of here.'

Emily pushed the trolley as they made their way to the car park. Toby was silent as they drove back to Montmartre. Once in the apartment he flopped on the sofa. Emily pulled his shoes off and gave him, *Le Monde Diplomatique*, *Liberation* and a glass of wine.

'Emily, bless you, cosseting and the promise of a delightful supper. You don't have bad news for me, do you?'

'Not at all, you've been away for ages and I miss you, the world is so dodgy and it's good to see you safely home. There may be something I want to talk about later, but that can wait. We'll eat in about half an hour, that'll give you time for a shower.'

'I'll do that now,' Toby said, getting up slowly, 'ritual purification is always a good move after being out of one's ground for a while.'

Aromatic wafts of thyme and rosemary from the veal, slowly softening in the oven, drifted in from the kitchen. Emily laid the table with a small posy of flowers in the centre and lit the candles. The early spring sun had gone down and she closed the shutters.

During the meal she listened to Toby. He talked about those things that development economists know to be the case but cannot say in public, or sometimes, even to each other.

'Now cherub, you've tolerated my ramblings for long enough. I recall you saying that there was something you wanted to air. I am all yours to dispose of.'

Emily laid her hands on the table and looked at Toby.

Two things. First, when Annabel was here, she met Jean-Marie and that made her curious about him and me. She said I was the first fag-hag she had known and did it mean I never had to worry about other women, how did I feel about Alexis, how was I going to cope with Jean-Marie being HIV positive?'

'Fag-hag – American English spares no blushes, does it?'

'It shocked me. As far as I know I'm with Jean-Marie because I am attracted to him, and he cares for me. I certainly didn't choose him for his sexuality.'

'How is J-M? I haven't asked because I guess I'm not too sure of the answer.'

Emily broke off a small piece of bread, dipped it into Toby's red wine and let it drip before popping it into her mouth.

'He and Alexis are fine. With any luck, the new retrovirals mean that their lives could go on more or less normally. Thankfully, Jean-Marie has calmed down and I'm just trying to be supportive. It's odd, he seems to have bonded with Alexis in a new way. They both came here for supper which was a first, and we had a good evening. I think they are trying out really trusting one another and doing well.'

'It can't be easy for them. Whichever way one looks at it there's this Damoclean edge to things,' Toby said.

'I feel a real connection to Jean-Marie.' Emily picked up her glass but did not drink. 'It's become complicated, our world has changed and so have we, neither of us has managed to say anything about the future.'

Emily got up and cleared the table, coming back with the cheese, bread and some clementines. Toby refilled their glasses. She cut herself a slice of soft ivory cheese and pushed the plate over to Toby.

'That's all good, I'm relieved that you're making sense of what is happening and keeping body and soul together.'

'It's very important to me right now, but what I wanted to talk about is my mother.'

Toby stopped eating and sat back in his chair. He wiped his mouth with his napkin and dropped it onto the table.

'Your mother?'

'Yes. You've been travelling all day and I'm sure you're tired, and I don't really want to spring stuff on you. You don't have to do it now but I want you to tell me about her. Tomorrow will give you time to sleep on it?'

'Tomorrow it is,' Toby said.

Emily lay in bed and asked herself why she had deliberately deferred, even if only by a few hours, finding out about her mother. Fear of what that might entail was plainly the answer.

∽

Emily and Toby, well muffled, sat on a bench along the perimeter of Montmartre cemetery. Wintry sun lit the wide carriageway down to the Avenue Rachel and glinted on the hundreds of tiny oratory roofs above the graves. Feral cats glided through the gaps between the tombs, doing the rounds of the sites where the good people of Montmartre habitually left them small piles of food.

'I want to know about my mother. Looking at my life there's an empty space. I can't say it is mother shaped, because I don't know what shape mothers are. I have no idea what it might have been filled with. When I was at school and girls would talk about their mothers, I would either keep quiet or talk about you. You are my omni-parent, the only person in the world that I totally love and completely trust. We have lived together for the whole of my life and I cannot imagine things to be different and if I'm honest, I don't want them to be.

'Maybe that's why I fell for Jean-Marie, he was never going to rock my boat. But now, he has. Before HIV I might well have said yes to marrying him simply because I couldn't imagine an alternative that I actually wanted, and it would have moved me on in my life without me having to think too deeply about it. I had thought the ménage might still be manageable if I had some legal protection – crazy girl?'

Emily stopped and looked at Toby, he held her hand but did not smile.

'I call you Toby more than papa because you're my best friend. You never try to hurt me, and I know that whatever happens in my world, I can rely on you. But I'm beginning to think I use your love as a place to hide from my life, and I'm not sure what to do about it. I thought my mother might be somewhere to start. I have no memory of her, and I simply never think about her. Biologically I know I must have had one, but that's as far as it goes.

'You knew her, must have loved her, I assume. But you've never encouraged me to be curious about her. I have never even seen a photograph of her. I don't know her address in America, and I am asking myself, why is this?'

The distant hum of traffic in the Avenue Rachel was the only sound. Toby put his arm round Emily's shoulder. He did not meet her eyes.

'Emily, for years I have anticipated this moment but haven't had the will or the courage to bring it about. I so treasure our life together that I have been too careful not to upset the apple cart. To say the least, I have been selfish.

'Your mother and I met when I was nearing thirty and devoted to my career, which was shaping up well. She had a secondment to Paris OECD. She wanted to see Europe, see what all the fuss was about, was how she put it. Our attraction was sudden, mutual and intense. Neither of us knew what we were up to. Lisa became pregnant despite our precautions and decided that she wanted to keep the baby, and to my surprise, she proposed that we get married. I hesitated but was persuaded. I adored her, but even then, looking back, I knew in my heart that I'd got it wrong.

'At some level she was dissatisfied with us, and more obscurely, despite her passion, she would not allow herself to be loved. Perhaps it would have made her too vulnerable to admit emotional dependence. She never took to Europe. She found us effete. Our interest in culture, in theatre, or art or even cheese, to her all this was simply taking one's eye off the ball. Capital ruled the world and economics was the way to power. She found Medicin Sans Frontiere ridiculously romantic.

'During the pregnancy she changed dramatically, she became almost paranoid. I thought this might be more or less normal hormonal swings and roundabouts. Then she wanted to go back to America to have the child, the hospitals were so much better, and it would ensure an American passport from birth. I strongly opposed and she finally gave in. I became increasingly anxious about what was happening to her and to us. There was no sense that this was a wonderful fulfilment of our relationship. For Lisa it was a project that needed to be managed. I began to fear that the initial sense of the madness of love was becoming simply madness. Emotionally I was shut out, the pregnancy and the baby were to be hers. She was young and fit and continued to work until the last minute.'

Toby's eyes watered in the cold breeze. He got out his handkerchief and wiped them. Emily sat mute.

'Your birth was scheduled. You were induced the day after an international colloquium and Lisa was hoping to go to a briefing at Chatham House, in London, a fortnight later. I was not allowed to be present at the birth. I came to visit, and I picked you up. You had weight, substance, a corporeal being in the world, newly sentient, you were a tiny miracle. I loved you immediately.'

An elderly English couple approached and politely asked them, in over formal and accented French, if they knew where the tomb of Emile Durkheim, the sociologist, might be. Toby directed them to the cemetery plan at the south gate and warned them not to expect a monument.

'Lisa wanted to mother you, to feed you. There were problems with her milk. Although you rooted vigorously it didn't always let down. Her nipples became cracked and sore. Creams and nipple shields were used, breast pumps. These things tried her patience and she could not get on with them. She became agitated and angry, finding herself suddenly and uniquely, incompetent. Because of the erratic milk flow mastitis set in which was painful and difficult to treat.

'Then suddenly she flipped. She became delusional and stopped functioning. We were responsible for a little life and she was neglecting you. I would find you in sopping nappies and unfed. When you cried she would just stare at you. She accused me of imprisoning her and of trying to make her mad. I engaged a nurse but Lisa would not cooperate and the nurse left. Finally, I had no choice but to call in a doctor who thought Lisa was psychotic and she had her committed to hospital. The diagnosis was post-natal depression and the prognosis, a full recovery.

'For me it was a terrifying time. I have never been so frightened. You were weeks old and we were on our own. Lisa's mother and brother came over from the States but barely spoke to me. They simply went to the courts to try and have you made their ward, in order to take you back to

America. I employed a full-time professional children's nurse to prove that I could look after you. I could not contemplate losing you and was afraid they might try and kidnap you. They were determined to take possession of Lisa's child. They could not believe that some hybrid Eurotrash, who must have tricked Lisa into marrying him and, undoubtedly made Lisa pregnant against her will, could reasonably have a valid claim. My *avocat* was good. I had permanent residency and qualified for French citizenship. I had secure, well-paid employment and, intended to stay in France and have you apply for citizenship at age sixteen. I don't know what else he said, but the judge ruled in my favour. Perhaps because there was no reason to suppose the mother would not be restored to health and, maternal competence, in due course. I was hugely relieved, the more so when my antagonists returned to the states after failing to persuade Lisa to leave and go with them.

'Lisa was in hospital for seven months. Throughout she would barely acknowledge me and remained implacably hostile. When I finally brought her back to the apartment, she would not look at you and she would not speak to me. All she did was pack a weekend bag, collect her passport and leave for Orly. That was the last time I saw her face to face.'

The rigidity of shock on Emily's face crumpled and she began to cry. Toby stood up and gave her his handkerchief. He put his arms round her as tears dropped on his shoulder.

'Papa, I had no idea.'

'There is more, I'm afraid. Do you want me to go on, or have you had enough for now?'

'I want to know everything, but it's too much to take in – that it's me and you we are talking about, but in a place I never knew existed.'

'I'm too cold to stay here,' Toby said, banging his hands together, 'and it will be dark soon. Let's go home and stop by the *traiteur* to collect something for supper. Going back hurts.' He put his arm round Emily's shoulder as they walked down the long, wide avenue to the street.

∽

Back in the apartment they sat on sofas facing one another across the sitting room. Gas from the fake log fire hissed faintly behind clear glass. Random street noises punctuated the silence. Little had been eaten.

'That was it,' Toby said, 'Lisa never spoke to me again. We were erased, as though we had never happened.'

Emily kicked off her slippers and curled her feet under her in the corner of the sofa.

'I was beside myself. I could not see how or why Lisa was abandoning us in such a way, and without explanation. I kept trying to think what I had done, or what I might do to bring her back, or at least get her to acknowledge you. I felt we were both being punished for some unfathomable crime. I found it hard to connect with work and the Director suggested I take time out, but I thought that without the anchor of rational demand I might mentally collapse myself.'

'I feel really apprehensive,' Emily said, 'but I know we survived because we are here. Did you try and contact her, did you go to America to find her?'

'She had been back in the US for a few weeks when she filed for divorce. I wrote to her via her attorney to try and get her to discuss access, I had given up the idea of reconciliation. She never replied. I tried to phone her mother. As soon as she knew it was me, she would hang up. The lawyers made it plain to me that she would not contest custody, nor seek access and that any future communication would be solely through them. We were excised from her life.

'Much later I began to see that perhaps this was for the best. After what had happened between us, I was not sure that Lisa and I would have been able to recover a workable relationship, one that would have allowed us to nurture you. But I still thought she would change her mind and certainly want you in her life in some way.

'We were so lucky to find Nicole. She looked after you for those crucial years, and gave you love. She saved us. Without her I would not have been able to travel with any sense of your security, and that would have been the end of my career.'

'I did love Nicole, papa, and it broke my heart when she went to Perpignan. She did mother me and I certainly took her for granted. I thought she would always be there, like you.'

Toby poured some brandy into his glass and raised an eyebrow at Emily. She shook her head.

'It was not easy to know what to do for the best. I often thought I should remarry, but the life we had made worked and changing it seemed a high-risk strategy. I know I was damaged by Lisa. You never took to any of the women that I brought home and my heart was not really in it, and so it never happened.'

Toby emptied his glass and sat biting his lower lip, his eyes cast down. Emily got up and put her arms around his shoulders. Toby took her hands and held them in front of him.

'Sit down, cherub,' he said, 'there is a final act to come that shows my absolute moral weakness and cowardice.'

Emily sat on the sofa, pulled a cushion onto her lap and hugged it.

'Development economics is a small world. I knew that your mother was in New York, working for a second-tier merchant bank and that her career had not gone particularly well. Le Gros had met her at a dinner and recognised her. I did nothing. Then when you were about twelve and ready to go to the Lycée, I got an express from her lawyers. I remember the formality of their language they might have been French. They regretted to inform me that Lisa had died in an automobile accident, no other vehicles or persons were involved. If necessary, they would inform me of the contents of her will. They never did.

'I decided almost instantly, I'm ashamed to say, that I would not share this with you. I felt no grief myself only a passing stab and a lingering sadness for what I conjecture was an unhappy life. I told myself that you would be unable to mourn someone you had never known, let alone been mothered by, and that you might find it emotionally confusing.'

'Confusing?' Emily said. 'Dear god, my mother has lived and now has died with me knowing nothing of her. That cannot be right. It feels as though you are talking about some other people's lives, not ours.' She threw the cushion on the floor and looked around the room, everywhere but at Toby.

'I've been living with only part of the script, like some poor Elizabethan actor. I don't know who I might have been. What about uncle James? Did you tell him never to mention her?'

'Of course not. James knew it all and there was no conspiracy. I guess he discovered you knew nothing, and probably thought the less of me because of it, but would not have seen it as his duty to fill in the gaps. He loved your company and unwittingly you helped him escape that negativity that had made him reclusive for so long. He was able to close his long mourning for Daisy, something that he would never speak about. I guess, at some point he was abandoned, like me. Why else would it be a closed book?

'Lisa's death made me think that I should be more

available for you. I left the institute for a few years, and you'll remember I took an academic job. Much less money but it gave me a lot more flexibility. I kept up with colleagues and when I thought that you were, more or less, through your adolescence I returned to the fray, thanks to my good friend the Director. As you know one is only measured by the size of one's latest grant and the prestige value of one's consultancies, and I was good at getting both.

'I enjoyed those few years. Not having a wife was an advantage in avoiding endless socialising with colleagues. I never truly enjoyed dinner parties and much preferred to spend my evenings with you, helping insofar as I was able, with the *devoir du soir*. And then it all seemed too late, how could I broach the topic of a dead mother with my teenage daughter? I should have been able to, but I was not. What can I say?'

'I don't understand, papa, how can I? I never thought I didn't have a mother, but there·was no evidence. Nothing there to ask questions about. Perhaps I imagined it might be a dark and dangerous place that would threaten our shared world, which is pretty much what you thought, isn't it?'

Toby poured more Calvados and this time Emily joined him.

'I've relied on us to see me through,' Toby said, 'allowed all our eggs to congregate in our little basket. I thought you would reject me as you got older. I braced myself for the adolescent rebellion, but it never came. To my surprise and I have to admit relief, we forged what felt to me like a mutually supportive adult *modus vivendi*. I fear that our interdependence has encouraged us to be more insular than is good for us, again, my selfishness. I never encouraged you to look beyond us to definitively become your own person. You've plenty of friends but I've never encouraged you to value them have I? I don't know what more to say, and I'm in danger of rambling. Am I a monster, Emily?'

Emily stood up her body sagged as though she had been punched. She ran her hands through her hair and looked blankly at Toby.

'I think you may be, papa, it's hard for me to judge right now.'

Emily went to her room and closed the door. Toby moved to the table and sat down. He folded his arms and laid his head on them. Thus, he fell asleep.

Emily lay on her bed feeling stunned, exhausted and wide awake. No sense could be made of what had occurred. Now I know that I will never know my mother, ever. She knew she still loved Toby, there was no way she could not. He must have suffered, and she hated the thought of his years of pain, alive within him, hidden from her. The unsettling thing was the continued hiding, that was deceit from the person she trusted most in the world. Perhaps she should get some distance.

Chapter 13

'JAMES, IS IT REALLY YOU?'

The man who stood in the cottage doorway, the morning sun at his back, was tanned with short hair, leaner than the young officer who had left the cottage in his staff car long ago. His coat was open, his tunic undone he wore no hat. Dropping his dirty grey kitbag he stepped forward put his hands on Daisy's shoulders and looked at her intently.

Daisy trembled as his arms encircled her and held her very tightly. She pulled back and touched his face, tracing lines round his mouth that were new. She looked down and gently took his hands. They were rough and red, like farmers' hands, not the white hands of the artist who had left for the war.

'Daisy.'

He kissed her at first softly, then with increasing ardour. They broke away and both burst out laughing.

'I suppose this is actually happening?' Daisy said, 'I'm not imagining you, am I?'

She pulled him into the sitting room, his dusty greatcoat fell to the floor and Daisy clasped him to her.

'It's been so long,' she said, 'so long.' She pressed her lips against his, her hands held his head as she kissed his cheeks, his eyes, his forehead. James wrapped his arms tightly round her. Daisy ran her hands along the hard contours of his back. For some time nothing was said as they held on to each other.

'I'm so sorry, I couldn't warn you. My papers arrived out of the blue, my CO let me go before they could be countermanded. I got a boat almost immediately, which was a great stroke of luck. It was chaos, food and water were hard to come by and we bathed in briny, but no-one cared, we were bound for Blighty. I did manage to get a shave at Southampton, but I must smell like a barnyard.'

Hilda came in from the garden, screamed, and rushed at James, who hugged her.

'James, welcome home, what a wonderful deliverance, it does my heart good to see you. Daisy, I'm so happy for you both, thank God, it really is a Red Letter Day.'

'Hilda, it's a miracle to me, to find the cottage still here, and you both still in it. It's odd, but everything seems a little bit unreal, as though I'm in a play or a picture, but my beautiful Daisy is real.'

He held Daisy's hands and stepped back, looking at her, his face creased in smiles. Daisy, who was not long out of bed as it was Saturday, cast her eyes down. She had on her shapeless orange jumper from schooldays, that hardly fitted anywhere, with rather muddy gardening trousers, and on her feet black plimsolls without laces. She raked the sides of her hair with her fingers.

'James, I must look such a fright. I never thought…'

'Transcendently beautiful,' James said, 'a Botticelli nymph, dressed for the outdoors.'

Daisy burst out laughing and put her arms round James' neck. Tears rolled down her cheeks.

'I'll put the kettle on,' Hilda said, 'if I'd known you were coming, I'd have baked a cake, as the song goes.' She called back from the kitchen, 'I can do you a couple of slices of toast and dripping.'

'Anything you can spare, gratefully received,' James called back, 'I haven't eaten for a while.'

Daisy pulled James to the hearth and put him in the carver. She sat on the hearthrug and put her head on his knee, slipping her arm round his legs. James stroked her hair. Winny sauntered in from the kitchen licking his lips and jumped up on James' lap. Hilda came in with the tea tray.

'I don't want to spoil things Daisy, but what are you going to do about the matinee this afternoon?' she said.

Daisy's face fell and she jumped up.

'James, this is awful. I'd completely forgotten. How can I leave you? I'll be afraid that this is a dream and when I get back, you'll be in Anzio or Berlin.'

'I don't want to lose you the second I've found you either, Daisy. I didn't realise, I hadn't thought of you working. But no matter, I promise you I am exhausted. I've barely eaten or slept for four days. I'll curl up with Winny while you're gone, I'm used to grabbing sleep when I can.'

Daisy leaned over and put her palms on his chest.

'James, I'm so sorry. I'll have to go, we all depend on one another, the cast are doubling and trebling roles as it is, and hardly anyone's word perfect, they're going to need a prompter. I don't have to do the evening performance, so I'll be back by six with any luck and I don't have to go until two o'clock. I'll make you as comfortable as I can before that.'

'Don't worry, Daisy,' Hilda said, 'I'm going over to Tom's to see what I can scrounge for supper and, when you go, James can put his feet up and rest for a bit.'

When Hilda had gone, they were quiet for a while. James stood up and stretched.

'Let's walk round the garden, I want to remind myself of

everything I left behind. I'm still amazed I'm here. We can say hello to Fanny, I'm glad your accident didn't put you off riding.'

'Not a bit,' Daisy said, 'I'm saving up for an Ariel Square Four. If I had one now, I could drive you to the cove.'

Clouds scudded across the horizon. Fitful shafts of brilliant morning light broke through. A light south westerly breeze ruffled the leaves that had begun to turn from green to russet. James stood by the shed door and looked at Fanny.

'It's not built for two and the engine is small, but one of us on the luggage rack might just work, if we go carefully, and slowly. You're lighter, so although it won't be comfortable, it would be safer if you rode pillion.'

'Worth a try,' Daisy said, 'I'll put something in a sack and tie it on.'

'I think you're both mad,' Hilda said, when Daisy asked for a cushion, 'take the well stuffed one off the Ottoman, and make sure you wear your helmet, and don't run over the Bobby.'

The route to the cove was mainly along little used lanes. There were only a couple of inclines where gravity won out and they had to get off and push. At the top of the cliffs they stopped and left Fanny in the lee of an abandoned miners' hut. Daisy rubbed her buttocks vigorously.

'Bags you're on the back on the way home,' she said, 'I'm black and blue. We must have looked ridiculous. Thank goodness we never had to do that when you met me from school, I would never have lived it down.'

'Too proud by half,' James said, 'that's not the spirit that won the war.'

He held Daisy's hand, pulled her to him and kissed her.

They began the precipitous descent, tacking along the paths cut in the side of the steep slopes of rock leading down to the narrow fissure, that opened into the cathedral grandeur of the semi-circle of ancient stone forming the walls of the cove. A carpet of glistening white sand shelved gently towards the sea.

'The storms weren't too bad last winter,' Daisy said, looking at the massive boulders strewn around the base of the cliff and filling the caves, 'so the furniture hasn't been rearranged much.'

They left their shoes and socks on a rock above the strand line. With trousers rolled up past their knees and, holding hands, they walked down towards the breakers. The soft wet sand was cold beneath their feet and the sea was icy.

'I've come here a lot while you've been away, to think about us and remember your big white cold feet that froze my armpits when I tried to warm you up. Now you're here I can scarcely credit it.'

Daisy shifted her stance as the ebb of the waves pulled at the sand, undermining her feet.

'I suppose we'll get used to things soon, then I won't have to keep looking at you to see if you've evaporated.'

'Too solid flesh I assure you,' James said.

Daisy cupped her hand and flicked some water at James' face.

'You can't do that to a Major it's against regulations.'

'You're not in the Army now, I can do what I want.'

James advanced on Daisy who splashed him again before wading to the beach and running back to the rocks.

'I'm still on reserve,' James said, 'they could call me back any time.'

'Don't say that, I'd die.'

They lay side by side on the sand looking up at the sky.

Daisy propped herself on one elbow and looked at James.

'What do we do now?' she said. 'What will happen to us?'

'That depends a lot on you, Daisy. We never became engaged because it seemed the wrong thing to do, but we did exchange our love tokens. Your cross has been with me since the last time we met. I gave you my ring and all my love, and you still have them both.'

Lifting Daisy's hand, he kissed the signet ring and looked into her face.

'Will you marry me, Daisy?'

Daisy closed her eyes and then reopened them.

'My darling, James, of course I will.'

Daisy leant over and kissed his lips. She stood up and pulled him to his feet. They walked along the beach around the headland to a cave sheltered by an outcrop of granite. They sat together on the sand. Below them a flock of teetering sandpipers darted back and forth along the foaming edge of the breaking waves. Daisy raised her jumper to her armpits and nestled James' head against her breast. He stroked her alabaster skin and kissed her nipples.

∽

On the way back they stopped at an inn, no more than the front parlour of a farmhouse with some racked barrels in a side room. They took their drinks outside and sat on a bench against the wall, looking out over a pasture where sheep slowly ambled, heads down. Daisy nibbled an Arrowroot biscuit.

'Cheers,' James said, 'my first English beer for years.'

The susurration of the breeze, birdsong and the occasional bleating of the sheep amiably filled the silence that fell between them.

'There's just too much to take in. It's like I've been on another planet, and now I'm back and it's hard to believe in that other world. It's as though my past belongs to someone else but it still feels so tangible, so close. I can't tell you what Italy was like. It wasn't a nightmare, some of the patriots were incredibly heroic and very good to us. But long periods of acute boredom, interrupted by brief periods of gut-wrenching fear is a very wearing existence.

'I felt responsible for my men and that kept me focused. But in the front of my mind I always had you to live for, and at times not wanting to die because I loved you was all that kept me going.'

Daisy put her hand in his and squeezed it. She lifted her head and kissed his cheek.

'We are real,' she said, 'I know we are'.

⁓

Daisy lay on the settee, her head on a cushion, her legs dangling over the armrest. Milling dust thickened the Autumn sun that fell across the polished wood and lit the Persian carpet making brilliant the pomegranate pinks and deep blues. From the gramophone, the words of Liu, the unhappy slave girl, singing to Turandot in a Peking garden, washed over her. Early in the day James had gone to Exeter on some business. Their visit to Fr Julian to talk about the wedding, she wanted the bells to peel and a choir, had made it all seem very real and imminent. It was going to happen.

Daisy was still unsure how she felt about it or how she should be feeling. She didn't dread it but weren't girls meant to be ecstatically happy, wasn't it supposed to be the most significant day of their lives? With her dad God knows where there was no-one to give her away. Hilda had volunteered, but

Fr Julian thought it might look a bit odd, and Daisy wanted her as Matron of Honour, so Hilda had asked Tom Dacre, whom, she said, was tickled pink by the idea. Daisy thought they could just forget it, it was only a bit part, but she kept quiet.

She got up and stood looking out of the window, down the garden to the trees in the lane. She had put off giving notice to the Theatre, had not even told them she was to be married. It would have to be done. And there was Alice who was to be a bridesmaid. Daisy had found herself thinking it would be nice if Alice could come and live with them, she was going to miss her terribly.

The record began to slow, Daisy lifted the heavy arm off the disc and ran her finger under the steel needle before unscrewing it and inserting another. After winding the gramophone, the new needle was gently lowered onto the shellac. James had said they would have an electric one when they moved to Campiston. He had shown Daisy some faded snapshots of a posh house and garden, but they didn't convey much. She had tried to imagine herself in some large Sussex country pile but her mind would not go there.

Since she and James had agreed to marry the texture of things seemed to have changed, even Hilda and Winny had taken on new meanings. While not exactly alien, the world had become uncomfortably temporary. I will continue, Daisy said to herself, but my world might end before it begins again.

The music stopped and was replaced by the repetitive scratching of a needle in a circular groove. Daisy returned the arm to its rest and switched the machine off.

Rex had let her come home to work on the designs for Me and my Girl. It was an ambitious choice for the small company, and he had taken on professional singers for the leads. He wanted to run it for a fortnight, or even longer if the reviews were good enough. If it flopped, then there would not be the wherewithal for a panto at Christmas. He could not give Daisy more money, but he was relieving her of much of the ASM donkey work. For a musical show the sets and costumes were critical to its success. Daisy was determined to make them brilliant, even though the budget was on the small side. Casting was done and rehearsals had started. Everyone was excited and willing the production to be fabulous. She tripped up the stairs to her room singing, The Sun Has Got His Hat On, and leafing through fashion plates from the early thirties.

∽

Daisy started at the unusual sound of a motorbike and the loud tooting of a horn. She flew downstairs and out into the garden. In the lane James sat astride a large red machine. He eased open the throttle as Daisy came down the path towards him, and the engine roared. Daisy stood in front of it with her mouth open.

'James, what have you done? It's a Square Four how did you get it?'

'Easy, I wrote the cheque and the man gave me the bike. Get your helmet and I'll show you what she can do.'

'James, how lovely, I can't believe it, please let me drive, please.'

'Not a chance, far too powerful for a mere slip of a girl.'

Daisy pouted and turned to go back to the cottage. She returned moments later swinging her helmet by the strap.

'It's very different to Fanny,' James said. 'I will teach you, but to begin with it weighs about four times as much and it goes three times as fast.'

Daisy got up behind James on the small pillion seat mounted above the rear mudguard. She put her arms round him, lay her head on his back and gave herself over to the thrill of speed. James threw the bike around the lanes and opened the throttle wide whenever the road would allow. He pulled up when they came to Marleigh wood. They walked hand in hand to the clearing where they would stop and kiss on the way back from school.

'James, that was wonderful,' Daisy said, 'being on the bike with you brought it all back, how much I loved you. I remember as you kissed me thinking that nothing in my life could ever approach the perfect happiness of being with you.'

James squeezed her and kissed her hair.

'My darling, Daisy, I could not love you more.'

On the way back to Yew Tree Cottage, Daisy felt inexplicably sad. I'm mourning my lost youth and I'm not much more than a child.

∽

'Blame the army,' James said. 'I prefer bikes. They're cheaper to run than a car easier to look after and more exciting, except when it's raining.'

They sat round the table in the kitchen. James wore civvies for the first time since his return.

'Puts little Fanny in the shade,' Hilda said, 'makes her seem quite sedate.'

'Porridge made with milk is so lovely and creamy, and Fanny doesn't give a fig,' Daisy said. She scraped the last traces of sticky oats from the bowl of the soup plate. 'Is there any more?'

'No, that's your lot,' Hilda said. 'I thought it would be a treat, provide a bit of ballast seeing as James has to ride all the way to Sussex today.'

'I wish I were going with you,' Daisy said, 'I'd love to see your house.'

'I can't take you, Daisy. The county would have a collective fit if I arrived with a beautiful young woman in tow before we were married.'

'If we bought a ring, I could just put it on,' Daisy said, 'no one would know.'

Hilda laughed.

'I bet you would as well. It's all those thesp's you mix with, morals of guttersnipes by all accounts.'

Daisy frowned.

'It's not practical, Daisy. I'll have to stay in Lewes for a few days before it's habitable. It's going to be quite odd to see the White Hart Inn again. I used to have tea there on the rare occasions I saw my parents. Some of the old waiters got honourable mentions in the Domesday book.'

'I wouldn't mind sleeping on the floor,' Daisy said.

'The house has been shut up for so long. The garden will be derelict, and I'll probably need a machete to find the front door. I want the house to be at least liveable in when we go there together.'

Daisy got up, cleared the plates from the table and piled them on the draining board beside the stone sink.

'I'll write as soon as I've seen the place and send you a report. I don't even know if the roof is still on. The furniture might be more riddled with woodworm than when I left. The kitchen and stuff like that can wait until we are both there. I used to paint in the drawing room as it had the best light. I'll have to build a studio, probably in the garden, I really need to get painting again.'

'Will I be able to use it?' Daisy said.

'Of course, and now I'd better get going.'

He picked up his helmet from the floor. I might as well

wear this, seeing as I bought it. I think it's my reflex about wanting to stay alive for you. I don't think I'd bother left to myself.'

Daisy went with him to get the bike from Fanny's shed and followed him out to the road.

'Things seem like they were, but they're not,' she said, 'go carefully, James. I suppose it's the war, but I don't want to let you out of my sight.'

'I'll be careful, and I'll be back as soon as I can be, shouldn't be more than a few days. I guess I'll move into Marleigh until the wedding. I've trespassed on Hilda's goodness too much as it is.'

'You don't have to you know that. Hilda loves you being here.' Daisy stroked his arm.

'I think I should. It won't be for long.' He kissed her.

James strapped his kitbag on the pillion, swung his leg over the bike and kick started the engine but it petered out. He tried again but it would not fire.

'Sorry, Daisy, too much choke, I'll get used to it, but for now how about a push?'

James pushed the bike forward and jumped into the saddle. Daisy put her hands on the pillion and ran down the lane. The engine fired and the bike accelerated away. He waved as he disappeared.

She stood in the lane listening to the fading engine, remembering another time she had pushed James on his bike. Hilda came out of the cottage and put her arm round Daisy.

'It's going to be awfully quiet round here when you're gone, my love.'

Daisy turned and buried her head in Hilda's shoulder.

'You've done it haven't you?' Alice said. 'You've actually had a fuck with James.'

'You are so coarse,' Daisy said, 'although it is true intimacy has taken place. Do you remember Esther Radcliffe said that it made you bandy legged.'

'Strange girl. Didn't Hilda hear you? It can be noisy, can't it?'

'Thankfully, the contingency didn't arise. We were al fresco, down at the cove, actually, and the sea made more noise than we did.'

'How long does it take?'

'I'm not sure, I foolishly forgot my virgin's stopwatch.'

'An hour, ten minutes, you must have some idea. What was it like? Did he have a Johnny? You might be pregnant, right now. What do you want a boy or a girl? Did you enjoy it?'

'Alice, give over. If you had given me your list of questions beforehand I could have taken notes.'

'Sorry,' Alice said, 'but you must admit it's all pretty amazing and there's no-one else I can ask, you're my best friend in the world.'

'I know,' Daisy said.

Blue hydrangeas nodded in the breeze. The two young women sat side by side in striped deckchairs on the smooth lawn, mown in dark and light stripes. On the low rattan table in front of them stood a glass jug of lemonade, a lace doily, weighted with coloured beads, covered the mouth of the jug. The still warm sun of an Indian summer shone through the trees. The only sound was the quiet hum of insects.

Alice stretched and took off her khaki ribbed jumper, pulling her arms inside the torso she lifted it over her head. She dropped it on the grass and shook her mass of dark hair. She turned to smile at Daisy and took her hand in her own to stroke it. Daisy got up and Alice lifted one of her legs. Daisy took the toe and heel of her boot and pulled, first one and then the other. She stood them upright beside the table. Daisy sat down and sipped her drink.

'Where did she get the lemons?' she said.

'Not a clue, probably some friend with a large conservatory. The farm I'm working on now has espaliered peaches along a south wall, but I doubt they amount to much.'

'It's delicious,' Daisy said, and lay back, her hands behind her head.

Alice sat up and looked at her.

'Come on, you've got to tell me all about it.'

'I'm not sure I can. It didn't seem completely real, or rather I felt I was part of it but also a sort of observer. I don't know what I was expecting, something soft and dreamy, but it certainly wasn't like that. Kissing was lovely but then things got a bit awkward.'

'Maybe it's like riding a bike,' Alice said, 'takes a bit of practice.'

'Perhaps, but when you and me are in bed together I feel connected to you, but it was almost the opposite with James, I felt rather alone. It was like he was doing something to me that I didn't need to be much involved with.'

They sat for a while, looking down the garden while the chiaroscuro played in the trees.

'I didn't feel romantic. He pushed his nob into me and moved it up and down, which was pleasant. It didn't seem to be going anywhere but he got very excited, then he pulled it out and sort of grunted and made my knickers all sticky with spunk. He gave me his handkerchief to wipe them, which was so embarrassing. I'm sorry, perhaps I shouldn't have told you, I don't want to put you off. I should have said it was just like the films, but it wasn't.'

'Sounds rather ghastly, and you'll have to do it all the time when you're married. What does it have to do with love?'

'I think you have to love someone to let them do it to you. Perhaps over time and if you're in the right mood it might be fine.'

'Blimey,' Alice said, 'I've been wondering if I should let Arthur. I think I'd rather eat mud. Did you have to touch his nob? What does it look like?'

'No, I didn't, and it looked like a wrinkly saveloy.'

Alice burst out laughing.

'What if he wants to do it every night and every morning before breakfast?' Alice said.

'I might have to pretend I've always got a period, I've just got no idea how often you're expected to do it.'

'It is funny,' Alice said, 'it's impossible to imagine my mum and dad at it. If he made her knickers sticky she'd scream. There's no chance of me risking that with Arthur he'd be sure to mess it all up in any case.'

Daisy shivered, the sun had slipped to the horizon and the breeze began to feel chill.

'I'm so glad I'm staying with you tonight. We must see one another as much as we can now the wedding date's fixed. After that you'll still be in Devon, and I'll be in Sussex.'

'I'm not even thinking about it,' Alice said, 'come on, let's go and play pontoon before we eat.'

Alice jumped up, pulled Daisy out of her chair and folded her in her arms. They stood in the fading light listening to the birds chirruping as they settled for the night.

Chapter 14

THE TRAIN WAS OVER AN HOUR LATE AS IT SNAKED OUT OF Gare du Nord. *Un perturbation* at the tunnel was the cause, nothing specific was ever mentioned. Emily sat and watched the suburbs slide by the window, occasionally punctuated by a shimmering logo, apparently suspended in mid-air floating in the murky morning light. Emily was intensely aware of herself, a sense that was so strong it gave her the uncomfortable illusion of her emotional state being visible to others. She could find no words to describe what she was feeling, it most certainly was not numb. Something somewhere was hurting. What she could not locate was the person she had been a few days before. Was her sense of herself in the world so tenuous, that she allowed something crucial, like the existence of a mother, to remain sequestered into her adulthood? And Toby, the lodestone of her life forever, how could he have kept it hidden for so many years? And now, am I running away? Physically, clearly yes. Leaving the internship would be a permanent blot on her CV, and with jobs so scarce did it make sense? No. Paris is a small town, it might be difficult to recover. Right now, she was not sufficiently connected to the outside to care.

Snow fell, flakes shot past the window in meteor showers. Emily was mesmerised by the whirling landscape, trees showed as grey blurs wheeling in arcs, as the train careened towards Pas de Calais. What had her mother looked like? How did she sound, move, smell, laugh? She had tried saying, mama, out loud but it sounded mawkish and repellent, trying to conjure the ghost of an unknown person.

Emily took the tube to Victoria where she texted Dan who was to meet her at Lewes. He had seemed unfazed when she called him earlier to say she was coming and so thankfully she did not have to explain her trip. Dan, slightly scrofulous and beaming was waiting at the barrier. He took her bag as they walked across the car park.

'This is a lovely surprise, I didn't expect to see you so soon,' he said.

'This is not a planned visit,' Emily said, 'I just wanted to get out of Paris for a while. I'm tired now, but I'll tell you all about it later.'

'That's fine. I dropped by and turned the heat on and lit the fire in the study, I think there might be a bit of damp in there,' Dan said. 'I've put a curry and stuff in the fridge in case you're peckish.'

'That's really kind, Dan, I don't deserve you.'

'A lot of people say that,' Dan said.

Emily leaned over and kissed his cheek.

'How are things with you?' She asked, 'How's college going?'

∽

Emily got up and went for a pee. She looked at her pale face and piggy eyes in the mirror and, briefly tried gurning to bring some animation to the image. She closed her eyes and turned away. Grind some coffee beans, if there are any, the smell might just invigorate. And coffee would help with the shock.

After a moment's disorientation on waking, she had recognised the dark tousled mop of hair and the plump white arm that lay on the duvet as belonging to Dan. This had not improved her hangover, and her immediate thought was, what have I done? Only mildly tempered by a vague remembrance of unexpected tenderness. She recalled Annabel's crass remark about Jean-Marie's sexuality saving Emily from "other women." For herself, being in a ménage put a necessary gloss on the idea of sexual fidelity, but this might not be the same for Annabel? And Dan, she must impress upon him that it was simply an expression of need in a vulnerable moment, and not a declaration of anything whatsoever. I've come here because I want some space and I've done this as soon as I arrive. It must be tidied up and cleared away, right now.

The face in the mirror was looking more human and capable, a good sign. An immense groan came from the bedroom, followed by the sound of feet flapping on the floorboards. Dan appeared, naked, at the bathroom door. He looked very white and where Jean-Marie had contoured muscle, Dan sported soft pneumatic curves. He yawned and ran his hands through his hair, showing black tufts underarm, where Jean-Marie had none at all. Dan vigorously rubbed his face and shook his head.

'Oh God, Emily, what can I say? I really didn't mean to, I am so, so sorry. I so don't want to fuck things up.'

'It's not the end of civilization, Dan. And don't be such a bloody chauvinist, it takes two to shag, and we did it. Perhaps it wasn't one of the best things we've done, and I admit I didn't see it coming…'

Dan grinned.

'For fuck's sake grow up. So far as I can see the only issue here is Annabel. We'll have some coffee and agree what to do.

I'm going to shower now and then I suggest you do. I'll see you in the kitchen shortly.'

Emily fetched her towelling robe. Dan started shaving with Toby's razor. She took a towel out of the airing cupboard and threw it to him.

'Catch, you'll find a guest toothbrush under the basin.'

Emily hung her robe up took off her nightdress and stepped into the shower. The blurred image of Dan at his ablutions could be seen through the glass. In the bedroom a phone rang.

'Ignore it,' she shouted, as Dan began to move.

'Just having a piss,' he said, and disappeared into the loo next door.

Emily wrapped herself in her robe, went back to her bedroom and quickly dressed. The call had been from Jean-Marie. He would like very much to come for the weekend arriving Friday, if that was alright with her.

Emily quickly texted.

'Of course, be lovely to see you. Let me know your ETA. I'll pick you up.'

Preoccupied as she was, the question of why he might want to see her was put to one side.

Dan came into the kitchen, pulled out a chair and sat on the opposite side of the table to Emily. She poured him some coffee but made no offer of breakfast.

'What do you think we should do about Annabel?' Emily said.

'I don't know. I guess we should tell her. It would be sort of dishonest if we didn't.'

'If we all had to own up to everything, life wouldn't work.' Emily said. 'Let's be clear. This is not the beginning of a love story. I have a perfectly competent lover and do not need, or want, another. Last night, I desperately needed comforting and you were good enough to stay. If we hadn't drunk so much it would never have happened. It's important we don't get it out of proportion.'

'No, I'm sorry, of course not,' Dan said, 'but…'

'But what?'

'Nothing, I guess, nothing.'

'I'm not being being cross with you,' Emily said, 'I'm angry with myself for letting it happen.'

She got up and fetched a pack of croissants from the cupboard. They bore the legend, 'Made with Charente Butter.' Breaking into the packet as she sat down, she offered one to Dan. He took one and put it on the table in front of him.

'We don't want anyone to be hurt. I know the English take sex seriously. How do you think Annabel will take it if we tell her?'

'I think she would be hurt but I hope she'd get over it,' Dan said. 'We've never discussed anything long term…'

Emily made more coffee and re-filled their mugs.

'So far as you and I are concerned, it happened and that's that and now back to good friends, am I right?' Emily said.

'Yes,' Dan said, 'if that's possible.'

'That's up to us. I'm not sure we should tell Annabel.' Emily said. 'We keep quiet and carry on as normal. What do you think?'

'Yes, I suppose we could,' Dan said.

'It might be a bit difficult right now, Dan, but the three of us get on so well. You're sort of my English family and I don't want to mess it up.'

'Right, of course,' Dan said. He got up and stood with his hands on the back of his chair. 'I'd best be going. I said I'd help Guy do some furniture moving this morning.'

He put on his boots and coat and stood by the garden door.

'There was something I wanted to go over with you, but it can wait,' he paused, 'It might have been a mistake, but I can't think that I've ever made a better one.'

Emily came around the table and kissed his forehead. She opened the door and Dan stood on the flags outside looking back into the kitchen.

'I think we'd better give it a few days before you come over,' Emily said, and gently closed the door.

Dan's car started and Emily listened to the engine as it bumped down the drive. She sat immobile for some minutes. I must find something to do she thought. I'll change the sheets.

∽

A few days passed and Emily was glad of the respite and looked forward to seeing Jean-Marie. From the window at breakfast she saw the studio and realised she had hardly taken notice of it since finding Daisy's portrait. The house and garden had claimed all her energy and attention. Perhaps it should be left as it is, a memento of James and Daisy, a place where she could imagine them working together side by side. She made some coffee, put on James' old Barbour and took it down the garden. The studio was as she had left it, except a few deck chairs had gathered against the wall.

Emily lit the stove and collected some of the sketchpads and piles of loose sheaves that lay around the place. The battered chest of drawers was full of the rubble of a working studio. One large drawer held dozens of dull metal paint tubes many hard with age. In another were bottles of oil and turpentine with rusted tops, tins of varnish, brushes of every size, many caked with paint, long marl sticks, paint knives with broken blades and rags stiff with pigment. Tucked into the side of the drawer she found three envelopes in the now familiar hand of Daisy all with James' BFPO address. Emily turned the grey dry paper over in her hands. Daisy must have written many letters to James but probably it was not easy to hang on to them while fighting a war in a foreign country.

She pushed the chaise nearer to the fire and sat down, tucking her legs underneath her and sipping her coffee. The first two envelopes proved disappointingly empty. The third postmarked September nineteen forty-six contained a single sheet of badly foxed thin paper. Daisy had written in a small hand to make the most of the paper.

Dearest Darling James,

This war is still confusing me. I thought the Italians surrendered years ago and yet you have been fighting the Germans there, it seems forever. Then the war ended in the Spring and I so much wanted to see you home, and they made you a Major with pips. I bet old Watson swanks with all the other batmen. But you say you have to stay there because you're young, unmarried and not a 'key man.' It's not fair and I think artists should be 'key men.' I'm sure lots of your paintings would be good for morale. Please try again to get some leave, it's seems cruel to me now it's over to keep you out there. By the time you get back I'll be an old lady and you won't want to be with me at all. As it is I doubt you'll recognise me. I keep getting taller and I've changed shape. I've 'filled out' Hilda says, less of a scrawny schoolgirl, not that I am one anymore, schoolgirl that is.

Working at the Marleigh Palace Theatre is still wonderful and makes me feel grown up and independent, but you really have to slave away for a measly pittance. I give pretty much all of it to Hilda, and I'm trying to save some. I don't need much for myself there's nothing in the shops to buy. We've just had a long run of a fortnight, which makes an ASM's life easier, but normally it has to be a week because we are up against the pictures. I don't know how the actors keep learning their lines, and as I'm prompter I can tell you, some of them don't.

Hilda's beginning to feel a bit worn out. She works too much, and it seems even if the war is over life doesn't get any easier. We had a min of food recipe leaflet that said to make margarine go further it would be a good idea to mix it up with mashed potato. At least it made Hilda laugh.

Hilda sends her love and so does my friend Alice, who has to endure me talking about you the whole time. I'm praying you'll get some leave for Christmas, and I love you more every day. I've borrowed some greasepaint so the kiss below is real, if a bit blurry. I had to blot it because of the grease. Write soon. Don't ever forget me.

Your Everloving, Daisy

Ps. Winnie caught three rats yesterday which is good and bad

Emily stared at the faded pink oval at the bottom of the page. It seemed so immediately present, redolent with Daisy's longing. She put her lips to the page where Daisy's had been. The sense of Daisy comforted as Emily looked through the sketchbooks. It was easy to distinguish James' academic style, carefully formed with firm lines, from the more impressionistic and less certain statements of Daisy, much of whose work was unfinished, some of it barely begun. Compared to James her style was profligate and restless.

A shaft of anxiety obtruded her thoughts she was still very angry with herself. Shall I tell Jean-Marie about Dan? Shall

I tell Toby? Jean-Marie might find it funny. It was faintly ridiculous. At a pinch he might even be cross. Toby would undoubtedly gloss it but think it poor form and an avoidable mistake. But then her normal self would never have dreamt of letting Dan anywhere near her bed. She must try and keep things cordial but cool for a while. There were no plans to meet Annabel and best not to make any, just yet. The story of her mother was still raw it would take time to settle. She needed to be alone for a while, to adjust.

She had been rifling through a sketchbook without seeing anything. Emily put it down on the chaise and stood looking out of the window, down the garden to the copse that failed to elicit the normal warm sense of attachment. The contained elegiac mood was gone, not to be recovered.

'Bugger, bugger, bugger,' Emily said out loud, as she left the studio, turned the key in the lock and returned it to the top of the lintel.

∽

Jean-Marie texted as he left Victoria. He would arrive at the station at four thirty. Emily grabbed James' Barbour and left by the back door. Outside the cloud was low, uniformly grey with a promise of snow, nothing in the garden stirred. Dan had suggested they hire a rotavator in the Spring and make a kitchen garden. Earlier he had detected the outlines of long forgotten beds around the glasshouse. The thought of Dan brought with it a vague anxiety. They had not spoken since he left a few days earlier. Perhaps she should get in touch after the weekend.

The old Peugeot reluctantly came to life and she slowly backed out of the barn. The steering wheel was ice cold and she stopped to put on gloves. After nearly freezing to death on the trip to Devon, it seemed less of a romantic wreck and more a dilapidated rust tub.

It would be good to see Jean-Marie. She missed him and wondered why he was wrenching himself away from Paris to stay in an isolated and draughty Campiston. The thought that he might be put off had stopped her asking him why he was to visit.

There was just time to go to the market. Hope over experience, as she said to herself. The vegetables were generally dull, the piles of sturdy salad leaves looked tempting, but Emily had found de-gritting them beyond her culinary skill. She left having bought nothing beyond some Cox's apples.

Jean-Marie appeared on the platform at Lewes station, looking his normal immaculate self in a tailored Vicuna overcoat that must have cost his mother a thousand euros. On one shoulder hung a soft leather backpack and he carried a paper carrier. Emily was surprised by how glad she was to see him and hugged him tightly. Jean-Marie kissed her and gave her the bag. It was full of large bulbous tomatoes.

'I had to scour the markets for these,' he said, 'I remembered how much you said you missed them in this gastronomic desert.'

Emily put her head in the bag to smell them. 'You're an angel,' she said, 'Thank you for thinking of me.' She kissed him again and held his hand as they walked to the car. Opening the door to the passenger seat Jean-Marie paused momentarily before risking his coat to the grimy interior.

'It's so good to see you.' Emily said. 'You will hardly recognise the place from your last visit.'

As they drove through the countryside Emily determined to keep the conversation light, chatting about the house and the continuing struggle to eat well.

After Jean-Marie had unpacked, he came down to the kitchen where Emily was blanching little purple topped turnips.

'Baked with bacon, to go with the pheasants,' she said, as Jean-Marie peered over her shoulder. 'Let me show you what's been going on outside before it gets too dark. Dan has transformed the place,' she said, looking at his gleaming brogues.

'Would you like a pair of wellies, rubber boots?'

'I'm fine, these are designed for the country,' Jean-Marie said.

They wandered round the now orderly garden and Jean-Marie admired the long glasshouse with its musky smell of fresh loam.

'All the work that's been done is outside,' Emily said. 'Apart from the kitchen we've left the house. I didn't want to buy anything much, in case, or when, I decide to sell.'

'You know what I think about that,' Jean-Marie said.

'I do, and I know it's the voice of reason but right now I'm glad I have somewhere I feel good about to come to.'

Jean-Marie put his arms round Emily and held her. 'It must be very hard for you,' he said, 'to suddenly have a mother but one you can never know.'

'Come on,' Emily said, 'there's one more thing I want to show you.'

In the newly electrified barn, the light shone down on the elegant lines of a half assembled dark green motorbike.

'Isn't it beautiful? I'll be able to ride it soon and it must be fifty years old.'

Jean-Marie ran a finger slowly along the curve of the petrol tank.

'Dan has taken photos of the stages of the reconstruction and he's going to make an album of them.'

'He does seem very much the polymath,' Jean-Marie said. 'Are there things he cannot do?'

'I doubt it, he has such enthusiasm and more energy and curiosity than a kitten.'

'Truly amazing.' Jean-Marie said.

Emily took him to admire the coppice and walk through the wood, now thinned with small piles of timber at intervals. The leafless trees showed black against a pewter sky. As they went back the sun was setting over the fields to the west of the house and a few flakes of snow drifted on the air.

In the kitchen Jean-Marie sat in the old carver that Toby had brought back from the cottage.

'Can I help?' he asked Emily.

'Yes, you can, would you light the fire in the study? When I've finished here we can have a glass of wine before we eat.'

Emily took some baked potatoes out of the oven and scooped the soft insides into a bowl. She beat in pepper, cream and some Dijon, turned it into an oval earthenware dish and scalloped the top with the back of a spoon. Sprinkled with some *fleur de sel,* it could go back into the oven with the birds.

In her room she changed her jumper for a shirt and brushed her hair. She wondered again whether to tell Jean-Marie about Dan. After all it had been an awkward and fairly pointless encounter, was there anything to be gained?

Back in the kitchen, she put the food in the oven, took a bottle out of the fridge, collected some glasses and joined Jean-Marie in the study.

'A treat to celebrate you being here,' she said, pulling the cork on the Pouilly Fuisse.

'Am I worth it?' Jean-Marie said, 'cheers.'

'When in Rome,' Emily said.

'Cheers does seem a very curious thing to say. I've no idea what it means.'

'Same as santé I guess. Let's play chess. I played with Toby, while he was in recovery mode.' She laid out the board on the little table, took two pawns and held them in her outstretched hands. Jean-Marie was white.

'I remember games taking rather a long time,' he said.

Ten minutes later, Emily said, 'Checkmate. We can have another game tomorrow, give you a chance to get even.'

'I'm not sure my ego could stand it,' he said. 'What if I lost again, and even more quickly?'

'How is your ego?' Emily said. 'I was surprised you wanted to come to Campiston, it's in England and it's in the country neither of which normally get you off.'

Jean-Marie slowly put the chess pieces back into their box.

'I came because you are here and I wanted to see you,' he said, without looking up. 'After you told me about your mother and then left Paris I was naturally concerned.' He leant over and stroked Emily's hair. 'I thought it would be a chance to talk about us here in deepest England.' He kissed her forehead. 'I haven't eaten since I left Paris and supper smells great.'

'The birds will done in minutes. We'll eat in here, it's warm. If you could make some space on the desk we'll need it as a sideboard.'

They sat either side of the table, lit by the desk lamp and an old standard with a tasselled shade.

After they had eaten, Jean-Marie leaned back in his chair and played with the stem of his glass.

'Hearing the story of your mother must have been so disturbing. One never really knows who one is. For my parents, who of course I depend upon, I act out some parody of me a person that I don't believe in. I saw you noticed my coat. It is lovely and my stipend most certainly would not have run to it. I think we may both be spoilt only children.'

Jean-Marie smiled and looked at Emily. She moistened her lips.

'Things have changed for both of us,' she said.

'Yes, they have.'

Emily filled their glasses.

'We are privileged but knowing that doesn't help. I still feel lost and would life be easier if we had to work to eat?'

'I think we do in our way,' Jean-Marie said, 'but, perhaps we do have to change.'

Emily stood up and cradled his head against her chest.

'Don't change too much,' she said, 'I like you just as you are. We haven't talked much lately, and it is so good to have you here where we can just be together for a while.'

Emily bent her head and kissed him on the lips.

∽

'Bo-Peep Bostel sounds ridiculous, even for England,' Jean-Marie said.

'It's down a charming byway and up a hill so incredibly steep that your ears pop on the way down. It's like you're landing a plane.' Emily said. 'Are you going to stick to those brogues?'

'Yes, I am. I have never worn rubber footwear and I won't start now, however quaint the name of where we are going.'

They turned into the narrow byway, drove past a few substantial houses and, began the ascent. Emily threw the old Peugeot round the dogleg bends that led to the car park at the summit. It was full of tweedy people with multiple large dogs.

Jean-Marie got out and waited for Emily to lock the car.

'Don't worry, she said the lock on the driver's door is jammed, no one in their right mind is going to steal it, just don't leave your wallet on the dash.'

They walked along the wide drove that followed the ridge

of the downs. Jean-Marie turned up his collar against the cold wind and stuffed his hands deep in the pockets of his coat, only to take them out again almost immediately.

'I'm torn between having warm hands and ruining the line of my coat.'

Emily peeled off her gloves.

'Here, have these,' she said, proffering them to Jean-Marie. 'Ancient Barbours don't have lines but they do have special pockets to keep hands snug.'

'Thanks a lot,' Jean-Marie said, and pulled on the yellow woollen gloves, splaying his fingers in front of him, 'they're rather nice.'

From the slopes and copses to the west there came the dull thud of shotguns and the barking of dogs.

'You often come across shoots on the Downs,' Emily said. 'Hunting is quite different over here. It's mainly the rich that shoot, but you can buy game cheaply. I get lots of fresh game for a few Euros from a farm shop in Piddinghoe, another silly name. We are having partridges for supper, with Kent Cox's apples, from over there.' Emily pointed vaguely across the weald that stretched out below them to a grey horizon. 'I know you like food that flies but geese cost a fortune here.'

'If we lived together, I would be as fat as a horse,' Jean-Marie said. 'I've never understood how you and Toby eat so much with at least one of you managing to keep their figure.'

'I blame him,' Emily said, 'and I think it's because he's never had a proper partner. It's one of the things I've suddenly woken up to. He and I are like a couple. In France, making food the centre of things isn't that remarkable, but it's not normally between a father and a daughter not in this century anyway. Perhaps I'm a bit like one of those slave girls, who half believe their lives are normal because they've never known anything else?'

Jean-Marie stopped and put a hand on Emily's shoulder.

'That's way too drastic. Toby may have got things wrong about your mother, but he's been a wonderfully loving father, certainly compared to the dried-up old stick that I've got.'

He let his hands fall to his sides and they resumed walking. The cloud had lifted, and the sun threw long shadows from the copses that clung to the slopes falling towards the weald. The air smelt faintly of spring and noisy tits and chaffinches darted among the bushes.

'In moments of madness I've imagined that I wanted to come out to my father that it might bring us closer together, but it would be awful. He wouldn't get angry. He would tell me not to be so stupid, and never to talk so lewdly in front of my mother. Then he would go to his study and shut the door and I wouldn't see him again for a week.'

Emily slipped her arm round his waist and squeezed him.

'You poor lamb, it must be so hard.'

'Out and proud, that's what they say here, but how can I be? I would probably be disowned and disinherited. My father would be terrified it would affect his law practice amongst the local money. My mother would never be able to face the bridge circle. It's still the nineteenth century in the provinces.'

Jean-Marie stopped again, put his arms round Emily and looked into her face. He bent forward and kissed her. Emily responded to the kiss and went to move on, but he held her and looked into her face.

'Emily, I do love you and when I spoke of us marrying, I meant it, and I know that you worried about me wanting you as some accessory to my career. If anything, I love you more now, but marriage does not seem right, and children would be reckless. Who knows what my future will be, and there is Alexis.'

Emily put her arms round him and kissed his face.

'Jean-Marie, I feel closer to you than ever, but even if we did marry there would always be three of us. When you and Alexis came to supper it was a great relief to me. He and I got on well and the three of us were relaxed together. I understand what you're saying about marriage. It might simply be taking on a load of stress we don't need. We've got on very well together without it. I can't say I have ever considered the idea of children. I haven't even got a cat.'

'Emily, there is something else I came here to tell you. I am leaving Paris, maybe for a long time, perhaps for good.'

Emily pulled away and stared at Jean-Marie.

'You're what? You can't be? What on earth for? What about your doctorate, your career? What about us?'

'Emily, I am so sorry, the very last thing I wish to do is hurt you in any way, but what has happened to Alexis and me has changed us irrevocably. We are just not living on the same old tariff and I've been forced into making a choice. Alexis has been taking retro-virals, he's been on AZT for a while now, and I must think about it for myself. He has asked for a posting in France-sur-Mer and the Quai D'Orsay have agreed to it. They haven't been kind and he goes to Reunion next month and I've said I'll go with him. I guess I shall have to teach school. I don't mind. My heart has gone out of my doctorate. It was never the substance, only the glory I was chasing, the chance of a job in a Grande Ecole. I feel I must follow Alexis and be there, if and when he needs me.'

'I don't understand.' Tears started to Emily's eyes. 'This cannot be true. You cannot go to Reunion, it's nowhere and they don't even speak proper French.'

'Emily, please, this is so hard. I may hate it, and not seeing you will be unbearable, I will miss us beyond everything. I told you I loved you in the Luxembourg, last Spring and you said nothing. When I suggested marriage, I felt you were angry, or worse, merely irritated. I never understood what was in your heart.'

Emily was shaking and tears ran down her cheeks. She brushed them away with the back of her hand.

'I don't understand anything,' she said. 'Why would you do this to yourself? Why do it to us? How can you say you love me and you're leaving me at the same time? Where's the sense in that? Surely, you don't have to martyr yourself for Alexis?'

'It's not martyrdom, Emily, it is a loving duty. I love you deeply, but we are separate people. I owe my standing here to Alexis. I did not know how to cope with who I was, and he saved my life.'

'Jean-Marie, this is too much for me. It's true I did wonder about us, whether you needed me for window dressing. I thought it was unnecessary, just your anxiety that being out would hold you back. But now you say you are giving up your life, and so I become expendable. No more dinners in my tiny black dress with your professors peering down my cleavage. No more being together, walking, laughing, eating, shagging and sharing each other.'

Emily began to sob, her shoulders heaving.

'I just don't get it,' she said.

They walked slowly back to the car. Jean-Marie put his arms round Emily's shoulders. She did not resist but neither did she respond. She drove fast down the hill and her ears did pop.

When they went into the house she ran upstairs to her room and slammed the door. She stood gazing sightlessly out of the window as the shadows lengthened and her body gradually ceased to quiver.

∽

Emily put the cup of coffee down on the small table beside Jean-Marie's bed. He sat up, rubbed his eyes, yawned and stretched. He ran his hands through his bouncy hair. Emily drew the curtains and turned to look at him. She came and sat on the bed, resting her hand on his thigh. Jean-Marie gently stroked her hand and smiled.

'Sorry for flouncing,' Emily said, 'I was so shocked and angry. I knew our future was uncertain, but it never occurred to me that we might not have one. You're the only man I've ever taken seriously. I thought the bond between us was unbreakable. I was wrong.'

Jean-Marie stroked Emily's hair, he folded her in his arms and kissed her face.

'The decision was not an easy one for me. You know who I am, my vulnerabilities, my needs. The only real consideration was you. In truth I don't know how I will survive without you. I'm just not thinking about life in Reunion.

'Alexis is frightened, and he needs me to be with him. I console myself with thinking that you have such an intensity of life in you, that whatever the odds, you will thrive. And in Toby, who I know mocks me, you have probably got the most kind and loving papa in France.'

Emily put her hands on Jean-Marie's cheeks and lifted his mouth to hers. He lay back against the pillows and pulled Emily close.

∽

Jean-Marie thought that it would probably be best if he went back to Paris and, Emily, who had little personal resource left to draw on, agreed. He managed to get a seat on an afternoon train.

'Shall I come with you to Waterloo?' Emily said.

'I should like that very much,' Jean-Marie said.

On the London train they sat together and held hands, there was little to be said. They had left in good time so that they could cross London by cab and avoid being herded on the metro.

In the twilight the streets shone as though they were wet. In the station bright lights and bustle both enclosed and separated them as they headed for the terminal. There was just time for a coffee. They sat opposite one another at a tiny round table each rapt in the other's presence.

'I can't believe this is happening,' Emily said.

'Nor can I,' Jean-Marie said, and squeezed her hand.

At the barrier they hugged for minutes. Emily lifted her face to be kissed and then Jean-Marie was gone.

Emily stood, her eyes clouded by tears, and looked out at an alien world. She felt unsure what to do next. She found the cab rank and headed back to Victoria.

∽

Emily arrived in Lewes to a fine drizzle driven by a gusting north-westerly. The car was cold and noisy as she drove up the hill from the station. Shopping seemed an impossible task, and so she drove straight through the town and headed to Campiston. The house was warm and calming. Upstairs she went to Jean-Marie's bedroom and buried her face in the scents of his pillows. All energy spent she slept.

Emily awoke, disorientated to find it was ten o'clock. She stared at herself in the mirror before going downstairs to the kitchen. In the fridge was a bottle of Pouilly Fuisse that was to have been their aperitif for supper. She poured a glass and took it to the study. She sat in the big leather chair still feeling numb. The pulsing green spot at the corner of her phone caught her eye and she automatically reached for it. Perhaps it was Jean-Marie? There was a long message from Annabel. Emily began to read it.

You complete bitch – how could you – I thought we were friends and you go and fuck Dan just for the hell of it and tell him to keep quiet – which of course he can't…

Emily switched the phone off and put it down. In the sitting room she collected a tumbler and a bottle of Calvados from the sideboard, walked slowly up the stairs to her bedroom and slammed the door as hard as she could. She splashed some brandy into the glass and raised it to the picture of Daisy.

'*Ciao Daisy*,' she said, '*priez pour nous.*'

Undressing slowly, she sipped her drink as she went along. A white broderie Anglaise nightdress lay across the back of a chair. It had been worn for Jean-Marie. She drained her glass and re-filled it to the brim before getting into bed and swallowing a few Paracetamol which induced nausea and she thought she would be sick. The feeling passed and she fell into a dreamless sleep.

∽

It was afternoon when Emily woke to the sound of sleet rattling against the window. She had not drawn the curtains and lay watching heavy black clouds bustling across the horizon. The room was dark and cold. Being conscious hurt.

Her eyes prickled and when she moved them her head felt almost unbearably painful. Her body did not feel like her own, except her bladder, which was bursting. Her lips were dry and hot. Standing up was not a great idea but had to be done. In the bathroom she avoided the mirror and filled a glass with water. She drank some and retched, her mouth filled with bile. She braved the mirror and when Hamlet's dilemma came to mind, she scolded herself for being melodramatic. Fumbling hands pulled on jeans and boots.

The Barbour over her shoulders, she went out by the back door and stood in drenching rain. The wind, that rattled the trees and shook the bushes, whipped her hair across her wet face. Emily thought she might be crying but couldn't be sure. After a while the positive abrasive effect of the elements abated, and she began to shiver uncontrollably.

Inside Emily shed her sodden clothes. Leaving them in a heap on the kitchen floor she ran up the stairs and stood under the hot shower waiting for her body to register something resembling normal. She put on moleskin jeans, thick socks and a heavy roll-neck sweater. They seemed the right sort of protection. Tired by the effort she lay down on the bed waiting for some strength to return. It was a day since she had eaten. Perhaps some green tea and plain toast might be worth risking, though her throat was sore from retching. The tea and toast soothed and despite a headache that suffused her entire being it allowed sufficient space within which Emily could wonder what to do next. She found the local directory and looked up – estate agents, Lewes – avoiding Annabel's firm she called the next one on the list.

Chapter 15

Dear Daisy,

The journey would have been more enjoyable if it weren't so long and the roads so slow. The bike [we must find her a name] is terrific and does eighty without even breathing hard. I know you'll love it when you get used to it. Powerful bikes are almost easier to ride than Fanny. The extra cc's make them more responsive and you can accelerate out of trouble when necessary.

Campiston House feels very odd. For one thing, I haven't been alone for years, it's a strange sensation, like the Marie Celeste. As I was bundled off to school so early in life, most of my memories of it are those of a child, and later I'd hardly settled in before I was called up. Luckily, Mrs Gauge, who used to be housekeeper, is still in the village and she and her daughter have been marvellous, scrubbing and polishing and washing all the old linen. I've borrowed two land girls from Bentley's farm next door, who have promised to make the garden at least accessible over the next few days.

Looking at it afresh everything is ridiculously old fashioned. The only way of getting hot water is by lighting the range. In fact the kitchen, like the bathroom basically a room with a bath in it, are museum pieces.

I'm not sure if you will take to all the old furniture either. It was never much cop and there's an awful lot of woodworm. I keep trying to look through your eyes, but it's not easy. I want to get on with things but I think we'll have to wait until we are both here.

The house isn't that big, but there are six bedrooms plus the old servants' rooms in the garret, and I think you will definitely need help. It would be a lot for one to manage and you will not want to devote your life to it.

I miss you and you are always in my mind. Give my love to Hilda. I'll write again in a day or so and be back just as soon as the place is habitable.

Your loving

James

Ps Mrs Gauge says she knows where my mother's lace wedding dress is. I'll bring it back you may like it.

Daisy read the letter over again. The house was real, and James was there. She imagined herself in a long dress with an enormous bunch of keys hanging from her waist, giving orders to the servants. Dust the sitting room, turn out the bedrooms, lay a fire in the bathroom. Six bedrooms sounds quite a lot, will I have to keep the beds made? Who on earth will sleep in them? Alice's house is the poshest I've ever been in and that only has three and a little one for the maid. Why would he want me to wear his mother's dress? It sounds creepy and in any case it's unlikely to fit. Daisy had thought of designing her own dress, the costumier at the theatre could make it for her. If it could be used in, Me and my Girl, she wouldn't even have to buy the material. She would only wear it for a few hours in the whole of her life so little point in making a fuss about it.

⌒

Daisy and Hilda came in from the garden, took off their boots and washed their hands under the tap.

'That's good, nearly done, we've got enough onions and marrows to last 'til next year,' Daisy said.

'With you gone to Sussex it'll be the year after.'

'You can always send us food parcels if there is a serious glut. I'm so hungry right now, what's for tea?'

Hilda took a bowl of brawn from the larder and put it on the kitchen table along with a loaf of bread. Daisy made up the fire.

'Tom's been so good to us, he gave me half a pig's head yesterday. You should have seen Winny while it was boiling, ecstatic.'

They sat down and Daisy cut a few slices of bread.

'I haven't told you, but James wants us to go on a honeymoon after we've moved into his house, by motorbike to the south of France. He says we can get a boat from Newhaven, which is quite near, and we'd be in Nice in three or four days. I'm not sure about going myself. He says no one speaks English and my French wasn't that brilliant, I was hopeless at oral. I've never even met a French person, all the teachers were English.'

'Of course you'll enjoy it. It'll be a real adventure. Seeing other countries opens your eyes to other ways of doing things. They're not like us, they've still got lots of peasant farmers and France is a lovely country by all accounts. If James had a side-car I'd ask if I could come.'

'I think I might like that as well,' Daisy said.

She cut another piece of jellied pig meat and put it between two slices of grey National Loaf.

'This is so good,' she said, 'I could eat the lot.'

'Contain yourself, there's another day tomorrow.'

'I worry that when I leave here I'm going to feel like a fish out of water. You know I've never been further than Exeter in the whole of my life.'

'New places are always hard to begin with, but you wouldn't want to stay in one place forever would you?'

'I suppose not,' Daisy said.

'It's different for me,' Hilda said, 'I'm content here now. I've got Tom and a few good friends but I'm thankful I had my years in the East. They really made me think about myself and about the Empire and I was fascinated by the other worlds around me. It put my little life in a bigger perspective.

'I think your friend Alice is a bit like me at her age. She's a lovely girl and I've grown fond of her. I think it's wonderful that coming here and helping us in the garden has given her a taste for working on the land. But you can see she's not content. It's a scandal the way she talks about that boyfriend of hers. She yearns for something more than Marleigh can deliver, an adventure in her life.'

Hilda got the tea caddy from the ledge above the range and put two spoons in the pot before filling it from the kettle. She brought it over to the table and Daisy put a cosy over it.

'I believe you two are the same deep down. You both want some control over your lives, to do what you want to do and not what others expect of you and I like that. Neither of you are girls who would settle for simply being housewives is my guess, but as long as you can do the things that you want for yourself, Daisy, I'm sure you can find happiness with James. It's quite clear that you love him even if you are, quite understandably, feeling unsure.'

Daisy put half a teaspoon of sugar and a saccharine tablet in her tea and stirred it.

'I think I've changed a lot in the last year or so. I love James but before he went overseas it all seemed quite simple.

All I needed was to be with him and everything would be fine, I don't think that's true anymore.

'When I left the shop to come here it felt like being let out of captivity. You left me to find what I wanted to be. You made it clear what the limits were, and you were quite strict, well, not really, except making me work in the garden, and I've come to love that. Alice and I have daydreamed about getting her dad to help us start a nursery together, I think we'd be good at it.

'Mum was always wary of James, never knew what to say to him. You made him welcome that first day, and it was for my sake. The pair of you gave me Fanny. That could never have happened with my dad. I still feel angry about him making me his drudge. When I look back, he gave nothing to me and mum and took anything he wanted. To all intents I suppose I'm an orphan now, not that it matters because you're here for me, and I love being here with you.'

Hilda gently shook the teapot.

'Do you think we could squeeze another cup out of that? I'll put the kettle back on.'

Daisy nodded.

'It hasn't always been that easy between us, Daisy. When you live on your own you get set, and I must say that I was bit apprehensive about being in charge of a teenage girl. But needs must in wartime, and as it turns out, you've brought me a lot of happiness.

'I think of your mum often, her being my only sister, and I still hope there could have been some mistake and she will come back and see what a fine young woman you've become. If you can see that being with James comes at a price, then that's to the good, it means you are going into it with your eyes open.'

Hilda took the gently steaming kettle off the hob and topped up the teapot.

'I hope my eyes aren't too wide. James just took it for granted that I would follow him to Sussex and leave my life behind. I tried to get him interested in living round here, but he didn't give it much thought. He said Campiston was his family home and he couldn't think of selling up, but he's hardly spent any time there himself. To sell his paintings he said he would need to be near London, for the galleries, and I guess that's true. He tells me there are plenty of theatres in Sussex, but Brighton is miles away and the nearest town, Lewes, is smaller than Marleigh and doesn't have one at all. There is an opera house quite near, which seems odd for the countryside, I might find something there.'

'I'm sure you will, love, you're not one to sit on your backside, and the way he talks about the garden, there'd be plenty to do there.'

Hilda looked up at Daisy.

'You won't want for anything. James is so generous and clearly well off. He bought that motorbike without flinching, and you say he's talking about furniture and improvements to the house.'

'He never mentions money and I'm too embarrassed by my lack of it to ever bring it up. I suppose I'll be a kept woman but I don't really mind about that. What I'm afraid of is that I'll find myself in a great big house with no idea how to manage it all, in a place that is totally strange. I just don't know what he expects of me except housework and cooking, and I'm not very good at either of them, am I?'

'A good plain cook,' Hilda said, and they both laughed.

'I hope I'm not being selfish, but I think he sees babies on the horizon, and I'm not sure that's what I want. It's obvious that people who love one another want to be together, and that means marriage, but somehow it seems so drastic.

'I'll lose the job that I love and all the people I work with, my best friend Alice, who makes me laugh and is like a sister to me, and the only person who has loved me and made me feel safe, and that's you.

'I truly love James and I want to be a good wife to him I would hate to make him unhappy in any way, but I wonder if I'm strong enough to cope with it all, can I change myself that much? I have to vow to, "honour and obey," and that scares me. I spent most of my life obeying a horrible man. I do trust James, but he'll sort of own me, won't he, like my dad?'

'I think you're being too morbid, love,' Hilda said, 'the marriage service is hundreds of years old and things have changed, women aren't the chattels they used to be, you're not a slave girl. You should be more positive, you are going to be able to live with the man you love, not everybody manages that.'

Hilda took out her hanky and blew her nose.

'I've never spoken of this before, but now's the time. There was a Chinese boy in Shanghai. We met at an Embassy reception, the bank couldn't find anybody else to represent them, so they sent me. I felt like Cinders going to the ball and I met this young Chinese and we hit it off and agreed to meet again. He was rich and upper class and had been educated in England, like quite a few of them. He liked English women, they had "spirit' he said. His family would never have approved and so we met when we could and mostly, we would just walk in the parks and talk. He took me to operas, which he loved, European and Chinese, which were very moving even though I didn't understand them. Quite soon we realised that we were in love, and we hoped to find a way to be together. Then his father found out about us, somehow, and made him stop seeing me. As far as the father was concerned, I was a lowly peon, and not fit to be the consort of his son. Lao was his name. He was quiet and beautiful and made me feel I really mattered.

'I cried for weeks, partly because I hoped he would defy

his father for me, but that's not the Chinese way. I don't know if he suffered, I wrote to him, but I never got a reply. I don't know if he got the letters. I like to think he didn't.'

Daisy turned and looked at her aunt.

'Hilda, that's terrible, and you've never said a word about it.' Daisy put her arms round her aunt and held her.

'How could you bear to lose him? I just go on about my own fears and anxieties, and I'm getting the chance to be with the man I love forever. How on earth did you manage being so far from home?'

It was a little while before Hilda spoke.

'I don't know. It hurt me in ways I couldn't understand in places I didn't know existed. There was nobody I could confide in. It left me feeling very vulnerable and wary. One of the managers was sweet on me but I just couldn't respond. Then, all of a sudden, we were told we had to leave or face being interned by the Japs. Some Brits who had houses and families stayed on hoping it wouldn't come to it. Goodness knows what happened to them, the Japs were known to be ruthless with anyone they captured. I found myself back here in the English countryside and grateful for it.

'I couldn't really have told your mother she wouldn't have got it, this is the first time I've been able to put it into words. Seeing you and James together has been wonderful, it's restored bits of me I thought had gone. I know I would do anything to help the two of you.'

Daisy kissed Hilda's cheek and sat down.

'I never guessed, and I never asked, did I? When there was a long gap in James' letters I couldn't concentrate at school and just felt sick for days.'

'Then you know what it's like, except for me after a while, I couldn't even hope. But now – I don't know. I'm glad to have Tom, he's been kind and I know he's "willing," as they say, but I don't want to be looking after a man, and that's what he'd expect. I'm not cut out for a farmer's wife. I've met a good few of them and, they're either in wellies all day or tied to the kitchen. To begin with I did feel a bit lonely out here, and I expect I may again when you go, but I've grown to appreciate my independence and I don't want to lose it.'

For a while they sat quietly. Hilda got up, kissed the top of Daisy's head, and began to clear the table.

'While I think of it,' Hilda said, 'I'm going to try and get the telephone. We've got the electric so the poles are all there. The GPO must be able to do it. I'll have to see how much it will cost. It would mean we could keep in touch more when you're in Sussex. I know trunk calls are expensive, but we can make them now and again.'

'That would be wonderful. I could still feel you were close.' Daisy sat slumped at the table, her hands holding up her head.

'Cheer up, Daisy, you know what they say, things are never so bad they can't get worse.' Hilda squeezed Daisy's shoulder. 'It'll be a new life for you, and you may well find it hard. But you have always been a clever and resourceful girl and one that most often gets what she wants.'

'You are right auntie I'm not a ninny and a lot of it may be first night nerves, I'll get over them. Hearing your story makes me feel ashamed.'

'There's no need to, my love. You're just more realistic than besotted which I like, just don't forget to count your blessings.'

∽

The light in the sitting room was beginning to fail as shadows thickened in the corners. Daisy switched on the standard lamp. Alice was at the table undoing a brown paper parcel.

'I'm so glad James' mother's wedding dress was too small, and by a mile. The lace was lovely, but the design was so old fashioned.'

'How about this?' Alice said. She lifted a veil out of its box and shook it out.

'It looks so theatrical,' Daisy said, 'but I suppose I will be playing a part, star billing in fact. It's much bigger than I thought it would be.'

Alice put the veil on Daisy's head, muslin and lace cascaded to her shoulders.

'I've got it the wrong way around,' Alice said, standing back to look. 'The long bit must go to the back, otherwise it looks top-heavy.' She swivelled it into place on Daisy's head and flounced it out around her face. She stood back again and put her head to one side.

'That's more like it, very mysterious. If you are a blushing bride no one will know.'

'I don't think that's the point. We're meant to be retiring virgins with no cause to blush. The man has to make the purchase before he gets a good look at the merchandise.'

Daisy pushed her head forward and peered from side to side, putting her arms out and feeling in front of her.

'It's pretty dim in the church, I hope I don't bump into people, there's normally quite a crowd for weddings, all the village ladies are bound to turn out and sit at the back. I'll have to rely on you to steer me down the aisle.'

'I'll tell mother you're thrilled with it then,' Alice said.

'I'm sorry, I don't mean to be ungrateful, it was very good of her to think of me, and you must thank her kindly. Very useful and it will count double "something old and something borrowed." I've already got "something new," that's the dress, so that only leaves "something blue." Do you think my fountain pen counts?'

'It might. But how are you going to wear it, we could put it on a chain round your neck?'

'Brilliant, then we're covered, Hilda will be pleased – phew. She's been full of old wives' tales and bits of folklore about marriage, I've no idea where she gets them from.'

'As long as she hasn't suggested a muslin bag full of dried newts' entrails to put under your pillow, I wouldn't worry too much.'

'She doesn't believe in it. The wonder is she knows it all, I suppose it's her generation.'

'The wedding itself is a bit like magic,' Alice said. 'You walk in there two separate people with different lives and you come out a bit later spliced for life.'

'Yes, but while you're in there you make solemn vows, it's not magic it's a contract. Fr Julian suggested a Nuptial Mass, as I'm one of his regulars, but I think it was a touch too Catholic for James' taste. I would have liked it, make more of a thing of it.'

'I'm with James,' Alice said, 'far too religious. You can go to mass any old time but you're only supposed to have one wedding, ever.'

'Fr Julian's got two others on the same day.'

'Blimey, sounds like a wedding factory, will they blow a whistle?'

'I think they are like James and me. Men coming back from the war and marrying their sweethearts.

'Fr Julian has been lovely. I went to mass yesterday, I wanted to thank him. If his fund hadn't paid my school fees I'd have had to leave, and whenever I was really anxious about James he would pray for us at mass.

'When we went to see him, he did go on a lot about the sacred nature of the vows, you'd have thought we were going into a nunnery, all duty and service. He's celibate, of course, so he can't really talk about it in a personal way. I've always thought he must be lonely, just him and the housekeeper in that gloomy old rectory. I hope they get on and don't bicker.

'The Sundays he read the banns at mass, he always smiled at me, which was kind. You know no-one is going to say anything, but it made me feel a bit vulnerable, asking if you're an honest woman in public. I'm glad it's going to be him.'

'Ah,' Alice said. She stretched and yawned. 'I shall have to be moving. I've promised I'll go and watch the cricket with my dad later, it's the last game of the season.'

'That doesn't sound like you.'

'I'm buttering him up. You know I have to get away from ma, she's driving me round the bend. Now you're getting hitched she's harping on about marriage the whole time, trying to set me up with eligible bachelors. I think she's rumbled that I'm hanging on to Arthur as a way of avoiding her evil designs. It's like living with the Gestapo. Endlessly criticising what I'm wearing, the state of my hair, why can't I be bothered to make up my face properly.

'My plan is to get my dad to buy me a cottage for me to live in. These farms I'm sent to all have empty worker's cottages because they don't need the men anymore, and we could probably get one for less than a hundred quid. As long as it was waterproof I wouldn't mind what state it was in, I'm quite used to outside lav's now, and I think mice are sweet. I could whitewash it all myself and I'd have a garden, and you could come and stay with me when you felt like a break.'

'That sounds a wonderful idea, but a hundred pounds is an awful lot of money.'

'But he wouldn't be losing it because he'd own the cottage. If I promise to work at improvements, he could sell it later for more money. The housing shortage won't go away overnight. So I'm putting it to him as an opportunity, he'd get a return on his capital he'll like the sound of that, as well as doing his only daughter a great favour.'

'You're going to be wasted as a farmer, you should work for the Bank of England.'

'I'd look silly in a top hat.'

Daisy took off the veil and put it back in its box. Alice put on her coat and tickled Winny who had jumped onto the table.

'I'll come with you to the bus stop.'

Daisy pounded up the stairs to get her greatcoat. Outside they linked arms and set off up the lane. The sun had come out and the remaining leaves glistened, a faint haze drifted over the fields.

'James is coming to tea tomorrow, then we'll go to the pictures and after that I shan't see him again until I meet him at the altar. His best man is a captain from the regiment. He thought a guard of honour would be nice for the major. James wasn't so sure, he said he wanted to try and forget the war not invite it to his wedding.'

'My dad will drive me over on Friday night. I'll bring my dress and nightie and stuff.'

'I'm so glad you are coming, I'm sure I won't sleep a wink, and you'll be with me in the morning. I can't really believe it's going to happen. I couldn't have two better dressers than you and Hilda for my starring role, a single perf, don't miss it.'

'Daisy, it will be wonderful, I know it will. I'm truly looking forward to it, especially the wedding breakfast.'

'A massive game pie and a ham, all from Hilda's Tom, of course. Then we go and stay in a hotel in Exeter and ride to Sussex on Sunday and that will be that, except for the honeymoon.'

At the end of the lane they crossed over and stood quietly looking down the Marleigh road for the bus. Alice put her arms round Daisy, and they held on to each other.

'You must write to me all the time,' Alice said.

'And you me. I'm going to miss you so much. You must come and stay you can have a different bedroom every night if you like.'

The dark green bus appeared on the horizon and rolled towards them.

The two girls kissed.

With a screeching of brakes, it came to a stop beside them. Alice pushed open the door and squeezed Daisy's hand.

'Goodbye, for now,' she said.

'Til Friday.'

Chapter 16

EMILY WATCHED FROM AN UPSTAIRS WINDOW AS A SCRUFFY English sports car crunched to a stop by the front steps. Sunshine dappled the long red bonnet. The tiny door swung open, and a pair of long legs clad in a blue grey chalk stripe emerged. A young man stood up, smoothed his unfashionably long hair and slowly looked about, taking in the house and grounds. He had no briefcase nor any obvious professional paraphernalia. He straightened a thin striped tie, school or even regiment, tripped lightly up the steps and gave the heavy knocker one loud thud. Emily waited a few moments looked in the mirror, came down the stairs and opened the door.

'Bruno Harper, I'm here to see Miss Emily Blount.'

'That's me, please come in.' Emily stood back to allow him to pass. He smiled and proffered his hand with the slightest inclination of the head.

'I understand you wanted some advice about possibly putting the house on the market. I was admiring it as I drove up, it's charming and has a natural affinity with its landscape. It must be a joy to live in?'

'Can I show you around,' Emily said, 'and then perhaps we might talk over coffee, if you would like some.'

'Delightful, that would suit me perfectly.'

'We'll do the house and then I'll leave you to roam around the grounds at your discretion.'

'Excellent.' He smiled again.

'Shall we start upstairs?' Emily led the way.

Later they sat in the sitting room, looking down the garden to the wood and drank coffee. The small plate of Madeleines lay untouched on the table.

After another encomium, the young man asked a lot of questions, about rights of way and tenures, and a few legal questions that Emily could not answer. She suggested he contact uncle James' lawyers.

'I cannot give you a reliable estimate of worth without doing some more work,' Bruno said, 'however, as this is not your principal residence you may not be in a tearing hurry to realise the value. Should that be the case you might like to consider applying for permissions to develop the property, it could readily yield two family sized apartments or four smaller units, and the studio would convert into an agreeable small flat. There's plenty of room for garages and gardens though the wood, given its size, might be an issue. It's certainly worth your considering. The house retains some lovely original features but not much has been done for half a century or so. Bringing it up to par is likely to be very costly. On sale with some permissions might be a way forward.'

He uncrossed his long legs and stood up. He took his wallet from an inside pocket and laid a card on the table.

'I'll get on to your solicitors, *tout de suite*, and they would certainly be happy to advise on the process of obtaining permissions.'

He stopped on the top step as he left and turned to Emily proffering his hand.

'Thank you so much Miss Blount, it's been a pleasure to meet you, and to see your delightful house. I can assure you that Proutt and Striker will help you find the best possible buyer for your property.' He smiled. 'I'll be in touch shortly.'

'*A bientot,*' Emily said, and shut the door. She walked around the house looking at the rooms. It felt as though it was already someone else's. It had been re-imagined in ways she hadn't considered. Annabel had said it would interest a developer when she first came. Emily put thoughts of Annabel to one side.

In a cupboard in the study she found the papers on the house that had been in the bundle along with James' will. There were some faded sketch maps, artfully coloured to show boundaries, buildings, woods, gardens and pathways. Why had she not thought to give all this to the young man?

Emily collected all the small artworks of Daisy's, mostly water colour drawings or brown pencil sketches of aspects of the house and kitchen garden at different times of year. There were some haunting pictures of the wood and pretty decorative works of interiors, the study and the studio, the sitting room looking out to the garden, a view from the morning room. With the folder on her lap she looked through the now familiar images. What had Campiston meant to Daisy? She would have liked a picture of her room. Was her own attachment to the house just a part of her fascination with the phantom presence of Daisy? Was her reluctance to sell a fear of losing the connection to someone she had never known and who only lived in her head?

Emily flipped open her purse and took out the passport size photo of Daisy she had found in the bureau. She stared at the image of a young woman who looked at once soft and strong, as enigmatic in this replica as in James' portraits. I guess I'm only looking to find myself. She put a log on the fire and watched it crackle into life. Now might be the time to grab the future, forget the English adventure, go back to

Paris and look for a job, perhaps with an NGO somewhere? First degrees don't have much of a shelf life, Toby had said, and she had already put a foot wrong by walking out on the internship. Paris may be a lonely place without Jean-Marie but it had shaped her life. Sussex was a new sort of delight but had done little to challenge the idea that the English were barely civilised, dwyle flonking said it all. Realistically what sort of future could she possibly make, or afford, in England? She had a momentary impulse to drop the photo of Daisy in the flames but could not do it.

∾

Emily took her coffee and sat on the step, lifting her face to the warm pale light. The rooks had already begun the noisy and laborious business of nest building in the tops of the beech and ash trees that bordered the drive. Their raucous calls drowned out all other birdsong. A taxi had been ordered and there were still a few things to be done before she could leave.

The young man from Proutt and Striker had been again and had taken a lot of measurements, inside and out, and had consulted various maps. The land ran to over three hectares. Most of it comprised the wood stretching from the end of the garden to the stream. It included the driveway that James' father had purchased. A price had been calculated for the entire freehold as it now stood that would comfortably cover an apartment in Paris, but Emily didn't want one. Toby would know what to do with the money. A developer with silver hair and a deep tan had already been to view, had stayed for about ten minutes, and put in a bid below the asking price that Emily had rejected. She worried that it was because she didn't like the thought of what he might do to the house, rather than the size of the offer. If she was going to go in any case, such considerations were definitely irrelevant.

Emily stood and stopped to watch the rooks. How did they make the first twig stay in place when they left to collect the second, and then the third and so on? The sound of a car could be heard underneath the cawing and no one was expected. A black mini stopped on the path and Annabel got out holding a bottle of champagne. She came over to where Emily stood put her arms round her and hugged her.

'Emily, I'm sorry to have been so awful please forgive me.'

'If it means we can be friends again, of course.' Emily smiled and held Annabel's hand.

'I am so relieved,' Annabel said and kissed Emily on the lips, 'I can't tell you how dreadful I've been feeling.'

'Me too.' Emily took the bottle to open it. 'Let's stay in the sun for bit, we can sit on the steps.' The cork hissed and she took a long swig.

'Cheers,' she said, 'to us,' she passed the wine over to Annabel.

'To us,' Annabel lifted the bottle to her lips, 'delicious, nice and toasty with good length.' They laughed and the bottle went back to Emily.

Emily brought some cushions and they sat in the comfortable declivities of the old steps and looked out down the slope to the weald and beyond to the blue line of the downs.

'I have missed you. I've been remembering that first evening I came here, and we just felt like friends and you shared Daisy, and the wine,' Annabel said, reaching for the bottle. 'When Dan told me it made me instantly angry, especially with him. First, why confess? It seemed so typically inept. I thought probably the reason was he was afraid I'd find out, and then what? Like, I'd have him arrested. And less charitably, was he such a weed that he had to tell me in the hope that I would in some way absolve him. I was burning with righteous indignation when I sent that text. I instantly realised it was stupid and that your silence was the only sensible response.'

Emily stroked Annabel's arm.

'I'm not sure what to do about Dan, myself,' Emily said.

'It's all a bit sad,' Annabel said. 'He can be a joy to have around. I love his infectious enthusiasms for things like trees and motorbikes and bread and, less endearingly, beer, but he's not much of a grown up. It even crossed my mind that he was secretly proud of having done something a bit adult and wanted me to know about it.

'The work I had to do to get him to college was nobody's business, but it's been good, and he has taken to it. The practical side is just what he wants and as long as I edit the essays, he'll get a degree.'

'That's good to hear,' Emily said, 'but what I haven't told you is that I'm selling Campiston. Realistically if I'm going to make a life and, critically, a living it will have to be in France.'

'I confess I already know,' Annabel said, 'Bruno told me he'd been instructed, and wondered why Proutt and Striker got the job and not me. It's partly what gave me the courage to come out with the olive branch. I thought if you left I might never see you again.'

'Things have not been going my way lately, Annabel, managing to screw up both Dan and then you made me think seriously about Campiston. As a weekend cottage it makes no sense. It's a big house to keep going even to keep warm.' Emily smiled and turned to Annabel. 'But to have you back on my side makes the world look a whole lot brighter. I'm going back to Paris this afternoon. I miss Toby and I need to see if I can find any sort of job close to development economics. I think

I'm better than my first degree might suggest because I've been talking economics with Toby since forever. I understand it, I like it and I know I could be good at it. So, I must give it a try. I'll have to go where the work might be, but that's fine. I'll be very lucky to find anything in Paris or London.'

'You might find a job somewhere warm and exotic and I can come and stay with you.'

'I guess it's likely to take a bit of time, but come and stay in Paris again soon, perhaps for a weekend.'

'I'd like that, we had a great time and I loved the city'.

The cloud thickened and darkened, and the wind became too cold for sitting outside.

'Let's go in. I'm afraid I've got to shut the house up and finish packing before the taxi comes.'

'Why not cancel it, then I could drive you to the station?'

'That'd be great, and it would be nice to be together for a bit longer.'

Emily shut the door behind them, and they went through to the kitchen. Annabel took the cushions back to the sitting room.

'Shall I close the shutters in here?' she called.

'Yes, please, the ones that actually do close. Security here is still in keeping with the décor, Second Empire. We've got plenty of locks and some keys, but no alarm system.'

Annabel joined Emily in her bedroom as she finished stuffing some badly folded clothes into her Samsonite case.

'That's a great case, looks bomb proof.'

'Probably is, it's Toby's. He lavishes money on luggage because he travels so much.'

'How is he?'

'He sounded pretty bouncy last time we spoke I just hope he hasn't started smoking the minute I'm off the case. I need him to last a bit longer.'

Annabel came and sat on the bed and put her arm round Emily.

'I don't want to sound like Dan's advocate, but what's to be done about him and the house now that you're going to sell? I haven't told him anything, but he's been carrying on with his practical woodland management and all the stuff in the gardens, and that old bike he's been obsessed with.'

Emily sighed and lay back on the bed.

'Yes, something will have to be done,' she said.

'If you don't feel you want to talk to him I'm happy to, but should he carry on for now or just drop everything? I know there were things he wanted to discuss with you about the land.'

Emily put her hands behind her head and stared at the ceiling.

'I'll have to think. I don't know what would be best. Let's finish shutting the place up and then we can talk in the car.'

They went around the garden securing the barn and the glasshouse. When they got to the studio Emily locked it and put the key on the lintel.

'I know it's bonkers, but that's where Toby and I found the key when we first came here, so we've always left it there. It's worked so far.'

'As a property person it makes me shudder,' Annabel said, 'but as it's you that's fine.'

Emily looked round the garden and down through the coppice to the wood.

'Time to go I guess,' she squeezed Annabel's hand.

The front door slammed behind them and Emily locked it. Without looking back she threw her suitcase onto the back seat and got in the car. Annabel nosed into the drive, through the rookery and turned onto the Lewes road.

'Perhaps you could ask him to carry on for now. I feel the house is safe with Dan around, and Bruno will be showing people over, so it has got to look loved. I asked the solicitor about planning permissions for development to improve the lustre of the property, but her advice was it might take an age, is not in itself cost free even if it's only outline permission, so why should I be bothered? She said I'd be more likely to get the asking price from a family than from a developer in any case. Perhaps Bruno was keen because it might make things a bit easier for him?'

'I couldn't comment,' Annabel said.

'It has certainly made me feel sort of transitional, but then I am, but it's not very comfortable. I tell myself the house was a windfall and one I'm very grateful for. I did come here as a teenie but now I feel I know the place and it has become a part of my life. If it hadn't happened, I should never have met Daisy or you.'

'I guess you'll miss it?'

'I am already.' Emily said, and smiled at Annabel. 'It came at a good time. I wanted some space to think about the future. Things have been changing, Jean-Marie came over to tell me he is leaving Paris. He's going to Reunion, to be with Alexis.'

'Emily, why didn't you say so earlier, that must have been awful. I can't even give you hug.' Annabel took one hand off the wheel and held Emily's. 'And you weren't expecting it?'

'No – it came from nowhere. At one point we'd even talked about marrying.'

'You poor angel, you must be shattered.'

The car swerved as Annabel turned to look at Emily.

'I'm still in the numb phase, I think. It's a bit hard to talk about. Paris will seem oddly empty without him. I realise I've been very neglectful of other people. I've let Toby and Jean-Marie take up so much space in my life.'

They pulled into the station car park, fringed with another tumultuous rookery. Annabel looked up.

'There were twenty-eight nests there last year,' she said, 'we had to count them every year when I was in first school and I just carried on.'

They walked onto the platform and stood looking across the track.

'Emily, I am so sorry to have been such a bitch, and just when you could easily have done without my tantrum. Let's keep in touch. I can manage Dan and keep an eye on Bruno. If you want to talk about any offers he comes up with, just call.'

'Thank you, I will. Tell Dan to carry on as usual. We will, that is Toby will, continue to pay him and I'll talk to him soon.'

The long caterpillar train slid into the station. They hugged and Emily disappeared behind the closing door. Annabel stood and watched as the carriages curved into the black tunnel and slowly made her way back to her car.

∽

The concierge got a more effusive greeting than was usual from Emily.

'It's good to see you again, Emily, I hope you enjoyed your stay in England. I've given your post to your father. There were no parcels.'

'Thank you, Manon, it's good to be back, I've missed Paris. The English countryside is just as quiet as ours.'

Emily lifted her case and carried it up the stairs. As she neared the apartment, she sniffed the air for tobacco smoke. She let herself in through the tall, black double doors.

'It's me – I'm back,' she called.

Toby, in jeans and a moth pocked cashmere jumper, specs on his forehead, emerged from his study. His face wreathed in smiles he came and put his arms round his daughter.

'Emily, it's so very good to see you. How was the journey?'

'Just fine, trains on time, but some MEP was holding court and making more noise than was necessary, so I had to move carriages.'

'Sorry to hear that. Ghastly gravy train for democratic detritus, best avoided I'm sure.'

Emily dropped her case and went into the sitting room, kicked off her shoes and lay on the sofa. Toby arrived with a glass of wine.

'It really is good to see you,' he said. 'How are you holding up? There's been a lot to contend with lately.'

'I'm not sure,' Emily said, 'floundering a bit maybe. Jean-Marie is still hard to believe, but I do understand in a way. I guess Alexis needs him more than I do.'

'I rather see it as the dear boy's stab at authenticity, he never seemed to have much of a vocation for academe, too anxious about it all. It must have taken some courage to give it up, nonetheless.'

'You're right. It leaves me feeling like I'm mourning, but I don't know what for.' She took a gulp of wine. 'I do know it's good to be back.'

'Good for me too,' Toby said. 'I've been too busy to buy supper and cook, so I thought we'd go to Lascotte. Would a hearty fish soup and monster sole suit?'

'Sounds great,' Emily said, jumping up and draining her glass, 'I'll just shower and I'm ready.'

∾

Emily watched the waiter at his sideboard deftly fillet the flat golden fish. They sat, Emily at the corner of a banquette, Toby opposite her on a chair, well into the dining room away from the noisy bar. The comfort of good food, the imperceptible service and the Chablis all worked to relax and soothe. Toby had recovered his ebullience and was full of entertaining gossip from L'Institut. By coffee and Calvados, Emily was beginning to feel more peaceful than she had for some time.

Toby twirled the stem of his glass and leant forward.

'There is one item of news I've yet to report,' he said. 'I've been invited to apply for a job with the Miracle Fund, as Director.'

Emily sat up with a start.

'I turn my back for a moment and you've been headhunted. I suppose you telling me at the end of a good supper means that you're interested?'

'Yes, I am. I'd love to do something new. I haven't had a change for a long time and now is about the right point in my career, before people start to think I've been around too long.'

Emily opened her eyes wide and looked at Toby.

'Wow – Director. They haven't got much of a presence in Paris, have they?'

'There's the rub. HQ is in NY and that's where I'd be expected to relocate. There'd be some travelling but less than I'm doing now, and I've made long weekends in Paris a condition of taking the job, and they seem entirely happy with that. Though I guess I'd have to be flexible.'

'Toby – so things have gone that far – you haven't accepted the post already, have you?'

Toby put his hands flat on the table and looked directly at Emily.

'I've agreed informally but I wouldn't sign until I'd had a chance to talk to you. You are more important than anything. And especially now Jean-Marie is no longer around, I don't want you to feel totally deserted.'

Emily sat, looking at Toby, unable to immediately respond.

'Even if I do accept, I still have contracts to run for the next few months that will mean returning to Paris regularly.'

'Of course, you must take it,' Emily said, 'as you say the timing is perfect.'

'I do want to be around to help you establish some direction, if that is what you want? I know you've made up your mind to sell Campiston and I'm sure that's the right decision, but should you want to hold on longer, I'm happy to continue helping.'

Emily closed her eyes.

'Toby, that's so kind and generous but also a bit destabilising. I've had trouble hanging on to the idea that the house must go, and I don't want anything to weaken my grip, but thank you.'

'I'm sorry,' Toby said, 'I realised the decision was rather fragile, and thought it might make life a little easier if you knew you could shelve it.'

'Don't apologise, papa, the problem is me. I'm trying to focus and move on, to somewhere or other, to take control of my life for the first time, but the ground keeps shifting. First Dan, then Jean-Marie leaves me, and Annabel throws a fit. I run back to Paris and you, quite reasonably, want to take a new and exciting job. I just feel like I'm being emptied out.'

'I know it's bit of a surprise. If you felt you'd like to, you might consider coming to New York. It would certainly be a change of scene, with a lot more going on than round here.'

'I don't think so. I can't follow you round the globe, papa, just because I can't find a life for myself.'

'It's not like that. I just want you to know you are not being abandoned. I know you to be clever and capable, you couldn't fail to find your way in life even if you tried very hard. You know I love you, Emily, and I shall always be here for you as long as I am here.'

They fell quiet and Toby sat looking down at the table.

'To be honest,' he said, 'I was amazed to be offered the job, there are better CV's than mine around, and also the speed with which they moved through the formalities after I had expressed my interest. My guess is they had someone lined up and he, or she, bailed out at the last minute. But I shall never get a better offer and I do want to take it.'

Emily looked directly at Toby.

'I suppose this is what real life is like. I keep thinking of your phrase, "no such thing as unalloyed pleasure." I do think it will be a great thing for you, you'll love it, but I can't help feeling sad. Since you told me about my mother, I'm in a new world and, it feels a lot harder than the old one.'

'I don't deserve your kindness, Emily, but I'm grateful for it, and I'm chastened by your magnanimity. Jean-Marie must have been a terrible blow. But it is, better to have loved, I've been telling myself that for the last twenty years. We won't lose one another. The pond isn't that big, and I'll spend as much time as I can in Paris. I'll miss you and our life together terribly. Enough for now? We can talk more tomorrow.'

'A good idea papa, I'm exhausted.'

'Bye the bye, Emily, what's up with young Dan?'

'I'll tell you on the way home.'

Chapter 17

DAISY SAT ON A STOOL IN THE SITTING ROOM IN HER nightie. The wedding dress was draped over one of the carvers. Alice resplendent in cream silk, was brushing Daisy's hair. Hilda came down the stairs and stood on the bottom rung with one hand on her hip.

'Hilda, you look lovely,' Alice said, 'your hair is perfect.'

'I expect Tom will propose again as soon as he sees you,' Daisy said, 'then if Arthur turns up, we can do the last act of Much Ado, and everyone could be married.'

'Go on with you, Daisy, we're too young to get married, aren't we Alice?'

'We certainly are,' Alice said, 'I think I might always be.'

∽

Dear Alice,

It was just as I feared. We stayed in this village and I tried to buy some bread. I don't know why I bothered it makes the National Loaf seem like cake. James says it's better in Paris but that's a few hundred miles away. Anyway, nobody understood a word I said and all I could do was to repeat myself and they kept talking to me in French and I couldn't understand anything, so finally

I just pointed, it's all stacked up behind the counter, and gave them a banknote. This got me a loaf that looks like a paving stone and a huge amount of change in coins. The people in the shop were unfriendly and clearly talking about me and probably thinking I was some sort of idiot girl.

We might stay at Menton later, where James says everyone speaks English because they are English. If I was on my own, I might starve. I don't think James' French is great, but at least people seem to know what he's on about, and he manages to talk naturally, whereas with me it's as if I'm doing French oral, it's hopeless.

I don't get the impression they like The English, so much for being liberators. Perhaps down here they still remember the hundred years war? I don't even know if our war got down as far as here, there's no sign of it. France seems enormous, we've been through endless acres of forest, and lots of mountains. Some are really high and wild, amazing to ride over with tumbling rivers and ravines. It is very Romantic, but only in the German sense, cold, drizzly and melancholy a lot of the time, which I really don't mind.

We get stopped by the unsmiling Gendarmerie a lot and have to show our papers, but so far nobody has tried to arrest us.

There are hundreds of tiny farms in the countryside, I haven't seen a single large herd yet. All the farmers wear blue work jackets, perhaps it's a government regulation? As we get further south, the oddest thing is all the vineyards, little knobbly grapevines, about a yard or so high, all planted in rows on slopes. We must have passed thousands of them. But I guess they need them as the working men seem to drink wine all the time, some of them from quite large bottles and in the street, while they smoke the most smelly cigarettes you could imagine. They must be just awful to kiss.

Most people look a bit shabby and dour. The landowners all live in huge chateaux, which often look run down and deserted, but James says they're not, the French just aren't as prissy as us.

It's a real education and James and me are getting on famously, although some of the places we've stayed in have been pretty dire, especially the beds. I'll write again soon and I miss you every day.

All my love

Daisy X

Ps: I must write to Hilda now and try to be more cheerful

❧

Dear Alice,

By the time we got back from France the builders had finished James' studio. It's very posh, big and light with room for two or three easels and lots of storage for canvases. Also, there's a stove and a chaise longue on which to drape a model I suppose, I didn't think they still existed outside the theatre, chaises that is – and electricity. [What a terrible sentence, Miss Granville would be ashamed of me].

James says there's plenty of room for me to work alongside him, but I don't think there is in truth. He likes to be on his own when he paints. He doesn't say so, but if I sit sketching, he just goes on like I'm not there and only grunts if I speak so it makes me feel uncomfortable. I think he's doing some good work, but he says times are difficult at the moment for artists and he talks about doing some illustrations for books, but by the way he says it I don't think he will.

I could have had one of the bedrooms as a studio but I'm not sure James would have approved so I've bagged the best of the old servants' quarters in the garret and made it into my workroom and boudoir, I'm writing in it now. It's got a window that looks down the garden to the woods at the end and a little fireplace, just like the one I had at Hilda's. It looks like my destiny is to live under the eaves.

It's very curious to see James in his big house in Sussex. He seems a bit like a different person. I'd only known him as a soldier and for most of that time he was in Italy, so I had to imagine him, and there was always anxiety. But now he's a country gentleman. Our nearest neighbours aren't farmers, like Tom Dacre with work roughened hands, they're landowners, who don't seem to do anything. There are two big local estates, each with its own real Lord of the Manor. James says they don't really get on because one family was for the King and the other for Cromwell in the civil war. Can you believe it? It is pretty feudal here.

The church, St Mary's, is thankfully Anglo Catholic, a huge barn of a place. There was no lovely Fr Julian, just a very stout priest, with a big red nose that looked as though it might have sniffed more port than was good for it. The front pews were for the quality and the tenants and workers had to sit at the back – guess where the usher put me? Then the verger recognised the new Mistress of Campiston House and I had to move to the front. Too embarrassing for words and too close to a really terrible choir.

The portly priest was very friendly afterwards, which is more than most people are, although it's not as bad as France. The people I see most of are Mrs Gauge, a sort of housekeeper and Penfold, which is what James calls him, or Jake which is what I call him, an old bloke who has been the gardener forever. There's a huge greenhouse, which needs a refit but could be wonderful. I'm trying to make a kitchen garden with Jake's help, which is a pretty big job. He is SO SLOW but usually gets there in the end.

In the summer I'll be able to go to the Opera house, which is only a few miles away, it's run by another aristocrat, so James says and was shut for the duration. I would love to get some work there. I'm keeping up my art and there's an amateur theatre in Lewes that I'd like to design for, but James says it's probably very cliquey, and he's probably right. Rex hated AmDram thought it gave theatre a bad name.

Do write soon and let me know how things are with you, I'm thrilled about your cottage and want to know all. I still miss you every day.

With much love
Daisy X

⁓

'Now then Mrs Blount, I've brought some lamb chops for your lunch, and after I've cleared away breakfast, I'll get the vegetables prepared for boiling. As it's Friday I got a nice piece of fish for your supper and I'll leave you a white sauce. Then there's a beef stew in the larder for tomorrow and a hand of pork in the meat safe for Sunday. In this cold it'll be fine. I've done a bit of apple sauce. I'll be back Monday after breakfast and then we can go through the week. How's that Mrs Blount?'

'Mrs Gauge, you're simply amazing. I just couldn't think that far ahead. Can't you call me Daisy, now that you know me, I'd feel more comfortable if you did.'

'I expect your missing your auntie, aren't you? I'll call you Daisy, if you like Mrs Blount, but not in front of Mr James, because I don't think he's quite ready for it. My name is Enid, but if you want me to be comfortable, then you'll call me Mrs Gauge, if that's all right with you – Daisy. Now then, do you want me to do out your room in the attic?'

'That's very kind of you but I use it like James uses his studio, so there are sketches and photos and bits of stuff everywhere. If you swept the floor and did a bit of dusting now and again, that would be lovely, and of course I'll call you Mrs Gauge.'

⁓

The north westerly wind whistled through the last leaves in the beech trees. It was unseasonably cold. Daisy came into the kitchen and shut the door, putting the folder of drawings on the table. There was a quiet hum from the newly installed refrigerator standing between the old Welsh dresser and the smart new cooker, with four gas hobs and two ovens, and to Daisy's delight, a grill that would toast bread in no time without the aid of a person holding a fork. She had resisted the tiling of the walls. They may be hygienic and easy to clean, but it would make the kitchen feel like a hospital, and it should be the warm heart of the house. The old range she hung on to, what if the gas supply failed? And on reflecting that there was no other fireplace in the kitchen, it would need to be lit in the winter months. Paraffin heaters were too smelly and dried the air.

James had deferred to her in these particulars, as he had on his plan to go to Heals and completely refurnish the principal rooms. Daisy thought the largely Victorian furniture in keeping with the house and that they should only jettison where woodworm had got the better of a piece or the room felt cluttered. In the event two horsehair settees, two occasional tables, seven chairs and a bureau that was falling to bits failed to pass muster. James insisted on a large modern, mahogany four-poster, which, when it arrived and had been assembled by the workmen, Daisy adored. It had thick velvet curtains on tiny little wheels that closed silently and completely. The pair of them spent a pleasant evening in their new bed poring over Heals' catalogue and selecting furniture they both liked that would not be out of place.

James would order them on his next visit to London. He had quickly established a habit. About once a fortnight he stayed at his bohemian club, The Chelsea Arts, where he was a country member. He enjoyed meeting with chaps he had studied with before the war and making connections with gallery owners and others in the art market. The food was good and the bed comfortable. James was clubbable.

∽

'When I were a youngster, I worked for Mr James's father for many a year. Just half a day a week in Winter and a day or so in the Summer, mostly. They weren't neither of 'em gardeners, not like you Mrs Blount. They just wanted it kept tidy, and a few nice flowers for the old Mrs Blount to pick through the summer, and a bit of veg now and again. They was good to me. When they went away they kept me on to keep things up to scratch and I'd be paid regular by the agent. But naturally when they died that all stopped. I missed it, nice house and a good bit of garden. I used to have a go at the wood but I were no woodsman and it went its own way.'

Jake finished the slow rolling of his cigarette, generously licked the edge of the paper and stuck it in his mouth. Rummaging in his pocket he brought out a battered Tommy lighter and lit up, sheltering the flame with a cupped hand.

'Now, what we up to today?'

'I think we've pretty much finished the easy bit,' Daisy said, 'it's laid out as near to the Victory garden I had with my Aunt as we can make it. I was surprised when I came here not to find a kitchen garden. Everyone in the country round me had one.'

'That'll be the war, then.'

'Two people managed to live off it most of the year round, and that's what I'm aiming for here.'

'I've only got a patch of garden meself,' Jake said, leaning on his spade and deeply inhaling, 'but most of the people I work for are very generous with their produce.'

'And so shall I be, Jake, when we've got some, so let's get a shift on. It's double digging today, but the more beds we can get done the more planting we can do before it gets too cold.'

Daisy pulled up her wellies and shouldered her spade.

'That's right, Mrs Blount. I expect Mrs G. will bring us a cup of tea before too long to wet our whistle, eh.'

'We'll start either end of that bed by the wall below the hothouse and aim to meet in the middle. That'll soon warm us up,' Daisy said.

The sun had not got much higher before Mrs Gauge appeared with a tray and set in on an upturned bushel box.

'There you are, the pair of you,' she said,' and I've brought you some seed cake to help you keep going. Jake, before you go come by the kitchen, I've got your Kate's eggs.'

'Thank you, Mrs G, I certainly will.'

Jake stuck his spade in the earth and took his half-smoked cigarette from behind his ear and lit up. Leaving it between his lips, he picked up a mug of tea and a slice of cake and grunted with contentment.

'My Kate's always been a bit of a gardener, but she's never done double digging like you can, Mrs Blount. Was you a land girl then?'

'No, my aunt taught me everything. Spring and Autumn we'd spend hours together in the garden. I came to enjoy it. There's real satisfaction in taking a carrot from seed to soup.'

'Right there is, and that's a neat way of putting it, I'll remember that.'

After a couple of hours Daisy had finished her half but Jake still had a way to go. Daisy cleaned off her spade with a stick.

'James and I are going out to lunch, so I'll have to make myself respectable. You stay as long as you like Jake and if you get done, we'll plant it out with brassicas tomorrow.'

'Right ho, Mrs Blount.' Jake stopped to lean on his spade and wiped his brow with a spotted handkerchief. He rummaged in his pocket and brought out his tobacco pouch.

'You leave it to me.'

Daisy smiled and headed for the house, reminding herself not to get irritated with Jake. He was getting on and it was difficult to find anybody to help with the garden. James had made it clear that he wasn't interested, he didn't have the time. However, he was happy to pay Jake for all the hours that Daisy wanted him.

∽

James had wheeled the Four Square out of the barn and pulled it onto its stand. He slid out the dipstick, wiped it on a rag and pushed it back into the sump before taking it slowly out again. He held it to the light to see the oil mark.

'Jolly good, that's fine for now. I'll ride pillion if you like?'

'Thanks.'

Daisy let the clutch in, and they bounced slowly down the long, rutted drive.

'It's on the way to Eastbourne,' James said, as they stopped before turning towards Lewes, 'about half-way to Polegate, I'll give you a nudge.'

'OK.' Daisy opened the throttle, the bike roared and accelerated down the narrow empty road.

The oblong house ran along one side of a square farmyard. Ramshackle barns and outbuildings were ranged at right angles to the house, leaving the fourth side open to the pastures and fields of winter wheat that rolled southwards towards the high downs and the sea. The bike skidded on the loose gravel as Daisy braked and came to a stop by the low front door.

In the ensuing quiet the house looked, at first sight, deserted. As they stood removing helmets goggles and gloves the door opened and a small dark man in shirt sleeves and braces emerged, his face lit by a broad smile under a mass of black curls.

'James – how wonderful to see you, you're looking gorgeous.' He vigorously pumped James' hands, holding on to them as he turned to Daisy. 'And you must be the new wife.'

James withdrew his hands and went to speak, but Daisy cut in.

'That's right, I'm Daisy.'

'Charmed' He took Daisy's hand and raised it to his lips, looking into her eyes. 'I'm Roddy.'

He swivelled round to James and clasped him in a brief bear hug, before turning back to Daisy.

'You're gorgeous too, lucky old James. Do you know he and I shared digs when we were at the Slade, happy days, and we haven't seen each other since…?'

'Must have been thirty-nine,' James said, 'before my call up.'

'Yes, I'm afraid I missed the whole show, LMF,' he turned to Daisy, "lacking in moral fibre" dear, they wouldn't even let me into the cadets at school, James will tell you all about it I'm sure. Now come on in out of the cold,' he clasped his upper arms and hunched his shoulders, 'we'll have pre-prandial tinkies in the studio because that's where the fire is lit.'

The farmhouse was a revelation. Pictures covered the walls from floor to ceiling. Chairs, tables, boxes, lampshades and many everyday objects were painted in pastel shades and abstract designs. This extended to the textiles, carpets, upholstery, curtains and shawls. The interior was dazzling.

Roddy made no reference to the exotic nature of the décor as he led them straight through the house. He stopped at the kitchen door. Inside, a tall angular woman in a floral wrap-over pinafore was busy at the central table.

'Mrs T be an angel and light the fire in the dining room or we'll all perish. Just let us know when lunch is ready, we'll be having a nourishing gin.'

The studio ran along one side of the house. It had once been a byre and iron rings were set into the walls at intervals. A catslide roof, pierced with long lights, made for a tolerable painting space. The floor was a mixture of flags and cobbles, gently sloped on two sides to the centre gully. It was covered with once brightly coloured rugs, now looking rather grimy. There was still a whiff of the cowshed. It was, even by bohemian standards, incredibly chaotic.

Debris was swept from a couple of rickety kitchen chairs and Roddy dragged them near to the stove which crackled comfortably, the black flue rising to meet the roof some way above them. He mixed large gins in water glasses and handed them to his guests.

'Chin, chin,' Roddy said, and raised his glass.

'James, this is such a joy,' he turned to Daisy, 'at Slade he was our guardian angel you know, pretty much the only one who managed to stay sane, or sober, for any length of time. We'd get into the most dreadful scrapes, being feckless and penniless to a man, and woman. But your James could always be relied upon to pull our chestnuts out of the fire.'

After this he spoke almost exclusively to James, who was not required to make much in the way of response. Now and then he would turn and smile at Daisy. The warm strong gin and flat tonic tasted awful, and Daisy was not relishing the now familiar experience of being ignored by James' friends.

'I'll go and see if your Mrs T would like any help with the lunch,' she said, and headed for the kitchen.

∽

'That's very kind of you, Mrs Blount, but everything's in hand. Is there anything I can get you? You might prefer a cup of tea to one of Roddy's gins, or a glass of sherry?'

'Tea would be lovely, thank you. Can I get it?'

'That would be a help,' said Mrs T, 'I'll get you a tray.' She quickly dried her hands and assembled what was necessary. 'I'd make it for you normally, but Roddy hasn't seen your James since before the war, and was so looking forward to it this morning that he had his first gin a bit early, so it's best for me to get lunch on the table sooner rather than later. They're all bohemians live here you know, mostly artists like your James. Roddy's on his own today. Normally it's like Piccadilly

Circus. They're good hearted but they can be a bit of handful, especially the ladies.'

'Have they made all the lovely objects and artworks? It gives the house a magical feeling, like it has its own character.'

'Well my dear, it's not like any farmhouse I've known, and I've been in a few over the years. They've even got statues in the garden. You should hear Isaac, the gardener. He doesn't hold with it. But then he's like most gardeners, because he works it, he thinks he owns it.'

'I can understand that. My aunt and I had a Victory garden round her cottage in Devon. There was always something to be done, even in the winter. When I came to Sussex, I missed it a lot. It was like living inside the seasons helping them along. I'm working on making a proper garden for James, but it's hard, there's years of neglect to get over.'

'You get your tea Mrs Blount and I'll just get these vegetables on the stove and put a match to the fire, and then if you'd like I'll show you Isaac's plot, might give you some ideas.'

Mrs T led Daisy out the back of the house to a large garden walled in rose brick. It was orderly and kempt, packed with good things and showed all the signs of being cherished. A pile of leaf mould in one corner gave off the familiar pungent odours of autumn. They walked round the remains of raised straw beds for strawberries and the rich loamy barrows for asparagus, neat frames for beans and netted squares for berries. The paths between the beds were narrow so as not to waste any more fertile ground than was necessary. A massive carved head of a Green Man, garlands of leaves curling from his mouth and nostrils, hung against the north wall.

'Right Mrs Blount, we'd better be getting back. If you'll finish laying up for me, I'd be grateful, and then get Roddy and your James in. I'll start getting the food on the table.'

'Of course, and thank you, Mrs T,' Daisy said, 'the garden is as magical as the house.'

Roddy had disappeared to the cellar. Daisy came in with two vegetable dishes and joined James on the painted chairs. James had a hectic flush and was more voluble than usual.

'Good news, Daisy. Roddy knows some of the opera people well and is more than happy to get you an introduction. You've got all the designs you did at Marleigh. It might be an idea to put a portfolio together so that you've got something to show them?'

Roddy came in and stood by the sideboard opening wine bottles and humming to himself. He put two bottles onto the table.

'No butler,' he explained, and filled glasses for Daisy and James.

Mrs T arrived with a steaming and fragrant pie dish and put it in the centre of the table. She gave the fire a quick rake and put more coal on. Standing by the door she took off her pinafore and rolled it up.

'I'll be off then Mr Roddy, back at tea-time to clear up,' she looked at Daisy, 'there's a pudding in the oven and a tray laid if you want it after lunch, Mrs Blount.'

'Thank you, Mrs T, I'll clear the table at least.'

'You don't have to, but if you did, it would be a kindness.'

She ducked out of the room and her pushbike sounded on the gravel moments later. Daisy dished up the food as it seemed to be expected. Roddy resumed his virtual monopoly of the conversation with rambling anecdotes that constantly referenced people, places and ideas with which Daisy had little or no acquaintance. Having broken in at one point to thank Roddy for recommending her to the opera, she lapsed into silence. Luckily, the minced chicken and mushroom pie in a light suet crust was in itself sufficiently engaging. Some more information about the opera house and Roddy's relationship with the company would have been good, but the chance to elicit this never came. Daisy wondered if Roddy had really meant it, or would be able to remember the favour, given the amount of drink the two men were sinking. After lunch she made tea, but only she drank it. Roddy had been back to the cellar. James was distinctly the worse for wear.

'James, we really must be going, I need to see Mrs Gauge before she leaves, and there are things that have to be seen to before supper.'

For a moment James stared at Daisy, rather glassily. Without waiting for a reply, she fetched their coats and helmets and eased James out of his chair. It still took a good twenty minutes to leave the house, with Roddy still in mid-anecdote as Daisy let in the clutch. Roddy shouted after them and waved goodbye with his red spotted handkerchief.

The ride back was a nightmare. James slumped heavily against Daisy's back and held her too tightly. He seemed incapable of leaning with the movement of the bike or shifting his weight in unison with her. This meant she had to keep the machine as upright as possible in order to keep some control. Bends had to be taken very slowly as did any curve in the road. Thus, they wound their slow way through the countryside.

When they reached Campiston, James stumbled off the bike, dropped his helmet and, mumbling some excuse disappeared into the studio. Daisy found him there later, overcoat still on, spreadeagled on the chaise snoring stertorously. She left him there and after telling Mrs Gauge they wouldn't be needing any supper, went to her room in the attic.

The fire provided some instant cheer and Daisy sat in its glow, staring at the flames and wondering. She rubbed her tummy, at least she hadn't felt nauseous. A little later she turned on the standard lamp behind the settee and with her writing slope on her lap she took out a tablet of paper and began.

Dear Alice,

Big news first. No poppies in the streets last month and I'm feeling a bit sick first thing. I'm pregnant. I can't believe it I can't even think about it and I haven't told James. I've tried but I can't find the words. I've decided to go to a doctor and have it confirmed first. That's all I can say at the moment. Do not congratulate me.

At least I'll be able to pay the doctor. James asked me if I wanted a dress allowance, apparently his mother had one. I said no thanks, but he insisted I needed 'independent money' so I've got a bank account with £100 in it and a cheque book that's the size of a tea towel. The bank is in London, but they are so famous everybody accepts their cheques. He said the King banks there, but he may have been pulling my leg. It's so kind of him, all I've bought so far is a dress for evening wear. It's very long and dove grey silk, it makes me look even taller and skinnier [if that's a word?]. He thinks I should wear jewellery like other women. I tried on some of his mother's but I just looked dreadful like a panto' dame. I think he secretly agrees because he hasn't mentioned it again.

It's all because of these excruciating outings to dinner that he insists we go to. I can manage sitting there and eating listening to the women's inane chatter. 'What sort of war did you have, darling?' I hadn't realised there were other wars on offer at the time. James says that it's code for did you manage to get out and spend the war in the colonies, having fun in South Africa.

323

After food the women all troop out to the drawing [we'd say sitting] room while the men smoke cigars and drink. This is where my heart sinks into my pretty heeled shoes and I feel abandoned. I can't do 'girl talk.' Their conversation is dreadful.

'Darling, isn't it just too wonderful that Barkers and Derry & Toms are getting back to normal. I can't wait for the roof garden to re-open, divine teas and wonderful views across London – and so riveting to see just who is having tea with whom – and such a relief now that the trains are beginning to run on time and they're not full of smelly, noisy squaddies.'

They all seem to be dying to get back to France and Italy but say it's impossible because their railways aren't running like ours, and the hotels are unreliable. I did try talking about our honeymoon in the South of France, but they just wanted to know if I stayed at the George V, in Menton, and of course we didn't, we were on a greasy motorbike and stayed in inns and lodging houses. I did say that the country was very beautiful but the people seemed desolate, but that was too serious, and so it was back to Barkers and Derry & Toms.

I try my best for James' sake, they are his people. He laughs at them and calls them the 'county' but doesn't see that he's one of them and I'm jolly well not. It's alright for him, he's their class, had a distinguished war, even if his medals are only campaign, I'm jolly proud of them. I'm a young, awkward country girl, with no family and not a trace of polish. I just don't meld darling.

Today we went to lunch with a friend of his in this very arty farmhouse where every inch of everything has been decorated by the artists who live there. Sort of William Morris, but modern designs. Our host more or less ignored me [although he did offer to get me an introduction to the local opera, but who knows] and James just abandoned me and they both got completely drunk.

James is sweet and I know he loves me, but he doesn't know what to do with me. I'm the one who has to change, who has to try and fit into his world and I cannot see it happening, at least, not in the way that he wants. It's not that I don't try I just can't manage it. Sometimes I feel stupid and inadequate, like I married him under false pretences. I wonder if he thinks he made a terrible mistake.

I haven't met a soul round here that I can imagine being friends with. Day to day it might look fine. But when I sit down to write to you, someone who really knows me, I can see more clearly what's wrong.

Sorry to moan, I guess I'm feeling put upon today. What I need is for you to come and give me a big hug and make me laugh.

With much love,
Your dear friend,
Daisy X

Chapter 18

EMILY CAME OUT OF THE PHARMACY AND HURRIED HOME. I've always been low on oestrogen, sometimes it's six weeks between periods. It might be just fine. She ran up the stairs slammed the front door and headed for the bathroom undoing her jeans as she crossed the floor. Once on the pedestal she put the spill between her legs and tried to pee. Finally, she relaxed and a stream of urine passed over the plastic strip. Up to three minutes wait, one bar pink equals not pregnant, two bars pregnant. Before a minute was up there were two pink bars clearly visible. Emily stared at the spill willing it to change. She immediately thought to get another kit this one could be faulty.

Still gripping the spill, she went to her room and fell heavily on the bed. It simply cannot be true, not now please. She lay back and closed her eyes her head teeming with anxious thoughts. Rolling off the bed she grabbed her coat on the way out and headed for the street, full as it would be with normal lives being led with apparent equanimity. Emily walked quickly dashing tears from her eyes. The world had changed in an instant. It was such a weird sensation. A short while ago I was me and the world was as it always is, it still looks exactly the same, but it all means something different. Mothers and children, not normally noticed, were surrounded by a neon aura. She wanted to talk to them, to ask questions but what about? Of course, I have this fearful choice, but it's mad, how can it be made? Emily laughed out loud. No data, I don't know any mothers or any children.

As the light began to fade the sound of bells tolling vespers could be heard from Sacre Coeur. She had been out for a long time and felt weary. There was no walking away and so she struggled to bring her mind to focus. What to do now? Keep to the prosaic – what to have for supper? That we still have to eat whatever happens, was a good thought to hold, and cooking a useful displacement activity. Perhaps a chicken, with lots of garlic, thyme, smoked bacon and Charlotte potatoes, one of their favourite suppers. Shop, then home.

∾

Emily poured vermouth into the hot juices in the Creuset, it sizzled creating wafts of fragrant steam. Next, someone to talk to before I implode. Jean-Marie, it would only be mid-evening in Reunion and she couldn't call Toby at l'Institut.

Eventually Emily managed a state of comparative calm. Having spoken to Jean-Marie, showered and changed her clothes, the sense of her alienation from herself diminished. The thought of telling Toby seemed daunting, perhaps because it would definitely make it real. Champagne was chilling, it hardly seemed appropriate, in fact rather odd as they very rarely drank it, but it would alert him to something potentially out of the ordinary.

With Toby ensconced with the newspapers. Emily quietly opened the Champagne and brought it in. Filling two coups to the brim, she handed one to Toby, who looked at her and raised one eyebrow.

327

'I'm pregnant.'

Toby slowly put the glass down untouched, and looked into Emily's face.

'You're pregnant. Are you sure?'

'The test was very clearly positive.'

'I'm lost for words. I guess this was not planned. How are you feeling?'

'Poleaxed.'

'Is the father Jean-Marie?'

'No, it's Dan.'

There was a long pause.

'Our youthful sylviculturist and general technical genius from England.'

'I told you, it was only once, the night I got to Campiston feeling rather dislocated.'

'Does he know?'

'No.'

'Holy heaven, when did you find out?'

'This afternoon, I didn't know what to do. I couldn't burst in on you so I called Jean-Marie. He was so lovely, he listened to me wailing and very calmly talked me through the possibilities. Telling me I'd got plenty of time to make a decision so not to rush it, that I could call him any time I wanted to talk. The choice seems to me impossible right now and my recent record on decision making isn't impressive. He said if I keep it, he wants to be a Godfather.' Emily, who had been looking down, smiled and raised her face. 'I was so grateful for his kindness. I do miss him.'

Toby came and put his arms round his daughter who lay her head on his shoulder.

'My dear Emily, this is amazing in so many unexpected ways.'

Toby picked up a coup and put the other in Emily's hand.

'Let's drink to the future, whatever it might hold,' he said, and drained his glass.

∽

Next morning Emily bought another pregnancy test of a different make, just to be sure, and walked back to the apartment at a normal pace. She sat with a coffee looking out of the window and wondered what to do next, and why she felt so calm. She half-heartedly tried a cost/benefit analysis but it didn't help. If there were any benefits, they were too nebulous to be weighed, debits on the other hand seemed to pile up fairly easily. Talking to Annabel about it seemed like a sensible idea. However, it was difficult to imagine that she would be thrilled and she might be mightily put out. She couldn't face telling Dan by phone, and email seemed too impersonal and she did not want to go to Campiston. Perhaps she should write him a letter. The tone could be kept cool and it would just explain the essentials. Perhaps telling Dan should be postponed? If she decided on an abortion she need never tell him. She was pregnant but nothing would be expected of him whatever she decided to do. But what if he got all macho about it and opposed an abortion? If she was not going to tell Dan then she could hardly saddle Annabel with the news. Emily decided to keep things to herself until she had made her decision and then present a fait accompli to the pair of them. The decision deadline was set at two, or at the outside three, weeks hence. Clearly rationality was not coming to her rescue and so she must wait and see how she felt. Having devised what she considered an excellent strategy, Emily went about her daily life but with a strong sense that something extraordinary was happening inside her.

∽

A mellow sun had drifted through the apartment all day and now glanced off the walls as it slowly dipped to the west. Emily had spent the morning alternately daydreaming and searching for new sites that might be useful places to send her CV and begging letter, which had already done the rounds of the obvious NGOs and research organisations. There just weren't that many in the frame and no jobs had come up for a beginner with a first degree. The couple of junior jobs that had appeared required experience. Emily was all too aware that she had little to recommend her in a competitive market. If she had stayed with her internship at least she would have something to suggest she was serious. Perhaps she needed to register for a higher degree. That might inspire a bit of confidence in her. Time to go and meet Toby. Knotting a favourite cashmere scarf round her neck, a present from Jean-Marie, she pulled the door closed behind her.

The long steps down to Abbesses were dotted with knots of children going home from school, playing noisily with shrill voices, oblivious in their own world. They made Emily smile but also feel uneasy. Getting off at St Sepulchre, she sat and watched the massive fountain in the piazza, soothed by the plays of light and the rhythmic sounds of the cascades. One winter when she was a child, the water had frozen and it seemed as though time itself had stopped.

In the Luxembourg there was a lot of activity around the perimeter of the ornamental pond. The little yachts, that could be hired, set off across the water and if they managed to avoid mishaps, the children ran around to meet their boat and turn it again into the choppy little waves.

Toby was at a seminar in the Senate and had suggested they meet in the tea rooms. Emily sat in the rather steamy atmosphere and sipped a Yellow label with cold milk, an affectation she had picked up in England. Toby, in a dark suit with a gleaming white silk shirt came in and joined her at the table. He squeezed her hand and looked around.

'It's looking rather seedy in here, let's go and get a drink.'

They walked past the gleaming windows of the Palais and out onto the street.

'Let's cross here and down that passage there's a bistro on the corner.' Toby said.

The single room had a clutter of small tables and chairs. Red curtains and buttoned banquettes lent it a faint old-fashioned charm. Lighting concealed above long wall mirrors reflected a cosy and comfortable space. They sat down and Emily ordered two Leffs. It was early evening and they were the only customers. A waiter moved quietly around the room laying up for dinner. Toby unknotted his tie, rolled it up, and put it in his pocket.

'I always find government seminars annoying. We are called to brief them on critical aspects of global economy.' He turned in his chair and asked the waiter for some peanuts. 'Half of them clearly have been sent by superiors and are openly uninterested, the half that listen seem unlikely to be swayed by anything they hear from us. No doubt their micro-political agendas have other, more pressing elements for them to contend with. It's all premised on the assumption of rational government and I've yet to come across one. Give me sceptical academics any day. Enough,' he took a long draught of his beer. 'How are you feeling about your dilemma? You seem to have been preoccupied but calm in the last few days, are you recovering from the shock?'

'I don't know whether it was shock or simply fear. A total dependant, for years to come – am I up to it? My only source of understanding is us, our lives. You were forced into being my only parent, you even had to fight for it. You made room for me in a life already full. You've kept your career, but you pretty much gave up on finding a life partner in order to spend your time, and your love, on me. I'm just beginning to think, on reflection as your sole beneficiary, that I might feel secure enough to try and do that myself. I've learnt so much recently about how my life has been shaped. I wonder if I could use my own experience of us to try and nurture a new person, to try and love as wisely and fully as I have been loved.'

'Stop.' Toby held up his hands 'That's too terribly romantic. You can't be hormonal already, can you? After the pain and joy of birth, and even without the complications that I had, there's an awful lot of blood, sweat and tears to get through. And signally, I was established when you came and joined me.

'If you want a career it demands masses of energy and flexibility, neither are commodities entirely consistent with babies, which is something to bear in mind. Having said that, sharing the world with you and watching you becoming a person has been the saving grace of my life.'

'Mine too,' Emily said, she looked round, the place was beginning to fill. 'Why not stay here and eat? It's too late to go and make supper.' She signalled for two more beers and asked for menus.

The waiter put before them small oval terrines of garlicky, crumbly pate de campagne with deeply bronzed domes and rose-pink meat. Toby ate a slice off his knife and murmured appreciation.

'I've been wondering if I should be drinking wine?' Emily said, picking up her glass.

'I should think so,' Toby said, 'just knock off the Calvados.' He paused. 'I have what might be a complicating factor to introduce.' Emily looked up. 'But a benign one,' he added. 'Angela Loiseau was there this afternoon and she has a smallish project coming up shortly that needs an economically literate dogsbody, part-time, at least initially, and I told her that you were qualified and currently on the market.'

Emily's jaw dropped.

'Papa, that is so good, oh, to be a dogsbody, it's beyond all my dreams.' She grabbed Toby's hands. 'You're a marvel, did you tell her it would be my first job and that at present I'm pregnant.'

Toby arched his back and wiped his mouth with his napkin.

'Yes, to the former and no, that's for you to negotiate. It's basically a research assistant, mainly Paris based with some limited travel.' He fished a card out of his breast pocket and handed it to Emily. 'If you are interested, get in touch with the project manager and make an application, you should get an interview.'

'Do you think the pregnancy will sink me?'

'I don't see why it should. It's not full time, at least not in the first phase. Angela trusts my judgment, even when it's my daughter. I told her you'd done a lot of work for me and done it well, which was true. She's always looking to get more women into the business.'

Emily leaned back in her chair her hands flat on the table.

'Papa, what shall I do?'

'I don't know,' Toby said.

∽

Emily left the metro at Cluny La Sorbonne and made her way along St Germain, turning off towards Pont au Double. She took comfort from looking at her reflection in the shop windows as she made her way to the College St Vincent. Her hair, heavy and bouncy in a reassuringly expensive sort of way, caught the sunlight as it moved. Neatly tailored black trousers, a plain cream silk blouse, with a choker of tiny seed pearls, another gift from Jean-Marie, that set off her milky neck, all came together with a dark tweed jacket of military cut. Momentarily she wondered if she had overdone it, she didn't often aspire to chic. Had she got it right? She was only off to an interview to be a *bonne a tout faire*, not tea with the president. What should she say about the pregnancy? How could it be introduced? 'Oh, by the way, I think I should mention…' sounded a bit flippant. But even worse was the fact that she hadn't even made up her mind, which would make her look impossibly flaky. She closed down the internal dialogue before it spiralled and checked the address.

The building, when she found it, was much older than expected with tall iron gates that opened onto a treeless courtyard, jammed with cars. It was entered by a short flight of worn stone steps. Little light penetrated inside, and it took Emily a moment to orientate herself. The lineaments of an old mansion house were still discernible, a panelled lobby punctuated with doors at regular intervals, ended in a wide central staircase. The predominant colour was dark brown. The concierge was lodged behind a large mahogany desk in front of a bank of bulging pigeonholes. He took her name and reached for his phone, inviting her, with a gesture, to sit on one of the ancient upright chairs.

'Dr Arpin will be with you shortly,' he said.

'Thank you.'

Drawn by the light Emily stood looking out of a bay window onto an unkempt inner garden. Moments later a young man tripped noisily down the uncarpeted stairs and strode over to where she stood. He proffered a long white hand and gave hers a firm shake while looking directly into her face.

'Raphael Arpin,' he said, 'would you like to follow me?'

'Yes, of course, I'm Emily Blount,' she said, partly to a receding back as he was already at the foot of the stairs. He stopped and turned, waiting for her to catch him up.

'You're here for a post with Prof Loiseau's upcoming North Africa project? How's your rural economics?'

'Pretty fair, though more Middle East, but I'm certainly au fait with current issues in North Africa.'

'Of course, you're Toby Blount's daughter.'

They hurried down a long dingy corridor. The air was chilly, no sounds came from behind the solid wooden doors on each side of them. He stopped at the end and stood back, holding the door open with arm fully extended and head slightly bowed to indicate that Emily should precede him.

The comfortable room was spacious and overlooked the courtyard. The décor was faded, the floor covered by an elderly Iranian rug, pomegranate and gold now faded to pink and ochre. Two heavy glass fronted bookcases, stuffed with papers and journals, gave it a domestic, donnish air.

'Please, be seated,' he said, indicating a battered chaise. Grabbing a sheaf of papers from a desk in front of the window, he wheeled an office chair across the room and sat opposite Emily. He dropped his papers on a small brass table that stood between them. His long black hair was pushed away from his forehead, where, as soon as he removed his hand, it returned.

'So, thanks for coming in. If you were the finance minister for Maroc, right now, what would your priorities be?'

Emily's eyes widened but she didn't blink.

'Well, for a non-oil economy the service and industrial sectors are in reasonable shape, as is tourism. The biggest issue must be the perennial one, agriculture, less than twenty per cent of GDP, but employing around half of the labour force.

It needs investment and modernisation, which is the focus of the project, as I understand it. But to avoid swelling the urban poor this needs to be linked to a growth of employment opportunities in other sectors, which means education and training. I'd be keeping a watchful eye on the Dirham and maintaining good relations with international bodies, IMF, World Bank, OECD and the Paris Club, to help manage debt.'

Dr Arpin nodded.

'Basically, I think you've nailed it, but there are other issues, economic and political. The sub-Saharan economies are all developing and so the competition for foreign investment is keen. The monarchy continues to support a moderate line on Islam, but in the current climate religion could become a destabilising factor.'

He smiled and crossed his legs, leaning back in his chair.

'If growth is low, and likely to remain so, and inflation difficult to control, what sort of economic development projects might help in promoting the rural economy, taking into account a certain political fragility?'

This was more complex and Emily had to think hard and fast, as she did for a series of scenarios that Dr Arpin laid out for her to comment on. Tea with the President could not have been more testing. The need to concentrate and monitor her performance was paramount, the awareness of time passing gave way to a constant demanding present. It was impossible to read Dr Arpin's evaluation of her contributions. At several points he probed her responses, asking for further explication. When they finally got around to discussing the project it sounded exciting and ambitious. Emily asked as many questions as she could think of and hoped they sounded incisive and intelligent.

After what now seemed like an age, she sensed things were drawing to a close, and still it was impossible to know whether she had made her case well. Dr Arpin remained friendly and polite throughout. Her heart began to thump. She must tell him. *If I don't mention the pregnancy now it means I have decided on a termination.* For a moment she felt a rising panic, but only for a moment. Her mind returned to Dr Arpin who was outlining the job.

'You would be managing the logistics for the lead rural field workers, keeping them supported and chasing their monthly reports. These would need some initial analysis before being fed into the data bank, though we might well have an analyst to do that, but a comprehensive summary report must be sent to me, along with assessments of progress and any problems arising. At an early point you would need to do a tour of the field to enable you to assess requests in context. You would be based here, and the post is initially point four, two days a week. The start is imminent.'

'Are you offering me the post, Dr Arpin?'

'Yes, it was a good application, your refs all speak very highly of you. You're familiar with the work culture, which is a big plus, and you've impressed me with your understanding of development work and its practical organisation.'

There was a pause. Emily sat up straight and looked at Dr Arpin.

'There is something I feel bound to tell you. I am currently pregnant.'

Dr Arpin leaned back and looked at the ceiling before slowly returning his gaze to Emily's face.

'Congratulations, Ms Blount. It is sensible of you to let me know. It is not a problem for us here at St Vincent. If we will not be socially progressive, then who will be? The question is rather the other way. Do you think you will be able to manage a new job, albeit part-time, and a new baby simultaneously, without either of them suffering? Also, would you be able to do the initial site visits before your confinement?'

'It's early days so travel should not be an issue. Later there might be some problems of time management, but if I get expert help and organise myself well, then I am sure that I can manage it.'

'If you can give me that assurance, then the post is yours if you want it. Perhaps you would like some time to think about it? I could mail you some homework to familiarise yourself with the organisation of the project.'

Emily found it hard to believe what had just happened and took a little while to respond. Her impulse was to go and hug Dr Arpin and thank him fulsomely, but she restrained herself.

'Thank you, I am sure I can manage to meet the demands of the post and would very much like to accept, it would be a marvellous opportunity for me, and I would give it all I've got. I'm ready to begin tomorrow.'

'That's admirable keenness. I suggest you take a couple of days to look over the homework and come back, shall we say Thursday at ten o'clock? That will give me time to get your contract agreed and drawn up. I'll mail it to you sometime Wednesday so that you will be ready to sign when I see you.'

Dr Arpin stood up and returned his papers to his desk. With unexpected courtesy he escorted Emily down the stairs, introduced her to the concierge and suggested he get a pigeonhole ready for her and a set of keys. They shook hands.

'You must call me Raffi, now,' he said, and smiled.

A moment later Emily was in the street wondering if it had actually happened. She breathed deeply and looked around to check the world was itself. I guess that's it, I seem to have made two amazing decisions. She looked down and rubbed her still flat tummy. On the way back she bought some Cremant de Bourgogne, best not to frighten Toby with another bottle of Champagne.

Chapter 19

IN THE BRIGHT KEEN AIR, THE ROOF OF THE STUDIO glistened white with a late frost. Daisy selected a long narrow spade and a rake from the barn and headed for the kitchen garden. A heap of rotted dung steamed gently in the sunlight. She and Jake had dug four straight trenches about a spit and a half deep. The compost was to be spread in the bottom and mixed with some topsoil. Although heavy manual work was now uncomfortable, Daisy continued to do what she could in the garden.

James had talked about there being asparagus beds when he was a child, and how much he had enjoyed the green shoots in a thick buttery sauce, and so she had offered to have a go at growing them, although they were known to be a temperamental crop and took time to establish. Daisy wrote to Alice for advice as she had only a vague idea about how to go about it.

With the small wheelbarrow half full of dung, she trudged to the end of the first trench and began to fill it. Standing in the trench she raked the dark crumbly mixture along the bed. With any luck Jake would appear soon and he could do the strenuous bits. She thought perhaps she should be a bit more careful. Although being slender she didn't have much to show, it wouldn't be very long before she would be forced to take things easier. Mrs Gauge definitely disapproved of her reluctance to give up the garden. 'Ladies with child' as she had quaintly put it, 'needed to have rest and eat good food.' Daisy had no intentions of resting. The farmers' wives where she came from never had a chance to rest yet managed to have a good many healthy children. She was determined that the business would not dominate her life quite yet. When the baby came she would devote herself to it, of course. She had fantasised that she might be able to find a wet nurse, like the old nobility, but James had just laughed, who would do such a thing nowadays?

∽

A letter for Daisy arrived with a crest impressed on the envelope, inviting her to visit and meet some of the people who were engaged in creating operas during the summer season. She stared at it for a long time. It was not expected, and the prospect brought butterflies to her tummy. James' friend Roddy had not only remembered, a feat in itself as he had most certainly been three sheets to the wind, but had put himself out on her behalf. He must be personally thanked for his kindness. However, daunted as she may feel by the aura of aristocracy, and she was, this chance could not be missed. A reply was written and she walked it down to the post box at Barcombe station.

When the time came, she wasn't at all sure she could go ahead with it. James said they were bohemian but in a rather smart way and that trousers would be fine, so she took the Square Four, despite his expressed anxieties about motorbikes and miscarriages.

The house was beautiful and put Campiston to shame,

the people she met were welcoming, interested in her and what she had done and in how she might become involved, in a small way to begin with, in their operatic enterprise.

For Daisy it was like an electric charge, she felt recognised and real in a way she had almost forgotten was possible. There was a lot of laughter and she joined in. It was a million miles away from Marleigh rep, for one thing all these people spoke posh, but unlike her starchy neighbours, they were relaxed, friendly, with no side. The whole thing smelt and felt like theatre and for the first time since she had left Devon, Daisy felt at home. They had promised to keep her in mind and get in touch later when preparations for the Summer season began. It was assumed that the impending baby would be no impediment.

On the way back she stopped off at the farmhouse to thank Roddy, who insisted she come in and pressed a warm Gin on her, adding a little Cassis to keep out the cold, which she accepted and even sipped.

∽

Daisy and James walked up the crescent drive, flanked with shrubberies of box, bay and hydrangeas to a grand Victorian house with mullioned bays each side of the Doric porch. To the left of the front door a discreet brass plate bore the legend, Merrivale.

James rang the bell and the door was opened by a young woman in a plain costume and court shoes who took them to Matron's office. Once there, they were greeted by a stout woman with peachy cheeks decked out in an impeccable uniform with a wide black belt, and a pie frill cap keeping every hair in place. She proffered a scrubbed pink hand.

'Welcome to Merrivale, Mr and Mrs Blount. I'm Matron.

Perhaps we might have a look round our excellent facilities and then we can answer any questions you might have over a cup of tea in my sitting room. Shall we start with the lounge and I could introduce Mrs. Blount to some of our ladies.'

'Thank you, Matron, that would be splendid,' James said.

Daisy smiled weakly and followed Matron down the corridor and through a set of double doors into a sitting room with furniture that made one sit up properly. A few noticeably pregnant young women sat around, reading or knitting. James coughed and went and studied the paintings around the walls. Daisy was duly introduced, and they seemed entirely friendly, but she could not think of anything to say to them. She had the curious thought that she was not pregnant in quite the same way as these mothers-to-be, who seemed entirely at ease with the whole business.

Matron wafted them through the facilities, the dining room, the writing room with a large wireless, a room where the practical side of early motherhood was explained and tried out on large dolls and a library full of useful books and magazines. In the wide corridors nurses in powder blue uniforms moved around quickly and quietly. Matron indicated a double door behind which was the medical side of things. This they did not enter. The spotless private rooms looked out over the well-tended gardens. There was a bed with a floral counterpane, a small writing table and an armchair, but not a cot.

Matron's sitting room was cosy with a lot of chintz. Tea was brought in by a white coated orderly, who smiled at Daisy and put a plate of Nice biscuits in front of her. Matron poured the tea and handed round the cups and saucers. They were briefly interrupted by a cheery and benign-looking doctor who shook hands.

'I very much look forward to meeting you again soon

Mrs. Blount and I can assure you that we offer the most up-to-date and convenient facilities for all aspects of modern motherhood.'

While the doctor entertained Daisy, Matron focused on talking money with James. When the doctor left, Matron asked Daisy if there was anything she would like to ask. Daisy said, no. She was assured that should anything occur to her she need only pick up the telephone. When it was time to leave Matron courteously saw them off the premises.

A broad avenue bordered with lofty Scots pines led down to the Hove sea front where they had left the Square Four.

'What a strange place,' Daisy said, as they put on their helmets and goggles. 'Somewhere between a hospital and a hotel and it felt just like school.'

'I was quite impressed,' James said, 'clean, efficient, well-run and competent looking staff. Just what one needs.'

Daisy said nothing. She insisted that James ride pillion as holding on to him on the back of the bike was getting too uncomfortable.

~

'I'd much rather have the baby at home. We've got a doctor, a district nurse and a midwife, they should be able to manage me between them, I'm not exactly delicate. I'm young and healthy and the pregnancy has gone without a hitch. Nurse Booth is looking after me and I'm taking notice of advice. I've already nearly stopped riding the bike. The only problem has been you and Mrs Gauge trying to make me lay down the whole time.' Daisy stared across the breakfast table at James, her brow furrowed and her mouth set.

'Who is having this baby, you or me? Surely, I can make up my own mind as to how my baby is born?

James put down his coffee and leant across the table. He looked Daisy squarely in the face.

'You're not being fair to me. I'm your husband and I have a responsibility for your welfare. Birth can be complicated and if you go to a nursing home, like most women do by the way, we know you would have the very best of care. I would have thought it's just common sense. People will think it very odd if we have the baby at home.'

'What does it have to do with other people? And we are not having the baby, James, I am.'

Daisy pushed her chair noisily under the table, before going upstairs to her room. Had she been able to run she would have. She lay on her bed and wiped her eyes. If I went to a nursing home I'd hate it. I'd get treated like an invalid and ordered about by starchy women calling me, madam, and secretly despising me. James would never understand. Dr Fraser and Nurse Booth are delivering babies all the time. He and James are friends. I trust them and they won't make me feel useless. I hate to quarrel, but I can't give in to his idea of common sense, it has to be on my terms.

Daisy breathed deeply and looked in the mirror to try and compose her face. She smoothed down her skirt. The stairs creaked heralding her arrival as she slowly descended to the morning room, where James still sat disconsolately munching toast. Daisy stood behind his chair, put her arms round his neck and kissed his cheek.

'I'm sorry,' she said.

James patted her hand.

'Me too, I should have discussed it with you properly rather than making assumptions. It never occurred to me that you might want something different. But I still don't understand your objections.'

'I know you want what's best, but I would feel so much

happier and more secure if you were near and, I was here at home, with Dr Fraser and a nurse I knew. I'd be much more scared having a baby surrounded by strangers in a hospital in Hove.'

'You've seen it, Daisy, it's not a hospital, it's a very comfortable nursing home and you'd have everything you needed and nothing to worry about at all for a couple of weeks, or longer if you wanted.'

Daisy pulled a chair up and sat down close to James. She put her hand on his thigh and looked him in the face.

'You are very kind and very generous, James, and I'm truly grateful, but you are not listening to me. I'm scared witless by the thought of having a baby and it has to be the way I think I can cope with it. There's nothing more I can say.'

James made a harrumphing noise.

'And I think we would be taking a wholly unnecessary risk, but if that is what you want then I'm willing to think about it. We should see what Dr Fraser says.'

'Why do we have to? Surely, it's a matter for us. Babies are born all over the place, every day. I'm afraid of the pain and how I will cope being a mother but honestly, nowadays it's not the risky business it was for our grandparents.'

෮

Dear Alice,

When it came to it, having the baby was a lot easier than I had imagined, and it has to be said, my imagination was running hard in the other direction. I've been thinking something dreadful was about to happen to me, something I would have absolutely no control over, but it is after all a natural process, if an amazingly painful one.

*It all seemed a bit casual at first. My waters broke, [I thought I'd wet myself] and Nurse Booth was sent round to examine me. She said I had hardly begun to dilate, which you have to do a lot of, and so she pedalled off home to have her tea. She came back later and kept checking me, and when the contractions were coming close together, and I thought I might fall to pieces at any moment, Dr Fraser appeared. He checked everything and listened to the heartbeat with a little ear trumpet, and then came the order to **push**. It was awful, like trying to pooh a boulder, I could not believe it was possible until it happened. Perhaps your sheep feel the same? I certainly have a lot of sympathy for them having to do it every year. Then the baby came splashing out [I hope I'm not putting you off] and they dash about frantically, cutting the cord, checking for defects, and getting the baby to breathe. Its first little wail was magical. Then they wrap it up and get it to latch on to the nipple of one of my glamorously inflated bosoms and that is that, apart from all the clearing up. It seemed to take forever and simultaneously no time at all. It was a lot messier than I expected.*

When I was cleaned up and in bed with baby all neatly wrapped in swaddling clothes James and Mrs G came in (to see baby), sex: female, weight: 7lbs 6oz, name: Augusta Blount (I had to be firm with James who wanted a whole string of female ancestors represented, all with hideous names). He was very sweet but too scared to pick her up, Mrs G was in 7th heaven, beaming and cooing, which was jolly nice as I've got no mum.

I'm ashamed to tell you but the thing I feared the most wasn't the pain but that I wouldn't like the baby or want to look after it, but it was love at first sight, literally. Nurse Booth says it's absolutely natural, it's our girls' hormones working their magic. Anyway, I'm besotted and – totally – exhausted. I'll write again when I get the time and the strength.

With love,

Daisy

Ps: Hope your lodger is behaving herself and feeding the chickens etc.

Pps: Miss you and do so wish you were here

X

For a couple of weeks after Gussie's appearance the neighbours came in succession to view the infant and make bright conversation. Daisy still found them hard work, their respective worlds being as far from each other as ever. The prettily knitted pink matinee sets, with matching bootees and ribbon laces, that they brought with them were wrapped in tissue paper and put in a drawer by Mrs Gauge.

The day now revolved around Gussie's needs. Mrs Gauge had increased her hours mainly to help with the mountains of nappies that had suddenly become a major feature of domestic routine. James had thoughtfully installed a twin tub washing machine that spun lots of the water out of the wet nappies making it easier to dry them. Daisy had thought Mrs Gauge's advice to get at least two dozen nappies rather excessive, but events had proved her right.

～

The sitting room was not as tidy as usual. Gussie lay asleep in a wicker Moses basket on a lambswool rug near the fire. James lounged in an armchair, a blue jewellers' box on his lap. Daisy poured from the large silver teapot they had taken to regularly using because of the unusual number of visitors and handed him a cup. A long cream silk baptismal gown trimmed with Guipure lace lay draped over the settee.

'I'm so glad we took Gussie to be baptised. Everyone was so welcoming, and the women made such a fuss of her afterwards. Father Luke was lovely. I thought he might drop her when he leant over the font, but I guess he's had a lot of practice. She was very good in church, but Mrs Gauge said the old women felt cheated because she didn't howl and cry out the devil.'

Daisy got up and bent over the sleeping Gussie, stroking her cheek with a little finger which the baby's head automatically turned towards.

'It's only ten weeks and it seems as though she has been here forever,' she said.

'She is extraordinary, isn't she? Eats, sleeps, eats again and creates dirty nappies in such a relentless way. All she has to do to win general approval is put on weight, like a prize pig.'

'Don't you listen to him Gussie, you're just getting established in the world, then you'll start doing all manner of things, won't you my angel?' Daisy gently kissed Gussie's brow and her eyes opened.

'I'm sure she will. It just seems like fathers are redundant at this stage. It'll be years before she can come to the study of an evening and prettily say goodnight to her pater.'

'I'll ignore that.'

'But I do have a lovely baptismal mug.' He took from the box a small silver mug with repousee flowers around the bowl and gleaming silver gilt on the inside.

Daisy took it and showed it to the baby, turning it to reflect the lights from the fire. She put it on the mantelpiece next to a silver candlestick.

'That's very pretty, James, it's such a lovely thing to do, thank you. Gussie will be quaffing her National Health orange juice from it in no time and banging it on the table for more.' Daisy picked up the hot water jug. 'Keep your eye on her while I fill this.'

'Just so long as I don't have to do anything.'

'I'm thinking of teaching you to change nappies, you can be a model dad.'

'Of course, I'd love to,' James said, 'but I fear I'd just be all fingers and thumbs, it looks rather specialised, all that folding and tucking and wielding those enormous safety pins without puncturing the poor child. It might just be too much for a humble artist.'

Daisy said nothing. When she returned Gussie was stirring, her tiny mouth puckering as she rooted for the breast. Daisy took her to the settee and laid her on her lap. She enjoyed the slight sensation of the milk letting down as Gussie latched onto her nipple. Leaning back into the cushions she closed her tired eyes. When she opened them James was looking at her.

'I love you,' he said.

∽

Daisy had a small notebook where she kept a record of Gussie's weight and recorded its steady increase. Nurse Booth had looked in every couple of days to begin with but now came once a week to see how they were faring and to weigh baby.

'She can get a bit fretful sometimes, and then it takes a bit longer before she's satisfied.'

'I shouldn't worry,' Nurse Booth said, 'it could be a bit of colic, half a teaspoon of gripe water often helps. Their little bodies have a lot to cope with in the first few months with everything developing and growing.'

Daisy and Gussie spent most of their time in the sitting room, by the fire, only using the nursery for sleeping and bathing. James and Mrs Gauge would often join in this very pleasant ritual of watching the cherubic Gussie splashing the water with her arms and shrieking with delight. Mrs Gauge liked to lift her out of the small porcelain bath onto a large white towel that had been warmed in front of the kitchen fire, and gently dry her. A little talcum powder was sprinkled under her armpits and between her legs to prevent chaffing before putting on the inevitable nappy.

It was Mrs Gauge who remarked that Gussie's hands and feet sometimes seemed cold even though the house was kept warm. Daisy was aware of her own inexperience and so reported this to Nurse Booth. After examining Gussie and checking her temperature and weight she thought that, just to be on the safe side, and although she could not see anything the matter, it might be a good time for Dr Fraser to come and see Gussie. When he came the reassuring stethoscope was deployed, the tiny pulse taken and a careful physical examination given.

'How is her sleeping, Mrs Blount?'

'She is very good most of the time, but she can wake up a bit crotchety.'

'And how would you say she is generally?'

'I don't know. She may be a bit more fractious than she used to be.'

'And is she feeding well?'

'I'm not sure. I think it may be taking a bit longer than before, but apart from that it's all fine.'

Dr Fraser smiled and chucked Gussie under her chin, she gurgled her appreciation.

'Is Gussie alright? Do I have anything to worry about?'

'I think she's doing very well, Mrs Blount, and I don't

want you to have any anxieties. We'll keep our eye on her development, as we do for all babies, but Gussie is a bonny lass, she's fine. Now, is there anything else? Are you keeping well yourself?'

∽

As the weather became warmer and Gussie began to take notice Daisy would wheel her out into the garden. Before the birth Daisy had sent for a catalogue that she and James pored over one evening. He wanted a large, regal looking perambulator of the sort seen pushed by nannies in Kensington Gardens. Daisy thought it impractical for the country and preferred one of the new 'strollers,' which James thought looked too much like an orange box on wheels but yielded to the argument that he wasn't the one who was to push it. In the event even the stroller had a job getting down the drive and pushing it through the lanes with their uneven surfaces and agricultural traffic made the enterprise rather arduous, especially as the maximum to be gained was the limited pleasures of Barcombe village.

As Daisy was so attached to the bike, James suggested they might get a sidecar. One afternoon they left Gussie with Mrs Gauge and rode to the motorcycle showrooms in Brighton. Daisy tried sitting in a couple of the dinky little carriages with their doll's house doors and perspex windows. They felt flimsy and there was very little room, and with Gussie on her lap there would be even less. She had not realised just how near to the ground they were, and the springs were pretty rudimentary. Every little dip and rut would be felt bouncing along those country lanes. There was something about being an outrider with no control over the machine, or any way of communicating with James, that made the whole thing seem like a bad idea. James agreed and thought that a car might be the only way forward, even though neither of them wanted one. They would definitely keep the Four Square.

Now that she was beginning to get some sleep, Daisy loved the mornings. After feeding and the morning routine, Gussie would be put to rest in the stroller and wheeled out into some shady spot in the garden. Daisy would sit beside her with a sketch pad or sometimes take her to the kitchen garden and do a bit of work. These were golden moments when Daisy felt a peace and contentment she had never had in her life. She looked at Gussie and put her little finger into her palm to feel the vice grip of those tiny hands. Daisy found herself continually awestruck by the astonishing beauty of this utterly dependent but emotionally other person. A being in the world that, in a way, she had made but without volition. Gussie made sense of life, conferred a new sense of self, and it wasn't exactly pride but something had shifted, she could share her life and love in a new way. Gussie was a true blessing.

∽

'Maybe she's teething,' Daisy said.

'That might be the case, Mrs Blount,' Nurse Booth said, 'but Gussie isn't quite making the weight gains we hope for and she does look a bit out of sorts. It could simply be her digestion, but I think it might be sensible to get Dr Fraser to have another look at her.'

Nurse Booth was holding Gussie and jiggling her in her arms. She moved to the window to check her observation of Gussie's colour. Her lips were definitely taking on a slight transparent hue, and her extremities remained cold despite the warmth of the room.

When Dr Fraser visited, a couple of days later, his

examination of Gussie seemed to be very thorough. He moved the stethoscope from her chest to her back several times, listening in different places. Frowning in concentration, he ran his hands over her skin and held her fingers and toes, regarding them minutely.

'Tell me now, how is the feeding going, Mrs Blount?'

Daisy paused before answering.

'Well, she can seem to make heavy weather of it sometimes. She snuffles and gets a bit hot and bothered. I've tried her with a bottle to see if that makes things easier, but there was no difference. Mrs Gauge is worried that she's not getting enough nourishment, but she's rarely very hungry.'

'I don't think we need to worry about malnutrition, Mrs Blount, but we must keep an eye on her weight, she could do with being a little more bonny.'

'I don't really understand what's going on. She still feeds often, but perhaps not for so long. Perhaps she's not getting as much milk as she needs? Perhaps there's something wrong with my milk?'

'I wouldn't think that's the case, Mrs Blount, just so long as you keep healthy yourself and eat properly. We'll just keep monitoring Gussie's progress a little more closely to make sure that everything goes as it should. I'll drop by in a few days.'

As she listened to Dr Fraser's car bouncing down the drive, Daisy found herself flooded by a wave of anxiety she had been resisting for some time. Even James had noticed a change in Gussie. He thought she had lost the roses in her cheeks, and he was right, Gussie did seem to be losing some of her vitality. Mrs Gauge didn't say much but exhibited an air of general concern. These things must be pointing in some direction, but where? Daisy had an inkling that there was something Dr Fraser was not telling her. She shrank from quizzing him outright, it would look as though she didn't trust him, and she did. Lewes, as the County Town, had a large library with an extensive reference section. She determined to go and research infant maladies and try to discover if Gussie's symptoms added up to anything. If she couldn't find out, she would definitely ask Dr Fraser what he really thought might be the matter.

⌒

The county library, a fine Victorian Gothic building lay at the eastern edge of Lewes, close to the river. The outside was distinctly ecclesial, inside there was a large hall where books rose in galleries from the floor to the decorated eves. Near the door were several reading desks where men and women stood perusing the national and local newspapers. A few mainly elderly men, surrounded by piles of books, sat at long tables ostensibly working. In the centre was a desk where two women librarians stood ready to stamp books and give advice. No one spoke. Daisy found it difficult to articulate precisely what she was looking for. The rather snooty young woman directed her to the general medical section, without a smile.

Daisy spent a while leafing through some bewildering, jargon filled, books and took the most likely candidates to a table. Most of them were hopelessly out of date and dealt with smallpox and herpes, rickets and tuberculosis. The photogravure images of distressed children were ugly and unsettling to see. There was only one recently published book on infant care that dealt with symptoms, their causes and significance. It covered a wide variety of ailments, including temporary jaundice in neonates, whooping cough, chicken pox, mumps and influenza and a host of minor problems of little significance but all of which might lead to fractiousness. There was nothing that corresponded to Gussie's chilled extremities, with her little fingers almost blue with cold sometimes, and neither anything on issues related to feeding or growth. All it had to say on slow weight gain was that all babies' metabolisms differed and so mothers should beware of making comparisons with other children. Daisy left the library feeling frustrated and disappointed, having found nothing to allay the solid knot of anxiety that she now carried with her.

She walked slowly up School Hill and put an order in to Flints, the grocer and general dealer, and another along the High Street to Marsh the butcher. Given her own way she would simply go in and buy things, but Mrs Gauge strongly advised against it, as some tradesmen were beginning to stop delivering out in the country, or were charging for it, and if they let things go, they'd end up having to traipse into Lewes for a pound of sausages. Walking back to where she had left the bike, Daisy renewed her resolve to ask Dr Fraser what he thought the issue might be.

∽

Gussie seemed quite animated as Daisy picked her up from the towel on the nursery table where Dr Fraser had finished his examination. It was good to sense her liveliness, especially as she had been rather listless for the previous couple of days. Daisy cleared her throat.

'Dr Fraser, every time I ask you about Gussie you more or less tell me she's fine and I'm not to worry. It's hard for me to be convinced when she is obviously not as well as she might be. Is it possible she might be sickening for something, and if so could you please be straight with me as I'm beginning to feel anxious about her progress? Do you think there is anything the matter?'

Dr Fraser finished packing his instruments into his black bag and turned to face Daisy. He stroked his chin.

'Well, as you ask me so directly Mrs Blount, I'll tell you what's in my mind. Little Gussie has developed some symptoms that we've all noticed, and while in themselves they are symptoms that a lot of children temporarily show signs of, they are also consistent with a condition called cyanosis, which, rarely, some infants go on to develop. That's why we're being sensible and keeping a close eye on Gussie's development. If the symptoms begin to fade, that will be fine, and that's what we're hoping for and expecting. If they persist we may have to think again, but we're not at that stage yet.'

Daisy looked down at Gussie and clasped her more tightly. She had to wait before she could trust herself to speak.

'So, there might be something wrong with her, something serious? How long before we can tell, one way or the other?'

'I'm afraid we can't be precise about that, Mrs Blount, we just have to keep monitoring to see how things are going. Let's look on the bright side, Gussie will probably be as right as rain in a few weeks.'

Dr Fraser picked up his bag, tickled Gussie's chin and smiled at Daisy.

'I'll drop by in a few days' time, you take care now and try not to let yourself worry. We'll see how things go.'

Daisy did worry, and it seemed to her that over the ensuing weeks Gussie gradually deteriorated before her eyes. Feeding became ever more fraught, tiny drops of moisture would form on her brow and Gussie at times was almost gasping for breath. The effort would leave her exhausted but unable to rest. She had ceased to take much notice of the world or her mother and would lay inert for long periods. The ghostly blue pallor of her skin could not be ignored, especially in her sad little face. Gussie was struggling and Daisy, gripped by an invasive fear, found herself in a state of perpetual alarm. She could barely eat or sleep and was almost unable to let Gussie out of her sight. The object of her deepest human feeling seemed gradually to be moving beyond her powers to nurture.

Dr Fraser came and went more frequently, constantly advising on nostrums to make Gussie a little more comfortable and dispensing assurances to Daisy that rang increasingly hollow. Her life seemed to be minutely focused on Gussie, nothing else existed.

∽

Both Gussie and Daisy had been managing to get some sleep. Feeding had become a little easier and Nurse Booth had recorded a near normal gain between weigh ins. After the morning feed Gussie dozed in the stroller. Daisy wheeled her into the bright garden where the fragrant air felt balmy. She parked in the shade under an old lime tree where the gentle rustling of the breeze through the leaves lulled the senses.

Daisy sat on a stool with a paper bloc on her lap, fountain pen poised. It was a while since she had written to Hilda, who, it turned out, much preferred a letter to a telephone call. Daisy's failure to write was partly because of her ambivalence about relaying anxiety, what could she say about Gussie? There was little point in alarming Hilda when there was nothing that she could do, and in any case Gussie might turn the corner any day and current anxieties become a thing of the past. Daisy set to and wrote about the baptism, which by now seemed a distant memory of another place, the new gallery in London who had taken James on and how things seemed to be picking up for him with commissions and some illustrating. She went into detail with her Victory

Garden surrogate, and how if she had Hilda and Alice with her, instead of having to rely on old Jake, they would be able to feed half the county by now, anything but telling Hilda about what was constantly gnawing at her heart. She stood up, put the writing pad on the stool and stretched. Gussie looked almost peaceful, some of the blue had faded from her cheeks, leaving them pale. Daisy leant over and stroked her cheek. It was icy cold. Daisy picked up her baby, suddenly heavy, and held her in her arms, the now lifeless head lolled on her shoulder.

∽

Coopers, of course, were the undertakers and everything was accomplished with a quiet dignity. Like the servants of royalty, Cooper and his men avoided eye contact. Fr Luke, rook-like in black vestments, said a requiem mass for the repose of Gussie's soul. James had rather baulked at this Romish idea. Insofar as he had any religion it held no metaphysical content. But faced with the enormity of Daisy's grief he had yielded instantly, as he had to the novel notion of a private funeral. Mrs Gauge came and sat at the front of church, with Daisy and James. Beside them, by the chancel steps, and lit by four black catafalque candles was the coffin. As it was too small to span the usual two trestles, a white board had been laid across them. Jake with his wife, Kate, and Nurse Booth sat at the back of the church. The sexton tolled the bell. There was no organ but Cooper's men who were all schooled in music, sang the psalm and an anthem a cappella. At the end of mass Daisy alone went to sprinkle the coffin with holy water. She leant over to kiss the small oak box that held her baby's dead body, and her legs gave way, her thin shoulders heaved with silent sobs. James gathered her up and held her. Intoning the Lazarus prayer, Fr Luke slowly led the short procession down the nave and out into the graveyard to the place where the Blount family were buried. Too small to be balanced on the men's shoulders, the little coffin was carried by its four handles. The grave was deep but so pathetically tiny and the slow lowering of Gussie's mortal remains to their final rest visibly affected all present. Daisy, James and Mrs Gauge each took a handful of earth and threw it into the grave. The rattle on the lid of the coffin wrenched Daisy's heart. Fr Luke came and touched her arm before walking back to the church. There was nothing to be said. Coopers' men folded the white lowering tapes, Mr Cooper turned, bowed deeply and they melted away, black against the sun. Daisy stood, no longer feeling anything at all. There was to be no wake. This could not have happened.

∽

Daisy found it impossible to reconcile herself to the loss of little Gussie. She was not herself. There seemed to be some barrier between her and her experience of the world. Even her own thoughts and feelings happened at a distance and everything was permeated by a sense of menace in all her waking moments and in her fitful sleep. She could recognise the world and James and Mrs Gauge, but they failed to signify.

Mrs Gauge was patient and attentive, forever trying to tempt Daisy's appetite with rabbit pudding or spotted dick, she thought her mistress was looking far too thin. As Daisy had become unresponsive, Mrs Gauge made her own decisions about keeping house, and if anything turned up she spoke to Mr James about it. Dr Fraser had prescribed blood tonics and recommended Swedish exercises for Daisy, which was rather radical for him. In truth he had little idea of what was wrong or of how to treat Daisy's symptoms. Given time, the great healer, this sort of thing usually cleared up of its own accord.

∽

Daisy watched the red viscous tonic slither down the sinkhole. She rinsed the bottle and set it on the draining board to dry. She caught sight of her hands and spread them out flat on the kitchen table, they looked so white and the knuckles too prominent. They did not look like her hands. A cup of tea might be good, but that would mean making it, she could wait for Mrs Gauge.

The house was quiet which was nice. James hadn't been up to stay at Chelsea Arts for quite some time, and it had been difficult to persuade him that she would be alright if he went to London for a few days. It was so clear that he was champing at the bit, although he may have suffered a twinge of guilt at abandoning her. Guilt was in the air. Women weren't supposed to have babies that died after a few months. And if they should be so unfortunate, it was incumbent upon them to rise to the occasion by behaving as though nothing particularly untoward had happened, and by getting pregnant again as soon as was compatible with good taste. Daisy sensed that James and Mrs Gauge blamed her for Gussie's death, even though blue baby syndrome was not uncommon and rarely spared the infants who contracted it. It was still beyond belief, how could a beautiful baby, a person that Daisy loved with all her being, wither on the bough so quickly.

She kept telling herself she must try harder, rally round – but how? There was no life energy to be had. A lot of time was spent in the garden, but she rarely lifted so much as a hoe, and all Jake could do was keep the weeds down and provide just enough vegetables to avoid getting the sack. As for painting or design or even photography, which was hardly physically demanding, there was just empty space where the interest and ability had once been. She had tried sitting in the studio with James while he worked, a sketchbook on her lap, her favourite brown pencil in her hand, and nothing would happen, so she had to leave before she began to cry.

Perhaps she was to blame. The poor wretched baby had struggled to live and breathe and finally gave up the ghost. As the life had drained from her so it did from Daisy, they had both drifted away. Daisy's only wish was that she could follow Gussie to wherever she now was, to caress her to make amends, to find where her own life had gone to.

Chapter 20

At the sight of Emily getting off the train, Annabel suppressed a laugh. A baby hung from a blue sling across her front, an explorer size rucksack from her back, and a shoulder bag was slung round her neck. The straight blond hair that normally framed her face was dragged into a knot on the top of her head. She stood at the barrier with commuters streaming past her, her face rumpled as she searched her jeans for the ticket. A woman in a peaked cap who took pity on her and opened the wide barrier to wave her through was rewarded with a beaming smile.

'Annabel, at last, how wonderful to see you. Crossing the Atlas Mountains was easy peasy compared to crossing the channel with young Daisy. She's only ten kilos but after a while it begins to feel like at least forty. I thought it would be better than driving because I could give all my attention to this gorgeous little bundle.'

Emily lifted up the baby to take the weight off her own shoulders for a moment.

'Say hello to Annabel, darling.'

The infant, in a pure white polar suit with a faux fur trimmed hood, obligingly craned her head to see what was about and shot her legs up and down while waving her arms and gurgling.

'I keep asking myself, how on earth did Toby manage me? Then I remember that, of course, he didn't. All that baby stuff was farmed out to professionals from the year dot. The other thing I have to constantly remind myself, still after all these months, is that I'm not the first mother in the universe, so shut up and get on with it. Give me a hug, it's so lovely to be back for more than a weekend.'

Emily opened her eyes wide and drew down the corners of her mouth.

'I'm gushing, aren't I? I never used to do this, frantic I never was, and you look terrific, beautiful and poised, unlike me.'

Annabel now laughed and hugged Emily as best she could, given the encumbrances. She kissed the baby's head and tickled her under her chin.

'Emily, it's great to have you back, you and Daisy are such an addition to life at the old house. When you leave, everything goes quiet and Dan and I feel positively middle aged. Let me help with the luggage.'

On the way to Campiston, Emily sat in the back of the Mini with the baby on her lap, wondering idly if there was a law on strapping infants in England. It was gorgeous to have her little baby close, to be able to smell her, see her, touch her, without her mind having to be partly elsewhere, and knowing that the encounter was strictly time limited. Ten days was unheard of luxury and she intended to luxuriate.

'How's Dan?'

'Blooming, as only he can. We're both anxious that we've bitten off more than we can chew, as my gran used to say, and all the big work falls to him, but he thrives on it. He is, of course, hugely looking forward to seeing the love of his life. He's prone to talking about 'my daughter' which can be occasionally puzzling, as we don't appear to have one. I've given up trying to explain the position and now just weather any looks of confusion.'

'I'm sorry if it's difficult, unintended consequences, the economists' nightmare. We could leave him in sole charge for a couple of weeks, endless nappies and a few broken nights would alter his perception. At the moment she's a bit like the princess across the water.'

'You're right, but I don't mind at all and, Dan, as you might imagine is oblivious.' Annabel swerved to avoid a pothole, and Emily held on to Daisy as she tumbled to the side. 'How's the baby/job balance going? It was getting stressful last time we spoke.'

'Gradually diminishing stress levels, I'm amazed what I can do when I have to. I was hoping to establish a routine but now that I've ditched the idea altogether, life's easier. I couldn't manage without Manon's daughter, Amelie. Takes it all in her stride and Daisy loves her, I get quite jealous sometimes. She's got a degree from Vincennes, but no job. Life for black girls in Paris is hard. I know I'm exploiting her, but she can stay whenever she wants, and I pay her well. That and baby supplies pretty much wipes out my salary, but we live frugally. Like the spoiled bourgeois parasite that I am, we rely on Toby to keep the roof over our heads and pay the taxes on the flat.'

Annabel swung into the drive, slowed down and braked gently in front of the house.

∽

The three of them sat round the kitchen table after supper. Emily ran her finger round the inside of the Creuset, now empty of the leek, bacon and potato soup that Annabel had made, and licked it. Dan was absently munching bread and cheddar and sipping a glass of red wine.

'I'll get the extra bedrooms ready tomorrow,' Emily said, 'Daisy in the master, Jean-Marie next to me and Toby in the Boudoir, because the table is the right height for him to work on. It's great your mum has come up with all the *linge de lit*.

'Bed linen'

'Thanks.'

Emily consulted a little black notebook.

'We'll have the *Reveillon* feast, on its traditional day, Christmas eve, when Guy's coming, but we'll eat before Midnight Mass not afterwards like people used to. The goose is ordered, plus a gammon and stuff for later. Toby is bringing wine and some caviar, which would be extravagant, but he says it's a corporate gift, which seems a bit insensitive for a development agency, maybe he chose it? He's also bringing a *Buche de Noel* and a load of cheese. No one will go hungry.'

'I've got a big box of Christmas crackers.' Dan said.

'We must make some extra thin toast for the caviar. I was just going to jump up and check the blessed infant, but thanks to Dan's intercom, I can do it from here. When big Daisy arrives, I suggest we call the baby little Daisy to avoid confusion.'

'Good idea Emily, it wouldn't do to start feeding big Daisy pureed veg and putting her down for a nap in the afternoon,' Annabel said, 'easy mistake to make what with there being only about eighty years between them.'

Annabel ruffled Emily's hair, who narrowed her eyes and stuck her tongue out.

'I'm up for it,' Dan said, 'I like the sound of little Daisy.'

'It's just my anxiety showing,' Emily said, 'what if she hates it here and it's a terrible mistake caused by me and my obsession.'

'Whatever happens, Emily, I'm sure you'll come out of it a better person. I'm dying to meet her, and so is Dan.'

'Toby said the same, she's a living link to his uncle. We'll soon see, I'm fetching her from the Victoria train tomorrow afternoon. Will I have the car, it's got the baby seat?'

'Sure thing,' Dan said. 'I'm helping Jack chop and deliver logs, seven 'til six, what's left of me should be back in time for supper. Right now, I'll go and get the Christmas tree in from the barn. It'll look baronial, decked out in the hall. Don't worry I can do it on my own. Are Toby and Jean-Marie due tomorrow?'

'How is Toby?' Annabel asked, 'and the answer is, no, Dan, Christmas eve.'

'I'm sure he's well, isn't he?' Dan said, looking at Emily, who smiled sweetly at him and nodded.

Annabel got up and with Emily's help started clearing the table and loading the dishwasher.

'Has he managed to get back to Paris much?'

'Occasionally, though much less than he intended. In some ways the US has changed him. It's only superficial, but he's become a bit of a VIP. You can tell he's boss class by the English cut of his suits with all that fine hand stitching, also the manicure, plus, the fact he's put on a bit of weight and has the general air of a man living on planet Toby. But underneath, he's still, papa, thank God. I ease him back into his old self in a couple of hours, cashmere sweater with moth holes, feet up on the sofa, a big glass of lightly chilled Chablis. He says in America they serve it so cold it might as well be anti-freeze so it's a blessing it comes in such small glasses, but with *Liberation* and *Le Monde Diplomatique* at his elbow he knows he's back in Paris.'

Emily took the tray of coffee into the sitting room where Annabel had rekindled a bit of life into the fire. They sat in front of it on the biggest sofa. Emily took her mug and tucked her legs under her.

'I've almost given up on Calvados. Brandy before bed just

isn't compatible with jobs and babies who might wake you at any moment, and keep you awake for as long as they think fit. One can't weigh making a person against any sensible criteria, but it certainly doesn't do the body any favours, my poor boobs have yet to recover from all those months of relentless sucking, and I'm thinner. Speaking of which, quite a lot of Dan seems to have disappeared, what's up?'

'It's simple, Dan, MW, that's Master of Wine, has given up the beer and only drinks wine. Dan now sees the vineyard as the future venture most likely to put meat on the table, and he's modelling himself appropriately, getting to know not only how to make it but how to appreciate it. He's joined the Wine Society and, although we can only afford to graze the lowest slopes of their formidable list, it's certainly the place to learn wine. I think he's right and I'm in favour of the new slimline edition.'

'It suits him, he's looking good and I'm with you both, wine is the way forward.'

'I'm glad you agree. We've got a five year plan with rough costings, we can look at it later. Weather permitting, Dan can do it. I just don't want him to grow a floppy forelock and start dressing like Bruno.'

'Relax, it could never happen.'

Annabel stretched. 'Do you want to bend your rule and try a teensy Calvados for old times' sake? You still have the baby but the job's gone for few days.'

'OK, *Un pour la route*.'

Annabel fetched the brandy and Emily mended the fire. For a while they sat watching the flames licking around the wood and tapering into the ether.

'I'm so relieved that the three of us have managed to stay together with the addition of little Daisy,' Emily said.

'Me too, it might have screwed us all, but you handled it

so well. Dan and I have come out stronger and you have an adorable daughter.'

'I'm still anxious about the future, especially now that Alexis is dead, and Jean-Marie is back in Paris.'

'That was so sad, it must have been awful for him, how is he coping?'

'He's more resilient than I had expected. After the death the family completely excluded him, even to the point of burying Alexis without letting him know. They're real bastards. They are even contesting the will. It's been a nightmare for Jean-Marie. At least his father, after ignoring him forever, has come round and is now handling the court case, probably because there is money involved.

'I've been seeing a lot of him. We're not sleeping together I don't feel I've got room for sex right now. I do want to help him through all this, I'm very attached to him. Even his gorgeous halo of auburn curls is beginning to show some wear. Having little Daisy makes me think about the future, for the first time it matters.'

Emily's shoulders fell and she stared into the fire.

'Little Daisy's got a father, it's Dan, who is going to be great at it, but that's not what I had, I lived with someone every day and night, who was always, or nearly always, there. I'm pretty sure Jean-Marie wants us to be her parents, ages ago he actually proposed, and he's besotted by Daisy. His dreams of academic stardom have faded, and he got to like teaching in Reunion. If we did share our lives, little Daisy would have a father figure at home. My fear would be that another Alexis would come along and break it all up. And I can't just forget his HIV status. It's possible he could get sick, even die, which I simply could not face.'

Annabel shifted onto the floor, arms wrapped around her knees and looked up at Emily.

368

'Emily, you've had a torrid time of it, hearing your mother's story, Jean-Marie leaving you, Toby going to New York, getting a job and having a baby – so much to deal with. Of course, the future becomes important if someone you love is going to inhabit it, but that doesn't make it any more under our control. You're doing famously, be proud.'

Annabel leaned forward, put her arms round Emily and kissed her.

∽

Daisy looked up at the dark wooden tester above her head. Her eyes blinked and her brow furrowed. She had been awoken from some intense dream, instantly dissolved, leaving only a trace of disturbance. Had she heard a child's cry? It sounded again from somewhere in the house. Was this still a dream? Through the dark shades of a winter morning her surroundings gradually took shape, her mind found the present. I'm in the lovely four poster that James got after we were married. I'm not dreaming the child, it's Emily's daughter who, to my surprise, is called Daisy, after me and is waking up on this winter's morning. The whole business is miraculous, some sort of enchantment that has brought me here, to now, to Campiston.

Since the moment Emily's letter had arrived at the cottage saying she was James' great niece and asking if she might visit, the story of Daisy's life had been thrown into deep disarray. The threads needed to be found and carefully reworked into a new narrative. No small thing to do in one's old age.

The clock on the mantle struck six, there would be no more sleep. Daisy sat up and slowly looked around. The room was familiar and strange. It smelled different and the rugs were new. She rubbed the top of her arms, it was cold. Her feet swung to the floor and she padded to the window and drew the curtains back. The garden – was it real? Outside, the world sparkled with a hoar frost, another miracle.

It was like meeting someone one had known well who had changed much over the years, but the lineaments remained the same. So far as she could make out only the study was exactly as she remembered. The old iron stove, the club furniture, even the humidor was still there, a relic.

Daisy put on a thick cable knit jumper and took the battered greatcoat from the peg on the door. It would be good to feel the crisp air on her face. The door opened quietly, and she headed for the kitchen.

∽

Daisy slowly climbed the short staircase that she had once sprinted up. They were to have tea in her old room. A fire crackled in the black iron grate before the old settee, the worktable was in place under the window. Daisy could immediately recall the sense of pleasure and relief that her own space had given her. A place where she could be herself and do the things that interested her or do nothing. So unlike the grimy refuge she had endured at the top of her father's shop.

Daisy thought she should give some sort of account of herself but found it hard to know where to begin. Emily's visit to the cottage had not lasted long, she had explained how she came to be there and that she was actually her great niece, which was news. Daisy knew about Toby, may even have met him, but not that he had a daughter, and one so engaging. The invitation to spend Christmas at Campiston had come as an aftershock and Daisy had politely refused. Emily left the matter open in case Daisy's plans for the season altered. She had spent sleepless nights, wanting to see the place for a last time, but fearful of how it might affect her, before writing to accept.

For a short while they sat together watching the fire take hold.

'I'm so pleased you are here to see little Daisy,' Emily said, 'between her and work I'm pretty much constantly exhausted, although I do have help. It's lovely to bring her here for a few days. It's good she and Annabel get on so well. It means we can sit in peace for a while.'

'Yes, of course.' Daisy looked at her hands folded in her lap. 'Emily, I want to tell you what happened, but I'm afraid I do not come out of it well as you will see.' Daisy paused, immobile. 'Your great uncle and I had not been married very long when we had a little girl, Gussie. She died after a few months and I lost my mind and fled to my friend, Alice, in Devon, where so many years later, you found me.'

Daisy slowly shook her head.

'I went to see my aunt Hilda who had been so kind and understanding to me and James when we first met. She told me my place was with my husband, and that I hadn't given him a chance and if the truth were known I didn't deserve him, and of course all that was true. People take sides, and she saw that the right was with James and she did all she could to get us back together, but I couldn't do it. Every Summer he would come and stay at Hilda's cottage. Once I went over to see him on the motorbike that I'd stolen from him when I bolted. He was kindness itself, not a note of recrimination. Seeing him, I knew I loved him, and it broke my heart. I'm glad that she and James were friends to the end. She left him the cottage so he could come and be near to me. She never forgave me for what I had done to him and never gave up on the hope of our being reconciled.'

Daisy put down her cup and folded her hands in her lap.

'For years I wished I could return to repair the terrible damage I had done to James, to us, but I could never find the courage. It seemed then that everything at Campiston was poisoned for me, Gussie had died, and I dreaded returning to the terrifying madness that had engulfed me there – here. As time passed the possibility of redemption slowly faded. James was so kind when he had every right to be angry. He wrote to me constantly, asking me to come back to him. Even when it was clear that I was frozen for good. He never sued for divorce, he used to send me regular cheques, but I could never bank them despite being perennially hard up.'

Daisy stopped and looked with watery eyes at Emily who reached out to hold her hand.

'Much later he wrote and asked if I truly wanted to have Campiston willed to me. As his wife I would naturally inherit. I did once love the place, this little room, the garden, his studio, our comfortable life. How could I go back to ghosts and failed promises? I had given my life to bitter grief rather than allow James to console me. I gave up any legal claim I might have. I did say give it to whoever you think will care for it, possibly your Toby.' Daisy fell quiet for a few moments. 'I never let go of the thought of what might have been, but for my fear and selfishness. It all still mattered, it still does.'

Emily put her arms round the thin shoulders and hugged Daisy.

'Daisy, that is so sad, and so unexpected. How you both must have suffered, poor things, it blighted your whole lives. When I used to stay here things always seemed a bit quiet after life with Toby, uncle James would spend hours in the studio and didn't encourage me to join him. There was an older lady who used to come in quite a lot and do stuff, otherwise it was just the pair of us. I liked it. We'd go for long walks on the downs in the late afternoon and I would try and make him laugh with stories about Toby and my life in Paris. I found him undemanding and comforting to be with, I'd just root about the place and sit in the woods and read all the English books. I remember meals were sometimes very odd, but I got used to the occasional cold lamb chop for breakfast, and I cooked for both of us whenever I could. I'd been cooking since I was strong enough to hold a skillet.'

'That's beautiful to hear, Emily, I'm sure you gave him some happiness and I'm so pleased that Campiston has come to you. The three of you seem committed to keeping it going and I find that a real comfort.'

'Are you happy to be here? I was so disappointed when you seemed to be set against it.'

'It was for you I came in the end. I felt I was trampling on your kindness, something I had done nothing to earn, and it might be my last chance to try and honour the memory of my James in some way. I'm afraid we lost touch. It was his solicitors who told me he was dead. I wasn't told of the funeral. Toby probably had no idea where I was. I'd like to visit James' grave, and little Gussie's, before I go back.'

'I was thrilled when you changed your mind, and if you want I could drive you to the churchyard any time, little Daisy permitting.'

Daisy looked at the tiny gold watch hanging loosely round her thin wrist. She moved it closer to her eyes.

'Thank you, Emily, my dear, and thank you for listening to me. It's curious, already the burden of terrible guilt seems to be breaking up a little now I'm here, but underneath is the most appalling sense of regret.' She turned her head to Emily and smiled. 'But enough, I should like to rest a little before seeing Dan. I like him, he would do well in, As You Like It, or Twelfth Night, he's got good presence, natural humour and he moves well. Before the light goes he's giving me a tour of the estate, as he calls it, which I think of as the garden. He's promised me a pleasant surprise.'

'Yes, I know, he told me, but I won't spoil it.'

Daisy manoeuvred herself to the edge of the settee and leaned forward to gain momentum for standing up. She smoothed her trousers and together they made their way down the narrow staircase.

∽

The wooden cot had a gabled canopy decorated with tiny carved daisies. It was set on rockers that allowed Daisy to gently soothe the baby with her foot as she sat, feeling she could not say what, and watched the tiny pink face with such enormous eyes peering, apparently inquisitively, into the world.

Dan cleared his throat as he came into the room.

'Do you like the cot? I used French oak, beautiful grain and the colour of dark honey, and after all, she is French. The design came from a medieval woodcut, nothing essential has changed since then, except rockers have disappeared. I thought I might paint it, but the sun on the grain flashes red and gold, it's gorgeous, like her. It's one of the best things I've done.'

'It is very fine, Dan, she looks so cosy and protected and such a lovely thing to do for Emily.'

'Yes, well, wood is a bit of a passion with me. I don't know if Emily has told you but I'm little Daisy's father.'

Daisy tilted her head to look at Dan.

'I'm sorry, I'm rather confused. I thought you and Annabel were a couple?'

'That's right, we are, devoted. I'm afraid the baby wasn't anything anyone had planned, she just sort of happened.'

374

'I see,' said Daisy, who didn't at all.

'It's how Emily wanted it. We all love little Daisy and it works pretty well.'

'It reminds me of the posh artists at Charleston. People said there were lots of children but the little lambs were never sure who their parents were.'

Dan kissed his finger and planted it on little Daisy's forehead.

'Anyway, let's tour the estate while there's still a bit of light.'

They went through to the kitchen and put on coats. Dan asked Annabel to keep an eye on little Daisy and they headed down the garden to the wood, through the fringe of coppiced willows and hazels to the taller pollards of ash, hornbeam and oak that Dan had revived.

'That's impressive, Dan. It was all pretty much wilderness when I was here, and I had no idea what to do with a wood. You've given it a new life.'

Daisy marvelled at the glasshouse, properly glazed with new heaters and clean soil.

'They are such pleasant and comfortable places to be in the winter, I see you've got an old armchair by the heater.'

'You're right, I keep my thermos in there when I'm working outside. I've been growing Marmande tomatoes. It was Emily's idea, and I can't grow enough, everybody wants them. I plan to put up a temporary growing tunnel in the spring which will double output, it'll be great.'

At the kitchen garden Daisy put her hand on Dan's arm.

'It looks so familiar. I laid it out to be like my aunt Hilda's Victory Garden. It was such hard work with only Jake to help me, he was ancient and much preferred rolling cigarettes and drinking tea to a spell of double digging. But surely there couldn't have been much trace of it left?'

'Dry summer, parch marks showed after I'd been over it all with a Hayter, I noticed the layout from an upstairs window, so I rotavated the beds and went on from there.'

'It's all so strange I don't feel sure about time anymore. If James were to walk out of the studio, would I be surprised?'

'It's amazing to think of you here so long ago and to be here now. It must feel like time travel, and I know what may well blow you away, if what I suspect is right. Let's go and find out.'

Dan crooked his arm, which Daisy took, and they made their way through the failing light to the barn.

'You've seen the vineyard, haven't you?'

'Yes, Emily showed me, perfectly neat rows going up the hill, I haven't seen vines since my honeymoon.'

'Annabel and I are so glad you decided to come back, you've been a presence all along, for us as well as Emily.'

Daisy squeezed Dan's arm but said nothing.

He pushed open the door and they stood momentarily on the threshold, staring into the gloom, before the space was flooded with light by lamps high in the rafters.

'Gosh, this was just a huge jumble of ancient rubbish in my day, and now it's ordered space, benches, cupboards, tools and intriguing bits of machinery, and all so neat and workmanlike. I can't imagine the energy this transformation took. You truly are a man of parts, Dan.'

Dan guided Daisy to the back of the barn. Where with a flourish he removed a tarpaulin. Daisy's hands went to her face and she gasped.

'Now this cannot be real.'

Her features crumpled and she took hold of Dan's arm. Her eyes blinked as she took in the elegant lines of a light framed motor bike, shining in full original livery.

'Dan, is this really Fanny? She was my bike when I was

still at school. Whenever I had the petrol, I would ride her there just to swank in front of the other girls. I had an officer for a boyfriend and this beautiful bike. It made me a princess in those days. I adored my bike it was the best present I've ever had in my life. How on earth did you restore her, she must have been a heap of rust?'

Dan held the bike upright and Daisy, after a couple of attempts, straddled Fanny and took the handlebars.

'I thought it had to be yours, and it's great that it is. It was a labour of love for me. The main thing was patience in finding what was needed. The engine was the easy bit, getting the tyres and the right colour paint was much more difficult. But it was certainly worth it, just to see you now. You can turn her over if you like, might need a bit of choke but she should start.'

Daisy looked down at the bike between her legs.

'I'm not sure I'm steady enough, Dan,' she said, but nonetheless, opened the choke, flicked out the starter pedal and stepped on it. It fired straight away and automatically she pushed in the choke to avoid flooding the carburettor. Daisy smiled as the purr of the little Villiers engine filled the barn.

∽

In the warm studio, a chrome yellow winter sun spilled around. Emily sat in a scruffy Victorian chair with little Daisy asleep on her lap. After the revelation of Gussie, Emily had worried that it might be difficult for Daisy to confront the baby, especially as she was the centre of attention and continually patted and petted by everyone. But Daisy found herself moved by her namesake, she felt there was some sort of redemption in being with little Daisy, an atonement for Gussie.

Daisy looked through some of her old sketchbooks and jottings with a sense of wonder. It was like discovering that someone thought to be dead was still alive. It was difficult but compelling to keep looking. Daisy's eyes periodically sought the watercolour portrait of herself that Emily had re-hung in its original position, where no direct light could fade the pigment. At first sight it had brought back so many tumbling and keen remembrances, she feared she would be overwhelmed by the past.

'I confess I still don't really understand,' Daisy said. 'It's not just how, but much more, why, did you try and unearth that schoolgirl?'

'Why, is difficult. Perhaps I needed someone, and I imagined that person in your image. I never had a truly close friend at school. I was odd, not altogether French, confirmed by having no family. Superficially popular, but not quite fitting the mould. It didn't matter so much at university but after I graduated, I found myself feeling alone and you, so to speak, came along.

'It began when Toby and I visited the house and found your portrait. You are clearly a schoolgirl, but you looked so enigmatic, so much going on behind those dark eyes, and it was painted with such tenderness. I wanted to know that person whose presence I instantly felt. I found a photograph of James and you so obviously together, and wondered what had happened.'

'That little watercolour was the beginning of my life,' Daisy said, 'it's astonishing to see it.'

'I did not for a moment think I would ever meet you, let alone have you with me here. It was absolute serendipity that I found you. Your Mrs Gauge's daughter had agreed to look through her mother's things to see if there were any letters from you that might give me a clue as to what happened.

There were none, which was disappointing. Then, Dan and Annabel came to Paris and they brought a message from Miss Gauge giving your address in Devon. She had found it in an old bloc of writing paper that her mother had used.'

Little Daisy wriggled and scrunched up her face. Emily put her on her shoulder and gently rubbed her back.

'At the beginning there were lots of traces when I looked, especially in your sitting room, lots of artwork, faded photos, I found some letters you had written. Later, at Yew Tree Cottage I discovered your journals. They were a revelation. I could almost touch the person behind the words, and they were so moving. They were not written for publication, and I'm afraid I did share them with Annabel, but of course I never thought...'

Daisy waved away Emily's scruples.

'I haven't thought of them for so many years, I've lost touch with that young girl and her world, I shut her out. It would be wonderful to hear from her again.'

'I brought them back from Paris, in their rusty biscuit tin, I'll put them in your room they are yours after all.'

Daisy laughed out loud and woke little Daisy, who turned her head briefly, her tiny hands clenched, before lolling back on Emily's shoulder.

'Emily, you're a wonder, a cross between a fairy godmother and the ghost of Christmas past. What will happen next? I don't want to be too inquisitive, I can now see why I might have been of passing interest, but why persist?'

'It's not entirely clear to me. After the journals I felt an affinity, your world was complex and demanding as mine is. For me I had to get out from under Toby's wing and make a life. And there was Campiston which meant something to me. I'd made a connection to it through you, and I knew it was important to the person I was becoming. It seemed like a haven but one I could never afford to keep. Toby generously kept it going while I dithered. On the point of selling, Dan and Annabel came up with their plan. Toby suggested we make a contract. It seemed over formal at the time, but it's helped us to stick together. I begin to hope we can hang on we all belong here now and especially you.'

'That would be wonderful, it's good to see the house alive with all the youth and energy you and your friends lavish on it. Now you must get on, I know how busy you are. I'll stay here a little and browse.'

∽

'Come in, come in, you're very welcome, mind all the foliage on the floor, feel free to have a look round. You just visiting?'

The smiling priest, in his black cassock, ushered Emily and Daisy into St Mary's and pushed shut the heavy oak door. Outside the world was cold and the ground hard with a frost that had lingered all morning. The church struck pleasantly warm. In the Lady Chapel candles flickered in the pricket set before a statue of the Virgin. Several women, and some children, were busy with flowers and some huge pieces of greenery, decorating the deep sills of the nave windows and the chancel, ready for the midnight mass. Others in aprons, hands encased in bright yellow Marigolds, rubbed vigorously at the lectern and the brasses. In the bottom of the tower where the bell ropes were looped against the walls, waiting to sound the Christmas peal, a tall fir tree stood, garlanded with strings of nuts and berries, green and red bows and tiny oranges. A light shone on the nativity scene with an empty manger, waiting for the coming of the infant Jesus. Chattering children ran up and down the nave in their socks, sliding on the newly polished wooden floor, bumping into one another and falling in laughing heaps. Christmas was very close. Emily and Daisy sat at the back of the church near the font where Gussie had been baptised and absorbed the benevolent bustle around them.

'I don't know what I had expected to see in the graveyard,' Daisy said, 'but it wasn't nothing at all, it makes me sad and angry, like Gussie wasn't worth remembering.'

'That can't be right,' Emily said, 'uncle James must have loved her, but I guess he found remembering painful and decided not to have a gravestone. We could talk to the priest, there must be a map of where people are buried.'

'I'm sure there is. We could have her remembered on James' stone I'd like that. I'm so glad to know where James is laid, it's reassuring, I feel closer to him, and I'll sort something out for Gussie after Christmas. Coming here has made me miss her, I still feel such pity for her little life, is that reasonable after more than half a century?'

'Of course, I can't imagine what it must have felt like.'

They sat for a while in silence.

'From what I've seen,' Daisy said, smiling at Emily, 'if we gave Dan a chisel and a hammer, he'd have it done in no time.'

'I'll wrap them up and put them in his stocking.'

Daisy got to her feet, Emily took her arm and they slowly walked around the church.

'This hasn't changed at all. I suppose churches don't. I'm looking forward to midnight mass, it's so good of Dan to offer to take me, he's never been to a mass in his life.'

They stopped at the tower where the Nativity figures were grouped around the base of the tree.

'Since Alice died the midnight has been my Christmas, I'm still moved by the blessing of the Bambino, so vulnerable in his little cot. For a brief moment peace, and love, seem possible and real, it gives me the strength to go back and carry on. I would have liked to share these moments with my friend Alice.'

'You must have spent a lot of your life with Alice. I met her in your journals, I've often wondered about her. She was clearly very special.'

'My darling Alice saved me as I knew she would.

'We were together until she died. There were some difficult times like any couple sharing lives, but together we had a life I could manage. She had some land, good pasture for sheep and an orchard, mainly cider apples. When her father died, she was able to buy a farm a few miles away. We managed, with a bit of help, for quite a while but it became too much for two women, just a bit past their prime, so Alice got tenants.

'I know that being with her was the line of least resistance, but it worked. There was deep affection and trust, all she wanted was for me to be there. With James it was so much more complex. I felt known by Alice and I hadn't realised how important that was, to know one another was to accept and I needed that more than anything in the world. James and I did love one another but we never really knew the other person, but then I never gave him much of a chance, did I?'

Daisy put her hand on Emily's arm.

'Before we go, Emily, I want to thank you. These few days haven't changed the past, but they have led me to begin to accept it gratefully, something I could not have imagined myself capable of. I can think of myself without flinching.'

Emily took Daisy's hand.

'I don't know what to say except that makes me very happy,'

The mini slid forward on the gravel as Emily braked too hard. Toby's car was in the drive, streaked with light from the house. It would be so good to see him after…she was not exactly sure how long. As she helped Daisy out of the car, she could hear his voice. They stepped into the hall where Toby stood with Annabel, admiring the tree, sparkling with white light. Seeing Emily his face broke into smiles and he came forward, arms wide.

'Darling cherub, it's been way too long.' He took her hands and kissed her on both cheeks.

'Papa, it's a joy to see you,' she gave him a hug, 'and it has been too long. I expect I've aged.' She turned to Daisy who was taking her coat off. 'This is Daisy, papa, who is staying with us for the holiday.'

'My dear, Daisy, I'm so glad you are with us.' He took her hand and raised it to his lips without kissing it, giving a slight bow.

Overdoing the Gallic charm, Emily thought, he must be nervous.

'I'm sure I met you here when I was a lad quite a while ago. They tell me there's tea in the sitting room. Let me give your coat to Emily, and we can go and see what can be salvaged from the past by our joint memories. But first,' he turned to Emily and handed over the coat. Emily bobbed a curtsey and caught Annabel's eye. 'how is little Daisy, and yes, I am fully briefed on current nomenclature.'

'She is on very good form, papa, as are you. I must feed her now and will bring her down shortly to see her *pepere*.'

'Excellent.'

Toby took Daisy's arm and steered her towards the sitting room.

'I love your dad,' Annabel said, 'he just wanders in and immediately the place is his, I wish I could do it.'

'Takes years of training I'm afraid. Where's Jean-Marie?'

'He's upstairs with little Daisy, which left me free to welcome Toby, and stash all the goodies he's come laden with. Dan's gone to fetch Guy. We're pretty much ready for *Reviellon*.'

'Thank you both so much, volunteering to serve the meal is beyond courageous. You've already done masses of stuff as well as helping with little Daisy, and I'm grateful. I've made the Dauphinoise and that's in the scullery. The goose will be cold by now and can be carved. Ask Toby, he's good at it. I'll do what you tell me, but not to have the responsibility, so I can keep an eye on baby is more than I hoped for. You could also ask Jean-Marie, he's kitchen savvy and loves it. Now I really must go and feed my little gannet.'

'Just come and see the dining room,' Annabel said.

The extended table was covered in a crisp white cloth. In the centre was an old epergne Annabel had found, filled with sprigs of holly and ivy, which were also draped above the pictures and lay on the mantelshelf. The glasses and cutlery sparkled in the firelight and every candlestick in the house was on the table or sideboard, waiting to be lit.

∽

Daisy sat in her room, pondering. She often conjured Alice, an absent witness, still able to validate Daisy's world. The meal had been pure theatre. So many people who talked and laughed the whole time, very clearly enjoying themselves. And such food, it was beyond her star. Before they sat down there was caviar in the sitting room. Dan had served teaspoonfuls on little pieces of thin, crisp toast, curiously with a white plastic teaspoon, she must ask him about that. The effect was inexplicably heavenly. A tiny burst of salty flavour, fugitive and delicious, so there

384

was no good reason not to keep on repeating the experience. Clearly everyone felt the same as the big round tin of what looked suspiciously like frog spawn had disappeared in no time. The champagne that went with it was too heady, and a few sips were ample. In the dining room things began with Christmas crackers which she hadn't seen for years. They were still full of terrible jokes and useless trinkets but they all went, BANG. Emily said it was an English thing, the French don't have them, and I could see their point.

It was thoughtful of her to put me between Guy and Toby, who both had known James. Guy as a young doctor had taken over when Dr Fraser retired, 'good hearted but out of date,' was how he described him. Guy would come over to Campiston to play chess, and in the Summer, they would walk the downs ending at Barcombe for a drink in the pub. His talking of James brought so much back that I thought I had lost. Dear James, I miss him and Gussie, which is so much better than feeling numb and disconnected.

Toby has been so solicitous, making sure of my comfort. He is a fund of witty anecdote, often at his expense, and told some affectionate stories of Emily when she was a child. They were close and they liked each other. Emily had talked about getting out from under Toby's wing and I thought, that would be some wing to get out from under. He can't help it he just gathers all before him. I don't think of my father at all, I doubt he came to a pretty end.

Jean-Marie was the only quiet one, apart from me. In the afternoon he came into the sitting room while I was playing with little Daisy. He's clearly another big fan. He was charming with lovely manners, but there was something solemn, as though he were carrying a hurt.

Towards the end of the meal, Dan and Annabel who had been hosting, were beginning to look a bit frazzled. Dan was constantly at the sideboard opening bottles of wine. I was amazed at how much everyone drank, including Annabel and Emily, but it didn't seem to make anyone tipsy, except perhaps they laughed more than they might have otherwise. Despite having an intercom Emily was up and down frequently, checking on little Daisy. At the end I felt like I used to coming out of the pictures into the real world, a bit disorientated.

∽

The rigours of the feast were over, Annabel's final shot was to put a tray of coffee in the sitting room, with a dish of petit fours. A little retro touch that only Guy and Toby took advantage of. They sat opposite one another, near the fire, with a chessboard between them and began a half-hearted game, soon abandoned in favour of coffee, conversation and brandy. Emily had made up a bed in the studio for Guy, and left the heat on all day, so he was allowing himself to get comfortable.

Jean-Marie was upstairs listening to Dan's plans for the estate, enunciated sotto voce, as they sat on Emily's bed, side by side, watching little Daisy sleeping in her cot. Later Jean-Marie was to go to mass with Dan and Daisy.

∽

'I'm the youngest by far,' Annabel said, 'my bro's are both married with standard issue wives and bratty children. I don't mention them because although they are kith and kin there's nothing going on between us. I only see them at Christmas. But now I've got Dan and there is so much to do at Campiston, especially with the mistress and her father in residence. My mum thinks you're very grand, so I let her think you are. That's not to say you're not grand, Emily. Mum thinks I'm some sort of species of servant, so Dan and I can only be spared for lunch on Boxing Day, which is great. We'll be back for supper.'

'Just make sure you're not late,' Emily said.

Emily and Annabel were in the kitchen battling to restore culinary order after the biggest meal Campiston had seen for decades. Annabel was unloading and then reloading the dishwasher while Emily dried the large dishes and pots and pans, putting them in cupboards and on the dresser.

'Do you think I'm bossy?'

'No,' Annabel said, 'you just tend to know what you want, and then tend to get it. At least that's what it looks like from the outside. Inside, I'm sure it's a different story.'

'It's just something that Daisy said. She was asking me about Dan and little Daisy and whether we'd talked things over when I got pregnant. I said, no, I had made the decision on my own. Which looked rather selfish. I suppose I thought Dan's such a softy that he wouldn't make a fuss.'

'The baby's head would have been engaged by the time Dan got around to making any sort of decision. I think if it's your body then it's your baby. It's not as though he did very much.'

'I don't really know,' Emily said, beginning to laugh, 'I honestly can't remember.'

Annabel started laughing and the pair of them held on to each other.

'That's not very flattering to my man, is it Emily?'

'We'll never know. I reserved a bit of caviar in a ramekin, I know it all goes in the blink of an eye. Let's call it a night, and finish it off with perhaps a thimbleful of Vodka?'

∽

At St Mary's the ringers spat on their hands and unhooked the bell ropes. Soon the grandsire triples would resound through the still cold air of the countryside, as locals and some cultural tourists, got ready to meet Christmas day in church. Fr Edwin had checked everything was in place. While not the holiest, it was the most magical mass of the calendar, although he had never understood why anyone in their right mind would come to mass in the middle of the night. He always kept the homily brief and his pyjamas on the radiator, there was another mass to be said in the morning.

∽

Daisy sat in a chair with the curtains open looking out on the garden, white with frost and lit by moonlight filtered through thin cloud. More had happened in the last few days than in the last twenty years. She had been reading her journals and recalled her and Alice when they were young. How innocent they had been, and kind to one another. The thought of Alice always brought her comfort, she could still see her dear face, feel her presence.

I'm glad I thanked Emily. It's odd but I feel she has saved me, and that in some way seeking the traces of me has helped her. It is a sort of love.

The chiaroscuro of pale light melted into the dark trees. She felt enormously tired. Beyond the tumult of recent days something more centred had emerged, was now in place. The sweet sound of the bells of St Mary's rolled across the dark fields to Campiston. Daisy lay back and closed her eyes. She could smell the damp cloakroom, hear Miss Hewitt clanging the end of school bell. The cold concrete floor, the rows of metal pegs, old black plimsoll bags in dusty corners. Girls chattering and laughing as they grabbed their blue Macintoshes and battered hats, and her young self, happy at last to be going home.

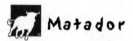